© Vanessa O'Neill

ΛBOUᴛ ᴛHE ΛUᴛHOR

TONY O'NEILL's books include *Digging the Vein* and *Down and Out on Murder Mile,* and coauthor of *Neon Angel* and the *New York Times* bestselling *Hero of the Underground.* His essays, poems, and short stories have appeared extensively online and in print. He is a survivor of heroin addiction, crack abuse, rehab, fatherhood, and stints in the Brian Jonestown Massacre, Kenickie, and Marc Almond's band. He lives in New York with his wife and daughter.

ALSO BY TONY O'NEILL

FICTION

Down and Out on Murder Mile

Digging the Vein

Seizure Wet Dreams

NONFICTION

Neon Angel by Cherie Currie (with Tony O'Neill)

Hero of the Underground by Jason Peter (with Tony O'Neill)

POETRY

Songs from the Shooting Gallery

S!CK
C!TY

A Novel

TONY O'NEILL

HARPER ⬤ PERENNIAL

NEW YORK • LONDON • TORONTO • SYDNEY • NEW DELHI • AUCKLAND

FOR MUM AND DAD,
ROSE AND FRANK O'NEILL

HARPER ● PERENNIAL

SICK CITY. Copyright © 2010 by Tony O'Neill. All rights reserved. Printed in the United States of America. No part of this book may be used or reproduced in any manner whatsoever without written permission except in the case of brief quotations embodied in critical articles and reviews. For information address HarperCollins Publishers, 10 East 53rd Street, New York, NY 10022.

HarperCollins books may be purchased for educational, business, or sales promotional use. For information please write: Special Markets Department, HarperCollins Publishers, 10 East 53rd Street, New York, NY 10022.

FIRST EDITION

Designed by Justin Dodd

Library of Congress Cataloging-in-Publication Data is available upon request.

ISBN 978-0-06-178974-8

10 11 12 13 14 OV/RRD 10 9 8 7 6 5 4 3 2 1

Success is stumbling from failure to failure without losing your enthusiasm.

—*Winston Churchill*

Once you choose hope, anything's possible.

—*Christopher Reeve*

PART ONE

ONE

By noon Jeffrey decided it was time to go in and wake up the old man. He found him dead. Jeffrey stared mutely at the body for a minute. He'd seen dead bodies before, but never one he'd fucked in the previous twenty-four hours. Looking up, Jeffrey caught his own reflection in the wardrobe mirror. Impassive, he studied the corrugated contours of his ribs poking through the skin of his stick-thin torso. His arms were a tapestry of cheap, blurry tattoos. Designs once meant to shock or even threaten now just looked like half-faded bruises on his bony body. Around his throat an India-ink necklace of barbed wire. His dark, thick hair stood straight out from his skull, adding another half inch to his gangly frame. His eyes were gray, sleepy, and full of lost hope. Jeffrey pulled the sheet over the old man's head and looked at his reflection again. He felt like a thirty-seven-year-old orphan.

He drifted back downstairs, poured another cup of coffee, and read the *LA Times* for a while. The television bleated something cheerfully moronic, so he turned it off again. Jeffrey sighed, and called Tyler, his on-again, off-again lover and OxyContin connection. Tyler sounded agitated and hungover.

"Yeah? What's up?"
"Bill died."
Tyler, on his end of the phone line, took a bite of his toast and looked at his kitchen clock. He suddenly exclaimed, "Dude, the *Steve Wilkos Show* is on right now!"

Jeffrey lit a cigarette and listened as Tyler bounded into another room and switched the TV on. The static roar of faraway applause.
"Shit, it's the pedophile one. I've seen this already. Check it out, Steve says, *'You should pick on someone your own size. Why dontcha pick on me?'* You seen this one, bro?"
"No. I don't watch TV."
"Dude, this one's awesome. Were you fucking him when he died?"
"No. He went in his sleep."
"What you guys do last night?"
"Partied with some whores from Santa Monica Boulevard."
"He was just watching and getting high?"
"Yeah."
"Coke and poppers?"
"Yeah."
"So, his heart finally gave out," Tyler announced with a coroner's certainty.
"Yeah. Maybe. I guess."

"So, uh, you wanna come over?"
"Shit, Tyler, I'm kinda freaking out right now, you know? I mean, what do I do *now*?"

"Come over and get high with me!"

"No, I mean money, all of that shit! It's so fucked up. I've been living with Bill for four fucking years, day in, day out, and now he's dead and I'm shit outta luck. I could have married some rich cunt in Vegas for like two weeks and I'd be entitled to something. Shit's so fucked up, man."

"You oughta write a letter to the governor. Look, look— he's gonna say it. *'Why dontcha pick on me!'* Dude, Steve's awesome."

Jeffrey listened to Tyler watching TV for a while. When the silence became uncomfortable he said, "Okay, I'll call you, bro."

"Yup," Tyler said, "let's hang."

Jeffrey re-cradled the phone, sat in his chair. Bill lay cooling in the bed upstairs.

———————

The silence lulled him into a dreamless half sleep. With a jerk, Jeffrey woke up in Bill's vast, modernist glass and steel house overlooking the Pacific Coast Highway. It seemed even more stark and cold with Bill having "left the building." A lot of people wondered how the old man could afford a place like this on a retired cop's salary. If anyone was bold enough to ask, the old man would just smile his cold predator's smile and say, "Investments."

If someone broached the subject with the old man's "personal assistant," Jeffrey would get a little defensive. "Shit, books! Do you even KNOW some of the cases Bill was involved in back in the day? He was one of the first cops on the scene at the Tate murders! He wrote a book about it. The first one, ever! I mean, it's outta print now, but in its day it was a big seller. He also . . . well, look, this is between you and me, right? 'Cos the higher-ups at the LAPD probably wouldn't like this . . . but he's written a few crime novels. Based on some of the cases he worked on. Under a pseudonym. Drake McKellen. Yeah, that's the old man . . . Drake McKellen."

This was usually enough. To most people, a few mass-market paperbacks on a drugstore rack were considered proof that the author must be independently wealthy. They didn't know that unless you were Stephen King or John Grisham those seven and a half percent paperback royalties would have barely afforded a one-bedroom apartment in Los Feliz. No, the books were a hobby, just like the boys were. The old man's tight-lipped defense of "investments" was actually pretty close to the truth.

Jeffrey went to the safe that lay behind the bloodred Warhol silkscreen of the electric chair. He entered the code. He removed one thousand dollars, one eight ball of cocaine, one ounce of marijuana, and a snub-nose, police-issue handgun. He left Bill's passport, police badge, and gold retirement clock. He locked the safe and gently placed the silkscreen back in its original position. Then he walked upstairs.

He walked into Bill's bedroom with a mixture of feelings—resignation, nausea, curiosity. He looked again at the body. Bill was now room temperature and stiff as a grotesque G.I. Joe doll. His mouth was pursed, wrinkled and tight like a puckered asshole. It gave the impression that when Bill had woken to find Death crawling over him, he had perversely decided to kiss it on the lips. The air hung heavy with the stench of stale farts. The room was silent and oppressive. The curtains were still drawn mid-afternoon, dust fragments danced lazily in a stray chink of sunlight. In another secret safe, the one that lay behind a false bookshelf loaded with novels by James Patterson, he typed in another code: 0765. The month and year that Bill joined the LAPD. From the secret safe, Jeffrey removed an external hard drive for a Macintosh computer, twelve CD-ROMs, a box of ancient metal film canisters, a jewelry box, another thousand dollars in cash, an eight ball of crack cocaine, and a half ounce of Chinese heroin.

Jeffrey held the film canister in his hands. It felt cool to the touch, yet still it radiated a kind of talismanic energy. He felt as if he were holding a newborn child in his hands, and that one sudden, spastic movement could prove disastrous, even fatal. In a way he *was* holding a life in his hands: the last remnants of the life of a Hollywood icon. The last performance by Sharon Tate, all that was left that had not been picked over by the media, the fans, the ghouls, and the curiosity seekers. In his hands was a film starring a slaughtered movie legend that had not been seen by anyone, other than a select crew of Hollywood degenerates, since it was originally shot decades ago.

He looked in Bill's closet and found a decent-sized suitcase with wheels. He packed it with the contents of the bedroom safe, relocked it, and wheeled the case over to Bill's bed. He kissed Bill's cold, rubbery forehead. He felt for the first time that he was kissing a little old man.

.   .   .

"Good-bye, Daddy," Jeffrey said.

Bill said nothing.

Jeffrey dragged the case downstairs. He packed away the contents of the downstairs safe before forcing the zipper on the suitcase shut. Jeffrey booked a cab and walked back to the guesthouse. In his bedroom Jeffrey shoved his unfolded clothes into a canvas bag. The guesthouse was small and Spartan. Some gym equipment tossed in one room, a computer in a second room, a single twin bed shoved in what would pass for a closet in Bill's house. This anonymous space had been Jeffrey's home for the past four years. In his whole time here Jeffrey had hung almost nothing of himself on the walls. Within twenty minutes, his home of four years was bare and unoccupied. An icy, desolate feeling came over him. He returned to the main house and waited for the car in silence.

He knew for certain that Bill's sons would be swarming over the house like locusts soon enough. Bill's estate would be carved up between them. Jeffrey would be entitled to nothing. The family knew no more about Jeffrey than they did of the contents of the safes. This, Jeffrey took as his inheritance. In these past four years, Jeffrey had taken on the roles of the old man's son, friend, wife, and lover. He had blended into Bill's life with perfect anonymity. He had never seen the family beyond the pictures of bucktoothed, teenaged prom dates that turned into fat, red-faced married men, and the single picture of a bony, long-dead wife. Bill had retained a cool distance from his kin, as one of them climbed the political ladder in Washington and another made his millions in the Laundromat business.

Jeffrey thought of the smell of Bill's hair oil, of trimming his nose hairs and grooming his mustache, of the taste of his urine. He knew his quick, silent departure, stealing trinkets of cash and cocaine like a grave robber taking rings and gold fillings, was what Bill would have wanted. The contents of the film canister alone represented what Jeffrey supposed was a small fortune. Unloading the items would have to be done with care and meticulous planning.

Jeffrey considered the drugs in his possession. A brief, mad thought flitted across his mind. He thought of holing up in Tyler's apartment for a while, and smoking and fucking his way to some kind of peace of mind. But Jeffrey was a pragmatist. He thought of how much trouble an eight ball of crack could cause, especially without Bill's steady, guiding hand. He thought of London, seven years earlier, a crack-fueled lovers' spat that resulted in his permanent exile from the city he'd most loved.

All of which had eventually brought him to Los Angeles, and to Bill. Now life had taken another unexpected turn. The decisions he made now would have repercussions that would be felt for a long, long time. On a sudden impulse, Jeffrey checked the Yellow Pages and ripped out a page. "Drug Rehabilitation" went into his back pocket. Jeffrey's cell phone rang. The taxi was here. LA Yellow Cab, *The name to trust since 1922.*

TWO

Dr. Mike adjusted his tie, fiddled with his cufflinks, and stared at his reflection one last time. There was a soft knock, and the door opened. A small, apologetic-looking man popped his shiny head through the door and said, "Dr. Mike? You're up in five."

"Okay, thanks."

Dr. Mike returned for a moment to his own reflection. He smoothed his gray temples. Then, as if remembering something important, he looked back at the bald man and smiled at him. The man seemed momentarily stunned to be caught in the glare of that smile. That all-white, dazzling smile had been shining from billboards, televisions, magazine covers, and computer screens with relentless regularity recently. Then, snapping out of his awe-induced silence, he stammered something about the good work the doctor was doing and quickly backed out of the room.

Dr. Mike looked at his watch. It was six fifteen a.m. On the green room's coffee table was the morning paper, with the headline DEAN THE DOPER: CORONER SUSPECTS OD IN MYSTERIOUS DEATH OF DEAN MICHAELS. Dr. Mike had read the paper in preparation for the interview. He was quietly taken aback by the timing of the young actor's death. A week before the new season of *Detoxing America* was due to air, Dr. Mike had ended up booked on every major network to speculate on the possible causes of the mysterious tragedy. And on every spot, he managed to turn the subject back around to his new reality show. Dr. Mike's manager had been particularly happy with his seasoned dexterity.

"You should call a wing of your new house the Dean Michaels Wing," he laughed.

Maybe I should hang the poor fucker's headshot in my guest bathroom, Dr. Mike thought. He laughed and said, "Maybe I'll do that. Maybe I'll do that."

Under the glare of studio lights, a pretty Asian girl patted Dr. Mike's face with a final layer of powder.

"Uh, Dr. Mike?" she half whispered.

The doctor puckered his mouth in annoyance and opened his eyes.

"Yes?"

"My name is Lai. I, uh, just wanted to say what a big fan I am. And, uh, I have a brother. He's an addict. I was just wondering if you had any advice. . . ."

Dr. Mike's eyes traveled down from her face, to her throat, and rested on her breasts, which dangled half an inch from his arm. The smell of her perfume. He cleared his throat. He smiled at her.

"Would you like an autograph?"

The girl smiled back.

"Oh . . . oh, sure . . . I have a pen . . ."

"No . . . not now. I need to prepare. When I'm done. Uh, well, I have this thing to do. Afterward. What time do you . . . *get off*?"

"Well—around noon, usually . . ."

"Would you like to meet for lunch? I'll be in the area around noon. I could . . . pick you up. Then we could . . . talk. About your brother."

She finished powdering his face, slightly breathless.

"Oh. I'd be . . . that would be great. I mean, are you sure?"

Dr. Mike brought out the smile. The girl felt herself get light in the belly, the sudden giddy lurch of vertigo.

"I'm sure."

He handed her a card, and she took it quickly. She slipped it into the back pocket of her jeans without anybody else seeing.

"Call me at noon," he whispered.

"Okay."

He watched her walk away.

"Dr. Mike! It's a pleasure!"

Dr. Mike turned. He found himself looking at the glowing, healthy face of Matthew Bower. This was the second time he had met the *Good Morning* show host, but it would be their first on-camera encounter. Bower had eased into baldness with the same quiet dignity that Dr. Mike had eased into premature grayness. Both men together represented the ultimate sexual fantasy of a large portion of American females over the age of forty.

They talked with a combination of an *"I'm a man in charge of my life"* friendly insincerity and a *"don't fuck with me"* professionalism.

"I wish we could be meeting under happier circumstances," Dr. Mike said, solemnly.
"True. It's a sad day. A very sad story all around. I really feel for his family."
"The disease of addiction is a chronic and incurable one."

When talking about addiction, Dr. Mike had a number of stock phrases—mostly bastardized or lifted outright from the *Big Book* of Alcoholics Anonymous—a book that he liked to use more for its "profile" than its content. Using the book like a preacher uses the Bible, he scoured it for key phrases, nuggets of wisdom, and platitudes to advance his own theories. While talking about the death of Dean Michaels to interviewers and reporters these past few days, Dr. Mike would sometimes zone out completely. He could not talk about the specifics of the Michaels case, as the young actor was not his patient. But each and every question could be answered by using a profoundly ambiguous phrase like: "For the addict, one pill, one line, one drink is too many . . . paradoxically, one thousand are never enough." The only time Dr. Mike really came alive was when he sensed it was the right moment to promote his show, *Detoxing America*. But even here there were stock phrases: "Revolutionary television," "Entertainment that educates," "The reality show that saves lives," and of course the advertising tagline: "America is SICK. But the DOCTOR is IN."

"Well," Bower was saying, "there'll be nothing hardball today . . . I know that you can't comment on the specifics of the case. Maybe I can talk to you about how crazy young Hollywood is acting these days, with the Lindsays and the Britneys . . ."

"Sure, sure . . ."

"Other than that—"

"GENTLEMEN! TWO MINUTES!"

"Well," Dr. Mike said apologetically, "it looks like we're up!"

"Good luck."

Bower sat down. The pretty girl again appeared at his side and began to powder him. As she bent slightly, she became aware of Dr. Mike's gaze on her. She half turned to him, smiled, and then scurried away.

"In four . . . three. Two. One."

It was showtime.

And in households across America, Dr. Mike's brilliant smile flashed in instantaneous transmission: it shone out indiscriminately from gargantuan flat-screen televisions mounted on the walls of monstrous Beverly Hills homes, battered black-and-white portables sitting atop ancient chests of drawers, color televisions glowing in dark bars where already a smattering of shaky, early-morning drinkers were waiting for their nerves to settle down.

" . . . so Dr. Mike, with the myriad perils you have mentioned in the world of celebrity . . . the, uh, easy access to drugs. The adoration. The pressure. I mean, what advice would you GIVE to someone like Britney Spears, who does seem to be having some very serious difficulties at the moment?"

"Well, Matthew," Dr. Mike said, leaning in, "in many ways you are touching upon something that makes my new show, *Detoxing America*, a revolutionary television event. Because what we are showing here is that there is NO difference between a celebrity who suffers from this terrible disease and the millions of ordinary Americans who struggle with addiction every day. I have made it my MISSION to bring recovery to those who cannot access it any other way. If you want my advice to Britney, I can give it to her right here and now."

Dr. Mike turned to the screen, and looked seriously through it. Across America people quieted down, sensing that something important was about to fall from the doctor's lips. Beers froze, hovering inches from the mouths of the drinkers.

"Britney. The new episode of *Detoxing America* goes out on VH1 at ten o'clock on Thursday evening. It is repeated on Fridays and Tuesdays. We have a full roster of recovering celebrities for this season, but next time I would be honored to have you as a guest. For now, like everybody else, just watch, and listen. Open your heart. Let go, and let God. Please don't shy away from the miracle of recovery."

Dr. Mike's eyes were glistening. They shone with the kind of sincerity that only comes with years of practice. And then it came, like the first rays of dawn bleeding across the horizon: the smile. It radiated from five million or so television screens in awesome synchronization, before reluctantly segueing into an advertisement for antidepressants.

THREE

Jeffrey made it to Tyler's place around three o'clock. So much for his resolution to stay away. It was a spacious, two-bedroom apartment on Franklin and Vermont. Outside the building a row of tall, raggedy palm trees rose up into the mercilessly bright skies like a parade of malnourished crack whores. He rang the bell, and Tyler buzzed him in. Tyler was on the ground floor. The door was unlocked.

"Oh, come ON, T! I NEED something . . . !"
Jeffrey could hear Trina's nauseating whine floating through the door. He knew this scene already. He opened the door.
"Tyler, what's up?"

Jeffrey walked into the dim cool of the apartment. He dragged the suitcase behind him. The wheels rattled against the polished hardwood floors. The living room was sparse, just an empty bookshelf, coffee table, leather couch, and flat-screen television. Trina and Tyler were on the couch. Tyler was stoned, regarding Jeffrey blankly through a haze of gray marijuana smoke. Trina was nervously crossing and uncrossing her legs, clacking her absurd high heels against the wooden floor. She was smoking a cigarette. The television was on. The television was always on.

"Hey, bitch," Tyler said to Jeffrey, "what's with the case? You moving in?"

Jeffrey closed the door behind him.

"Can I hang out today? I'm checking into rehab tomorrow. I need a place to stay until a bed becomes free."

Tyler cocked his thumb at Trina.

"You wanna take this cunt with you?"

"Hey, FUCK YOU, T!" Trina snarled.

"What's up, Trina?" Jeffrey said.

"What's UP," Tyler sighed, "is that little Miss Silicone here thinks she can blow all of her cash on titty jobs, and then come here begging for freebies!"

Ah, thought Jeffrey. New titties. So *that's* what's different about her. She had gone for that classic '80s porn star look, and now her painful, shiny-looking tits were pointing straight out from her ribs, making her waist seem even more ridiculously tiny. Trina's pockmarked face darkened.

"It was a work-related expense! I need these for my career!"

"Oh," Tyler sneered, "dancing at Crazy Girls is a *CA-REER* now! Who knew?"

Jeffrey walked over to her. "They look good," he said.

"Thanks! Wanna feel?"

Trina popped a swollen breast out of her top and presented it to Jeffrey.

"Gurl . . ." Tyler laughed, rolling his eyes.

Jeffrey gave the absurd breast a squeeze. It seemed ready to burst. The nipple stood out a good inch from the breast, in a state of permanent, numb excitement.

"Feels really . . . *big*."

"Thanks! So I was just explaining to Scrooge here that I need some Oxy for work. It's my first day back. I'm out of refills and I'm getting sick. I had to take three weeks off to recover, you know. . . ."

Jeffrey joined them on the couch.

"I get off at eleven p.m.! I'll pay you then!"

"I don't do loans, Trina. If I front you today, I'll have every one of those pill-popping bitches from the club hanging out here with their hands out. It's bad business!"

Trina pouted. "I won't tell."

"Trina, hon, you got a big mouth. The answer's no."

"Just TWO!"

"No. Come back with some money and we can talk."

Trina looked at Jeffrey. "Hey, can you lend me eighty bucks until tonight?"

"I'm flat broke," Jeffrey lied. "Sorry."

"Okay, okay," Trina sighed, as if Tyler had just negotiated a major concession from her. "I'll fuck you. But I want four pills to fuck you."

There was a moment of silence. Tyler looked at Jeffrey. Then they both burst out laughing.

"What? WHAT?" she whined.

"Girl, are you smoking crack?" Tyler demanded. "You ain't got the right equipment for me! You'd better go see that surgeon again if you wanna fuck me!"

"What? What's so funny? You've fucked me before! Shit, a hole's a hole. You said it yourself!"

Tyler rolled his eyes. "I was on METH, hon. World of difference."

"I have some meth," Trina said, quietly.

Jeffrey watched the television for a moment and quickly remembered why he didn't own a set himself. Trina had finally gotten a break.

"Okay, Christ. Lemme have some ice."

Trina handed him a small baggie containing a dirty gray powder. Tyler dipped his knife into it and paused with the tip inches from his nose.

"Two pills," he warned her. "This is a sympathy fuck. Two pills, okay?"

"Shit, okay."

Tyler hoovered up the meth.

"You wanna watch TV for a bit, Jeffrey? We won't be long. . . ."

"Okay."

Trina got up and *clip-clopped* to the bedroom. Tyler turned to Jeffrey and whispered, "This is the LAST time. This bitch is driving me crazy!"

Later, Jeffrey and Tyler were watching *The View* on TiVo. Trina had already left for Crazy Girls, with the Oxy-Contin. Tyler was wearing sweatpants and an ancient, faded "Frankie Says Relax" T-shirt. He was still tweaked and shiny with sweat.

"You know who I'd like to fuck?" Tyler asked.

"Who?"

"That Hasselbeck bitch."

"Who?"

Tyler pointed to the television. On-screen several un-
attractive women were talking about the death of a
Hollywood actor.

"That one. The little blonde with the mean, pinched
face."

"HER?"

"Yup."

"You know something? I think you're going straight. I
mean, you're banging strippers left and right, and now
you wanna fuck . . . *her?*"

"Do you watch this show?"

"I don't watch TV."

"Dude, she's a total bitch. I mean, she's a Republican,
stuck up, a real churchgoing cunt. The worst kind of a
cunt. She probably has a Bible on her nightstand."

"Uh . . . right. And?"

"And she's a WOMAN. I mean, I've fucked Republicans
before, they're the sickest fucks out there. But she's a
Bush-lover, a Christian, a fucking *woman*, you know? I find
her, like, so fucking REPULSIVE, I just wanna fuck her.
You know what I mean? To, like, teach her a lesson."

Jeffrey took a pull on Tyler's joint.

"Seriously, bro, I think you need to lay off the meth. It's
like fucking up your brain. You should hear the shit you
say when you're on it, sometimes. You freak me out."

"You're so boring, dude."

"Please . . . welcome the host of *Detoxing America*, Dr.
Mike!" said the television.

Applause.

On-screen a studious, gray-haired doctor walked onstage. He waved to the crowd and gave a semi-apologetic
"Aw shucks, me?" grin.

. . .

"I hate this motherfucker, too," Tyler announced.

"Who's this guy?"

"He's a fucking doctor. Dr. *Mike*—can ya believe that name? Dr. Mike! He's like he's something off of *Sesame Street* or something. Imagine having a doctor called Dr. fucking Mike? He runs a rehab. He's like Mr. Recovery. Every time I turn on my goddamned TV this fucking clown is on it talking about somebody. Britney, that dead actor, what's-his-face Michaels, anybody. He's such a fucking whore."

"He has a TV show?"

"Yeah, dumbshit! *Detoxing America*. They get a bunch of washed-up celebrities and put 'em through detox. Only most of 'em don't have a real drug problem. They're just desperate to be on TV. He has that rehab, Clean and Serene, out in Pasadena. The one that Robert Downey was always in. . . ."

"What? What did you say his place was called?"

"Clean and Serene."

Jeffrey was pulling a piece of paper from his back pocket. He looked at the paper. Tyler watched the television impassively. Dr. Mike was talking about why young Hollywood uses drugs.

"Because drugs feel great!" Tyler shouted at the screen.

"*. . . the addictive personality is certainly encouraged by the excess of Hollywood, which is something that I discuss in detail in my new book,* Narcissism and Narcotics *. . . ,*" Dr Mike was saying.

"Bro, you ain't gonna believe this," Jeffrey said.

"What?"

"That's the place I'm going to tomorrow. Clean and Serene in Pasadena."

. . .

Tyler looked at Jeffrey. He whistled. "For real?"

"Yeah."

"Wow, that's a nice place. Did the old man pay for it?"

"Well, yeah. Kind of."

"That's wild. You'll probably see tons of famous people in there. Can you take pictures?"

"I don't think so."

"That sucks."

Jeffrey watched the television for a moment. Dr. Mike was talking about his television show, telling the women of *The View* that *Detoxing America* is reality television that saves lives.

"Wanna smoke some crack?" Jeffrey said.

"Oh, sure. Hey, dude, you should totally fuck Dr. Mike."

"Yeah, maybe I should . . . ," said Jeffrey, as he started pulling the coke and the pipe out of his bag.

FOUR

In the dream Randal was looking out toward a perfectly clear horizon. The powder blue sky lay hard against
the sapphire blue of the farthest point of the ocean. The
water was crystalline, lapping at the shoreline with a
gentle undulation. He was sitting on a beach chair. The
one-eared girl was sitting in front of him, just as she
had been before. Her single earring, a large hoop bear-
ing the legend "Esmeralda" in script, twinkled in the
sunlight. This hypnotic twinkling, in time with the
bus's steady lurches, had lulled him to sleep originally.
It kept up its steady rhythm here, as he ran his hands
over her smooth, oiled back.

Then they stood up on the hot sand and walked toward
the water hand in hand. The water was warm. As they
walked, their feet at first smushed into the soft white
sand. Farther on, they found themselves in a patch of
dark green sea grass. Here they stopped. She sat, so only
her head was poking above the water. As Randal sat

beside her, he felt the warm slush of the sand and the slimy weeds collecting around his ass and his thighs. It was this sensation, warm, viscous, that began to bring him around. That and the driver with the bulldog neck, who applied the brakes and frantically looked back over his shoulder, barking, "YOU! SIR! Wake up! Get off my goddamned bus!!!"

He blinked. The mid-afternoon sunlight burned his face through the scarred glass. Someone had scrawled "FUCK THE LAPD" in Magic Marker here. There was a rank stench. Esmeralda was here, too, on her feet and looking down on him with unconcealed disgust. The smell of his own shit made him gag. He looked over toward the driver, who was standing now, about to walk toward Randal and physically drag him off the bus. An old Latin lady stood behind the driver guiltily, having informed him of what had happened. Half retching, Randal staggered to his feet and said, "I'm going!"

Delirious, he staggered off the bus and onto the sidewalk, leaving a trail of excrement in his wake. He sat under the Hollywood sun with crap leaking from the legs of his destroyed $1,500 Yves Saint Laurent suit. The bus tore away from him, and he was alone on the hard plastic bench.

Randal's receding hair was dyed platinum. His once handsome face was hollowed out beyond recognition. He still had the eyes, though. Soulful eyes. Eyes that earned more forgiveness than even he thought he deserved.

He was on the corner of Hollywood and Highland. He walked toward a pay phone, noting the dinosaur bursting from the roof of Ripley's Believe It or Not, with a clock clamped between its jaws. He called his brother collect. Across the city, white-knuckled behind the wheel of his Lexus, Harvey accepted the charges.

"You're a motherfucker," Harvey said.
"Harvey. It's Randal!"
"I know who it is. Nobody else calls me collect on a regular basis. I guess you're calling to see how the funeral went? It was good. A lot of people showed up. Susan Sarandon was there, the Cruises, Bobby De Niro came. Can you believe that? It's been, like, what? Fifteen years since they'd worked together? He showed anyway."

"Harvey, man, listen—"
"Shut the fuck up for a moment, okay? I'm telling you about Pop's funeral. Don't interrupt me. You're so fucking RUDE sometimes! Anyway, De Niro spoke, oh and shit, you'll never believe who was there. Sidney Poitier. Sidney fucking Poitier. Can you believe that shit?"
"Wild."

"Yup. So you calling me with some brilliant excuse for why you didn't show up?"
"It's not an excuse. I just got out of the psych ward. They held me for seventy-two hours, dosed me with lithium, the whole fuckin' bit. I woke up strapped to a bed, in a ward with a bunch of nut jobs. There was this chick that kept trying to catch invisible butterflies and a guy with shaved eyebrows who screamed all night. I called the suicide hotline when I was fucked up. . . ."
"Again? My goodness, aren't you the reckless one. Well, I'll be sure to let Mom know. . . ."

.   .   .

"You're such a callous prick sometimes, Harvey. I'm sick. I lost my wallet. I got shit in my pants. They gave me a fucking bus token and sent me off into Hollywood. I'm standing outside of Ripley's Believe It or Not."

"You ought to be inside of it. Hold on. HEY, ASSHOLE. WHATCHA DOING? INDICATE, FUCK FACE! YEAH! THAT'S RIGHT! YOU DUMBSHIT." Harvey sighed, "Hey, shitpants. You still there?"

"Yeah."

"Okay, Randal, listen. Here's the deal. Mom, Lori, and I had planned an intervention for you. We like flew this professional interventionist called Autumn down from fucking San Francisco, and we all wrote letters about how much we loved you but we don't wanna see you die, all of that shit. But, uh, I guess you were indisposed. So I'm gonna give you the Cliff Notes. You're goin' to rehab or you're cut off. No apartment, no credit cards, nothing."

"Can you come pick me up?"

"Hold on, shitpants. Don't cut me off before I get to the best bit. Randal, are you willing to accept the gift of recovery that we're offering you?"

"Sure. Whatever. Can you send a limo? I need to change."

"No changing. You're going straight to rehab."

"I need clean pants. I shit in my pants!"

"Don't be a pussy. I'll bring you some fucking pants, okay? You're meant to be experiencing a, uh, rock bottom right now. So experience it. They're waiting for you to check in. It's a good place. The guy who runs it has that TV show, *Detoxing America*. You seen it?"

"Yeah, I've seen that asshole. I do have a TV, you know."

"Well, anyway. He seems like a good guy. He deals with celebrities, so I'm sure he's used to spoiled fucking speed freak assholes like you. Just hold on, 'Kay? I'm calling a car service."

Randal returned to the bench. He waited. Was this a rock bottom? He wasn't sure. When money is not an object, rock bottoms are hard to find. There are mostly trapdoors, which lead to ever more dark and deep caverns of degradation. He thought about scoring some more meth before the car service arrived. It was hopeless, though. Drug dealers never accept collect calls.

Every year or two Randal had to make the trip to rehab at his family's behest, or face the prospect of being cut out of his inheritance. Now that his father was dead, Harvey would no doubt be in charge of the estate. Dad had been senile and soft, prone to bouts of sentimentality and sudden forgiveness when he was drunk. Harvey, though, could be a hard-nosed bastard. The prolonged infantilism that Randal's meth habit brought about had changed their relationship as siblings, twisting Harvey into the tough-loving older brother. Only these days it was more toughness than love.

As Randal waited for his car, he supposed that there were worse things than rehab. He would have a bed, meals, and he'd met more than one girlfriend while undergoing treatment. After all, there's no icebreaker in the world like a shared love of hard narcotics.

Randal limped to a nearby Jack in the Box and headed straight for the bathroom. He tried to clean the drying shit off of himself as best he could. He used the abrasive brown paper towels and cold water to scrub some of the stench away. He shoved the shitty, wet paper towels in the toilet bowl. When he had done all he could, he flushed the toilet. It immediately backed up, and started to flood. He fled the bathroom and walked as nonchalantly as possible past the customers waiting for their Jumbo Jacks with Cheese. He staggered out to the sunlight again as filthy water began to seep out from under the door and into the restaurant.

When he made it back to the bus stop the car was waiting for him. Randal slid into the backseat and opened the window wide. The driver, an enormous, sweating black man with a shaved head and an ill-fitting polyester uniform, took off without saying a word.

"Hey, man. What's your name?"

"Christian," the driver replied, with a heavy African accent.

"Hey, Christian. My name is Randal. I was just wondering if we could make a stop on the way. . . ."

"No stop. Mister Earnest specified no stops. No stops until the hospital."

Christian turned the radio up to signal that the conversation was at an end. *Goddamn, Harvey!* Hopeless, Randal closed his eyes and enjoyed the breeze against his face. After a while he heard some off-key singing and opened one eye. Christian was singing along in a weird, fractured falsetto to Jennifer Rush's "The Power of Love." He looked at one of the business cards that had been left in the backseat. DIVINE LIMO, it read, IT'S NOT JUST WHEN YOU GET THERE—IT'S HOW YOU GET THERE! Groaning, he closed his eyes again and waited for sleep.

F!VE

After lunch at Spago Beverly Hills, cocktails at Bar 19, and a furtive blow job in the backseat of his Mercedes-Benz, Dr. Mike was adjusting his tie in the rearview mirror when Lai said, "So, I take it from the ring that you're married?"

Dr. Mike smiled without any emotion and said, "Yes. Happily married with two children. But I'm sure you already knew that. I assume you are familiar with Google?"

Chastised, Lai quieted down. This was Hollywood, after all. Everybody involved knew what the deal was.

Lai had no illusions that she would ever have the opportunity to talk to Dr. Mike once this encounter was over. But she had got half of what she came for: the addictive, instantaneous thrill of bedding a celebrity. As far as that went, Dr. Mike was okay. Not as exciting as getting head from Dave Navarro in a back room of the Sky Bar, but definitely better than last year's coke-fueled bathroom sex with stand-up comedian Randy Dick. She looked at the full condom, knotted in the ashtray. Catching her gaze on it, Dr. Mike said, "You know, if you'd like to, uh, freshen up . . . I have a travel-size Scope right there in the glove compartment."

Lai shook her head. There was only one more thing she needed.

"We never had the chance to talk about my brother. . . ."
"Your who?"
"My brother."
"Oh, yes. An alcoholic, yes?" Dr. Mike began to shake his head. "I've dealt with many alcoholics in my time. . . ."
"He's addicted to cocaine, Dr. Mike. Crack cocaine."
"Oh, oh, yes. Yes. Where do you live?"
"Oh. Los Feliz."
"We can talk while I drive you over there. . . ."

———————————

They were heading down Sunset, toward Vermont. Lai was talking, and NPR was droning softly in the background. Dr. Mike's face was cocked at an angle, and he was dreamily listening to what Lai had to say. Her brother was indeed a habitual user of crack cocaine, but not only that, he was a transgender who made for a more than convincing woman. When Lai had pulled out the picture of her and her brother, Dr. Mike had scrunched his eyes, disbelieving. Never in his years of trawling the underbelly of Los Angeles had he seen a more beautiful and convincing transvestite.

.   .   .

"You see . . . Joseph is . . . well, my parents are very old-fashioned. Very traditional. He's the only son and—they prefer to think of him as DEAD rather than deal with the fact that he's . . . like THAT. He doesn't even like me to call him Joseph anymore. He insists on being referred to as . . . *Champagne*."

"Hm. This complicates matters somewhat. Dual-diagnosis patients are much more difficult to treat—"

"Dual diagnosis?"

"When there are obvious . . . psychological problems unrelated to the addiction itself. Dual diagnosis is a broad term. It can cover anything from manic depression to a case like your brother's where there are, uh, sexual issues. . . ."

"I mean—I love my brother. And I accept him. But the way he's living his life . . . I suspect he's supporting his drug habit . . . by . . . by *prostitution*. There are always these creepy old men around him, and I know that Joseph would never dream of hanging out with these guys unless they were supporting him."

Dr. Mike looked at the picture again. Dr. Mike had thought that Lai was pretty, maybe not stunning, but definitely pretty. However, next to her brother, Lai looked hopelessly plain, nondescript even. Champagne was beautiful, truly stunning. He wondered if Lai was upset that he made a prettier female than she did.

"Has he sought any kind of treatment for his drug use?"

Lai shook her head. "He says that he's happy. But I know that he isn't. I know him. I can see the scared little boy underneath the makeup."

When she said that, Dr. Mike felt his breath get wet and heavy in his throat. His hand trembling slightly, he passed the photograph back to Lai.

"Write your brother's number on the back," he said. "I can't promise anything, but I can at least call him to offer my advice. If he wants to seek treatment . . ." Dr. Mike shrugged. "Well, I can see if I'm in a position to help him. But as I said, I can't promise anything."

"Sure, sure. Thank you. . . ."

Lai scribbled the number on the back of the picture and handed it to the doctor. He slipped it into his suit pocket.

"You understand that we won't really be able to . . . continue to see each other after this. . . ."

"You don't have to give me the speech. I'm a big girl. I just want you to help my brother."

"I can promise to try. That's it."

"That's good enough."

He pulled up. Lai looked at Dr. Mike. He smiled at her. She hugged him awkwardly. What to say now? "It was fun"? "Say hello to your wife"? "I hope you enjoyed the blow job"? I mean, what do you say in this situation?

"It was nice to . . . meet you," Dr. Mike said.

"Yeah, you too. Do you have any smokes?"

Dr. Mike shook his head, and she got out of the car.

"You really shouldn't smoke those things, you know," he called after her. "They'll kill you one day."

And then with a roar, he was gone. She was back in the disappointing realm of reality once more. She went inside, turned on the TV, and another stupid day passed like a dream.

S!X

"So tell me, Randal, what brings you here?"

Randal was sitting across from an impossibly young drug counselor. He looked to be, what, twelve? Thirteen? He was wearing a Circle Jerks T-shirt, and Randal noticed that he had a Misfits tattoo on his arm. I mean, did this kid really have any clue about who the Circle Jerks were? Or did he just think the T-shirt looked cool?

"Uh, what?" Hearing that the kid's voice had gone up expectantly at the end, Randal snapped out of his thoughts. "How do you mean? I came in a taxi."
"No, I mean . . . why do you feel you need treatment?"
Randal was wearing a pair of ill-fitting tracksuit bottoms and a huge Denver Nuggets T-shirt. Both items of clothing had been taken from the lost and found box. Randal's filthy suit was in a trash bag, next to his feet. Upon arriving he had been immediately led to the

showers. The warm water felt good against his aching muscles. The sensation was fleeting. Now Randal was agitated again, and there seemed to be endless rounds of paperwork to be completed before he would be dosed with medication and allowed to pass out.

And on top of it all . . . there was this wannabe punk rock kid, with his stupid fucking questions.

"Look," Randal said, "I'm here because my brother is gonna take away my credit cards if I don't get clean."
"And you do meth, correct?"
"Yeah."
"How long?"
"Until it runs out."
"I mean, how long have you been doing meth?"
"Shit, I dunno. Years. Put down 'years.' I can't think straight right now. I'm crashing. When do I get my medication?"
"When we complete your paperwork, and the nurse checks you out."

Randal watched the kid as he filled out the form on his Mac notebook. Everything in the office looked new, expensive, and shiny. The building itself was vast and painfully white. It smelled of bleach and new carpets. Clean, happy, productive, neat, new. The staff walked around here with cultish smiles on their faces, attacking him at every turn with attempted hugs and cries of "Welcome!" All of the friendliness made Randal want to puke.

"So you work for, uh, Dr. Mike, the TV doctor, huh?"
The kid pursed his lips.

"Dr. Mike is very much a REAL doctor."

"But I mean—I just mean, the one on TV?"

"Yes."

"Will he be treating me?"

"Dr. Mike treats all of the patients. It's a common mis-understanding that he's some kind of a Dr. Phil char-acter, a 'TV doctor,' as you say. But Dr. Mike has always retained a regular practice here, and meets with every patient on a one-to-one basis."

"Is he here now?"

"He's only here on Fridays. The rest of the time you'll have your day-to-day counselor. You'll be assigned one. Do you attend AA meetings, Randal?"

"No."

"Have you ever attended AA meetings?"

"Only when I'm in rehab."

"The meetings are mandatory here. Just so you know. We believe that the twelve-step program is an essential backbone to any attempt at recovery."

"So my room won't have a minibar?"

"No," the kid said without cracking a smile, "it won't have a minibar."

———

"Okay, spread 'em, buddy."

Next Randal was looking into the face of a puffy South-ern ex-drunk, with a bristly red mustache and ruptured blood vessels all over his face. The top row of teeth was missing. He was wearing a T-shirt with the Confederate flag on it, and chunky silver rings adorned eight of his fingers. He had a soft lilt to his voice, but there was steel underneath it.

"I beg your pardon?"

Randal was in another closed, antiseptic room. "Big Jim" had directed him here after his meeting with the punk rock kid. By way of introduction Big Jim had looked into Randal's eyes and muttered, "Say ah."
"Ah?"
"Longer. Like at the dentist. I'm checking your mouth for contraband. Say AH."
"Aaaaahhhhhhh."

"You got some fucked-up teeth in there. You a meth-head?" Jim asked when he was done poking around in there.
"Yeah. You got some pretty fucked-up teeth yourself, Jim. You do meth, too?"
"Been clean for comin' up to thirteen years. But, nuh, I was a drunk. I just liked to kick the shit sometimes. And sometimes, I got the shit kicked outta me."

Big Jim shot Randal a big, toothless grin. Then—maybe deciding that the time for small talk was over—Big Jim said:

"Okay, spread 'em, buddy."

Sensing Randal's confusion, he clarified: "Drop the pants, turn around, bend over, and spread your cheeks. I gotta check for contraband."
"I don't have contraband."
"Sure. Nobody has contraband. We still gotta check."

Randal sighed. He had been through this routine be-fore. He dropped the sweatpants, turned around, and halfheartedly pulled his ass cheeks apart. Big Jim pulled out his key chain. He had a little pocket flashlight attached on there. He flashed it into Randal's asshole.

"Nice job you got there," Randal said, gritting his teeth. "Your mom must be real proud."

"My momma's dead. She was a drunk, too, only she didn't see the light in time. Okay, buddy, you can get dressed."

Randal straightened up. He turned and looked at Big Jim reproachfully. Big Jim just grinned at him.

"And anyway, it ain't a job."

"Uh?"

"I said, this ain't a job for me. Nuh-uh. I've been doing this for thirteen years, and it ain't a job. It's a vocation. There's no better feeling than watchin' some sorry sack of shit like yourself walk into this place thinking they know it all, thinking that the program don't got nuthin' to show them, thinking that they can still do it their way . . . watching the moment come around that they finally GET IT. Finally let go, and let God. That's what gets me outta bed in the morning."

"I guess it's nice to have a vocation," Randal said.

Big Jim was on his cell phone. "Yeah, he's ready. You can take him up."

A few moments later the punk rock kid reappeared and said, "It's time to get you medicated."

"Halle-fuckin-lujah."

Randal's feet squeaked against the tiles as he was led to the detox unit. The unit consisted of several rooms, each with three beds, a bathroom, and a single television bolted to the wall. There was a nurse's station and a small kitchen. He was left with the nurse, an older woman with frizzy red hair. She had a vague beaten-up look about her face that suggested she had once been a drunk or a doper. Randal silently had his blood pressure taken, his eyes, ears, and throat examined, his weight assessed. Finally the nurse went to the medicine closet and returned with a paper cup full of pills.

"Something to help you sleep," she said, pushing a pill toward him.
"Some diazepam to help with your anxiety.
"Some clonodine to regulate your blood pressure.
"Some Tylenol to take away your aches and pains."

Randal scooped up the pills, popped them into his mouth, and swallowed them with a practiced efficiency. He wondered if the diazepam would be enough to make him feel something. As the nurse explained his dosing regimen to him, he started making instantaneous calculations. He would receive a 10 mg diazepam three times a day. If he saved them up, he could maybe cop a buzz at bedtime. It would be better than nothing. Even in a place like this, Randal knew that it was always possible to work the angles.
"And this is chloral hydrate."
The nurse passed Randal a small cup of toxic-looking green goo. Before she could say any more, he gulped the contents down.
"Say," he said, "isn't that the shit that killed Marilyn Monroe?" The nurse just shrugged.

He smiled at her, already feeling better. Just the idea that his stomach was digesting these little miracles and that soon the chemicals would be in his blood and he would again feel like a real human being—however briefly—was a great comfort.

"Is there food?" Randal asked, smiling sweetly, momentarily filled with artificial goodwill.

"There's bread and fruit in the kitchen. Cereal, too."

Randal stood. "I'm hungry."

"Mr. Earnest—"

"Randal, please."

"Randal—you may start to feel a little unsteady soon. Maybe you should wait a moment before you—"

Randal shook his head.

"I'm feeling great. Shit, I could drive a car on stronger shit than this."

"The chloral hydrate will take effect pretty quickly. I'd suggest just lying down for a moment to see how it affects you. . . ."

Randal laughed a little and made for the kitchen anyway. The nurse shrugged and turned away to finish her paperwork. In the detoxification unit it was silent. The only other patient was an older woman whom Randal glimpsed as she shuffled from a bedroom to a bathroom, heavily medicated.

"If you need me," the nurse said over her shoulder, "just whistle."

"Yup."

She found him in the kitchen, twenty minutes later, with the toast cold in the toaster, the plastic knife still in his hand, facedown in a pool of saliva at the kitchen table.

"Aw shit! We got another sleeper!" she yelled.

SEVEN

In the shitty part of Hollywood where all-night news-stands, peep shows, transient hotels, and check-cash stores bordered uneasily the desolate ass end of the tourist strip, Bee was getting hassles from his old lady. He hissed into his cell phone:

"I toldja. I'm coming back now. I'm gonna get a ride with Pat."

"All of these shady fucking speed freaks sitting around the place lookin' to score. . . . The fucking apartment is getting like Union fucking Station! And then fuckin' Henry shows up with his girlfriend a couple of fucking granolas from San Francisco . . . I mean, he's just bringing random people who he bumped into at the club over now? This is my HOME. I don't want it to turn into some kind of fucking crash pad for Henry and his dopey friends. . . ."

"I heardja! Listen, babe, I'll talk to Henry about showing up unannounced like that, okay? That shit ain't cool. I swear. Look, Pat wasn't at the hotel, he was over in the

Spotlight, I had to go find him. Then we had to wait for some guy to show up so he could do business. Now we had to walk to pick up his car. . . ."

"Yeah, yeah, whatever, just make sure you get over here before this dreadlocked bitch starts burning some fuckin' patchouli or talking to me about my aura, okay?"

"Okay, okay, babe."

He snapped the phone shut. Pat stepped out of the bodega, ripping open a packet of Parliaments. His garish Hawaiian shirt billowed around his taut, muscular frame. He looked like some strange cross between an alcoholic country singer on the skids and an aging Hells Angel. But despite the face that had worn out like twenty miles of unpaved road after decades of pummeling himself with booze and methamphetamines, the eyes still burned with an astounding intensity. And like the eyes of a rabid dog, if you stared into them for too long you ran the risk of having your face ripped off.

The older man lit a cigarette and twisted his eyes up against the rays of the dying sun. Then Pat playfully clipped Bee around the back of his head and growled in his two-packs-a-day gurgle: "C'mon, shithead, the car's right here. S'yer old lady on your back again?"

Bee just shrugged as they walked toward a rust-bucket red 1984 Toyota Corolla. The tinted windows were filthy, the paint peeling. Pat wrenched the door open. It hadn't been locked. Nobody would want to steal this piece of shit anyway.

"What happened to the Trans Am?"

"Scrapped it. Fuckin' transmission gave out."

Bee's thick, greasy hair was combed back flat against his skull and his red eyes were hidden behind a pair of bootleg Ray-Ban Wayfarers. As they sailed down Hollywood Boulevard, Bee said: "Every time I see you, you got another piece a shit car. Why dontcha just buy a decent one?"

Pat shrugged. The reason was simple. In his line of work it helped to switch vehicles often. That's why he routinely bought junkers and drove them until they died, then dumped 'em and replaced 'em. He didn't need the heat noticing him because he was driving some fancy-ass car around making deliveries. In fact, the only car he'd ever kept was an ancient Volkswagen Bug that just kept going and going. But after four years he got sick of looking at it, so he traded it to a whore for two eight balls of cocaine. The fucking Krauts sure as hell knew how to build cars. But he didn't need to tell the kid any of that. Instead, he said: "Those beaner chicks can be ballbusters, huh?"

Bee was staring at his cell phone absently, waiting for it to buzz into life again with more of Carla's screams. "Huh?"

"Ballbusters. The Mexicans. Ah was married to one for a year ana half, back when I was a young buck. Almost broke her goddamned neck a few times."

"Huh? What, Carla? She's Dominican."

"It's that fuckin' Indian blood . . . ," Pat went on, ignoring him. "Makes 'em crazy. Does she drink?"

"Uh, no, not really. She mostly just likes to get high."

"You're lucky. They get crazy on that goddamned firewater. Get a few drinks into Maria and—whoo!—watch out, boy. The bitch would flip the fuck out. Came at me with a kitchen knife once, calling me a no good son of a bitch, sayin' I was screwing around on her. That's how I got this. . . ." Pat raised his chin, exposing a thin scar across the Adam's apple. "I had to knock her ass out! She comes around the next day and shakes me awake. *'Pat! Pat! My tooth's missing! What happened to my tooth?'* I tole her that she fell in the bathroom and hit her face on the sink. Fuckin' dumb bitch believed it, too. She couldn't remember a goddamned thing. Turn that radio on."

Bee turned it on, caught some lousy station playing country music.

"Were you? Screwing around on her?"

"Shit, of course. She knew goddamn well! Only really bothered her when she was drunk. Turn that hick shit off. Find something decent, man."

Bee started turning the dial. "What happened to Maria?"

"She ain't around no more," Pat replied.

Bee nervously switched the station. Pat glared at Bee for a moment like he was thinking of snapping his spine. Then he looked back to the road. A flat-toned woman was talking about the Dow Jones.

"Switch it."

A hip-hop station.

"Yeah, right. Switch it."

An alternative rock station.

"Fuck that. Switch."

A '70s rock station. "Sweet Home Alabama" by Lynyrd Skynyrd. Bee almost pulled his hand back, sure that Pat would say "Stop." Instead he barked, "No."

Bee switched. Pulsing electronic beats.

"Fuck off."

Phil Collins singing "Against All Odds." Bee's hand hovered by the radio.

"Don't touch that motherfucking dial. Listen, man. Listen to this fucker's voice."

Bee watched Pat out of the corner of his eye. It looked as though Pat was driving with his eyes closed. His head swayed in time with the lilting piano.

"You like music, right?" Pat snapped suddenly, fixing Bee in a cold stare.

"Yeah. I like drum and bass."

"Drum and bass? What is that? Some kinda faggot music?"

Pat's eyes, as cold as long-dead stars, glared at Bee. Bee shut the fuck up. Pat's leathery face remained cool, but the voice dripped with barely concealed violence. The twinkling of Pat's pendant, as the sun turned the sky a dirty shade of gold. Then Pat started laughing, which was a disconcerting sound, like the wheeze of a deflating air bed.

"How can I just let you walk away . . . ?"

"Just let you leave without a trace?"

"Fucking beautiful song, man. You HEAR that motherfucker? You hear that VOICE? THAT'S the blues. I tell you, that's BLUER than any nigger blues singer I ever heard. That's PAIN, baby. That's real pain. That's from the fuckin' soul, man."

"Yeah," Bee croaked.

Pat gripped the steering wheel, momentarily lost in the swelling of the song. His skull rings twinkled as he drummed his fingers. His head was shaved. His high cheekbones cast deep shadows on his sucked-in cheeks. A graying handlebar mustache gave him the look of a starved vulture. An inked thunderbolt on the throat marked him as a killer, and a spiderweb on the left cheek as a habitual prisoner.

"Okay, listen, this is the bit I'm talking about. The chorus. Shhh."

Bee was a twenty-one-year-old aspiring tattoo artist and speed freak. A character collector. The kind of guy who relished going into shitty bars in the bad part of town and talking to the locals, just so he could go back like some explorer returning from a desolate, forgotten continent, and repeat the stories verbatim to all and sundry. However, he was completely out of his depth with someone like Pat, and he knew it. Pat was a lifelong meth freak and career criminal. Pat's once amusing anecdotes had gotten progressively darker over time, until Bee started feeling more like an accomplice to Pat's criminality than just another member of Pat's constantly rotating audience. A part of Bee aspired toward the outlaw cool of a man like Pat. But only a small part. Mostly, Pat scared the shit out of Bee. If Pat didn't have the hookup for some of the finest methamphetamines in Los Angeles County, Bee would have surely limited his contact with the crazy old bastard already.

Suddenly, unexpectedly, drums kicked in at the top of the second verse. *Thud, thudthud, thud-thud-thud-thud!* Pat cranked the volume to its maximum level. The interior of the car vibrated, as the speakers rattled and protested, distorting and crackling ominously.

"This was a fucking golden era for music. This was the last era of the fuckin' troubadour. The last era of the great love song. . . ."

Pat had not slept in many days. In the two years that Bee had known Pat, he had never known him to sleep or eat. The music was painfully loud. Phil Collins's voice burrowed into Bee's skull.

"I mean, shit, I don't think that no one out there—NO ONE—has written a better song about the fucking horror and absurdity of relationships. Of what love does to a man. I mean—bitches fuck you up! That's what Phil is saying here, you know what I mean?"

The meth he had smoked earlier was making Bee's head throb and his chest hurt. Pat was still talking, he had never stopped, his voice was getting louder, and louder, more insistent and hectoring.

"Phil Collins! Man—you can't fake that shit! That's a man who obviously had his nuts handed to him by a broad, you dig?"

Bee noticed beads of sweat standing out on Pat's brow. Goddamn, Pat looked like his heart was about to explode.

"YOU KNOW SOMETHING? IF SOMEONE . . . IF SOME MOTHERFUCKER SAT WHERE YOU ARE SITTING RIGHT NOW AND TOLD ME THAT THIS SONG DIDN'T MAKE THEM FEEL SOMETHING, YOU KNOW WHAT? I'D HAVE TO BUST THEIR FUCKING ASS. I'D FUCK THEM UP. YOU KNOW WHY? YOU KNOW WHY, BEE?"

Unsure of how to answer, Bee just shrugged.

"BECAUSE THEY'D BE FUCKING WITH ME. YOU COULD ONLY SAY SOMETHING SO STUPID IF YOU WERE TRYING TO FUCK WITH ME. I MEAN, SHIT. IF THIS SONG DON'T MAKE YA FEEL SOMETHING YOU GOTTA BE DEAD OR A FAGGOT OR SOMETHING. GODDAMN. AM I RIGHT? HUH? AM I RIGHT, BEE, HUH?"

"You got it, man," Bee answered quickly. "It's a classic. A total classic. None better."

Pat smiled. He lowered the music slightly. He seemed calmer now. His eyes were wet, gleaming.

"He sure was an ugly son of a bitch, though," Pat mumbled to himself as they sailed past Rampart. "Kind of amazing he managed to get laid in the first place, if ya think about it. . . ."

When they arrived at Bee's tiny apartment, Carla's pissy mood relented somewhat now that Pat was here with the speed. Pat knocked on the door and cooed, "Home honey, we're high," and laughed a crackly laugh at his own joke. Carla opened the door and ushered them inside, dead-bolting it afterward. "Here comes the candy man." Pat grinned, giving Carla a kiss on the cheek. "How are ya, baby?"

"Doin' better now." Carla smiled, handing Pat some twenties.

"Ain't that the truth. . . ."

Henry, his girl Heather, and the girl from San Francisco with the dyed green dreadlocks immediately flocked toward Pat to buy. When everybody was fixed up, Pat lingered for a while to bang a little speed himself. They sat around the apartment, loading the pipe, cutting up the rocky gray powder with razor blades, absorbed

in the process of preparing the drugs. Pat noticed the
dreadlocked couple watching him hungrily as he pre-
pared his shot. Pat instinctively recognized that they
were junkies. New junkies for sure, baby junkies, but
junkies just the same. It was the way that they stared
at the needle as if it were a twenty-dollar steak. They
looked young and clueless. The boy, whose name was
Sunray, was wearing what looked to be a pair of girl's
jeans slung low at the hips. The girl was pale and pretty
despite her ridiculous dyed green dreadlocks.

"You guys from San Francisco?" Pat said to Sunray ab-
sently, as he tapped the air bubbles from his syringe.
"Yeah, how d'you know?"
"Just a hunch."

Pat returned his attention to the needle. You never
could tell who was or wasn't a faggot in San Francisco.
He slid the spike into his scarred, leathery forearm, pulling back the plunger, sending a plume of thick blood
blossoming into the syringe. Then he pushed the speed
in, his lips pulled back, exposing yellow teeth, worn flat
by decades of meth-induced grinding.

When Pat withdrew the needle from his arm and sucked
away the black-red bloodspot that bubbled from the
crook there, the girl with dreadlocks asked, "Uh, that's
a cool pendant. Who is it?"

The meth made the blood pound in Pat's ears. His jaw
was clamped in a grimace of pure euphoria. He said,
"What's your name, baby?"
His eyes burrowed into her. She stammered, "Salvia."
"Salvia . . ." He grinned, breaking her gaze and address-

ing the room while pointing to the pendant. It was on a gold chain and featured a portrait of a man with a neckerchief and mustache, rendered in semiprecious stones in a religious-iconic style. "This is Jesus Malverde. The patron saint of drug dealers. Old Jesus here was a Mexican bandit who was executed in 1909. He's a bit of a folk hero south of the border. The beaners believe that wearing an image of this guy will keep you alive when you're in . . . my line of business."

"Wow . . . where did you get it?"

"I took it. I'm not one for patron saints and shit like that. But the spics, that's a different story. They're a superstitious bunch."

Pat looked over to Carla, and then to Henry. Henry dropped his gaze.

"No offense," he grinned, "I don't mean to talk bad of all y'all. I'm sure there's plenty of you who don't believe in all of that shit. Just in my experience it seems that most of ya do."

Pat was thirty years the senior of anybody in the room. His weathered face exuded a quiet authority. The stench of cooking meth filled the room as the pipe went around. The others sat in rapt attention before him.

"Now, the other day I had a bit of business around Westlake. I went there to meet a friend. I found out that my friend was having some . . . problems. There was some other motherfucker filling in for him. The prick was a real smart-mouthed little beaner. Mouth fulla gold, thought he was real fuckin' smooth."

Listening, Henry felt his jaw tighten. He glanced at the girl he was here with. She was staring at Pat, rapt, oblivious to Henry's discomfort. He began to feel anger rise in his chest but knew better than to talk back to the man with the drugs.

"So I tell this guy that I want five balloons. He tells me, no, eighty bucks only buys four balloons. I tell him I've been buying dope around here for a long time, and I want five. Eventually the little bastard relents and gives me the other balloon. I make a mental note to check the merchandise later. Sure enough, when I pull over the car and open it up, it's bunk. The last balloon is a piece of gum, wrapped in wax paper. Not fucking cool. So I turn the car around, and go back to express my *displeasure*."

The pipe and lighter made their way to Pat. He paused long enough to heat the glass bulb with the butane flame and suck in the pungent chemical fumes. He passed the pipe on and exhaled a cloud of gray smoke.
"So that's where I picked up Mr. Malverde, and also this. . . ." Pat had been digging around in his pocket as he spoke, and on the word "this" he produced something small and shiny. The others strained to look. It was a gold tooth, bent out of shape a little, but still recognizable, twinkling in the dim light.

"That's the last time that goddamn spic'll try an' stiff me on a deal, I tellya. I dragged that motherfucker four city blocks by his goddamned head, before I let him go."

"Hey, man!"
All eyes turned to Henry. He glared at Pat.

"Problem, kid?"

"Why don't you quit it with all of that spic shit, man? It ain't cool. My mom is Colombian. Carla's *dominicano*. You got two spics sitting right here."

Pat stared at Henry with blank, insect eyes. Henry was a slight kid, pretty and young. Pat smirked. He took in the diamond earrings and the neatly trimmed goatee. He was pretty sure the kid was more naïve than ballsy. Bee tried to catch Henry's gaze so he could motion for him to shut the fuck up. Pat leaned toward Henry, who remained oblivious to Bee's warnings.

"You ever been to prison, kid? I don't mean county jail. I mean prison."

Henry shook his head, slowly.

"Well, I have. That's where you really get to see people as they truly are. I watched the fucking spics hold down a white boy no older than you are now and fuck the shit outta him. Just because he wasn't affiliated. Because he didn't believe in choosing his friends carefully. So they took him for their lapdog. Seven or eight of them broke him in like that, knocked him around until he was about ready to do anything they asked. He was real screwy after that. They knocked something outta his head, and he never got it back. Inside, boy . . . that's where you get to smell the STINK of humanity up close. A spell inside the pen will knock that we're-all-in-this-together peace, love, an' harmony shit outta ya straightaway. You get me?"

There was an uncomfortable silence for a moment. Henry relented, smiled a weak smile, and stared at his shoes. He could not meet Pat's gaze again for a long

while. Salvia and her boyfriend, Sunray, gave each
other a look.

"Ask him," Sunray hissed.

"I will, shut up!"

"What's up, honey?" Pat grinned, turning his attention
to her.

"Do you have any dope? We just came down from San
Francisco, and uh, we're both getting a bit . . . anxious."

"Heroin?"

"Yeah."

"Shit. If you'da asked me an hour ago, I'd have said
yeah. I don't touch that stuff myself. That stuff is bad
news. But I got some buddies who are into it, and . . . I
buy and sell it once in a while . . . shit, I could maybe, uh
. . . you kids need it tonight?"

Sunray nodded, "Yeah."

"You wanna go for a ride? I think I know one guy who'll
be around this time of the evening. . . ."

Sunray looked doubtful, but Salvia said, "Sure. I mean,
if you think you can get hold of someone. . . ."

"Yeah, Uncle Pat'll take care of ya."

He stood. Looked around the room, hooked his thumbs
in his belt. "You take care, man," he said to Bee. "I'll be
seein' ya."

Salvia and Sunray stood: "Nice to meet you, Carla. . . ."

Carla nodded and returned her attention to the pipe.

"Nice to meet you, too, Henry . . . ," Salvia said.

Henry stood, hugged them awkwardly. "Yeah. Take
care." He watched them go with Pat, uneasily. Well,
fuck it. At least he was out of here now.

The three of them walked out into the balmy night and walked toward the car. Sunray went to get into the passenger side, and Pat stopped him.

"Backseat, hombre. The lady gets to ride shotgun."

As Sunray slinked into the backseat, Pat opened the passenger door for Salvia and winked at her.

"Go ahead, hon. Maybe some of my manners'll rub off on the kid before the night's out. . . ."

He slammed the door behind her, and whistled that Phil Collins tune again, as he walked around to get into the driver's side, jangling his keys as he went.

EIGHT

Jeffrey woke up and screamed, "Jesus!" He was on Tyler's couch. Tyler was crouched down at the other end of it. He had the toes of Jeffrey's left foot in his mouth. When Jeffrey screamed "Jesus!" Tyler froze, and looked up to Jeffrey's uncomprehending face. He took the toes out of his mouth.

"Okay, I know this looks bad," he said, "but . . . I was . . . oh, Jesus, man, I don't have an excuse. I was fucking loaded, and horny, and your feet just looked . . . well, they looked *spectacular*."

Jeffrey pulled his feet away from Tyler and sat up.
"Oh, God," he said. "What time is it?"
"It's like three a.m."
"Why are you awake?"
"I've been up all night. That coke you gave me was amazing. Is there any more?"
"Yeah. There's more. Jesus, I gotta check into treat-

ment today. Why couldn't you have let me sleep?"
"I tried not to wake you up, dude. I saw your toes and I
couldn't help myself. Sorry."

Jeffrey reached for his lighter and lit a cigarette. He
looked around and said, "Where's my stuff?"
"Safe. I put all of the valuables in a tote bag and stuck it
up in the crawlspace. I figured you'd need the suitcase
for rehab. No point you dragging all of that other fucking junk around with you."
"It isn't junk. . . ."
"Well, whatever it is, it's safe as fucking houses, man.
The bag's a collector's item, bro. From the last movie I
worked on—*The Adventures of Pluto Nash*. Did you ever see
that one?"
"Nah. Don't think I did."

Before he had started dealing drugs full-time, Tyler had
been moonlighting as a set dresser's assistant. This basically meant that he did all of the grunt labor on the set,
for cheap. When it came to the movies, though, Tyler
had a kind of reverse Midas touch. No matter how big
the budget, no matter how hot the star, whatever movie
Tyler worked on seemed to sink without a trace. Luckily
for the movie industry, Tyler soon lost interest in that
career and decided to get into drug dealing instead.

"It's a great fucking movie, bro. Eddie Murphy plays a
nightclub owner on Mars. It's like one of his best roles,
so fucking underappreciated. Anyway, dude, you can
hang on to the bag. It's yours. You're gonna make a fortune on eBay with that fucker one day."
"As long as my shit's safe, man. My whole fucking life is
in that bag. It's all I got."

"Don't stress! I'll guard it with my fucking life, okay? Anyway—dude, we're amigos, yeah? I got your back. You can count on Tyler."

Jeffrey coughed and rubbed his eyes. "I need it. The rest of the dope is in there." He checked his watch. "This is my last day of freedom. Better make the most of it."
"I'll get it!" Tyler sang, jumping to his feet. "I'll get some more of that coke, too."

Later that day, Jeffrey found himself surrounded by the kind of jeans that cost two hundred dollars and looked like they'd gone through a shredder. The plasma screens at J. Ransom on La Brea were playing some shitty song by Coldplay, but Jeffrey had drowned out the noise with his own headphones. David Bowie was singing about drawing something awful on his carpet. He leafed through the designer labels, and his mind turned once again to Bill. It was Bill who had first brought him to this place. His first suit—at least his first suit not bought specifically for a court appearance—was a black Dior number that Bill had picked up for his birthday. He knew that he was wasting valuable cash by buying the clothes he'd need for a stint in treatment at a place where socks started at the sixty-dollar mark, but he could not resist one last stroll around the place. The staff had all known Bill's face and would trip over themselves to fawn over him. Alone, Jeffrey was just another civilian, now totally ignored by the snooty little bastards.

Sex and commerce. It had always been this way. The main thing that growing up sharing a double bed with three brothers in a Belfast council flat had taught Jeffrey was that he didn't want to struggle for the rest of his life. His mother seemed to take some pride in how desperately they all lived, as if by enduring hell on earth she would somehow be guaranteed paradise on the other end. Apart from this sense of martyrdom Jeffrey didn't remember too much else about his mother. When he left Belfast at fifteen and never returned, his abiding impressions of her were about her fetish for crucifixes and the empty bottles of diazepam she'd leave lying around the place. Nobody in the family mourned Jeffrey's departure. There was no room at home for a smart-mouthed, snobby kid who thought he was too good to live this way. Especially one kicked out of the Christian Brothers school for forming "inappropriate relationships" with the older boys.

His late teens and twenties had been a time of borderline alcoholism and risky sex. London's Piccadilly was his entire universe, and the all-night cafés, where he ate pills and waited for anxious men in suits to buy his time, were the closest thing to a real home he knew up until then. In the other hustlers, strays, and addicts of Piccadilly Jeffrey found something approximating a real family. When his friends would be beaten senseless by a client, get robbed, or locked up, it caused him deep, genuine pain. That's why he got his first tattoo, the necklace of barbed wire. Back then a tattoo like that had the power to unnerve potential clients, pacify them even. Not like today. Jeffrey looked over at one kid folding a Ralph Lauren sweater, with diamond earrings and a skull tattoo on his forearm. He had a platinum streak in his hair and wore two-hundred-dollar designer frames. Now tattoos implied as much threat as a fucking low-fat mocha latte.

When Bill had come along, it had been the right place and the right time. Without Bill, Jeffrey was just another rent boy who was getting too long in the tooth. Most of his contemporaries sank into chronic alcoholism and drug abuse once their looks started to go. But in Bill, Jeffrey had found the holy fucking grail, the thing that prostitutes the world over dream of: the ideal sugar daddy. Bill had been caring, considerate, generous, and—once Jeffrey got over the fact that he was almost forty years older than him—attractive. Maybe Jeffrey only had a hard-on for Bill's status, but a hard-on was a hard-on just the same. Jeffrey wondered, not for the first time that morning, why the fuck Bill had to go and die on him.

He looked up again at the video screens. It was that stupid fucking "Rehab" song, sung by the girl who looked like Ronnie Spector after going through a car wash. Jeffrey looked at his watch. Minus two hours and counting. He was already wondering if he was doing the right thing by checking into rehab again. In his back pocket was a carefully folded square of aluminum foil, with cocaine and heroin melted onto it. In his breast pocket, a pack of Marlboro Lights with an aluminum pipe carefully squirreled away in there. Suddenly he needed more, and he needed it right now. Trembling, he placed the ninety-dollar boxer shorts back where he'd found them and stumbled out onto the street, gulping the air down.

Later, Jeffrey was in the back of a gypsy cab, on the way to Clean and Serene. They had made a stop at a Del Taco drive-thru line. He had paid the driver an extra forty to let him smoke in the back. The driver was listening to

talk radio. On it, some ranting right-wing commentator was suggesting that America nuke Venezuela. The
driver was Indian and agreed loudly with most of what
the commentator said. An air freshener shaped like Old
Glory hung from the rearview mirror.

They were waiting to pick up a Macho Burrito and a
strawberry milk shake, and Jeffrey was smoking a
speedball off of the square of aluminum foil. He blew
the smoke out the window as the cab lurched forward.
The server said, "Four twenty-seven," and Jeffrey passed
the money over. He took the food and the driver pulled
out of the drive-thru lane.

When he was sufficiently high, Jeffrey could once again
recognize that his only option was rehab. If he wasn't
together enough to sell off the merchandise then he
would be truly screwed. All of the years he had put in
with Bill would have been for nothing. There was no
place else to go. He hadn't spoken to his family in years
and had no experience as anything but a kept man.
He had one shot to get his life in order, and this was it.
Getting clean was the only possible first step. This was
always the way: Jeffrey could only seriously consider
getting clean when he was high. Then the terror loos-
ened somewhat.

As they headed to rehab, Jeffrey forced the burrito
down. The cocaine had sapped his appetite, but he was
determined to eat something good this morning before
he was forced to survive on a diet of shitty institutional
food. He drank the milk shake and chased it all with
a few more hits off of the foil. He made the driver pull
over so he could get out and vomit the whole lot back

up again in front of several horrified people waiting at a bus stop. Once he did that, he felt good. He was ready.

Jeffrey looked out to the streets. Los Angeles was such a garish, ugly place. He'd noticed that the first day he arrived from England. Nothing matched. The faux 1950s motel signs, the raggedy palm trees, the screaming billboards, the tacky neon . . . all of it a collision of styles, colors, and mismatched eras that made no sense together. Yet, somehow, there was something almost hypnotic about it. It had drawn him in all of those years ago when Bill had first brought him here after meeting in an Internet chat room.

"This place gets under your skin," Bill had told him then, "and it never really leaves. Kind of like having a drug habit, you know? You can leave this city, but a part of it will always be lodged in your brain, calling you back. It becomes a part of you."

He wondered if he would really be strong enough to leave LA once and for all. Or was he doomed to return, like a helpless junkie to the needle? The radio spewed, and the sirens wailed. Jeffrey picked up the foil and continued toward the bright, clean corridors of Clean and Serene. In an hour there would be interviews, paperwork, payment up front, and the first dose of medication. There would be several days of sweating and twisting on thin cotton sheets, drifting in and out of consciousness while the opiates worked their way out of his system. But for now, that was all still an abstract concern. With the coke and heroin inside of him, Jeffrey feared nothing at all.

N!NE

They drove in silence. Champagne stole a few glances at the doctor as they glided down the Pacific Coast Highway in his gleaming black Mercedes. His eyes were fixed dead ahead, and she could see something churning within him, some battle raging, barely concealed, beneath the surface. His smile was fixed onto his face, almost a grimace now, his mouth twitched as if unable to form the words that sat heavy on his tongue. She smiled to herself and watched the road. He wordlessly put a CD on to break the silence. She recognized it. *Blood Sugar Sex Magik* by the Red Hot Chili Peppers. *White boy music,* she thought. There was something vaguely ridiculous about the sight of him with his gray hair and his sober business suit driving his Mercedes and listening to the Chili Peppers. She felt momentarily disgusted, like she had noticed he was wearing a toupee.

She caught a glimpse of herself reflected in the tinted passenger windows. Her long straight hair was parted in

the middle, framing a face that had—over the years—
earned Champagne a lot of money. She was born with
surprisingly delicate features, and naturally full lips. The
cocaine had eaten away at her puppy fat, just enough to
accentuate the dramatic angles of her cheekbones. Her
eyes seemed almost too big for her face, but the eyes were
what kept them coming back. Mostly they were empty,
but through some quirk of genetics, men tended to see
what they wanted reflected in them. They saw feeling
glimpses of unfathomable depth in those eyes, so sleepy,
and sad. In some instinctual way Champagne understood
this and made sure never to disrupt the fantasy. Part of
being a good whore was learning when not to speak,
knowing how to use silence effectively. Now, her features
teetered on the brink: soon, the starved look around the
eyes would harden her face and eat away at her beauty.
But now, as she was caught between gorgeousness and
devastation, she looked more desirable than ever.

When she first got the call, Champagne assumed that
it was some jerk-off dirtbag pulling a prank. Ever since
putting her picture and number in the back of the *LA
Weekly* a year ago, she'd gotten a lot of those. Some fucking freak asking her if she could take a fist in her ass,
while he was frenziedly jerking off down the line. No
intention of ever seeing her or spending money: ninety
percent of the guys out there just wanted to see what
they could get for free. They reminded her of dogs,
panting wetly and dry-humping lampposts in the summer heat. Champagne was well aware of Dr. Mike, just
as anybody with a TV set would be.

"Yeah, right," Champagne had laughed, "you're Dr.
Mike from the TV. And you have my cell number, and

you're calling me personally. Keep talking, fuckhead."
But the more the doctor had spoken, mentioning Lai,
and the *Good Morning* show, she realized that somehow
this was all true. Dr. Mike, the celebrity doctor from
the television, was calling Champagne to talk about
her drug problem. For a moment, Champagne was
furious with Lai for her seemingly endless attempts to
interfere with Champagne's private life. But as Champagne's mom had once told her when she was a little
boy: angels come in all kinds of disguises. She kept him
on the line, talking. Thankfully, she started to realize
that recovery wasn't all that was on the doctor's mind.

It was in the way that he insisted he would have to see
her "in private" in a voice that quivered with nerves.
The way he told her that her sister had told him a lot
about the "special circumstances" of her case, and that
he felt he could be a "comfort" to her. The biggest sign-
post of all was that he made her agree not to breathe a
word of this to anyone. *"If you can't agree to that, we cannot
see each other, and I cannot offer my services to you. I treat all of my
clients on the promise of anonymity, and I ask that you respect my
boundaries also."*

Champagne knew little about the world of celebrity, but
she knew enough to realize when a man with wealth
and power was offering a mutually beneficial arrangement.

As they started the ascent to the house, she tried her
best to look unfazed. After all, a lot of wealthy men had
taken her on dates before. The wealthy were the worst.
The ones with wives, kids. They were the ones who
wanted it the nastiest. The ones who strove to give off

the air of normalcy. The ones who would vote against gay marriage or liberalizing the drug laws. They were always the ones who wanted to be tied up, pissed on, fucked in the ass. The straighter the outward appearance, the kinkier they were in the bedroom.

But even by the standards of her wealthiest johns, the building that they were approaching was eye-popping. It was a huge terra-cotta-colored mansion, with luscious palm trees and thriving vegetation surrounding it, with a gate and intercom system that wouldn't have been out of place on a maximum-security prison. When they pulled up, the doctor said, "Here we are!" and the cheeriness of the comment seemed forced, out of place. He was nervous, she could sense that. She looked him straight in the eye and said, "Thank you, Doctor." He never seemed to quite meet her gaze. In person, there was something obscenely insincere about him. They got out of the car, and she looked around. The afternoon was bright and mild, and for once the smog was clear. She could see the city splayed before her—glittering and empty, like a just-paid whore.

She took the pipe and the baggie of rocks out of her purse as they stood there. She said, "You don't mind if I smoke, do you?"
He watched her, leaning against his car. Her legs were long and tan, and the thought of what was underneath her minidress made his mouth dry. He shook his head, stammering, "There's no one around. Go ahead."

She put it to her lips. Held the lighter, twirled the pipe expertly, and exhaled a plume of chemical gray smoke. Dr. Mike caught a scent that was at once alien and familiar to him. He watched her as she closed her eyes, swaying, as if dancing to a slow song that only she could hear. He waited a moment, cleared his throat, and said, "Shall we go inside?"

The house was palatial and very cold. Or maybe that was the effect of the crack. Everything seemed to gleam— perfect, in place, new. Champagne ran her hands over the marble countertops and said, "Nice place. Lots of room."

"Hm-hm," Dr. Mike said. He emerged from the kitchen with two glasses in his hand.

"Is Absolut okay?" he asked. "I'm afraid we're out of the good stuff. I just keep this around the house so that the cleaning lady won't steal the Grey Goose."

She took the glass and said, "So this is where you fix your patients, huh?"

Dr. Mike shook his head.

"I maintain a private practice in Pasadena. I do see patients here sometimes. But only certain . . . select clients."

"Celebrities?"

Dr. Mike nodded his head slightly. "You could say that," he said.

Champagne looked at the glass in her hand. It was full of crushed ice and had a slice of lime in it. She took a sip and handed it back to him. "Needs more vodka," Champagne said. "This tastes like lemonade."

Dr. Mike returned to the kitchen and topped up her drink. When he came back to the living room, Cham-

pagne was sitting on the white leather couch, unbut-
toning her shirt a little. He stood there and took in the
long, smooth legs. The leather boots. The necklace
with her name spelled out in silver that sat between her
breasts. He felt momentarily breathless with revulsion
and desire.

"Why are we here, Doctor?"
"I told you. Your sister asked that I—"
"Why are we here, Doctor?" Champagne asked again.
Dr. Mike was a little taken aback by how utterly unfazed Champagne was by the house, the situation . . .
by him. He had expected it to be different. It had always
been different before. It was almost as if she didn't know
who he was. He felt himself getting tense and a hard
lump forming in his throat.

"You interest me," he said eventually. "Your case inter-
ests me."
Champagne smirked at him. As she did, he noticed the
Adam's apple. Slight, almost imperceptible, but definitely there. He noticed that his skin was clammy. He
felt like a bumbling fifteen-year-old boy again, and he
liked it. He hadn't felt like this in as long as he could
remember.

"My case? There's thousands like me in this city alone.
My case isn't very special. Now"—Champagne opened
her legs slightly when she said this, and he followed the
smooth brown of her inner thigh up, up until just below
the crotch, where it became engulfed in shadows—"I'll
ask you again. And if you don't answer me honestly,
then you better call me a cab. You call *me* up, out of the
blue, telling me that you want to *help me*. You want me

to keep everything on the down low, and you pick me
up from a side street in a car with tinted windows. You
take me back to your big, empty house and pour me a
drink. We're all alone. Nobody knows we're here. So . . .
what exactly are you looking for, Doctor?"

They stared at each other in silence. The moment went
on and on. After what felt like an unbearable number
of minutes Dr. Mike said, in a low, strangulated voice,
"I don't know."

"Yeah, I figured that. I think I know what you want. You
said you maintain a private practice?"

"Yes, that's correct."

"You see, I've been having some problems. Trouble
sleeping. Back pain. I don't have health insurance. Do
you think that you might be able to help me out?"

The doctor shrugged. "Well, it would be hard to make
a diagnosis without seeing your medical history. . . . I
suppose, uh . . ."

"Maybe you could write me a prescription? A little
something for my back, a little something for my
nerves? Something to help me sleep? You know,
Doctor . . . I would be very *grateful*."

Dr. Mike paused for a moment and then crept toward
Champagne like a guilty schoolboy. He stood before
her. There was barely a foot between them.

"You know . . . for someone like me—it's difficult. It's
difficult because I have much that I need to keep quiet.
Discretion is of the utmost importance to me."

"I understand."

"I have something I could give you. I keep some medication around the house, for emergencies. I suppose we
could come to some kind of . . . arrangement."

"An *arrangement*. Yeah, I like that. An arrangement sounds good. Come closer. Close your eyes."

Dr. Mike was about to talk, but then he thought better of it. He closed his eyes. In the darkness, he listened to the beating of his own heart, the roaring of the blood in his ears. He waited. He started to feel foolish. He thought about opening them again. He had never felt as self-conscious as he did at this moment in time. He fought the urge. He waited. Then he felt her, tugging at his belt. She opened it and pulled it out of the loops. He heard it land on the floor with a dull clunk. He sensed her repositioning herself, closer to him. He felt the pants unbutton, the zipper coming down. Then they fell to the ground, followed by his underwear. He felt momentarily embarrassed by his hard-on. He shivered slightly when he felt the cool air against his bare flesh. He felt like he might faint as the blood rushed from his head.

"My, my . . . ," he heard Champagne mutter. Then he felt her lips, and the furnacelike heat of her mouth clos- ing around him. He felt confused. He still had the glass in his hand. Should he put it down? Should he stay put? Should he . . . oh, Jesus.

Dr. Mike let out a low, guttural groan. It was a groan that—to him—felt as if it had been inside of him for many, many years. He dropped the glass on the floor, allowing its contents to splash out over the wood. He felt the furious heat of her mouth as she began to work him expertly. She took his penis from her mouth for a moment and said, "I think I'd like some of that medica- tion now. It helps me to concentrate . . . *Doctor*."

He opened his eyes and looked down at her. She was looking up at him, those sad brown eyes meeting his gaze, her mouth half open, resting against the head of his cock, smiling a little. Dr. Mike stammered something and started to straighten his clothes.

"Hurry up," Champagne said, "I'll be waiting."

As the doctor hurried off to locate the pills, Champagne smiled to herself, finishing off her drink with a long slug.

TEN

After five glorious days in detox, Randal was transferred to population. Detox was always a breeze for Randal. Unless you were kicking cold turkey in some shitty charity ward, the stimulant users had it much easier in detox than the heroin addicts or the drinkers. The physical habit to meth is negligible. Once you are removed from your sources of supply the drug craving becomes disembodied and futile. There is nothing much else to do but eat sleeping pills and watch television in your pajamas. Occasionally they would have him attend a twelve-step meeting, held in the "smokers' lounge" outside in the mild, cricket-chirping California air, but these too seemed more bearable than usual with the addition of a steady supply of downers.

Harvey arrived on day three, with Randal's clothes. Randal regarded his brother through heavy, medicated eyes.

"How's Lori?" Randal asked. "Is she mad at me?"

"Everybody's mad at you," Harvey sniffed. "I mean, the family starts to get used to what a fucking animal you are, and you always find some way to lower our expectations even further. She's threatening never to see you again."

"You got a cigarette?" Randal asked.

"Since when did you smoke? No!"

"I'm starting today. If I can't get high, then I'm gonna smoke. I gotta do something to pass the time in here."

"Why don't you concentrate on getting better, dickhead? You're getting too old for this shit. I haven't touched a drink in fourteen years, and I feel better than ever."

Randal laughed sadly to himself. He walked slowly over to the window.

"I like this place," he said softly. "They don't treat you so bad in here. I could make a go of this if they'd let me move in permanently. Give me my meds three times a day; let me watch the *Tyra Banks Show*. Thing is, that bitch is a whole lot more bearable when you're on medication, you know?"

"Randal, I'm just telling you—if you can't keep it together this time, then you're out. You're on your own. The family can no longer support you. We've done all we can do. We have spent hundreds of thousands of dollars trying to help you, but you won't even meet us halfway."

"I know . . . I know. Look, I want you to know that I wouldn't be doing this if . . . if I had any choice in the matter. I'm not in control of this anymore. I'm struggling, bro. I'm struggling."

Harvey smiled, coldly. "I know. And I've heard this from you before. I've seen sorry-ass Randal, just like I've seen don't-give-a-fuck Randal. If you want me to believe that things will be different, then take this program seriously. We cleaned out your apartment, because when you come out of here, you're moving in with me. I'm gonna personally monitor your recovery."

"Oh, come on!"

"You don't have a choice. You live under my roof, you stay close to the family, or you go your own way. I'm not having everything my father worked for pissed away by a selfish fuckup like you."

Harvey stood and walked over to his brother.

"I can help you. Just let me."

Randal shrugged. He looked out the window again. Harvey didn't move.

"If you're waiting for a hug, or some fucking thing, you're out of luck," Randal snapped after a few awkward moments.

"Whatever, bro. Your clothes are in the suitcase. I guess I'll see you on visiting day."

"Don't bother. I don't wanna see anyone right now."

"Whatever."

When Randal was moved to population he was taken over to the main building by Jay, another one of the long-term patients. Jay was an enormous Mexican. He walked with a limp, and had an "LA" tattoo on his cheek. He didn't go in much for small talk. The lobby was bright and stark, a kind of faux Frank Lloyd Wright glass structure. Once you made it to the dormitories, the surroundings were slightly less palatial. He was taken by elevator to the third floor. They walked a little down the corridor, stopped outside of a room, and knocked. From the other side, the sound of reggae music was reverberating. The door opened, and a tall, skinny white kid stood there, with tiny little dreadlocks sticking out at angles from his head.

"Levi," the kid said, slapping Randal on the palm when he held out his hand. "Respect, mon."

Randal's new roommate was Levi Stanson, a twenty-year-old heroin dealer, in for an addiction to the same substance that he once sold. He wore a baggy T-shirt with an image of a lion wearing a crown, and spoke with an accent that was some strange bastardization of Jamaican patois. When Jay split, Randal was left with this kid, who was blasting his music on an expensive-looking stereo system and dancing around the room examining a sheet of paper.

Randal said, "What you listening to?"

"Yah man, it a Dennis Brown selection, init?" Levi said, with an easy grin. "Ah say one. You into da reggae?"

"I don't know much about it."

"Ah Dennis Brown, 'im a bad bwoy. Check it doh—dis 'ere is my sound system. I listen to reggae, yeah? If you ain't down wit' dat, you better get some earplugs, init?"

"I don't care about music," Randal said, putting his case away. "You can listen to whatever the fuck you like. I don't follow that shit."

"Yeah? So whatcha like, mon?"

"I like getting fucked up. You?"

Levi laughed. "Bash! You a bad bwoy, Randal. First time?"

"Nope. Yours?"

"Yup. First and last, mon."

"How long do you have left?"

"Tree months. I's on parole, yeah? Me nah finish treatment, me gets a tek back to jail. . . ."

"So you're here for the long haul. . . ."

"Da long haul. Ras. . . ."

"You from LA?" Randal asked. "You got an accent."

"Nah, mon. I an' I from Philly. You a from LA?"

"Yeah, born and fucking bred," Randal said. He pointed to the paper in Levi's hand. "What are you doing?"

"Essay. On mi *higher power*. For di doctor. Him a big bout yah. Nuff money 'n' fame! You met him yet?"

"Nope."

"Him a smart bwoy. Chatting 'bout how Jah-Jah has a purpose for us, yeah? You, him, an' Levi."

"Really," Randal said, "I don't have the first fucking clue about what you're saying."

"Ah. Take it easy, mon. Unpack. I don't wanna chat you with the good stuff too soon."

Randal started unpacking, and the kid bopped around the room, examining the crumpled sheet of paper in his hand, occasionally pulling his pen from behind his ear, and crossing something out, adding a word here or there.

Once he was done, Randal looked around the room. Two twin beds, separated by a nightstand. Anonymous furnishings, and a single window that looked out over a parking lot. There were two pictures on the nightstand. One was a photograph of a beautiful young black woman sitting on a beach towel. She was squinting in the sun, smiling at the camera. The other was a black-and-white image of a bearded man wearing some kind of tall, ceremonial headdress. "Who's the guy in the big hat?" Randal asked.

"That is Haile Selassie I, Conquering Lion of Judah, Lord of Lords. Jah Rastafari."

Randal looked at the picture again. He seemed like an unassuming kind of guy. "What about the girl?"

"Mi likkle jubee, Michelle. She's waiting for me. She's a good girl, mon. When I get out, I'm gonna take her home."

"To Philly?"

"Bloodclaat! Nah, mon. To Jamaica. We gonna have a bunch of little café au lait babies runnin' around in the sand, yeah? It's gonna be beautiful."

"You're gonna go to Jamaica? For real?"

"Yeah, mon. Dere's nah way I an' I can stay clean here. All the good stuff that Dr. Mike teaching us in here is one thing, mon, but it's a nuff problem if there's people slinging dope just down the road from my crib, yeah? I mean, what iz I gwan do when I get out? Me can't go back to selling shit no more. There's nuthin' for me here, mon."

"So what are you gonna do in Jamaica?"

"Jah will provide. I'm a singer, yeah? A DJ. My gwan rock the dancehalls."

"They got drugs in Jamaica, too."

"Not *drugs*," Levi said with a smile. "They got that good Jamaican collie. For Rastafarians, collie weed is sacred. Nah an impure drug, like heroin. They naw got heroin on di island."

"No heroin on the island? What about speed?"

"Speed?" Levi laughed. "Dere's nah fuckin' speed in Jamaica. That's your shit? Speed?"

"Yeah."

"That's a baldhead drug, mon. Nah offense. We a naw tek speed in Jamaica. We likes to take our time."

Randal looked at this kid again. He felt bad for him. He obviously was going through some kind of intense identity crisis.

"So you're gonna complete your time here, and split to Jamaica with your girl. That's cool."

"Big up! Dat's the shit that keeps me going, mon. Three more months of dis, and we'll be outta Babylon. Easy."

Somewhere outside of their room, a bell rang.

"Come on, mon, forward . . ."

"What is that?"

"Time for our morning meeting, mon. Come wit' me. I'll get you orientated."

"So what does the good doctor say about weed being a sacrament?"

"We disagree on dat. So I tell 'im what him want to hear. Only one man can judge me . . ." Levi turned his eyes up to the ceiling fan. . . . "The creator. The root of David. Ites . . . me nah want all da bagels to be gone by the time we gets downstairs."

ELEVEN

The girls sat around and talked. It was early afternoon, and Crazy Girls seemed even more lonesome, the air a little more stale, and the darkness a little more pervasive at this time of day. The stray sliver of sun that crept in past the doorman had an accusatory look about it. It made the holiday garlands that hung from the entrance to the stage shimmer slightly. They drank vodka to combat the effect of the uppers. Onstage a chubby Dominican girl called Lupita danced to Lil Wayne's grunts and implorations. Trina had just started her shift. She was drinking with some of the other girls, waiting for the club to start to fill with the early-afternoon crowd.

"Look at this shit," Trina said, putting a crumpled piece of paper on the table.

"What is it?"

"A fucking eviction notice. That bitch is trying to throw me out of the apartment now. Says I got three days to vacate or they're gonna change the locks."

.   .   .

The saga of Trina's apartment was an ongoing topic of discussion at Crazy Girls. The actual landlord was a hunched-over little soft touch with a beaten, hangdog face called Manny. Manny wasn't the problem, though. The problem was his wife: a fake-titted Eurotrash cunt who had shown up on Trina's doorstep a week after she'd moved in, brandishing an early '80s copy of *Greek Penthouse* in which she was the centerfold. She was there to warn Trina away from her husband.

"Manny say you are model . . . ," she had said through tight lips. "Well, I am model, too. And Manny is happy with this model, yes? I don't want you to come shaking your ass around my husband thinking you get special treatment. If you have problem with apartment, then you come to ME."

After a month or so when a virtual army of cockroaches and mice had emerged from the walls and taken over the apartment, suddenly Manny was nowhere to be found. She could hear armies of creatures scuttling across her ceiling in the small hours, and the poison that she put down for them only seemed to turn their shit neon blue. Aside from that, the little bastards seemed to quite enjoy it. "This is Los Angeles, darling," the wife told her when she complained. "You must get used to vermin, yes?"

When Trina retaliated by withholding the rent, a standoff ensued. The neighbors, all Armenian like the landlord and his wife, became openly hostile to her. The men spat as she walked past, and the women would not make eye contact with her. Her car was often boxed in, and nobody ever seemed to know who owned the offending car. There were drunken phone calls in the middle of the night from the wife: "You pay what you owe us, bitch, or you get what comes to you!" And now notice to quit the apartment. This was not a good day.

A hard-faced redhead called Cherry picked up the paper and looked at it.

"I got these before," she said. "Go to the courthouse downtown. If you file the right papers, you can drag this shit out forever. . . ."

"Bitch, just pay your rent!" chimed in another girl, who danced under the name Foxy. "You ain't broke!"

Trina snatched the paper up.

"I ain't paying shit! The place has fucking mice, roaches, nothin' works. The city TOLD me to stop paying rent until they fix that shit."

"Don't sweat it, girl," Cherry said. "They can't do shit. They're just trying to scare you."

Trina said, "Fucking A. That bitch can suck my dick!" She picked up her glass.

"Talking of being scared . . . ," Cherry said, "you know that little jackass Derrick? Last night, he more'n got his ass handed to him. So he was drunk, as usual. Over by the bar. He was talking shit. . . ."

"He's a pervert," Foxy said. "He keeps asking me to touch his dick and call him Daddy."

"Well, anyways, he's pretty drunk—you know when he gets all sweaty and red-faced? And all of a sudden he makes a grab for my titty! And the little fucker spills a beer all over me. I told him to keep his goddamned paws to himself, and he gets up in my face—bitch this, and bitch that—I thought the little fucker was gonna take a swing at me."

Cherry paused for effect.

"Before I could even call for security he got grabbed from behind, and I guess Derrick knew who the dude was—because he was stuttering and apologizing . . . I mean, more to him than me! And boy, he couldn't get his ass outta here quick enough. Derrick pulls out the bills for the drinks and tries to leave but the dude grabs him and then he gives Derrick this look. . . . Well, shit, then Derrick like totally empties his wallet out on the bar and splits. Left a hundred-dollar tip for two drinks. Derrick was scared of him, I mean really fucking scared."

"Who? Scared of Juan?" Trina asked, craning her neck to look at the door guy. He was sitting on his stool by the door, shoveling takeout pad thai into his face with a plastic fork. Manhandling a customer seemed out of character for Juan, who was a lazy motherfucker and only got the job because he was a cousin of the owner.
"Juan? Please, girl! I'm talking about Pat! You know I heard . . ."
Trina—and the other girls—leaned in as Cherry's voice became barely audible over the music.
"I heard he killed a man. Up in Frisco. Something to do with a robbery. Somebody tried to screw him on his cut and . . ." Cherry trailed off, and a look came over her face that suggested blood and vengeance.

"No, no, that ain't how it went down!" interrupted Foxy. "It was a debt. Pat's a dealer. He got more niggas underneath him than the fuckin' World Trade Center. He's *cold*. Friend of my cousin worked for him. That motherfucker cut off one of his thumbs over some money shit. Kept it, too. They say he got a collection. Every motherfucker who ever dealt with that bastard got a story."

"I heard he collects teeth," Cherry said, her authority suddenly undermined by Foxy's cousin's friend, "that he's half Cherokee, and that it's a tradition. A ritual. You know, back when those people useta paint their faces and scalp cowboys'n shit."

"Hush up," Foxy said. "Speak of the devil. . . ."

Pat was standing by the entrance, talking to Juan. Pat laughed, slapped Juan on the shoulder, and made his way into the bar. He had been making a daily pilgrimage to Crazy Girls for three weeks now. He appeared one day out of nowhere and insinuated himself into the daily workings of the club so seamlessly that it seemed like he had been there since the place opened. He was the only customer in living memory who'd ever received free drinks from the bartender. He'd come in at four p.m. and drink and flirt with the girls until seven. Then he'd check his watch, leave a pile of money on the bar and say "duty calls" with a crooked grin, and disappear until the next day. He had talked and flirted with nearly every girl in the place, but nobody seemed to know much about him except for the most gothic and outrageous of rumors. These were breathlessly passed around, minor acts of violence and criminality were added and elaborated upon until Pat took on an almost superhuman aspect. He was like some old god, full of implied wrath and vengeance, sitting there nursing his drink and furrowing his brow.

"He's handsome," Trina said, looking over to Pat as he sat at the bar and ordered a drink. He was wearing a black leather jacket over his wifebeater, Levi's 501s turned up at the cuff, and scuffed motorcycle boots. He looked casually over to Lupita as she danced and then to the girls, giving an easy wink to Trina when he caught her eye on him. Trina smirked at him flirtatiously, then looked back to the other girls. "I mean, handsome for an old dude. How old do you think he is?"

Nobody had an answer for that. Lil Wayne had stopped singing. "Lupita! Lupita, ladies and gentlemen . . . give her a big hand . . . ," the DJ roared before lining up another record, "Candy" by Cameo. Besides Pat and a lone Mexican well on his way to unconsciousness, the place was empty. The Mexican's eyes were heavy as he sat in a booth, while a one-armed stripper called Little Five-O rubbed her ass against his crotch. Trina stood.
"I'm gonna see if he wants to buy me a drink."
As she walked away, Foxy raised a plucked eyebrow and said, "Something about that combination don't sit well with me. That bitch ain't got no sense. She'd better be careful. . . ."

The others uh-huhed, and drank their drinks, and looked sadly toward the light outside, which was becoming ever more abstract and unreal to them. In this place it was somehow always three a.m.

TWELVE

Once his paperwork had been processed, Jeffrey hunkered down to undergo detoxification. As the dope worked its way out of his system, he sweated and twisted on the thin mattress and his dreams were vivid, full-color nightmares of piles of pure, white Chinese heroin, Bill's shriveled-up old corpse dancing as if suspended on marionette strings, and rocks of crack the size and shape of boulders. Sleep came in fits and starts, but he underwent his withdrawal with the stoicism of someone who had been through this routine many times before.

On the fourth day of detox, Jeffrey saw a ghost. Not an emissary from another plane, rattling chains and groaning. This one happened to be alive, but it was a ghost just the same.

The nurse poked her head around the door to Jeffrey's room and said, "It's time for your meeting."

"Meeting?" Jeffrey groaned, twisted up inside of a sweat-soaked duvet.

"We're having a meeting. Out in the smokers' lounge. Come on!"

Reluctantly Jeffrey splashed water on his face and looked at himself in the mirror. By day three, the worst of the physical symptoms had peaked. Still, if he wasn't on a large amount of drugs right now, he would be barely standing. Even with the addition of a cocktail of chemicals intended to mask the worst of his symptoms, Jeffrey still felt like shit. His asshole was burning and raw, from enduring endless bouts of violent diarrhea. He looked to have lost at least five pounds, and his skin looked an even paler shade of corpse than usual. His head felt like it had been stuffed full of cotton wool. He tried to brush his teeth, but the taste of the toothpaste made him retch.

He shuffled out to the smokers' lounge in his slippers, feeling like a little old man. Out here there were three nonpatients, sitting around the table, drinking coffee and chain-smoking. There were two other shell-shocked patients in their nightgowns, looking as miserable as Jeffrey was. Jeffrey was about to take a seat when he saw him. He was sitting there, lighting the butt end of a cigarette, trying to suck the last of the nicotine out of it. At first Jeffrey thought that this was some kind of flashback, a hallucination brought on by the effects of the withdrawal. He blinked his eyes, looked away, and then stared once more at the man who sat at the table.

He had the vaguely handsome, bland look of a newscaster. His skin glowed with good living and wealth. He smiled, showing dazzling white teeth. With or without the leather Gestapo getup, there was no doubting that this was a sick fucker who went by the name of Brian Hammer.

"The Hammer" was a longtime regular at Bill's legendary "Extreme Halloween" parties. That was until the first Halloween that Jeffrey came on the scene. Catching sight of him, Jeffrey felt his asshole twitch, as if it had some kind of sentient memory of the Hammer's brutal excesses that year.

Just then the Hammer looked up and caught Jeffrey's gaze.
"Welcome!" he said. "Come—come! Sit down. We're about to start."
Jeffrey stood there, frozen, his mouth flapping open a little. The others turned now—a well-to-do-looking black man in a suit and a red-faced ex-drunk with jug ears. They all smiled welcomingly and beckoned for him to take the seat next to the Hammer.

Be cool, motherfucker. Be cool. He doesn't recognize you. Not dressed like this.

"Welcome, everybody," the Hammer said. The voice was chillingly familiar. Nasal, dry, the hint of a Kentucky accent. Jeffrey felt his palms getting sweaty.

"Now, normally we don't do this, but I'm feeling particularly thankful to be here today. It's my fourteenth sober birthday, and what better way to mark the occasion than by coming back to the place that saved my life? So if y'all don't mind, I'd like us to join hands, bow our heads, and say the Lord's Prayer. . . ."

. .

Before he knew what was happening, the Hammer had slipped his hand over Jeffrey's. His grip was powerful. The others, oblivious to Jeffrey's discomfort, all bowed their heads.

"Our Father," the Hammer began, "Who art in heaven . . ."

The last time Jeffrey had seen the Hammer was four Halloweens ago. Bill's Extreme Halloween parties had been a strictly invite-only occasion and were famous among the perverts, drug fiends, and thrill seekers in Bill's inner circle as *the* social event of the year. Hired help walked around with silver trays loaded with a brain-cell-massacring array of uppers, downers, and halluci-nogenic substances brought in from every corner of the globe. The finest Peruvian flake cocaine and the purest Chinese heroin were among the more vanilla selec-tions. There were vintage intoxicants from the LAPD's seizure rooms, stuff that brought back memories of bell-bottoms and roller-disco, like PCP and Quaaludes. A priceless batch of original Owsley acid was dragged out of the freezer and handed out like party favors. There were a variety of rare pharmaceuticals imported from all over the world, including Diconal, Palfium, Eu-kodal, and temazepam jellies. The booze ran the gamut from a $100,000 bottle of 1947 Cheval Blanc to a case of original Ripple wine procured from a private collector for an undisclosed sum.

That night Jeffrey was in a blood-splattered white dress and blond wig, with a shattered tiara on his head. Bill looked unrecognizable—his skin pigmentation had been professionally altered to give him a vaguely Middle Eastern appearance. A wig of tight black curls blended in with his head seamlessly. He was wearing a torn-up Armani suit, and was covered in blood. A piece of glass looked to be sticking out of his neck, and the coup de grace was a foot or so of intestine that snaked out of his belly and had been casually slung over one shoulder like a feather boa made of raw meat. This year they were Princess Diana and Dodi Al-Fayed, back from the grave.

There were eighteen boys rounded up by Bill to make themselves available to his guests. They were a mix of rent boys, junkies, and unfortunate kids who had run afoul of the LAPD and whose asses now literally belonged to Bill. Ever since his retirement from the force, a few of the prettier and more desperate of the LAPD's young male victims were sometimes offered a free pass in exchange for one night's work. For the older decadents still on the force, being able to rustle up some young boys too terrified to say no to being used as semen receptacles for Bill's guests was powerful leverage in scoring an invite to the party. You could tell who the newbies were. They stood around, naked, huddling in groups, stiff and nervous when someone would sidle up to them to say that their services were required.

Taking in the chaotic splendor of the party, Jeffrey found himself watching the Hammer as he went for one of the boys, grabbing his buttock like a man appraising an animal at market. Another of Bill's guests, a wealthy California media mogul dressed as John Wayne Gacy, leaned in and whispered, "Who did your catering? You have some fantastic hors d'oeuvres. . . ."

.   .   .

The Hammer, who never imbibed anything stronger than caffeine and tobacco, took his boy into a private screening room. There, while some of the most extreme Ukrainian snuff movies on the market played out on the sixty-inch plasma screens, he locked the door behind them with a dark smile on his lips. When he emerged from the room forty minutes later he looked slightly apologetic. Jeffrey noted the curious look on his face as the Hammer called Bill over, and both of them disappeared into the screening room. When Bill called Jeffrey inside, he knew from Bill's expression that it wasn't good news.

The room had several rows of vintage red velvet cinema seats in it, all facing toward the plasma screen that dominated one wall. On-screen, a movie that Jeffrey had seen before: a gang of feral Eastern European youths riding around in a car with a handgun. As their digital camera rolled they pulled up next to a teenage boy on a bicycle, shot him in the face, and sped away laughing.

"The kid must have overdosed," the Hammer was saying. "He just stopped breathing!"
Jeffrey looked down at the brutalized, twisted kid on the floor. He was nude and lying very still and very bloody on the floor underneath the screen. He was dead, no doubt about that.
"What the fuck happened?" Jeffrey said.
"Well, Brian says that he just stopped breathing. He was, uh, inserting something into the kid, and he had some kind of seizure."

"What the fuck were you inserting?" Jeffrey said.

The Hammer puffed out his chest. "Who the fuck do you think you're talking to, kid? Watch your fuckin' tone of voice with me!"

Bill raised a hand and looked at the Hammer.

"We'll have none of that, okay, Brian? Now calm down. What happened?"

"The kid—he kept telling me to stick it in his ass. He said he could take it. He kept telling me to put it farther in. More and more. The kid was a fucking screwball. He asked for it, so I gave it to him. The next thing I fuckin' know he's rolling around on the floor and twitching and shit. I slapped him around a little bit to bring him out of it, but . . ."

Jeffrey looked at the kid's bloodied nose and busted lip.

"Yeah. You did a good job of slapping him around, all right. What did you use—a tire iron?"

"I'm warning you, Princess—one more fuckin' word out of you and we'll be dumping two bodies tonight."

At this, Bill turned and grabbed the Hammer by the throat. The Hammer immediately started trying to wiggle away, but Bill's grip was iron. Despite his age, Bill was strong. He pressed the Hammer against the wall, slowly choking the air out of him.

"You don't fuckin' talk to him like that, okay? He's mine. Nobody fuckin' talks to him like that. If I have to dispose of a fucking extra body tonight it ain't gonna be HIS. You got me?"

He let go, and the Hammer started coughing and gasping for breath.

"Shit! Bill! I'm sorry, man! I'm just . . . I'm just a little freaked out is all!"

"What were you sticking in his ass?" Jeffrey asked.

"Uh, the dildo. The dildo."

"Well . . . where is it?"

"Well . . . right before . . . you know, the seizure . . . I guess I shoved it too hard or something, but it just . . . It fucking disappeared. Schluup! It vanished right up there. All fourteen fucking inches of it."

"Aw, Christ," Bill said. "It's inside of him? Anything else we should know?"

"Yeah . . . ," the Hammer said, "I need it back. It's traceable. The fucking thing is custom-made. Monogrammed. I—I had it modeled after my own, you know. That's why they call me the Hammer. The head is kind of . . . well, I guess you'd have to see it. . . ."

He smiled a kind of aw-shucks grin. Bill looked around. "We'd better lock up this room until afterward. We'll figure out what to do once the guests clear out. So one of the boys goes missing. No big deal. Brian—you're staying. I ain't getting that fucking dildo out. That's on you."

Jeffrey looked at the corpse, and then back at Bill, shell-shocked. "So you're just going to dump the body? Where?"

"Don't worry about that," Bill said, "I know a good spot."

"Lead us not into temptation and deliver us from evil. Amen."

"Amen," the group chimed.

"Well," the Hammer said, addressing the group, "I guess I'll get this started. Fourteen years ago I was a drug addict and an alcoholic. Today I have a job that I love, a beautiful wife, and two gorgeous children. Today I no longer look at myself in the mirror and wonder who that son of a bitch is. Clean and Serene gave me a second shot at life, a chance to feel like a worthwhile human being. And for that, I am truly grateful. I'd like to introduce you all to Roman, who will be sharing his story with us today. . . ."

After the meeting, Jeffrey went straight back to his room. He lay down on the bed, his guts churning. The nurse peeked in at him and asked if he was all right.

"Yeah. I'm just feeling tired. I need to rest. . . ."

"Well, if you need anything, I'm right out here. . . ."

He lay like that for a while. When the Hammer and Bill had left after the party to dispose of the body he had done something similar. He lay alone in bed until four a.m., when he heard Bill's steady footsteps outside of his door.

"You awake?" Bill said.

"Yeah."

"You freaked out by what happened?"

"Yeah. That was some fucked-up shit. He was eighteen. He didn't deserve to die like that."

"Nobody deserves to die," Bill said, "but they do. We're just animals, Jeffrey, and we do what we do because of instinct. Nobody mourns for a fucking gazelle that gets eaten by a lion. You don't need to mourn this kid. He was born to die. We're all dying from the moment we're shat out into this world."

"Did the Hammer get his dildo back?"

"Yeah. It was messy, but he got it."

"Jesus Christ."

"Look, kid, if it makes you feel better I'll keep him away next year. That motherfucker has just about used up all of my good graces already. We'll get some fresh faces next year, okay?"

"Okay."

"Now I gotta explain that one of these kids is AWOL and make sure nobody stole the silver. Get some sleep. Good night, kid."

On the thin institutional mattress Jeffrey turned on his side, pushed the scratchy blanket to his face, and muttered into it, "Good night, Bill."

TH!RTEEN

On the way back from lunch, Randal stopped by his room and pressed his ear to the door. Thank Christ, there was no music. Randal had come to regret his initial comments that he didn't care what kind of music Levi played in there. After a week of nothing but reggae, loud, repetitive fucking reggae, Randal couldn't take it anymore.

"Can you turn that fucking shit off?" he'd barked eventually. "This fucking music is driving me crazy."

"This is Prince Far I, mon. Bumbaclaat!"

"It sounds exactly like all of the other stuff you play. How can you tell this stuff apart? It all sounds exactly the fucking same. It's driving me crazy, Levi. Have a heart, man!"

"Well, mon," Levi sighed, "you have cloth ears. Maybe you'd appreciate dis better if you had a smoke."

"You got anything?"

"Nah. . . . Even mi fucking mouthwash is alcohol-free. . . ."

Thankful not to hear the relentless beat of Levi's music, Randal pushed the door open. The room was in darkness. He thought he had the place to himself for a moment, before he noticed that Levi was sitting in the room with the blinds drawn. He was perched on the edge of his bed, with his head in his hands.

"Levi? Are you okay?"

Levi shook his head quickly and turned away from Randal. "Get out, mon. Me need some space."

From the sound of his voice, Randal knew that Levi was crying. Randal crept forward.

"What happened? Are you okay?"

Randal looked around the room. On the floor were ripped-up shreds of paper. He looked over at the nightstand. Haile Selassie was up there, alone. He looked back at the floor. The shards of paper were all that was left of the picture of Michelle.

"Is that your girl on the floor?" he asked.

Levi looked up, his eyes bloodshot and his cheeks wet. "Nosy motherfucker, ain't you?" he hissed.

Randal shrugged, but did not leave.

"Yeah. Bitch up and left. Said she can't wait for me. Wants to move back in with her mom."

"She'll come around. Just give her some space. . . ."

"Space? The bitch GOT space. That's the problem. And it's not just that. She's fucking some dude. I need to get the fuck out of here and talk to her."

"But your parole . . ."

"Fuck my parole. I know a guy who can get me a passport, yeah? I could pick her ass up and we could be out of here before they even know I'm gone."

"I dunno, man. That sounds like a bad idea, listen . . ."

Randal walked over to Levi. He placed a hand on Levi's shoulder. He felt Levi tense up under his touch, so he pulled back a little. "Just . . . look, I just came here to pick up my copy of the *Big Book*. I have a meeting. Just don't do anything stupid, okay? We'll talk it out when I get back."

"Yeah, mon. Sure," Levi said. Randal nodded and picked up the book. He looked back at Levi.

"Take it easy," he said. "It's going to be all right."

Levi sniffed, and said, "You know what the worst fucking part is? The part that really fucking kills me?"

"What?"

Levi shook with rage as he hissed, "She's fucking a nigger. As if leaving me wasn't enough, as if crushing my fucking dreams wasn't enough, now she's fucking a *nigger*. GodDAMN!"

Levi started to bawl, like a little child. Randal looked over at the picture of Haile Selassie, and then back at Levi, who was balling his fists and trembling as he sobbed. "Look, I'll see you in a little while," he said, before he crept out, softly closing the door behind him. He moved on down the corridor for his daily meeting.

By the time he made it back to his room, Levi, the stereo system, Haile Selassie, and all of that fucking reggae music was gone. All that remained were the torn-up fragments of Michelle's picture. Randal walked back downstairs to the front office and asked for some tape.

"What for?"

"There's a rip in my copy of the *Big Book*."

The kid behind the counter sniffed and passed over the tape. "Make sure you bring it back," he said.

"Yes, captain."

Randal returned to the room and silently gathered the pieces of the photograph together. He laid them out flat on the nightstand and arranged them like a jigsaw puzzle. It was tricky, and it took a while, but he was able to repair the picture. It looked messy, and most of the rips were plainly visible, but it was better than nothing.

"It's just you and me now, Michelle," he said to the picture, "you and me."

Randal placed the picture under his pillow. Tomorrow there would be questions asked about Levi's departure, but for tonight he had his own room, and a girl in a bikini to keep him company. Life was good.

FOURTEEN

After the prayers and the coffee, Jeffrey sat staring at the men in the circle sullenly. It was his first meeting, and surprise sur-FUCKING-prise—it was the same bullshit as always. Jeffrey looked around at the collection of grinning, evangelical ex-dopers and -drunks, banging on about the *Big Book*, and the twelve steps, with the lobotomized zeal of the newly saved.

The detox had been several days of barely conscious sweating and hallucinating madness. The incident with the Hammer had unnerved him greatly. For days afterward, Jeffrey expected to wake up in his detox bed to find the Hammer looming over him in his SS gear, ready to administer some bloody revenge with a gigantic sex toy. By the fifth day the worst of the opiate withdrawals were over, and the paranoia started to fade, but Jeffrey was left with a post-kick reservoir of rage and hatred inside of his soul, which was not being soothed away by having to sit in this pointless, airless meeting on his first day in population.

Jeffrey cast an unimpressed eye around the room. *Look at these fucking jokers*, he thought. *It doesn't take a fucking genius to work out where they came from. Let's see. This fucker here, with the gut and the shiny, comfortable-looking face. Drinker. Probably got a family, and a nice house in the Palisades. Probably here because his wife is sick of him getting drunk and making an ass of himself at important social gatherings. Or maybe he groped the maid after a few mid-afternoon cocktails, and she complained to the wife. Either way, he'll be clean and serene in his allotted thirty days, and will probably become a twelve-step lifer. It's like joining the country club for people like him, except they just talk about getting drunk instead of actually doing it.*

Jeffrey shifted uncomfortably in his hard plastic seat. He was only marginally aware that the meeting's main speaker was still talking.

This guy . . . man, opposite end of the spectrum. Those tattoos are prison tattoos. No fucking doubt about it. He's probably here on condition that he completes, otherwise he's going back to jail. He's Latino, so he probably got busted with an amount of coke that a white guy would have walked for, and now he's caught up in this bullshit system and will have to play along with all of it. This poor fucker will do everything by the book, graduate, relapse, and be locked up again within twelve months.

This chick here is a painkiller freak. You can spot them a mile off. That smoothed-over, alien face of the wealthy and the bored. Hm. OxyContin, Ambien, Xanax, maybe a glass of red wine. Probably been doing that for forty years. Maybe she's getting divorced, and this shit is about to get brought up in the case, and she's doing this to ensure she gets a big enough chunk of her husband's assets.

.   .   .

"That's when I was at my lowest ebb . . . ," the guy was saying, "that's when I knew I'd reached my rock bottom. Finally, with no other options, I somehow found the strength to let go, and let God. I picked up the *Big Book* one more time, and I started to read. . . ."

I mean, that's the fucking problem with this fucking shit, Jeffrey thought, sulkily, *nobody REALLY buys it. It's like some kind of Chinese face-saving ritual. Everybody goes along with it for whatever reason—fat boy over here doesn't want his wife to kick him out because he groped Esmeralda, this poor fucker over here doesn't want to go back to jail because he enjoys smoking a pipe at the end of a bullshit week of cleaning dishes for white people, and this rich old cunt wants to make sure she isn't painted as a drunk and a pill freak in the divorce proceedings so she can truly screw over her cheating rat bastard of a husband.*

And what is everybody's get-out clause? God. That's why the fucking twelve steps have such a place in this society, because all of them, all of these fucking Americans are so fucking strung out on God that they's start shitting their pants if he was taken away. Not spirituality, of course. Nothing so demanding as having to actually consider the idea of something greater than themselves. Just a word: "God." God as an abstract idea. God: the word that wipes away the sins of unfaithful politicians, crooked lawyers, drug-using heiresses, and soap actors who drive drunk. "I found a relationship with God." And all of America waves their hand like a gin-soaked priest after confession. "Go forth, your sins are forgiven."

After less than two hours out of the detox ward, Jeffrey was beginning to wonder if he hadn't in fact made a very stupid decision by agreeing to the minimum two-week stay in population. Maybe he should have just split after getting out of the detox ward. I mean, Christ, what exactly did he hope to achieve by staying here longer than was absolutely necessary?

The meeting's chair had shared an interminable story in which he detailed a short burst of drug use, followed by thirty years of hanging around AA meetings sharing his "experience." When he opened the meeting up, everybody sat there, sullen and silent for a moment. Then someone raised his hand.

"Hi, my name is Randal, and I'm an addict."
"Hi, Randal," the room chimed.

Jeffrey took in this guy and smiled. He had some of his own sullen indifference in his face at least. There was something eerily familiar about the face. Was he a celebrity? He had spotted one disgraced local politician and a girl who was either a model or an anorexic, looking extremely uncomfortable in the lunch queue. Not a great celebrity-to-nobody ratio. Tyler would have been disappointed. But this guy . . . there was something that rang a bell with Jeffrey. Maybe he used to be famous. He was handsome, but there was a certain hardness to the face now, probably the result of decades of drug use.

"So uh, I've been here for a week now," the guy said. "I mean in population. I'm feeling a mixture of emotions. Mostly I'm wondering just why the fuck I'm putting myself through this again. I thank you for sharing your story with us, but Jesus, every time I'm in these places, all I wanna do is get fucked up. I mean, really, AA makes me want to smoke meth. Ah, well, fuck that. Everything makes me want to smoke meth. I was tying my shoes this morning, and that made me want to smoke meth. I mean, my problem with not smoking meth is that everything seems so fucking boring now. I get the program. I really do. I understand! But I wonder if I get with the program, and say that's it—no more drugs, no more booze, no more fucking around . . . I mean, I might live to be eighty or something, but Jesus Christ it sounds like hell, you know?"

This elicited some nervous giggles from the room. The guy had a model's cheekbones in a certain light, though he was slightly demented-looking. He was in his late thirties and had dyed his thinning hair platinum, and that gave him a strange, permanently startled look. He was wearing expensive-looking clothes, out of place with his on-the-skids persona.

"I mean . . . ," Randal went on, "it's totally cool that you've been clean for thirty years, and I'm not trying to belittle your life or your experience . . . but you know, I don't know if it's for me. I mean, thirty years sober would seem like a life sentence to me."

Then Randal fell silent. He looked at his shoes. He was done sharing. There was an awkward quiet in the room while everybody waited for someone else to raise their hand. After a few moments the shiny-faced fat guy raised his hand and started talking about how his drinking had been getting out of control and his wife and daughter were pissed at him.

"It came to a head . . . at a party over at the Weinsteins' house, when I, uh, got drunk and, well, I did something I'm pretty ashamed of. Something inappropriate. With . . . with one of the Weinsteins' hired help. I mean, uh, I don't really remember much of what went on, but everybody else certainly does, and I doubt my wife is going to forget it in a hurry. . . ."

Back to our regularly scheduled programming, Jeffrey thought, sitting back in his chair and closing his eyes. . . .

Later that day Jeffrey was introduced to Luke, a balding ex–crack smoker from New York with a dirty smoker's laugh and graying stubble on his square jaw. Luke was to be Jeffrey's mentor for the first few days.
"Just till we get ya situated, y'know? You're gonna be on the third floor. You been in treatment before?"
"Yes."
Luke smirked. "Yeah, I kinda figured. You can usually tell the returnees from the candy-asses. Well, you don't need the sales pitch from me then. But they're a nice bunch here. You're rooming with a new guy. Well, uh . . ."
Luke leaned in conspiratorially.
"This guy's kind of a problem, to be honest. From what I see of him, he's a real example of self-will run riot. I'm not keen on putting a new guy with him, but his room is the only one with a spare bed at the moment. If you have any concerns, you just talk to me, okay?"
"Sure thing."

They walked up two flights of stairs and into a long corridor with staticky, electric blue carpeting. The place had the look of a vaguely high-end European youth hostel. The air smelled faintly of Pine-Sol and air freshener, and off in the distance the whine of vacuum cleaners toiled away. When they came to the right door Luke knocked. There was no reply. He knocked again and walked in.

.   .   .

The room was nondescript and clean. There were two twin beds separated by a nightstand with a lamp on it. On the farther bed lay Randal, the guy Jeffrey had seen in the meeting earlier in the day. Randal was reading a magazine and blasting music in his headphones. Sensing movement, he looked up. He jumped to his feet and said, "Shit, sorry, didn't hear you guys!"

"Randal—I'd like you to meet Jeff."

"Jeffrey," Jeffrey corrected, shaking Randal's hand.

"Nice to meet you."

"Saw you in the meeting this morning. You were talking about tying your shoelaces."

"Oh. Oh, yeah. Right."

"What are you reading?" Luke asked.

"Oh, uh, nuthin'. Just a magazine."

"Is it recovery-related?"

"Uh?"

"Recovery. As you know, Randal, we have a rule here that only recovery-related literature is allowed inside of the facility."

"Actually, Luke, yes, yes, it is. I'm actually reading a pretty inspiring story of one man's struggle to overcome addiction, and, uh, I think that there's some lessons in here that I can apply to my own, uh . . ."

"May I see it?"

Jeffrey watched with amusement as Randal tried to fast-talk Luke. "Well, uh, I mean if you'd like to . . ."

He reluctantly handed it over.

"ADDICTED TO PUSSY," Luke read, "THE MAN WHO CLAIMS TO HAVE SLEPT WITH OVER 10,000 PROSTITUTES."

"It's actually very inspiring. He, um, well, I think he's just getting to the part where he weaned himself off of, you know, the hookers. . . ."

"This isn't recovery-orientated, Randal, and you damn well know it. This is going to have to go into the confiscated box."

"How is this not recovery-related? Sexual addiction is a problem I can relate to. . . ."

"Then read the *Big Book*, or read one of Dr. Mike's own books on sexual compulsion and addiction. Don't try to tell me that *Sexual Tourist* magazine has anything to offer you right now. I mean, Jesus, *Sexual Tourist* magazine? Where did you find this?"

"There's a great twenty-four-hour newsstand on Hollywood and Cahuenga."

"Hm. Anyway, can you try to keep this kind of bullshit to a minimum? I don't want you fucking with other people's recovery. If Jeffrey tells me that there are any more fucking shenanigans in this room, we'll bounce your ass right out of here. Capisce?"

"Sure."

Jeffrey tossed his bag to the floor.

"I'll see you boys downstairs," Luke said, turning to leave. "We have our afternoon meeting in thirty minutes."

"Okay."

And with that Luke was gone. Randal flopped back onto his bed.

"What the fuck is up with that guy, man? You heard the way that jerk-off talks? Who the fuck uses the words 'shenanigans' and 'capisce' in the same fucking sentence?"

"He seems a little high-strung," Jeffrey agreed.

Jeffrey started to unpack his bag.

"Hey, listen . . . you an actor or something?" Jeffrey asked. "You seem kind of familiar. . . ."

"An actor? No, thank Christ. You aren't an actor, are you?"

"Nah. I'm no one."

"You seem familiar, too. You been in treatment before? Don't I know you from Tarzana?"

"I was there in oh-six," Jeffrey said, "sixty-day bit in the summer, I think."

"Hm. I wasn't there in oh-six—oh-three, I think. You been to Utah?"

"What, Cirque Lodge?"

"No, for the fuckin' nightlife. Yeah, Cirque Lodge."

"Nah."

"Fun place. I was in there with Lindsay Lohan. Word on the grapevine was that she fucked her way through every crackhead and drunk in that place. She split before I got a turn though. Pure Hollywood trash."

As he shoved his clothes into drawers, Jeffrey suddenly said: "Cri-Help. You were in Cri-Help!"

"Sure. That woulda been . . . fuck, ninety-six? Seven?"

"Ninety-seven!" Jeffrey laughed. "I remember you. You roomed with Big Mike. Jesus, you keep in contact with any of those guys?"

Randal shrugged. "You remember Don? The truck driver?"

"Yeah. Crackhead, right?"

"Yeah. That's him. He died. Heart attack. Was doing, like, sixty miles an hour at the time. Went off the freeway and demolished a roadside diner."

"Holy shit."

"Yeah. Recognized his face on the news report. Besides that . . . ah, I don't really keep in touch with people from these places. It's not like I'm ever gonna see them again, you know? You?"

Jeffrey shrugged. "Bumped into a few of them at meetings, you know, right after I got out. Freebase Alex, Georgie the Pimp . . . but I didn't keep it up. Those fucking meetings depress me. Did you graduate?"

"They booted me out over some bullshit. It wasn't the first time. Too many fucking rules, you know?"

"Listen, Randal, I don't want you to think that I'll be busting your balls or running off to Luke to go tell stories. What you do is your own business, man. I'm here for fourteen days and then I'm getting the fuck outta Dodge. What are you in here for?"

"You mean what drugs, or why am I putting myself through this bullshit again?"

"Both."

Randal shrugged. "Meth. Really, I'm here because I don't have a choice. You?"

"Something similar to you, I guess. I got nowhere I need to be."

"Have you met Dr. fucking Mike yet?"

Jeffrey shrugged. "Nope."

"Me neither. He showed up last Friday and gave a fucking pep talk in the canteen, but that could have just been some asshole in a gray wig for all I know. I'm beginning to think that he's like the Wizard of Oz. Pay no attention to the doctor behind the curtain. . . ."

"You think they'll wheel in a television set so he can talk to us?"

Randal yawned. "You hungry? The one thing they do have in this place that's okay is the bagels. No poppy seed, though. They say it dirties up the urine tests or some bullshit. C'mon . . . I'll show you around. . . ."

FIFTEEN

After getting off the stage with the final chords of "Dazed and Confused" ringing out through the club's PA, Trina saw Pat by the bar. He was drinking, and one of the other girls was hanging around him. They made eye contact, and he waved at her. She walked over and shoved her way in between them.

"Hey, baby," she said.

"Trina! I saw you dancing, girl. That was real hot shit, baby. You pick your own music? It was way better than the garbage most of these chicks dance to."

"Yeah. I won't dance to anything but Zeppelin. That shit just makes me *move*."

At this the other girl left, scowling, looking for trade.

"So how you doin', sweetie?"

"Good, I guess. Quiet tonight. You gonna buy me a drink?"

Pat pushed a twenty over to the barman and said, "Whatever she's drinking."

"Just a Pepsi."

Pat looked at her. "That's the second time I bought you a drink, and the second time you ordered a Pepsi. You the clean-living type or something?"

Trina shook her head. "Nuh-uh. I don't drink at work."

"I know why you don't drink," Pat said, smiling.

"Oh yeah?"

Pat leaned in close. "Yeah. It's all in your eyes. Or at least your pupils."

Trina was silent for a moment. The barkeep brought the soda. She sipped it through the straw. She looked back at Pat again.

"I'm sure I don't know what you're talking about," she said, smirking.

"Sure, baby. You got a steady supply for that stuff?"

Trina nodded. "Steady enough."

"Well, you let Uncle Pat know if you need anything. *Anything*." He leaned in and whispered in her ear, "Coke, heroin, speed, pills, whatever. You let me know, 'kay?"

He leaned back again. Trina smiled at him.

"Whereja get those scratches from?"

"Oh, these?" Pat raised a large hand with fingers like clubs to his face, and touched the red marks that ran down the sides of his cheeks. "I, uh, I guess you could say that I got them in the heat of passion."

"Hmmm. Who's the lucky girl?"

For a moment Pat's eyes glazed over. He thought about Salvia's face, pressed hard into the mattress, struggling for breath as he tore her ass up. How he had twisted those stinking fucking dreadlocks around his fist and yanked on them so hard that the mattress barely muted her screams. How he'd had to knock some sense into her when he was done, and she'd been dumb enough to come at him with her fucking bitch nails.

"No one," Pat said, shaking himself out of his thoughts, "I don't think I'll be seeing her again."

Trina leaned in close. "You don't like the rough stuff, huh?"

"With the right lady, I like anything. You know something? You got a great smile, honey. A real knockout."

"Thank you. You're sweet."

"That's me," Pat said, "a real fuckin' sweetheart. Say, what time do you knock off at?"

"Two a.m."

"You wanna go eat afterward?"

Trina looked around. Making dates with the clients was frowned upon. The barkeep was busy mixing a drink for one of the girls. There was no one in earshot. Trina said, "Sure. But, uh, meet me somewhere else. If they saw that we were hanging out, you know, away from the club, they wouldn't like it."

"Oh, honey," Pat said with a cold smile, "they wouldn't do shit, believe me. But whatever you'd like to do is cool. You wanna meet me at Astro Burger? Around two twenty?"

"M'kay."

"It's a date," Pat said.

"Is it?"

He shrugged, smiled at her, and then stood up. He looked at his watch. "That's me. Duty calls."

———————

It was four thirty in the morning and Pat had blood on his face. He was driving away from Trina's apartment building at a good clip. Trina was kneeling in the passenger seat, looking through the back window.

"There's no one following us," she said.

"There'd better not be," Pat growled. Then, looking in the rearview mirror, "The cops'll be there soon."

"Shit," Trina hissed, turning around. "They have witnesses. This is fucked up."

"They have one witness, and I dunno if he's gonna be talking for a while. They don't know who I am. It's cool. Nobody saw you. It was a break and enter gone wrong, that's all."

"GodDAMN that fucking bitch!" Trina hissed. "Don't they need to give me notice before they change the locks?"

Pat shrugged. Trina thought about the piles of unopened mail from Manny's lawyers. She looked around the inside of the car.

"You got my stuff, right?"

"It's all here. Don't worry."

After talking for an hour at Astro Burger, Pat had asked if Trina wanted to stop by his room. She said sure, but she needed to pick up her medication from her apartment first. They drove in tandem to Pat's motel on Hollywood Boulevard, and then took Trina's car over to her place. They pulled up outside of the building around four in the morning, and Pat waited in the car while Trina crept across the deserted forecourt to get her stuff.

Pat was fiddling with the radio when Trina wrenched the car's door open moments later.

"Motherfucker!" she spat. "Look at this shit!"

She handed a piece of paper to Pat. She had found it

taped to her front door. Pat looked the eviction notice over, and then tossed it on the floor. "They changed your locks already?"

"Yeah. Fuck, man, all of my shit is in there. My fucking clothes, my drugs, everything is in there. That fucking bitch! The housing court said that they couldn't do this. . . ."

"Listen," Pat said, "I can get in there for you. But I won't have a lot of time. We'll load up the car and split. You can crash at my place if you like. I got plenty of room. It's a nice motel; they got free HBO and an ice machine in the corridor. It'll be an adventure. You up for an adventure?"

Trina looked out at the deserted street. The skies were still inky. "Sure," she said, "I guess."

"Okay, come on."

They got out of the car, and Pat opened the trunk. Inside there was an assortment of tools. Pat picked up a stubby metal crowbar and a claw hammer and said, "We're gonna have to be quick. Grab the shit you need fast. It's gonna make some noise when I open the door, so the fuckin' neighbors are gonna be lookin', okay?"

"Okay."

Now, as they drove away from her apartment with everything she could grab shoved into a bag, Trina said, "You're bleeding."

"It ain't mine. Who the fuck was that bastard anyway?"

"The landlord. Musta heard you breaking in. Shit. What if he IDs us?"

"He ain't gonna be talking. I got him good with the

crowbar. If he even wakes up, that motherfucker's brain is gonna be scrambled. Nobody's ID'ing nobody. You wanna get some booze? I can stop at a liquor store."

Once they were a safe distance away and sure they weren't being followed, Pat slowed the car down and merged with the traffic on Hollywood Boulevard.

When the excitement had died down, Trina said, "Shit, man. I'm sorry. I didn't mean to get you caught up in all of this drama."

Pat laughed. "It's cool. I kinda like it. Is your life always so fuckin' exciting?"

"Feels like it."

"Well, I think we're gonna get on then." Pat reached over and placed a hand on the back of Trina's neck. "You're shaking."

"I'm all fucked up. My nerves are shot."

Pat started massaging her neck with a strong heavy hand. Trina half closed her eyes and let her head flop back a little.

"You got your stuff. We'll pick up a bottle, go back to my place, and you can unwind. This kind of shit is always for the best. Think of it as a new start."

Trina laughed. "Yeah. A new start. I left most of my shit in that fucking apartment. All of my outfits for work. Goddamn."

"I'll take you shopping. Tomorrow. We'll go to Rodeo fucking Drive if you like. Howzat sound?"

Trina looked over to Pat and smiled. "It sounds like bullshit. But I like it. Keep talking. . . ."

S!XTEEN

Sundays were cleaning day. Each "client" at the center was assigned a task—everything from cleaning out the ashtrays along the length and breadth of the building to working in the laundry room, raking the sand in the recreation area, or cleaning the bathrooms. With Luke assigning jobs for their section, Randal and Jeffrey found themselves with the shittiest work detail available: bathroom cleanup. The bathrooms were cavernous and stale, and as filthy as you would imagine a bathroom that accommodated one hundred men would be. Randal was at work in the showers, scrubbing the mildew from the walls with a filthy sponge. Jeffrey was looking at the stinking row of toilet stalls with a dejected look on his face.

"How come I have to do the fucking bogs?"
"The what?"
"The bogs. The toilets! I want to do the showers."
"Fuck off. The showers are my gig. It says it on the

worksheet. Randal—showers and glass. You're on the
toilets."

"Jesus."

Of course the staff framed this unpaid manual labor as
being somehow essential to their recovery. They had to
learn to take responsibility, their caseworkers said, they
had to relearn basic skills like keeping a clean home.

"Clean home," Jeffrey's caseworker had explained, "clean
mind."

It seemed like a bullshit excuse to Jeffrey. Just another
scam to save money, just like the shitty food and the
itchy, prison-issue bedsheets. They charged enough
money to be here. Couldn't they afford a professional
cleaning crew? Jeffrey started to unload his cart of
cleaning equipment. Randal looked over to his partner.

"And, Jeffrey—take your time, okay?"

"Why?"

"Because they'll assign you some other bullshit job.
I made that mistake already. That ball-busting cunt
Luke'll work you like a bitch if you let him. You'll
be sent over to one of the other bathrooms to help
that crew, or some shit like that. Don't think that
if you rush through this they'll let you go smoke a
cigarette, or put your feet up. It doesn't work like
that."

Jeffrey had already had his fill of the section supervisor.
He had been on Jeffrey's back lately, too, reprimanding
him earlier in the day for saying good morning to a female client.

"Talking with the female patients is forbidden, Jeffrey."

"I said good morning. That's all."

"It doesn't matter. We don't want the complication of people forming romantic relationships while in therapy. So to keep it simple, we enforce a strict noncommunication rule between the men and women."

"But, Luke—I'm gay. You do know that, right? So really it's YOU I shouldn't be talking to."

"If you continue with this insubordinate attitude, I will have to bring it up with Dr. Mike at our next meeting. . . ."

Jeffrey looked around the filthy bathroom, and then at Randal.

"Jesus, fuck. What is that asshole's problem anyway?"

"Same as mine. Same as yours. He's pissed off he can't get high. He just won't admit it."

They scrubbed in silence for a while, each lost in his private miseries. Finding his attention wavering, Jeffrey looked over to Randal again. So far his new roommate had been tight-lipped about everything besides how much he hated the facility, and how he'd rather be anywhere else but here. Beyond that, he wasn't the type to spill his guts about himself in the regular group meetings. That trait was pretty unusual in this place. People seemed to trip over themselves in their hurry to reveal their darkest, most intimate secrets to rooms full of strangers. This was of course encouraged, but it made Jeffrey profoundly uncomfortable. For someone raised in an Irish Catholic household where emotions were never discussed, the urge to confess all to a room full of strangers, to share your most hidden thoughts, to cry in front of other people, was totally unfathomable. Jeffrey knew that if he wanted to "participate in the recovery process" he would have to get over this phobia, but he wasn't sure he could do it. He could not understand how someone who had been in treatment for only a day or two could discuss the sexual abuse they suffered as a child, or the secret self-loathing that had fueled their drug use so readily. Jeffrey couldn't help respecting Randal's stoicism, despite the fact that the others—and especially the counselors—seemed to take it as a direct challenge to their authority.

Something else about Randal intrigued Jeffrey. There was an aspect of Randal's character that reminded him in a way of Bill. He had that same air of authority. It was hard to pinpoint—maybe it was just in the way he carried himself physically, or in his ability to take control of a group of people and steer the conversation without even trying, but Jeffrey guessed that on the outside Randal was someone who commanded quite a bit of respect. Even in his current, pitiful position, hunched over so he could scrub the crap out of the communal showers, Randal seemed like somebody important. Curious, Jeffrey took the opportunity to ask, "So what happened? I mean, really, how did you end up in here?"

Randal paused. He looked back to Jeffrey. For a moment Jeffrey thought Randal was going to bat the question aside, like he usually did whenever someone tried to get him to talk about himself in group. Instead, as Randal started scrubbing again, he talked.
"I woke up on a city bus. I'd shit my pants, my father was dead, and I'd missed the funeral. My brother told me I had to get to rehab or they'd cut me off."

Jeffrey quietly said, "Oh, sorry. I mean, I'm sorry to hear about your father."

"It's okay. It wasn't a shock. My father had been dying for a long time. Cancer. It had eaten away at the old man so much that all they could do was pump him full of morphine to try to stop him waking up the other patients with his screaming. I'd known it was coming. Everybody knew. It didn't make it any easier. . . . I'd been clean for, shit, six months. No meth, no booze, no nothing. Longest six months of my life. I was dealing with these soulless movie assholes all day long. You see, my family is in the movie business. My pop founded Metro Studios."

There was a pause as Jeffrey processed this information.

"He *founded* Metro Studios?"

"Uh-huh."

"Holy shit, really? That's big-time."

"Yeah, that's what they say. I grew up in the industry. A real son of Hollywood. When I got out of rehab last time, the family decided that I should start working for my brother, Harvey. I guess they wanted to prove to me that I could live a productive life, or something. He gave me some bullshit job in one of his offices in Studio City. So for a while I'd have to put on my shirt and pants, and show up to the office at nine in the morning. A genuine working stiff. It was hard. I mean, every day it was a struggle not to get high. But I did it! I don't know how, but I fucking did it. I was going crazy, holed up in my little cubicle, making small talk with all of the assholes my brother employed. I mean, I was the only person over twenty-five, and they were all so fucking *enthusiastic* and *insincere* it made me wanna puke. I grew up in that world. I know what a fucking despicable, shitty, inhu-man business the movies are. And these stupid assholes just couldn't wait to clamp their jaws on that teat and start sucking.

"They had come from all over the fucking country, all of them lured to Hollywood by the promise of the movie industry. My brother paid them peanuts, the studio was churning out crap endlessly, every so often some brain-dead actor would come in for a meeting and curse them out because they didn't put the right kind of soy milk in the coffee, and yet these kids thought they were the luckiest motherfuckers alive. When it comes to the movies, people just . . . man, they can't think straight. They'll put up with anything! I don't get it."

Randal scrubbed the dark brown gunk from in between the tiles of the cubicle with a little more fervor than be-fore when he said this. He sprayed more cleaning so-lution on there. The brown shit started to come away. Over his shoulder he could hear Jeffrey scrubbing the toilets, waiting for Randal to continue the story. Down the halls were yells, screams, whistles, and laughs. The song of cleaning day.

"The thing is, my old man was the only person in this world I still gave a shit about. Not Harvey, not Mom, none of the others, just Pop. Pop was the one who was always there to help me out when shit got too crazy. You know, my father had Harvey, and Harvey was the one who had Pop's business head, and his knack for making money. He was the good son, you know? All I got from the old man was a receding fucking hairline. That, and enough money to REALLY fuck myself up.

I mean, they sent me to the best fucking schools in the country. They even sent me to this fucking Swiss finishing school up in the fucking mountains until I got kicked outta there for screwing the broad that was teaching us French. I mean . . . they tried anything and everything to get me to stop screwing up. But I couldn't. I didn't want to stop! From the beginning I was this way, always into something . . . huffing paint fumes, or shooting speed, or showing up to class with a head full of strong acid. Whatever I could get my hands on, that was what I wanted. That's what they didn't understand. I never came to them on my knees, begging for their help to stop. As bad as it ever got, I never really wanted to quit. There was no problem that my drug use ever caused that I figured couldn't be solved with more drugs. Pop was the only one in the family who seemed to have accepted the way I was. I mean, shit, that's who I am. He figured it was best not to rock the boat, and let's just try to keep me alive, you know?"

Jeffrey gingerly wiped another stray pubic hair from the rim of the toilet. It seemed impossible that these filthy crap receptacles had been cleaned at all in the last month. The smell of stale piss and bleach made his stomach flutter.

" . . . So the call comes one day, and basically my pop is about to die, and if we want to say our good-byes, then now is the time to do it. It finally dawns on me that my own father is about to die, and I am never going to see him again. Not only that, but fucking Harvey is gonna be in charge of the estate, the houses, the money, and basically everything . . . well, man, the only logical response to that was to get fucked up, you know? So instead of going to the hospital I call up my connection. He hasn't spoken to me in six months. He says, *'Hey, Randal, I thought you were dead or some shit.'*

" *'Nah. Worse. I've been straight. I want to pick up two ounces.'* "

"So I walk outta the office without even saying goodbye. I tell you, that was a great feeling walking out of there and never looking back. It was like suddenly the birds started chirping in the trees, and the sky turned a perfect shade of blue. Finally, I didn't have to think about my father at all. I didn't have to think about anything. I practically skipped all the way over to my connection."

"Wait," Jeffrey interrupted, slightly dazed by the way that Randal had suddenly opened up to him, "you gotta explain this to me. Your pop founded Metro Studios. So you're part of the Earnest dynasty?"

"Randal P. Earnest, that's me."

"So your brother is Harvey Earnest."

"Yeah."

"Owner of Dreamscape Studios?"

"Yeah. And the biggest douchebag in Hollywood, bar none."

"Holy fuck."

"Yeah. He thinks I need it tough this time. And with Pop gone, Harvey signs the checks. I really don't know what I'm going to do this time. Without Pop around, Harvey finally has me where he wants me. He'll never let me live by my own rules. He's a fucking control freak shithead. That's why he's so fucking rich. You don't get to run a place like Dreamscape without being the world's biggest asshole."

"I guess not."

"All I ever wanted was to be left alone by my fucking family. To be free from that fucking weight of expectation. Like I'm supposed to be impressed by Jack fucking Nicholson because my pop worked for him? I'm meant to kiss his ass when he comes around the house and pretend to care? Fuck that! I'm supposed to enjoy the company of these fucking people? Ugh. I mean, have you ever heard a bunch of movie people when they actually get together and talk? There's nothing more boring than an actor without a script. De Niro, Nicholson, it doesn't matter. They're basically props with speaking roles. I can't begin to tell you how much I fucking hate that world. There was no way I could handle it, you know, straight."

"Why don't you leave Hollywood?" Jeffrey said, as he moved onto the next toilet. "Start over somewhere else? Away from your family?"

Randal laughed. "I've thought about that just about every day of my life. But go where? With what money? Harvey would cut me off in a heartbeat. I mean, if I just said, "Fuck Harvey" and set out on my own, what would I do? Get a job? Put on a fucking suit five days a week and show up to an office, again? Nah, that ain't me. I can't do that. The only kind of career I could ever have would be in the industry. No matter how fucked up I am, I will always be able to make a living in Hollywood. Anywhere else in the world, and I'd be totally fucking unemployable. The movie business is worse than the fucking Mafia. You can't escape a name like my father's that easily. When Pop was alive I could get away with agreeing to rehab twice a year, and things would pretty much carry on as normal. Now everything's different. This is shaping up to be a pretty lousy year. . . ."

"What are you two ladies talking about in here?"

Randal and Jeffrey looked up, and there was Luke standing in the doorway, scowling. He was in his uniform of acid-washed jeans and a lumberjack shirt, with his pudgy thumbs hooked into the waistband. His beady eyes glared at them.

"There's too much fucking talking going on here for my liking. If you ladies have time to talk, then maybe you need some extra tasks."

Luke was the kind of asshole who was corrupted totally by whatever token bit of power the facility had bestowed upon him.

Randal stood and turned to Luke.

"We're working, Luke. Nobody said we had to do it in silence. This ain't a fuckin' monastery, man."

"Yeah, well, it ain't a fucking vacation camp neither. Why don't you stop dicking around, or maybe you want me to write you up?"

"For what?" Randal laughed. "Having a fucking conversation? Kiss my ass."

Luke walked over to the showers. He pulled back the plastic curtain and peered into the first stall.

"So you're done with this one?" he asked Randal.

"Sure."

"Come here."

Luke crouched down and ripped up the slip mat, flipping it over.

"Look at this."

"Look at what?"

"Look at this mildew."

Randal peered closer. Around the suckers that held the slip mat in place there were a few remaining traces of mildew. "Oh," Randal said.

"Oh, indeed. I suggest you scrub that off straightaway, unless you want me to write this up."

Luke entered the shower stall to look closer.

"Luke! Come on, man! You're fucking standing in my clean stall with your fucking boots, man!"

Luke glared at him.

"This stall ain't clean. I'm doing you a favor. You need to start over and stop half-assing it. You know your problem, Randal?"

Randal folded his arms.

"No. I guess you're gonna tell me, though."

"You half-ass everything. You half-ass this shower stall. You half-ass your recovery. It's no wonder you are where you are. With all of the opportunities you've had handed to you in life, you've found yourself on your knees cleaning a fucking shower stall. That must suck."

Randal smirked.

"You think it's funny?"

Randal started to laugh and just shrugged.

"You think you're a tough motherfucker," Luke snarled.

"Well, I got news for you. You ain't tough. You ain't tough at all. I've shat tougher things than you."

With that, Luke stormed out. Randal and Jeffrey looked at each other for a moment, before erupting. When the laughter came it was free and easy. The first honest-to-

God laugh either of them had had since checking into this place.

"He's shat tougher things than you!" Jeffrey wheezed, gasping for air.

"Oh, Jesus. That fucker has a way with words."

"What a fucking asswipe!"

When the laughter subsided, they began scrubbing again with renewed vigor. Luke's interference had actually improved their mood. It felt good to be united in their hatred for the balding, wannabe tough guy.

"Oh, boy, I've come across dickheads like that in every rehab I've been in," Jeffrey said.

"How many times you been in these places?"

"Six or seven. Some back in England. That's where I started using. I'm Irish, originally, but I went over to London when I was fifteen. Got into it there. A boyfriend introduced me to it originally. You know I'm a fag, right?"

Randal shrugged.

"Don't make much difference to me either way. But you don't scream it out or anything."

"Yeah, well, I was never one for the feminine boys who listen to techno and dig *Will and Grace*. Where I grew up, if you were a fag you kept it hidden."

"Six or seven rehabs, huh? Why do you keep coming back?"

"I guess I keep thinking that the next time will be different. A lot of those other times I went because there was someone, usually some wealthy boyfriend, who wanted me to get my shit together. My relationships always seem to follow the same fucking pattern. I'll be twenty years younger than them, and they'll want to save me. They'll always think it will just take love, or money, to fix me. It even took *me* a while to realize that you can't fix people. Life's all about learning how to live with everything that's wrong with you. It got so that I started to think that sending someone to rehab was a normal first step for any long-term relationship."

Jeffrey smiled, without any real humor.

"Of course it never worked like that. I was always able to stop for a while. I mean, this whole recovery thing was never really a factor in how long it lasted. It was always a conscious decision to start using again. Because without getting high, man, I would be so *bored*. And I'd realize just how boring everybody else was. In the end I figured I'd start using again to save whatever relationship I was in at the time. I even told one guy: *'I'm smoking crack because you're too uninteresting when I'm not smoking it. As long as I'm sober, I feel that I'm too good for you.'*"

Randal laughed. "Wow. I've been dumped a bunch of times, but no one ever used that line on me."

"That guy said something similar actually. That one ended particularly badly, and I had to leave London. Long story. . . ."

"So that's why you ended up in LA?"

"Well, that was Bill. My last boyfriend. I met him online. He flew out to Manchester, where I was staying at the time, to see me. At first I was kinda shocked when I saw him. He was older than he looked in his pictures, a lot older than my usual guys. But he was handsome. And he had charisma. He just had something that I liked."

"What? Money?"

"Yeah, well, there was that. But something else. Power. A kind of quiet power. Bill looked after me good. Nobody knew about us. But he looked after me. Got me my paperwork for the U.S., no questions asked. He was everything to me. . . ."

"So what happened?"

"Bill died. Went in his sleep. And I don't know what the fuck to do next. I need to start over. I'm just hoping that this time it's different for me. I need to stop this shit. At least for now."

"But why come here?" Randal asked. "Why not just go on vacation? Take a fucking break. Hang out on the beach. It'd probably be cheaper than coming to this fucking place."

Jeffrey shrugged.

"I have a lot of stuff going on right now. My living situation just changed, everything just changed. I just know I won't be able to deal with all of that if I'm fucked up. Who knows? Maybe something will stick. Maybe I'll come out of this place full of the joys of sobriety."

Randal snorted. "Yeah, maybe. Ya never fuckin' know, right? It's a nice idea."

Somewhere in the building a bell rang. Randal dropped his sponge.

"Fuck this. Sounds like it's time for coffee."

"Thank Christ."

They stood up and surveyed the bathroom one last time.

"You know it's gonna look like shit within the hour," Jeffrey said.

"Yeah, well, fuck that. That's life."

"I guess."

.   .   .

They walked down the corridors together, joining the other men who came flooding out of the bedrooms and the stairwells, all drawn by the bell out into the cafeteria, where for a few minutes at least they could forget sobriety and just shoot the shit and laugh. At least until the bell rang again and it all started up all over again.

SEVENTEEN

When Friday rolled around, Randal finally had the chance to meet the fabled Dr. Mike. He was given an appointment slip and sent up to the third-floor offices fifteen minutes before. He waited with a bored-looking receptionist until Dr. Mike's prior patient finally emerged. He was beaming. He backed out of the room muttering, "Thank you, Dr. Mike . . . thank you . . . yes, I'll see you soon. . . ."

The secretary smiled at the guy as he left, and said, "Randal? You're next."

Randal closed the door behind him.

"Dr. Mike, it's a pleasure to finally meet you. I was beginning to think you were a figment of the collective imagination over here."

Dr. Mike looked at Randal, but did not stand up. The doctor was handsome and tanned, possessing the anonymous good looks of a daytime soap actor. When he spoke, dazzling white teeth peeked out from between his thin lips. He wore wire-rimmed glasses, and his gray hair was neat, trimmed close to the skull. He wore a navy shirt and salmon pink tie. Good living radiated out from him, and Randal had the impression that if he stood close to Dr. Mike, he would smell fragrant, freshly scrubbed. The doctor held his hand up to Randal and clutched the phone closer to his ear. "Yes . . . ," he said, "yes, I understand that, but you must tell him no. No more medication. None. I'm with— I'm with— I'm— Listen, I'm with a client. If he keeps screaming, let him scream. This is a tantrum, that's all. The pain is not real. It's psychological. Yes. Yes. Okay. *I'm with a client.* Yes. Good-bye."

He hung up the phone.

"Sorry about that," he said, without a hint of apology in his voice. "Sit down, please, Mr. . . ."

"Earnest. Randal Earnest."

"Ah, yes. Randal."

They sat there like that for a while, Dr. Mike studying a sheet of paper with a furrowed brow. He stopped, leaned forward, and said, "So how are you feeling today, Randal?"

"Okay," Randal said.

"You've been in population for two weeks, yes? How are you finding it?"

"Fine. I know the routine. I've done this before."

"Yes." Dr. Mike consulted his sheet. "I see several admissions here. Wat Tham Krabok, in Thailand, was the most recent."

"Uh-huh."

Dr. Mike laughed a little.

"You've tried it all now, yes? You've tried to quit on your own accord, you've tried self-will, you've tried denial, and you've even tried voodoo. And here you are."

"Voodoo?"

"The Thai retreat. Wat Tham Krabok."

"It's not voodoo. It's an herbal purification system. It's all about, uh, looking inside of yourself, flushing the toxins from inside of you. . . ."

Dr. Mike snorted.

"*Voodoo*, Randal. I don't mean people in grass skirts dancing around and drinking chicken blood. I mean voodoo in the general sense of the word. Snake oil. As long as there have been addicts, there have been charlatans queuing up to take advantage of their desperation. I'm sure it cost you a pretty penny."

"A little less than here, actually."

"And what good did all of this introspection do you? That detox took place in the spring. And now here you are."

Randal thought about the monastery. About the silent monks who made vile-tasting herbal concoctions that literally made him vomit the toxins out of his body. When he had arrived back in LA he had looked thinner, healthier than ever. He was high within twenty-four hours, though.

"The problem was," Randal said, "that when I looked inside of myself I didn't see anything. Nothing at all. In fact, when I looked inside of myself I realized that I am only truly happy when I'm high."

"Hm. That is your disease talking, Randal. The sooner

you realize that, the better. What are your plans? When you get out of here. What are your goals?"

"Financial independence."

"And . . . meetings?"

"Maybe."

"If you don't attend meetings," Dr. Mike said, "you will die. This disease is a chronic and incurable one, but with diligence and care it can be arrested."

"I've heard this before, Doctor. As well as Thai voodoo, I have plenty of experience of the American variety, too."

Dr. Mike smiled, coldly.

"If you don't want to be helped then there really is nothing anyone can do for you."

The phone rang again.

"Excuse me, Randal." Dr. Mike picked up the phone. "Yes? Yes, I can hear him. This is a tantrum. He has *who* on the phone? His surgeon? I don't need to speak to his surgeon. I— I— Yes, I am well aware of his medical condition. I will say it again. No painkillers. The pain is psychological. He is an addict. Yes. Yes. Look, I'm with a patient. I know. I'd suggest earplugs. Good-bye."

"Sounds rough," Randal said, as Dr. Mike hung up the phone.

"Just another addict angling for pills. You get used to it. Addicts are by their very nature cunning and devious. They use pity and emotional blackmail on the outside to get what they want, so why should it be any different in here?"

"Dr. Mike, do I have any other options besides AA?"

"Sure. You can continue to use drugs and die. Nothing else has been proven as effective in arresting the disease of addiction as the twelve-step program. Total abstinence is the only solution."

"My father died of cancer recently," Randal said quietly.

"And how did that make you feel?"

Dr. Mike was back on familiar ground. He pressed home his unexpected advantage. "I'm sure that those negative emotions made your disease stronger."

"Well, that's just it. My pop wasted away in a hospital bed. All they could do was give him morphine to stop *him* from screaming. You see, my pop had a disease. It wasn't his fault. One day he went to the doctor, they stuck a finger up his asshole, and told him he was rotting away from the inside out. It was an awful slow, painful death."

"I'm terribly sorry to hear that," Dr. Mike said in a monotone.

"I am addicted to drugs because I've been taking them daily since the age of fourteen. Really, this is all my fault. I didn't contract a disease. I chose this life."

Dr. Mike shook his head. "You didn't *choose* this. It chose *you*. Usually it's a combination of things. Genetics. Was your father an addict?"

"No."

"Really? He never drank?"

Randal laughed. "Sure, he drank. But he wasn't an alcoholic."

"Are you sure of that? Not all alcoholics can be found pushing a shopping cart full of bottles down skid row.

A functioning alcoholic can still have a healthy family life; in fact, he can seem perfectly normal in every way...."

"So what, then? If his life is unaffected, how is he an alcoholic? If he has a glass of wine with dinner, or cocktails at six, how is he an alcoholic exactly?"

"The disease, Randal. It is all about the disease. Genetics is one factor. Childhood trauma is another. There are many factors that go into making an addict."

"Cancer is a disease," Randal said quietly. "I just like to get high."

"I want you to be a success. I've spoken to your brother about your case, and I feel that with due diligence on your part we can help you. He's very concerned about you. He loves you."

Randal smirked.

"What are your success rates?"

"How do you mean?"

"Here at Clean and Serene. When people graduate, and they attend meetings like you suggest, what are the success rates?"

"This is a serious disease. Most people inside of this facility will not make it. You should take a look around. Within a year some of these people will be dead. Many of them will be back on drugs at least. A small percentage will remain clean."

"Jesus," Randal said, "if I joined fucking Weight Watchers and they told me that in a year half of the class would be fatter than ever, some would have adult-onset diabetes, and maybe one or two would actually lose weight, I'd be asking for my money back. I read this thing I'd like to talk to you about...."

Dr. Mike sat back in his seat and sighed. He looked at his watch.

"Make it quick, Randal. We have a few minutes only. And please, try to keep it recovery-related. I'm not here to debate you. I'm here to help you."

"You see, I've read a lot about the twelve steps, because Harvey lives and breathes that stuff. I mean, I just wanted to find out what the statistics were, because none of it seemed to add up to me. I read this thing about Dr. George Vaillant. He's on the Alcoholics Anonymous World Service Board of Trustees. You see, he did this study—"

"Oh, Christ," Dr. Mike said, rolling his eyes. "This old story again?"

"No, wait—listen. He's an AA guy. He did the only study of treatment outcomes for people who do the whole AA thing. . . ."

"Randal—"

"He followed one hundred people who were trying to quit drinking with AA for eight years—"

"Intellectualization, Randal! You are trying to intellectualize your problem—"

"And he found that—please—let me finish—he found that only five percent made it, which is the same—"

"Randal, our time is up. I suggest that we—"

"Which is THE SAME percentage of people who spontaneously quit on their own!" Randal began to recite the part of the study that had stuck with him. To Randal, it had the same resonant power that the *Big Book* of Alcoholics Anonymous had to others in recovery. As Randal spoke, Dr. Mike stood and walked toward the door.

"After initial discharge, only five patients in the Clinic sample never relapsed to alcoholic drinking, and there is compelling evidence that the results of our treatment were no better than the natural history of the disease."

"Thank you, Randal," Dr. Mike was saying, "our time is up. We can continue this discussion at a later date."

"But don't you see? It doesn't work. IT DOESN'T FUCK-ING WORK. So why are you selling me this?"

Dr. Mike walked over to Randal.

"Mr. Earnest," he said, "this attitude is not going to be helpful to you in your recovery. If you don't like the way my facility works, then you know where the front entrance is, and I will tell you again that door is NOT locked."

Randal stood. He was shaking slightly. He looked the doctor in the eyes.

"But I WANT to quit. I don't want to stay like this." He was almost crying now. "I want to get better. But I don't want to do it this way. . . ."

Dr. Mike smiled, his face suddenly full of compassion. It caught Randal off guard slightly. The doctor moved toward him and held Randal's hand, tenderly. Randal almost recoiled, but stopped himself. His hand was shaking.

"Randal," the doctor said, softly. *"Randal. You've tried it your way. Yes? You've tried it your way. You've tried analyzing it, and overthinking it, and reading studies, and flying off to monasteries, and therapists, yes? You've tried it. Look at this. Look at your hands."*

Randal looked down. Dr. Mike held Randal's hand in his palm. The back of the hand was facing up. The skin was white and heavily scarred from years of the needle probing his flesh looking for working veins. Even now the wounds were fresh and angry. There were solid masses of toxins under the skin and discolored patches where it seemed that the hand was rotting away from some hideous disease.

"This is where your way got you, Randal. Here. We follow a very simple program. You just do as you are instructed. One of our mottos here is *Keep it simple, stupid.* Keep it simple. Listen, and follow instruction. Okay?"

In that moment, Randal realized why the doctor was where he was in life. Randal was dumbstruck. He just shook, and he could feel tears coming. He fought them back with all of his might, feeling used and pathetic. He croaked out, "Thank you, Doctor," and left the office with the uneasy feeling that he had been taken advantage of, without quite knowing how.

Dr. Mike closed the door and locked it. He sat down and called his wife. It went straight to her voice mail. Today she was in Beverly Hills, shopping. He left a message.

"Hi, honey, it's me. Just checking in with you. Hope you're having a good day. It's been crazy here today, so I wanted to call you quickly before it starts up again. I might be home a little late, so you'll have to pick up the kids. I'll e-mail you if I get a chance. Bye."

He pressed the receiver down and got a dial tone. He took the photograph out of his wallet and dialed the number on the back. On the third ring she picked up. "Hey. It's, uh, it's Mike. Are you at the hotel? Yeah. And it was all taken care of, yes? You didn't need to sign in, show ID, any of that, correct? Okay, listen, I'm leaving now and I'll be there shortly. Remember—don't make any calls to room service, and stay in the room for now. As far as they're concerned you're a high-profile case of mine who wishes to remain anonymous. The staff have been instructed to stay away. Yes, I have the medication. See you soon."

He pressed the receiver again. He dialed 0.

"Daisy? Hold all of my calls. I have an emergency with a client. Yes. I need to go off-site to deal with this; I'll be back later. No. If it's an emergency, e-mail me marked urgent if it really can't wait. I have my BlackBerry. No calls. Thank you."

EIGHTEEN

"You awake, Randal?"

"Yeah. Can't sleep."

"Me neither."

They lay there for a few moments. The darkness in their room was almost total. The only light was a stray glimmer that crept in under the door.

"What did you think of the doctor?" Jeffrey said.

"I dunno, man. He seems to be saying the same shit they always say. He just does it with a movie star smile, that's all."

"But don't you think he has something?" Jeffrey said. "Something weird. Like a power . . . ah, I dunno."

"Celebrity," Randal said. "He has celebrity. It IS a power. You know, at one point today he held my hand, and looked me in the eye, and told me that I was going to die if I didn't do what he said."

"Yeah. He said something similar to me."

"But you know something? Even though I knew what

that fucker was doing—even though I've been given this speech before—somehow, I felt for a moment that he was really empathizing with me. That he . . . *understood* me. I got choked up. I almost cried."

"Wow. You see? I think that there's something different about him. You know, he talked to me about Bill. He said some stuff . . . about my father. Stuff I hadn't thought about in a long time. About our relationship. It was pretty intense."

"That's just it," Randal said, "that's what I don't like about him. He has this fucking knack for getting inside of your head, but when he talks, it's all of the same old shit. It's just the way he presents it. I mean, think about it—hasn't every drug counselor you've ever had tried to blame what you do on your parents?"

"Well . . . well, yeah."

"And isn't it a bit of a tired old fucking cliché that you were living with Bill because you saw him as some sort of surrogate father figure? I mean, haven't you heard that old story before?"

"Yeah. All the time from fucking therapists who don't know the first thing about what Bill and I had."

"But Dr. Mike just said the same old shit to you, but somehow, he made it seem profound. It's like when fucking De Niro is in a shitty movie. He can be working with the worst piece of shit script and somehow he sells it. Right?"

"Yeah. Christopher Walken can do that shit, too."

"Right. I had that same feeling you get when you sit through the fucking *Wedding Crashers* or whatever, just to see if Walken still has some of that same *Deer Hunter* magic. You walk out of the theater thinking that Christopher Walken can act his ass off, but kinda pissed off that you had to sit through two hours of shit to see it happen. I dunno. I've been around celebrities a lot. And you know something, when he comes over to your house, De Niro has something kind of unreal about him. Inhuman. Like he can only really be a human being on the screen. When he's sitting on your couch, drinking brandy with your pop, there's something weirdly artificial about him. Like he's half a person. That's what I feel about Dr. Mike. That motherfucker is half a person."

They fell into silence again. Randal heard Jeffrey sitting up in the darkness.

"Can I ask you a question?"

"Shoot."

"What kind of connections do you have? I mean in the industry?"

Randal laughed a little. "Shit, I got connections. I know most of the big guys on a first-name basis, and the rest I can get to within a couple of phone calls. What, you gonna tell me you have a great idea for a fuckin' movie or something?"

"No."

"You ARE an actor. I fucking KNEW it!"

"No, nothing like that."

There was a long pause as Jeffrey debated with himself one last time whether to really go ahead and talk to Randal about the tapes. He knew that Randal might just be the one person uniquely positioned to be able to help him with his problem, so he shoved his reservations aside and said, "I have a movie. I have a movie that I think is worth a lot of fucking money. The movie . . . it's all I fucking have. It's all I have to my name right now. But I don't know what it's worth or even what the fuck to do with it."

"I don't follow you. You a filmmaker or something?"
"No."
They lay there in silence for a moment. Randal had the vague idea that Jeffrey might turn out to be just another wannabe asshole who wouldn't be able to get over his famous surname. When he signed checks in restaurants, he invariably had to listen to the waiter's spiel that he was only doing this until the right part came along, or until he could get someone to buy his idea for a TV show about a crime-fighting dog with telekinetic powers. He remembered one bitch launching into a David Mamet monologue in the line at Ralph's when all Randal wanted to do was get his groceries and get the fuck out of there.

"Okay, here's the story. I didn't tell you this when we were talking the other day, but Bill used to be a cop. LAPD, homicide division. He was retired when I met him, and his family had no idea of the life he lived, especially in his later years, after his wife was dead and he could do what he wanted. There was a lot he had to keep secret. There was no room for a fag who wasn't firmly in the closet in the force, especially back then."
"I can imagine."
"But that's not all. Bill was a drug user. No, fuck that. That sounds wrong. Bill was a drug *connoisseur*. He liked his boys young and his drugs pure. He was into some dark shit. The macabre, you know? Over the years he collected a lot of stuff. Stuff from the high-profile cases he worked. Stuff that the right collectors would pay a lot of money for."
"Okay. So, what?"
"So when he died, I inherited what was left of his collection. A lot of the bigger items were sold off toward the

end. He'd had a few surgeries, a heart bypass and a cancer scare. A lot of hospital bills. So a lot of it was gone before . . . before he passed. All of it except the movie."

In the gloom, Jeffrey heard Randal reposition himself. He was sitting up now, wide awake. Jeffrey had his attention, at least.

"Okay, nice buildup," Randal said. "I'm intrigued. So what's the movie?"

"Bill was one of the first cops on the scene at the Tate house, the night of the Manson murders. August 9, 1969. He said it was a fucking bloodbath. That's the thing—over the years the whole fucking incident got so mythologized that it's almost like it never happened in concrete reality. Like it was always some fucking awful movie about the death of the sixties. That night, though, nobody knew anything about what had gone on, and Bill was just a rookie cop showing up to a call about a murder. He was there with some old-timers on the force, and more than one tossed their fucking cookies when they saw the state the killers had left the victims in. He said the place looked like a slaughterhouse. Bill was a big movie buff. He knew who Sharon Tate was. He said it was the weirdest thing to see someone like Sharon Tate in that condition. I mean, she was beautiful. Totally beautiful and they fucking DESTROYED her. I know that Bill was never really the same after that night. That whole experience left a real mark on him."

"Anyway, he took some things. Said he had the feeling that this was history, you know? In all of the chaos it was easy for some items to . . . go astray. Things weren't as strict back then, with forensics and all of that stuff. People were walking in and out of the crime scene unchecked. So he pocketed a few things. One of the bigger items he took was a box of film canisters. Eight millimeter and sixteen millimeter. Home movies, shit like that."

"Go on."

"Well, he'd had the film for a while before he managed to get hold of a projector and actually check what was on there. Turned out that one of these film reels contained something pretty fucking crazy. Listen, I'm willing to tell you this, but you have to agree that I'm doing it on the understanding that it goes no further than this room. Yes?"

Feeling slightly ridiculous, Randal said, "Jesus. Okay . . . sure."

Dropping his voice to a whisper, Jeffrey continued, "It was a movie shot at their house. It was a party scene. With some pretty big people. Steve McQueen was there. Sharon. Roman Polanski. Lee Van Cleef. Mama Cass."

"Jesus Christ. Sounds like an interesting dinner party."

"Interesting is an understatement. The other tapes had similar things, even bigger celebrities floating in and out. . . . I mean, that was their world, right? It was before the fucking tabloids would stake you out and report on every little thing celebrities got up to . . . so it was just a different time. Even before Bill saw THIS tape, he thought that the others were special. You really got to see these people with their guards down, relaxing . . . candid."

"So what goes on in this last tape that's so astonishing?"

"Well, according to Bill, a lot of shit that they wouldn't want to be made public. Drugs. Pills, booze. Everybody's acting pretty loose, you know? And then as the fucking camera runs, everybody takes off their clothes, and they all take a pop at Sharon Tate."

"What?"

Randal was not quite sure he was hearing right.

"They all fuck her. Steve McQueen fucks her, and then he rolls off of her, and Yul Brynner has a go. Mama fuckin' Cass is naked and eating her pussy, while someone is screwing her from behind. I mean, according to Bill it was a full-on drug and sex orgy. Twenty minutes or so of hard-core, uncensored fucking."

"No. I don't buy it. Have you seen it with your own eyes?"

"No."

"He was fucking with you, man. Seriously, something like that . . . I mean, you couldn't keep a lid on it. You seriously expect me to believe that this boyfriend of yours sat on something like that for like, what? Thirty years? And he just goes and dies, leaving it to you? It doesn't make sense."

Jeffrey remained silent for a moment.

"I know that it sounds ridiculous," he said deliberately, "but you don't know Bill. I never saw the tape because in the whole time I was with Bill he wouldn't let it out of the safe. But I saw other shit. Serious shit. He'd buy and sell and trade stuff with other guys in the force. I mean, unbelievable shit. You know Charles Ng?"

"No. What's he? A kung fu guy?"

"No, a serial killer. Leonard Lake?"

"I dunno."

"Well, Bill had some of the tapes that they shot. That stuff has never been made public. They were a team. A serial killing supergroup. There were hundreds of these fucking tapes. They would kidnap girls, take them to this compound, and just film themselves . . . *torturing* these women. Rape, mutilation, I mean, horrendous fucking shit. I saw some of those, they were on videocassette. Seriously fucking disgusting. I mean, I couldn't watch more than ten minutes of it. It was like some crazy fucking Japanese porno gore movie, except everything was for real. But the cops, man, they would trade those fucking things like they were baseball cards. Arrange screenings in cop bars. Sit around Bill's place, drinking beers and cheering those sick fucks on. Pretty fucked-up shit."

"Okay," Randal said, "okay. I believe you that Bill had access to some pretty insane shit. But as for the Sharon Tate thing . . . why are you telling me about it? What's your angle?"

There was a pause. It seemed as if even Jeffrey was trying to work out why he had brought this up.

"How much do you think something like that might be worth?"

There were a few moments of silence. Then with a sigh, Randal spoke.

"Well . . . I mean, IF it existed, and if it was real . . . I mean, it's priceless. It's a lot of money. If. But that's a big if, you know?"

"Would you help me check it out?"

"Oh, Jesus. Listen, Jeffrey, I like you. And that's saying something because I hate most people. But I don't *know* you. Not really. Not outside of this place. I mean, Jeffrey, I don't have time to get involved in something like this. I have problems of my own to deal with without getting tied up with the shit you have going on right now. . . . I mean, the last thing I need is to get involved in something that might end up being nothing at all. . . ."

"Half."

"Huh?"

"Half. I'll give you half. Straight down the middle, no questions asked. Look, man, I need help with this. I don't know anyone else who would be able to help me to get this to the right people. You could, you said it yourself. You know those people. That's your world. How much do you think it might be worth to the right collector?"

"Fuck. I dunno. A million? Two? Ten? I mean, you can't even quantify something like this. It's like—it's like you're telling me you have the Holy Grail, or the Shroud of fucking Turin."

"You know people in porno?"

"Some . . . but that's not the way to go. Something like this has to stay in the hands of a private collector. If it ever gets out, then it becomes worthless. It would be all over the Internet in a heartbeat, and no more valuable than a used copy of *One Night in Paris*. No, somebody is gonna want to pay money to keep this under wraps."

"What? The family? You mean blackmail them?"

"Blackmail? Not unless you want to see the inside of a jail cell. I mean we need to find the kind of person who wants to be the only one who can see this, who even knows of its existence. A freak. A collector. No offense . . . but someone just like your boyfriend."

They both lay in the darkness for a while. Jeffrey wondered silently just how much he could trust Randal. Just talking about the film with his new roommate filled him with uneasy reservations. But Jeffrey knew that the time to act was now. In a matter of days he would be out of the relative security of Clean and Serene, and if he wasn't in a position to find a buyer for the tape, then he was well and truly screwed. What else was he going to do? The only other person he knew with connections in the film industry was a strung-out gay porn actor called Spider. Spider was hardly the kind of person you could trust with something like this. At least Randal had his famous surname, and his connections in the industry. As for his reliability, Jeffrey would have to take a chance.

"Half?" Randal asked, breaking the silence.
"Half."
"Jesus Christ."

They again lay there in silence for a long time, but neither slept. They lay there, separately turning over what it could mean to sell this film to the right person. To Randal it represented freedom from his family. To Jeffrey it represented a clean break, a chance to start over somewhere new. There was no more talk after that, but no sleep either. Silent, surrounded by the darkness, calculating, imagining, making silent, secret plans.

N!NETEEN

There was a palpable excitement at Clean and Serene that day. Word had begun to spread around the place that not only would Dr. Mike be making one of his irregular appearances, but he would also have some of his celebrity patients from *Detoxing America* in tow. They were filming the reunion episode, where the assorted celebrity flameouts were brought into a treatment center to attend a meeting with "real addicts."

"How did you hear all of this?" Jeffrey asked Johnny D, an old black junkie who claimed that he once played bass for Sly Stone.

"I heard it from Big Jim."
Johnny D nodded over toward the aforementioned man mountain, who sat with his plate piled high with soggy-looking Eggos. "You know how those crackheads are. Gossipy motherfuckers. Like a bunch of old women."

As Johnny D moved on down the line, Jeffrey turned back to Randal. "You hear that?"

"Yup."

"Who's on the show? You even know?"

"Who gives a shit? A bunch of fucking D-list nobodies who are getting involved in this circle jerk with Dr. Mike so that they can get one more hit of kinda, sorta fame."

"You're such a fucking cynic, man. I dunno. I thought Dr. Mike was kind of an asshole, too, but when I met him. . . . You know, he seemed sincere. I mean, I don't know if I buy all of this twelve-step stuff, but he was sincere. He made me wanna believe it."

"Of course he made you wanna believe it. That's his shtick. He's selling you something that totally falls apart under any kind of critical scrutiny. But he has a nice smile, clean teeth, and he smells good, so you wanna buy it. I'm not saying he's not charming. Nobody gets big in this town unless they got a good way with people. I just get the feeling that if he weren't in this line of business he'd be on QVC selling mops and fucking lawn chairs."

Jeffrey laughed, and asked for a plate of home fries and bacon.

The rumors continued to spread around the facility. When people have been smoking crack, robbing banks, drinking vodka for breakfast, or injecting meth daily for the last bunch of years, sobriety can seem pretty dull by comparison. So even the most tenuous chance for excitement is seized upon.

The celebrities would be coming in at noon to start filming and would attend a one p.m. "in house" meeting. There were three meetings held inside. There was one on the third floor, next to the meditation rooms. People jokingly referred to that one as "the Cuckoo's Nest": the dual-diagnosis meeting. They put people who were crazy as bat-shit, even without drugs, in the dual meetings. That's where the likes of Running Deer went. Running Deer was a Native American Vietnam vet with a taste for whiskey and bar fights. He was a nice, sweet old guy who had spent twenty years of his life in solitary confinement before being allowed to transition into a residential drug rehab. He had straight, thick hair down to his ass, and his arms and portions of his face were covered in prison ink. His predominant tattoo was an India-ink swastika on the forehead. The swastika was the reason that a lot of people avoided Running Deer; it gave them the impression that he was some kind of insane Native American Nazi. One day in group therapy Randal heard somebody ask Running Deer about the swastika. He'd pointed to his forehead and said, "This is the symbol of the whirling winds. A sacred and ancient design, used by the Navaho. Not a swastika. This is a link to my own history. This is a link to the proud and mighty Navaho people." People still tended to avoid him though, unnerved by his frequent "episodes," which came on without warning.

Running Deer had a habit of barricading himself in his room and screaming very, very loudly for hours at a time. He would be shouting orders in there, or yelling about incoming enemy fire and ranting about the fucking gooks. There seemed to be no pattern to it, and as a result Running Deer was the only person in the facility without a roommate and was made to attend the Cuckoo's Nest. The staff tolerated him and had on more than one occasion threatened to kick him out if he trashed his room again, but there seemed to be a general consensus that Running Deer was harmless. Eccentric, but harmless.

Another Cuckoo's Nest regular was Jimmy the Gimp, a tubby, pasty kid from the Midwest who was reportedly a convicted sex offender and a recovering methhead. Jimmy had one leg three inches shorter than the other and had a habit of staring off into some vague middle distance, effectively zoning out of all that was going on around him. This seemed to happen pretty regularly, especially in slow meetings. Randal had only talked to Jimmy once, during a cigarette break. Jimmy had joined them at the table and out of the blue began to talk about the differences between fucking a guy and a girl.

"I mean, when you're inside you gotta fuck guys, because there's nothing else around. But they just feel different. Even if you close your eyes and picture Brooke Shields, they still feel different."
The others stared at Jimmy, but Randal had taken the bait and laughed. "Brooke Shields? You got a thing for Brooke Shields?"
Jimmy grinned nastily and sucked on his Parliament.
"You ever see that bitch in *Pretty Baby*? I've had a hard-on for that cunt for like twenty years now."

The other two meetings were a pretty evenly matched bunch. It was obvious that they tried to balance out the cynics with the true believers, the gleaming converts to the words of Dr. Mike and the twelve steps. The meetings were expertly gerrymandered, so that those more inclined to call bullshit on some of the good doctor's more ridiculous statements were heavily outnumbered by those who would be willing to raise their hands and thank God and Dr. Mike for another glorious day of drug-free living.

As they ate breakfast, Jeffrey said, "I heard that the drummer from the Nosebleeds is one of the celebrities."

"Those fucking eighties cheese-balls? They couldn't even get the singer?"

"The Nosebleeds were cool. They had some songs."

"They sucked, man. They were poseurs. Any fucking person from a band who does one of these shows is a joke. You don't see Chuck D doing this kind of shit."

"But Flavor Flav has a show on VH1. A dating show."

"Exactly."

The day carried on with its usual annoyances. The pressure in the place seemed to be building until at last the lunch bell rang. As they all started shuffling in to get reheated soggy tacos and frozen French fries, it became immediately apparent that the men and women of Clean and Serene were in the presence of greatness. Off in the corner of the vast cafeteria, at the farthest table, sat five people, surrounded by lights and cameras. Randal vaguely recognized some of them. There was Sasha Jones, the actress most famous for her role in the 1980s sitcom *The Mikey Forrester Show*. Since that show's heyday, she'd released a memoir, *Flowers in the Dirt*, about her struggles with alcoholism and depression. She'd even made it onto *Oprah* once, shoved in between two other guests who'd managed to fuck up their shots at fame. But Randal hadn't seen her on TV for years now.

She looked older, bigger, the cute face that had once landed her the role as Mikey's love interest all but bankrupted now.

There was a guy in leather pants with long blond hair who must have been the drummer from the Nosebleeds, a glam rock band who had a few hit singles before grunge came along and rendered them has-beens virtually overnight. He looked weak and shaky; the poor bastard had obviously blown out the circuitry in an important part of the brain with drugs, and no amount of therapy in the world can fix that. There was a skinny woman with a strange, plastic surgery face, who might have been a long-ago Playboy Playmate of the Year. The junkie lead singer from a one his wonder LA rap-metal band who had gone bald and put on fifty pounds since he'd last been seen on television. And a onetime semifinalist from *American Idol* who made the news by getting kicked off the show when she was arrested driving under the influence of booze and MDMA.

Jesus, Randal thought, *the fucking A-list is here.*

As they took their food and sat down to eat, Randal noticed that whenever someone tried to take a table too close to the celebrities they would be blocked and shooed away by the camera crew. The cafeteria was filling up fast, yet there was a ring of empty tables around the celebrities. In fact, all you could really see were the cables that snaked around the tables and the asses of the men filming them. Occasionally there would be a glimpse of the side of Sasha Jones's face, or the Nosebleeds guy's long blond hair, but that was it. And of course, Dr. Mike sitting at the head of the table like Jesus among his disciples.

Johnny D slinked back after unsuccessfully trying to get close to the group and joined Randal instead.

"What's up?" Randal asked.

"They told me to sit somewhere else. Didn't want me bothering the famous people."

"Really? They said that?"

"They said they wanted the shots to be natural. Just them, eating their tacos. They said that if the regular population got too close, then they would act differently."

"Celebrities are a touchy bunch."

"Celebrities?" Johnny D laughed. "You're being kinda generous there, son."

After a carefully stage-managed lunch, Dr. Mike stood at the front and addressed the cafeteria. The after-lunch announcement was nothing new, but the fact that Dr. Mike was doing it was. This usually fell on the shoulders of the regular staff; people like Dave Bones, the old biker with the hole in his trachea, or New Orleans Suzie with the glass eye and scar on her cheek.

"Welcome," Dr. Mike said.

There was a mumble from the cafeteria. The cameras were on Dr. Mike and on the table of celebrities, catching their every reaction to Dr. Mike's speech. The doctor looked even more artificial than usual, the effect of his makeup and the unnatural lighting.

"Addiction," Dr. Mike began, "is a disease that does not differentiate. Addiction is a disease that affects the young, the old, the rich, and the poor. I have a group of very special patients who are joining us today, a group of very brave individuals who have waived their right to anonymity and have decided to take part in the great experiment that is *Detoxing America*. Finally, the general public now has access to what really goes on in a treatment center. I think that this is vitally important to raise the consciousness of the general public, and to help people empathize with the plight of the addict. Don't let their celebrity status fool you. These people are disease-ridden—just like you. I'm sure you will all join me in a round of applause for these brave, brave people."

At that Dr. Mike started clapping. The staff joined in enthusiastically, and soon the rest of the patients slapped their palms in appreciation, while Randal shook his head in disgust. Dr. Mike raised his hands, and the room fell into silence again.

"Having completed treatment, our guests are now paying a visit to us at Clean and Serene to attend an AA meeting and see what goes on here at this facility. Now, this does mean that there will be some releases for you to sign. If you are not comfortable with appearing on television you must let us know, and you will be made anonymous in the editing room. For those of you who don't read English, the staff will be more than happy to assist you. Now, without further ado . . ."

As Dr. Mike said this, there was a scream from the table of celebrities. While the attention was focused on Dr. Mike's speech, Running Deer—who had been standing at the back of the room—had crept over toward Sasha Jones with a pen and a piece of paper.

"Miss Jones?" he had said, lightly touching her on the shoulder. Running Deer had been incarcerated during the 1980s for drunkenly killing a man in a bar fight, and during that time he had watched *The Mikey Forrester Show* religiously. Running Deer had never seen an honest-to-God celebrity before. Sensing that this was an opportunity that would never arise again, Running Deer took his chances.

As he placed his hand on her shoulder, Jones turned around and was faced with an American Indian Vietnam vet with a swastika tattooed on his forehead. He was grinning at her and trying to shove something into her hand. She let out a shriek of horror and leapt to her feet.

Immediately the scene was chaos. When Jones shrieked, so did Running Deer. In fact, he crouched down in the fetal position, covered his head with his hands, and started howling like a kicked dog. One of the film crew dived at Running Deer even though he was no longer in contact with Jones, knocking him to the ground. The two of them sprawled over each other as the cameras rolled, capturing every second of it. The cafeteria erupted in screams and yells, and people craned their necks to see the action.

Running Deer head-butted his assailant on the nose, splitting the skin and eliciting yells of support from the crowd. Seeing the blood, Johnny D practically pushed Randal over, screaming, "KILL THAT MOTHERFUCKA, CHIEF! TAKE IT HOME, BABY!"

Dr. Mike pushed his way through the crowd, and the staff descended on Running Deer, attempting to restrain him. The bleeding cameraman staggered off, his

face in his hands, blood running through his fingers.
Sasha Jones was screaming at the camera crew, "Get
me OUT of this place! That Nazi motherfucker almost
killed me!"

Within seconds, it seemed, the crew, Dr. Mike, and all
the celebrities had been rushed out of the room.

The population of Clean and Serene booed as Running Deer was dragged from the cafeteria, still struggling. One red-faced staff member was screaming,
"That's IT, motherfucker! You're out of here. They're
gonna lock you up for good, Chief Shithead!"
The whole time Running Deer was screaming, "Incoming! Incoming!"

It took a while for things to settle down. Sensing rebel-
lion in the air, the staff came in and announced that the
meetings were beginning immediately. The patients
were quickly split into groups and taken upstairs.

As they were being herded out of the cafeteria, Randal
nudged Jeffrey and said, "I guess that fucked up their
reunion special."
"I guess."
"You think they'll really kick the Chief out? I mean,
that fucking camera guy overreacted. He started it."
"Tough break. Some people don't have any luck, you
know?"
"I can't wait to get the fuck outta here. This place is
bullshit, man. Total fucking bullshit. I wish I was splitting when you are. A week! You lucky bastard."
"I don't feel lucky. I feel anxious, man. Tense."
Randal put his arm around Jeffrey's shoulders.

"You'll be cool. Just don't fuck up, and it will be fine. I'll be out in two weeks. If we keep it together we can make our own luck for a change. No more bullshit cures. We can get as far away from here as we like. . . ."

Jeffrey smiled. "I like that. I like that a whole lot."

TWENTY

When she first landed in Los Angeles from Reno fifteen years ago, Trina didn't have much. Just seven hundred dollars from a stolen credit card and a bag with everything she owned stuffed in it. It was mostly clothes that barely fit her anymore, unwashed and shoved in there in a hurry. The only sentimental item that she had was a Rainbow Brite doll whose face had worn away because of her habit of rubbing her nose against it at night to get to sleep. When she stepped off the bus a handsome young boy who went by the name of Ugly John stared at her so hard that she asked him what the fucking idea was. Trina had learned over the years that you had to be tough and that you couldn't let anybody give you any shit. Otherwise people would eat you alive.

He was standing there casual, eyeing her up and down, sucking a soda pop through a straw. Ugly John didn't take her abuse badly, though, and he asked what her name was. After they'd talked for a while he took her to McDonald's for lunch. He bought her a Happy Meal and wrote down a list of addresses for her. Mostly hotels that had cheap rooms and a few phone numbers in case she wanted to score drugs. When he saw the look on her face when he brought up drugs, he offered her some blow. Trina was fifteen and she had only ever drank booze or huffed industrial solvents before. Cocaine seemed to be impossibly glamorous, something rock stars and actors did. They went into the bathroom, and Ugly John cut out a generous line for her. He handed her a fifty-dollar bill, and she rolled it up and inhaled. The coke tasted clean and sparkly, like winter frost. The first time that she snorted cocaine, Trina realized that she wanted to feel this way always. Her brain seemed to finally catch up with her mouth. For the first time in her life, Trina felt comfortable in her own skin.

Trina ended up sleeping with Ugly John. He rented a room for them in a dilapidated hotel downtown called the Cecil. For someone so young, Ugly John seemed to have a lot of money, and Trina liked that. There was a bar next door to the Cecil that smelled of damp and rat poison. It had an unlit neon Santa Claus off in the corner next to the cigarette machine. It was April. The barmaid was from Juarez and did not ask for IDs. The only other customers were barflies silently drinking from dirty glasses and watching a Lakers game. Trina had never drank in a bar before. She suddenly had the impression that she was no longer a kid. She had made it from awkward adolescent to adulthood in the space of seven hours. She knew that she had done the right thing when she snuck out of the house last night.

After drinks and more coke they went upstairs to-gether. Trina had had sex many times but she had never had sex on cocaine before. Trina decided that sex was a lot better on cocaine. Instead of the anxious, fleet-ing couplings that she'd had with other kids at school, or with the nervous married men who arrived at the house with heavy brown paper bags from liquor stores, this lasted for at least ten minutes, and it felt real good while it was happening. Ugly John put his mouth to her pussy and did something that made her feel amazing and self-conscious at the same time. When Ugly John told her that she had a sweet pussy, Trina's heart flut-tered, and she fought back the urge to say, "You really mean it?" in a voice dripping with childlike wonder.

She stayed in that room at the Cecil for two months. After the first forty-eight hours of drinking, screwing, and snorting, Ugly John told her that she had to pay him for the cocaine and the room. He said she owed him a thousand dollars. When she refused to give him money, Ugly John pulled a knife on her and took her bag away. He found the seven hundred dollars and took it. "Down payment," he said. He told her that she was going to work off the rest of the debt, otherwise he'd kill her.

"Ain't nobody gonna come looking for you, bitch. No-body. You better start acting right, girl, otherwise you're gonna see what a son of a bitch I can be when I need to be. . . ."

Trina was sure he was right. With no money and no bag, she decided she'd better do what he told her. Ugly John would leave in the early afternoon and start rounding up men. They were mostly Mexicans who didn't speak much English, or the occasional drunk in a crumpled business suit. On a busy day, he'd show up with two or three at once, and they'd have to queue up in the hallway for their turn. Once or twice they'd ask to do her at the same time, and Ugly John would charge extra. Mostly they were drunk and useless and would sweat and breathe whiskey smells all over her, pumping furiously, calling her names, and pulling her hair.

Once she had started doing as she was told, Ugly John would act nice with her. He would give her some of the money she'd earned. All the money went through Ugly John, and she wasn't even sure of how much she charged for sex. "Go buy yourself something," he'd say. He started letting her leave the hotel, and she'd wander through the cheap trinket stores on Broadway spending her earnings on stuff that she didn't need: "I LOVE LA" stickers that she thought she might send to her kid sister back at home, dolls from Mexican TV shows she'd never seen, costume jewelry, malt liquor, candy bars, that kind of stuff. Ugly John returned her Rainbow Brite, but the doll seemed stupid and childish now, so she handed it to a little Mexican girl she saw loitering in front of the hotel one afternoon. In the evenings, before things would get busy, Ugly John would show up with tacos, and they'd eat. Mostly, though, they did cocaine. She didn't like to fuck unless she had coke, and the more coke she snorted, the more money Ugly John kept to pay for the drugs. If she complained about Ugly John taking too much of her money, he'd beat her. This was not the first time she had been beaten by a man. In fact, since she had come to LA the only new things she had experienced were the cocaine and the Mexican food.

.   .   .

One day she told Ugly John that she wanted to go to Beverly Hills. Ugly John laughed at her. "I came all the way to Los Angeles and all I see is this hotel room and your little dick! You never take me anywhere!" Ugly John told her to shut the fuck up. She called him a dirty nigger. He called her a cunt, and a whore, and beat the living shit out of her. He bloodied her up and knocked one of her teeth out. The men didn't seem to mind that she looked that way. When things went back to the way they were, she started saving the money that Ugly John gave her. When she had two hundred dollars in her pocket she left and never came back.

One thing that Ugly John taught her was that a girl had to choose her man carefully if she wanted to get by in this world. A good man was hard to find, and Trina had the scars to prove it.

They were in Pat's hotel room. Pat was staying in a place called the Motor Home Lodge, on Sunset Boulevard. There were ten apartments on their floor, and the interiors were a murky brown color. The television was black and white, and one channel showed a continuous porn loop with a wavy, grainy picture. They had been here for a day now. She didn't like this place as much as the place where Pat had brought her originally, but she knew that it wouldn't be forever. Pat told her that every month or so he liked to switch hotels.

"I don't like it if too many people know where I live," he had told Trina when they had boxed up and moved out of the Deville Motel. "It's bad for business."

.   .   .

Pat was preparing a pipe for them. He was wearing his grease-stained Levi's and a once-white undershirt. He looked over to Trina and said, "What you thinking about?"

Trina jerked out of her thoughts. "Hm?"

"I said, 'What you thinking about?'"

Trina smiled a little and looked coy.

"I was just thinking," she said, "about how a good man is hard to find."

Pat flicked on the lighter. The flame was strong and blue. He smiled to himself a little, maybe about what Trina had said, maybe because of the drugs he was about to smoke.

"You look after me, Daddy," she said, "and I like that."

In the closet hung almost a thousand dollars' worth of clothes that Pat had bought for her at the mall at Hollywood and Highland. He'd put the cash in an envelope and waited in the car for her. "Buy something sexy," he'd instructed. After the incident with her apartment, Pat told her it would be better for her to keep a low profile for now, so he called the club and told them that she would not be in for a while. Just like that, Pat and Trina were living together, and Pat was supporting her. It was the happiest that Trina could remember feeling.

She went over to Pat, and while he started smoking, she tugged at his jeans and started working his cock with her mouth. From a boom box on the nightstand "Thru These Walls" by Phil Collins played quietly.

As she was sucking him, her cell phone went off. She stopped, walked over, glanced at the number, and put the phone down again.

"Who was that?" Pat asked, handing her the pipe.

"Tyler. He's calling about that money again."

"How much you owe him?"

"Two hundred."

Pat nodded over to a pile of cash on the nightstand.

"Pay him. Seems like every time I'm about to bust a nut, that motherfucker calls and ruins the moment."

Trina made a face. "Fuck that. I don't wanna give that bastard the money. He hung me up, made me beg for credit. If I was a fucking boy, he'd be handing pills out like they're fucking candy. He's a faggot. He hates women."

"You want me to talk to him? Straighten homeboy out?"

Trina laughed at the thought. "He'd about shit a brick. I dunno how he fucking keeps in business. That's why he only sells to women and faggots! He sits in that apartment of his with fucking suitcases of money and fucking pills, and he don't even got a gun."

Now Pat was interested. He leaned forward.

"You serious?"

"Yeah! People are walking in and out all day and night, and half the time he's so out of it on his own shit he doesn't know who's there. One day somebody is gonna take that boy for everything he has, then he'll have bigger problems than my two hundred fucking dollars!"

Taking her hit, Trina got back down between Pat's legs. White clouds billowed from her nose and she said, "Sorry, Daddy, where were we . . . ?"

Pat pushed her head away from his cock. Now it was his turn to look thoughtful.

"You know . . . I'm thinking that maybe we should be the ones to benefit from this motherfucker's stupidity."

Trina looked up at Pat. "What, you mean . . . ?"

"Let's rob this faggot. Why not? He ain't a friend of yours, is he?"

"No. He's a real cocksucker."

"And he don't even know who I am."

"Uh-huh."

"So if I was to pay him a little visit, maybe persuade him to hand over the money and the drugs . . ."

Trina smiled. The idea seemed thrilling, adventurous. Like a movie.

"Seems like a no-brainer to me. We could get out of town for a little while. Live it up. You ever been to San Francisco?"

Trina shook her head.

"Beautiful city, girl. Here . . ."

Pat got up and grabbed a bunch of bank notes. He counted out three hundred and handed them to Trina.

"Pay him," he said, "buy some more. Get in his good books. And let's try to figure out when he gets his bulk delivered. Where he keeps the money. I wanna know exactly what weapons he has in there and who his supplier is."

Trina took the money.

"Sounds complicated."

"All I need you to do right now is pay off that two hundred and get some more shit. You said he has pills?"

"Uh-huh."

"Try'n get some Dilaudid. I haven't had Dilaudid in a dog's age."

"Okay, Daddy."

.   .   .

Trina didn't need to be asked twice to go and buy drugs. She was already pulling her clothes on, slipping her cell phone in her pocket. She gave Pat a long, hard kiss on the lips. Pat slapped her on the ass.

"I'll be back soon . . . ," she said.

"Sure thing, sweet cheeks."

Trina smiled as the door closed behind her and walked toward her car. She clicked on the cell and found Tyler's number.

"T, it's me. Cool to stop by? Okay. See you in fifteen."

TWENTY-ONE

"I'm stiff," Tyler complained, stretching like a cat. "I've been on the couch forever."

"I've been trying to get his ass to Chico's house all afternoon," Spider grumbled. Spider was tweaked as usual, edgy and sweaty, his eyes darting around the room as if he were hearing noises all over that nobody else could perceive. Trina rolled her eyes.

"Fuck that shit," said Tyler to the monstrous pile of blow on the coffee table, "I've been busy. Can't you see how busy I am?"

Trina clacked her heels on the bamboo floor as she uncrossed and recrossed her legs incredulously. "Yeah," she said, looking at Spider, or through Spider, or what did it matter? "I don't know how he fits it all in."

Tyler snuffled and wiped his nose with a shaking hand. "Always, with these fucking mooches in my apartment! Why are you here, man?"

Spider immediately launched into a long, convoluted

story about a guy named Chico who wanted to trade painkillers for meth. Tyler started to zone out, eyeing the cocaine again hungrily. Another one of Spider's elaborate schemes to get something for nothing. The television was on. He looked over to it; something familiar was cutting through the chatter of the others, something familiar, something that interrupted his train of thought for a moment. He saw the eyes first. *"You've followed their ups and downs, but how are they doing since completing the program?"* Dr. Mike's plastic face was burning with calculated sincerity from the plasma screen. The eyes fell upon Tyler like the eyes of God. An old god, one full of judgment and condemnation. A god who wore a starched blue shirt, who smelled faintly of soap and a delicate, feminine fragrance, a god who had facials and manicures. A god at once fearsome and strangely emasculated. "Turn that shit off!" Tyler barked at no one in particular.

"Fuck this shit!" Spider hissed, getting to his feet, suddenly filled with indignation. "If you don't want my custom I'll take it elsewhere."
"Take your ass to Walgreens if you don't like the way I do business!" Tyler said, and Spider stomped out, slamming the door.

"So, uh, about that money I owe you . . . ," Trina said.
"Here we go. You spend it on ass implants?"
"No. I got it right here."
Trina reached into her bra and counted out the bills. Tyler watched her, silently.
"You got any Dilaudid?"
"Sure. I got the crazy eights and the fives."
"I'll take four of the eights."

Tyler shuffled off to his bedroom, and Trina cut herself a line. When Tyler returned, he counted out the money.

"It's all there," she said coldly.

"Just checking. This is a business, not a hobby, ya know?"

"Yeah. I know."

Tyler sat down again. "I'm fucked," he said.

"You look burnt out, man. You need to slow down."

"Yeah. Fucking Jeffrey left a bag full of fucking drugs and shit here. When he went to rehab. Valuables, he told me. I ain't kidding, he had a fucking envelope stuffed full of fucking China white. I took a little out. Sniffed it. Just a tiny bump. No shit, I nearly fucking died. Haven't had dope that pure in a long time. I could feel my fucking lungs shutting down. Like someone was sitting on my chest. I put that shit back, but I ain't felt right since."

"Jesus. What's Jeffrey gonna say about that?"

"Nothin'. He ain't gonna know." Tyler stared at Trina. "Right?"

"Hey, it's none of my fuckin' business."

"And anyway, he knew I was gonna dip in. You don't tell the fox to keep an eye on the chicken coop, right?"

"I gotta split, T."

"Sure. What day is it?"

"Thursday."

"Fuck. Jeffrey's due home tomorrow. I haven't had my dick sucked in a long time. Maybe he'll be feeling horny."

"Why don't you just go buy a boy?"

"And leave the house? I dunno."

"You're the laziest fucking crackhead I ever met."

.   .   .

Tyler looked at her, and smiled coldly.

"You don't wanna take care of me? I'll give you a freebie."

"It ain't a freebie if I have to suck dick for it. And I don't know where that little thing has been, T. Anyways, I got a boyfriend now. I'm in a relationship."

"A stripper relationship. How does that work? If it lasts for more than a few days, does he get a weekly rate or something?"

"I ain't gonna strip no more. I moved in with him. He's an entrepreneur. A businessman. He's taking care of me."

"Yeah, right. A businessman. You're funny, you know that?"

Trina got up.

"I'll see you around, T."

"Peace."

Trina left, and Tyler looked around the house. God-damnit, maybe he would have to go out and buy some ass. It was Thursday night in Hollywood. It wasn't as if he were going to stay in and read a *book*.

———————

The kid was fifteen, but looked younger. That's why he worked so much. He'd told Tyler that he had been in LA for six months now. He would be well on his way to a small fortune if every dollar that he'd made hooking didn't go into funding his crack habit. Still, he was a pretty kid, and Tyler figured he probably had another year or two left in him before his face gave out altogether.

"So, you know, I'm really an actor. This isn't my full-time gig or anything; I'm, like, in between jobs right now," the kid said, wincing as he hoovered up the last line of meth.

Tyler was wearing a bathrobe and Speedos. The kid said his name was Maestro. Maestro had been hanging out on Santa Monica Boulevard at two in the morning when Tyler was buying tacos and looking for trade. That was last night. Now that he had got what he needed Tyler was agitated by Maestro's presence. It was time to move on. Tyler watched the kid with bored eyes. "You planning on sticking around much longer?" he asked.

The buzzer interrupted them. Tyler peeked through the blinds, nervously, and then sighed when he saw who it was. He buzzed Spider in.

Bad luck emanated from Spider. If you had the right kind of eyes you could spot it straightaway. He was short and stocky with an ugly, scrunched-up face. He had a variety of unsuccessful hustles going, none of which seemed to bring in very much money. Spider was a professional moocher. He was dressed in a baseball cap, dark jacket, and jeans. Today, he had a smoothed-over, anonymous look about him. He dragged a black suitcase behind him. He looked around the room, with his small burned-out eyes screwed up a little. "What's up?" he said, to no one in particular.

"Hey, Spider. Back so soon? This is Maestro. . . ."
Maestro held out his hand, but Spider just looked at it, seemingly unwilling to touch the boy's hand.

"You been on vacation?" Maestro asked, awkwardly withdrawing it.

"Nope."

"Spider's never been out of LA. Right, Spider?" Tyler laughed. He was rolling a spliff.

Spider shrugged. "I got all I need right here."

He sat down next to Maestro, putting the case at his feet. He looked over to the kid sourly. Maestro thought there was something rotten about this guy's face, something degenerate and nauseating behind those eyes. He'd dealt with enough freaks in his life to know one when he saw one. Maestro smiled at him a little, cool and noncommittal.

"So what's with the case?" he asked.

"Stole it."

He bent over and opened the case, pulling out clothes and toiletries. He was hurriedly checking the clothes for designer labels.

Tyler sighed, and then looked over to Maestro, delivering his explanation in the neutral tones of the narrator of a nature documentary.

"Spider hangs out at LAX. By the luggage carousel. He takes cases. Then he usually shows up here trying to trade whatever motley collection of junk he has scored for drugs. It's all getting rather boring, to be honest."

"Shut up, faggot!" Spider spat, examining a blouse and then tossing it in a heap on the floor. "Goddamnit. It's garbage, man. *Forever 21!* Fucking shit. There was a nice Louis Vuitton suitcase that went around three times, but it was too obvious, man. They could have been staking the place out, you know?"

Maestro took a drag off his cigarette. "You ever been caught?"

"Yeah. A couple of times. You mind putting that thing out? I'm trying to breathe here."

"This motherfucker's been caught, what—six, seven times?" Tyler clarified.

Spider shrugged, and then went back to work. "I've been banned from LAX. That's why I grew the mustache. And dyed the hair platinum. Switching my look up."

"Yeah," Tyler sneered, "I don't know where he gets off calling me a faggot when he looks like a reject from the Village People. Nothing more disquieting than a self-hating homo."

"I ain't a homo."

"You fuck guys."

"For money."

"You fuck guys, though."

"So?" Spider said, stopping what he was doing and staring at Tyler. "If I cut someone's lawn for ten bucks, it don't make me a landscaper."

Maestro looked over at Tyler and smirked. Tyler made a face and mouthed "closet queen" at him silently. Maestro laughed a little, getting into the game, blowing more smoke in Spider's direction. Spider ignored them, rummaging through the side pockets now in desperation. Triumphantly he produced a wad of alien-looking notes and started counting them frantically.

"Two thousand Jamaican dollars," he said triumphantly. "What can I get for this?"

Tyler shook his head. "Don't you have any real money?"

"This IS real money."

"Don't let the palm trees fool ya, Spider. This ain't fucking Jamaica."

"Come on. Don't give me any shit, man."

"Will you do me a favor? You got your car?"

"Yeah."

"I'm supposed to pick up Jeffrey. Like, half an hour ago. And Maestro needs a ride back to his place."

"All right," Spider scowled, stuffing the money into his pockets, "but I'm keeping the bread. And fuck me! Bitch, put that cigarette out!"

"Fuck you, faggot," Maestro enunciated, slowly and clearly.

TWENTY-TWO

It was rent day in the Hotel Barbarossa, and as usual Atef was left chasing up money from the scum and the deadbeats who had run this place into the dirt over the years. When his father had come from Pakistan in the '60s, they had decent clients then. Poor, but honest. Wannabe actresses, musicians, screenwriters, all drawn to the West Coast by the lure of the film industry.

Atef's memories of growing up here were mostly positive: at least, up until the '70s. That was when his father had started drinking, and the neighborhood's slow decline had started to become the hotel's decline. As Mexicans and Guatemalans replaced the Filipinos and Jews, gang activity around the park had turned the hotel into a haven for drug dealers, prostitutes, and addicts. His father was too old, drunk, and tired to try to maintain the place, and by the time the old man died of a heart attack in the early '80s, Atef found himself inheriting a notorious flophouse.

.   .   .

The place barely survived year to year, and Atef treated his residents with as much disdain as they treated the building. One of his regular Thursday rituals was the rent collection. Walking the floors, hammering on the doors, warning the clients that they would be thrown out if they didn't pay up today. Sometimes they would try to ignore his warnings, and at least once a month he had to chase someone out with a baseball bat. Mostly, though, they paid, albeit reluctantly.

"Hello? Rent day!" Atef screamed through the door again, beating against it with his fist. He repeated his yell and placed an ear to the door. Nothing. Sighing, he slid his key into the lock and let himself in.

He half expected the room to be empty. Most of them just took off in the middle of the night, off to other hotels, maybe to a period of sleeping on the streets. But not today. As he opened the door, he saw her lying in the bed, naked, the sheets bunched up around her belly. He took in the peaceful look on her face, and then the breasts, which just sat there pointing upward, tying his tongue for a moment.
"Hello? Miss, hello?"
There was no reply. Outside he could hear the drilling of concrete, the screams of people driven insane by the heat already, but in this room everything was still, quiet. He crept forward.

Her mouth was hanging open slightly, giving her a slightly mongoloid look. He stared at her breasts and noted that her chest was not rising and falling. As his eyes lingered on them, he felt himself getting hard.

He'd had a hard-on for this bitch for a while now. Always hoping somewhere in the back of his mind that she would come to him with money problems, looking for some kind of arrangement to keep her room. It never happened, though, not with this one. There were a few of the girls who paid with furtive blowjobs and hurried fucks in the dreary front office, but this one always had the money at the end of the week. Atef wasn't surprised. She was by far the most beautiful whore in the place.

He reached out, touched her throat. The skin was icy to the touch, and there was no pulse. He allowed his hand to travel down her body, coming to rest on her breast. Even cool like this, it was still firm. He ran his thumb over her nipple. Then clearing his throat, he straightened up and went back to the door. He closed it and clicked the lock in place.

He looked around the room. On the bedside cabinet were several prescription bottles. One for diazepam, one for Xanax, one for something called Dilaudid, and another for Ambien. Large bottles. The only one with any remaining pills was the Ambien. He pocketed the remainder, and noticed her purse on the floor next to the bed. He went through it, removing eighty dollars and some Trojans. Then he returned his attention to the woman. Another fucking OD. Well used to this routine by now, Atef took his time. Glancing at the door one more time, he unzipped himself and started playing with his aching cock.

"Now you're fucking dead, you bitch . . . ," he said to her. "Now I can do anything I want to you, huh? You like this, don't you? You like watching me jerk off. . . ."

With his free hand he touched the dead girl's breasts. Then, frowning, he put his finger to her jaw and forced the mouth shut. That was better.

As he started to beat faster and faster, he pulled the sheet away, to further expose her naked body. As the sheet fluttered to the ground, he froze. He immediately felt a shudder run through his body. He muttered, "Jesus CHRIST!" and pulled his hand away from the sheet as if he had received an electric shock. He felt his dick go limp in his hand. He scurried to the bathroom and splashed cold water on his face, stuffing his penis back in his pants guiltily. He ran his hands through his wet hair and looked at himself in the mirror. He retched a little, barely believing what he had seen. He went back to the door and looked over at the bed. *Jesus fucking Christ*, he thought, *when you think they can't get any worse, they do!*

He looked again at the huge, out-of-place penis between the girl's legs over there on the bed. He noted, a little ashamed, that it looked bigger than his. She was so beautiful, so feminine, and small, yet there was this thick, ugly penis sprouting out of her like some monstrous challenge to nature. Atef shuddered. *People PAY for this?* he thought, outraged. *There are some real sick motherfuckers out there!*

Taking one last look around the room for valuables, he finally stormed out, locking the door behind him, so he could make that familiar 911 call. He knew that the cops would take their sweet goddamned time, as always. He poured a larger than usual finger of whiskey into his mid-morning coffee and waited. Champagne was a fucking MAN. He shuddered with disgust and raised the cracked cup to his lips.

TWENTY-THREE

After almost two hours of waiting in the lobby of Clean
and Serene, Jeffrey grabbed his case and stepped out
onto the street. He couldn't take the looks the receptionist was giving him anymore. *Poor bastard,* her face
said, *he's doomed.*

Outside, there was nothing around, except for a
two-lane highway and a McDonald's. This was a
neighborhood in name only, nothing more than
a collection of anonymous buildings built to be
observed through the unreal lens of a car's wind-
shield.

Earlier that day, he had scribbled his cell number on
a napkin and handed it to Randal. Randal had smiled
and pocketed it. "Two weeks, man," Randal had said,
"I'll catch up with you in two weeks. Don't go fuckin'
OD'ing on me or something."
"I'll be okay. I gotta find a place to live, and all of that

bullshit. Call me when you get out, and we can take care of business."

"Got it."

Then Jeffrey had gone downstairs to start the process of checking out.

He called Tyler's cell again. There was no answer.

The sun felt good against Jeffrey's skin. It was nice to be away from the incessant air-conditioning. He looked to his left and noticed there was a liquor store. He wondered if the treatment center or the liquor store had come first. It seemed like a perfectly symbiotic relationship. Everybody wins if a drunk walks out of this place and buys a bottle of booze. Everybody except the drunk.

A rusted 1980 AMC Pacer pulled up beside Jeffrey, belching fetid black smoke. The horn honked three good, long blasts. Jeffrey peered in and cursed under his breath. It was Spider. He pulled open the door.

"Where's Tyler?"

"Home. He sent me. Jesus Christ, ya shoulda seen the fucking swish he had me drop off. Goddamn. Fruitier bastard I've never seen before. No offense, man. But the kid was a fag with a capital F, ya know?"

Jeffrey shoved the case in the backseat and got in. Spider was manic and sweating up a storm. Tweaked out, as usual.

"I'm going to kick Tyler's ass," Jeffrey said.

"Huh?"

"Nothing."

Spider stuck the car into Drive, and they squealed away. As they weaved in and out of traffic, Spider talked a machine-gun monologue, cutting through traffic and slamming his fist against the horn whenever anyone got in his way. At Jeffrey's feet something that looked like meat lasagna was ground into the rubber slip mats and the inside of the car smelled of fried onions and toxic sweat. "So, uh, you're clean now, huh?" Spider was saying. "Clean and serene. Goddamn. That's a good thing. I'm proud of you, man. So what's next? Uh, you got any plans?"

"I think I'm gonna get out of LA."

"Really? Why?"

Jeffrey shrugged. "I just need a change of scene."

"Well, whatever floats your boat, man. But you know, where are you gonna go? This is LA, man. The center of the universe. We got everything here. I'm so sick of people putting this place down, like we're not cool or something. Like we're not New York. Man, *fuck* New York. I never met anyone from New York I liked. They can keep it, you know? What, you wanna go to New York?"

Jeffrey shrugged.

"No. Maybe get out of the States for a while. I dunno."

At this, Spider slammed on the brakes. An SUV directly behind them swerved, and the wailing horn faded into the distance as it barreled past them, nearly mounting the sidewalk in the process. Spider looked over at Jeffrey, incredulous.

"Leave the STATES?"

"Sure, why not?"

Spider sniffed and twitched a little. Then he took off again, muttering to himself. He seemed genuinely aggrieved by the idea that Jeffrey might leave the U.S.

"Crazy shit, man. You know people are like riding on fucking rafts made out of banana crates right now, trying to get in here? Jumping over walls and shit. And you wanna leave? Where the fuck are you gonna go? Leave the States! Jesus Christ!"

They rode for a while in silence. They took the 101 to Hollywood and Jeffrey instructed Spider to take the exit at Vine. Then Jeffrey said: "Stop the car."
"What? I thought we're goin' to Tyler's place!"
"No. I need to make a stop. Tell Tyler I'll swing by tomorrow night."
"You sure?"
"Yeah."

They pulled up by the Pantages Theater. Jeffrey grabbed his bag and said, "I'll catch you soon, Spider."
"Take it easy."
Outside, the streets were balmy. He walked west, until he hit a favorite bar of his, Bob's Frolic Room. He walked into the cool, dark space. On one wall, a colorful mural depicted various Hollywood legends who had surely never set foot in the place. At the bar were a handful of afternoon drinkers. On the television, *The Young and the Restless* was playing and the barmaid, an impossibly tiny Russian lady, was watching it, rapt as she polished a glass. Jeffrey took his seat at the bar. To his right was an old man with a gray beard reading *LA Weekly*. He was eating popcorn and drinking a beer.
"Whattya have, hon?"
"Corona."
"Sure thing."

He left a twenty on the bar, and she pushed the frosty bottle over to him. Jeffrey opened up his bag and there, sitting reproachfully on top of his clothes, was his copy of the *Big Book* of Alcoholics Anonymous. He took it out and placed it on the empty bar stool next to his. He looked at his own reflection in the mirror that lined the bar and the rows of bottles. Each one promising freedom, wit, good times. He thought about Dr. Mike's smooth, airbrushed face, and the smooth, assured baritone of his voice. How sobriety had seemed so easy, so logical inside of the doctor's office. He took a pull of the beer. The beer tasted good. The beer tasted better than good—it tasted wonderful.

There were two weeks to wait before Randal finished his treatment. All he had to do was find a place to lay low until then, and they could work on making enough money to split LA forever. The idea of having to hold it together for even a couple of weeks was strangely terrifying. It seemed like an impossibly long time.

No drugs, he told himself. Just booze. You can still make the meetings, but if you need to get fucked up stick to booze. You can hold it together. He thought momentarily about having to step foot in Tyler's place, and the temptations that would entail. That's why he couldn't go tonight. He felt too fragile. It was too early. He needed to have a few drinks, unwind, find a place to stay for the night, and then in the morning he could make it to Tyler's. No worries. No worries.

Jeffrey closed his eyes, thankful to at last be back where he felt at home. He put the bottle to his lips and took a long slug. He slid the empty bottle away from him and signaled for another.

TWENTY-FOUR

Pat sat behind the wheel of the rusted red Toyota, watching the apartment building. He had the patience of a crab. His eyes were milky white in the dim sun. Trina was filing her nails. She was hunched down in her seat, with her knees on the dash. Fine strands of her hair were plastered to her forehead with perspiration, and her brow was furrowed in concentration. She looked like an impatient, petulant child.

There was a Carl's Jr. bag at Pat's feet. It contained onion rings. Pat reached into the bag absentmindedly without taking his eyes off the building across the street. The windows of the car were rolled down, and the air outside was murky, heavy with the scent of juniper and the chirps of crickets.

"I don't know how you can eat that shit," Trina said without looking up from her nails.

"These onion rings are superior in every way to the onion rings from Jack in the Box," Pat said.

"What about Fatburger?"

"Fatburger has good onion rings. But I don't like their French fries."

He took a bite.

"Anyways I don't mean THAT," Trina said, looking admiringly at her nails and putting the nail file back in her purse, next to the duct tape. "I just mean I don't know how you can eat anything. I'm too nervous."

"Nuthin' to be nervous about, girl. He don't got a gun, right?"

"He's got a gun. I told you that. He don't got bullets. He's got a gun that he bought someplace, but he just takes it out when he's trying to impress boys. Even if he did have bullets, he wouldn't know how to use it."

"He don't keep it on him."

"Right."

"Then that's what I mean. There's nothing to be nervous about. Here . . ."

He reached into the bag and handed an onion ring to Trina. She took it, looking unsure. Pat grinned at her. After smoking meth earlier her stomach felt disembodied, obsolete. She couldn't remember what hunger felt like. Her nerves were on edge in a way that was both unbearable and delicious. It felt like she was about to score drugs. She took a bite anyway and then quickly shook her head, dropping the rest of the ring into Pat's outstretched hand.

"I prefer In-N-Out's," she said.

Pat shushed her. A shadowy figure emerged from the building dragging a suitcase behind him.

"That's him, right? His buddy?"

"Uh-huh. Sure is."

They watched as Spider fumbled with his keys, cursed, wrenched open the door of the car, and tossed the case inside. Then he got behind the wheel and looked at his reflection in the rearview mirror.

With a squeal of tires, Spider tore off down the road, signifying that Tyler was home alone.

———————

When the knocks came, Tyler assumed that it was Spider trying to haggle more drugs from him. "Son of a BITCH," he said, getting up from the couch. He put his eye to the peephole and saw Trina standing there, alone. She was biting her nails and fidgeting from foot to foot. She looked like she was working her nerve up to something. Great. Another fucking mooch. This was turning out to be a fucked-up kind of a night.

"Bitch," Tyler started yelling to her as he pulled back the four dead bolts one after the other. "You'd better not be looking for handouts. I've had about all I can take tonight. I'm getting sick of you cunts treating this place like it's—"

He was going to say "Bank of America," but before he could get the words out, the door—which he had started to pull open—was violently kicked from the other side. It smashed into his face, making the world go gray for a moment. He staggered back a couple of steps before his legs buckled underneath him. There was movement all around him. Suddenly a pair of strong hands grabbed Tyler by his eighty-dollar vintage Joan Jett T-shirt and hauled him to his feet. Tyler was staring into a mouth full of yellow, ground-down teeth.

"Who ya callin' a bitch, pretty boy? Huh? Who you callin' a bitch?" the mouth screamed at him.
"Uh? Uh?" Tyler grunted. He was roughly shoved
against the wall, knocking the wind out of him again.
Pat punched him in the gut.

Tyler groaned and retched.

He heard Trina scraping the dead bolts back into place,
locking them all inside.

More punches landed, thudding against his face, knocking his vision out of whack.
THUNKTHUNKTHUNK
One blow connected squarely with his left ear, and
everything went quiet for a moment

before the world ERUPTED with the screaming of a
thousand unearthly alarm bells.

Tyler looked up, confused.

He didn't recognize the face in front of him.

"The money and the drugs, faggot. Where are they?"
the face was demanding. "If you get stupid with me, so
help me fucking God I'll kill you. . . ."
Pat grabbed Tyler by the balls. He gripped them hard.
He held Tyler up by the throat with the other hand. He
started to twist Tyler's balls violently. Tyler wept and
keened in a terrified, agonized way.

"I will fuck your pansy ass up if you don't start talking. You got me?"

Tyler struggled some more. Pat gave the nuts a further twist. It felt as if he were trying to tear them off. The agony made Tyler double up, but as he did so, Pat choked him and forced him upright again.

"GOT ME?"

"Yes!" Tyler screeched. Pat let him go, and Tyler collapsed into a pile on the floor, breathing ragged huffs.

As Tyler lay there trembling, Pat threw something round and shiny over to Trina. "It's gonna get noisy in here," he said. "Crank the volume on this. Track seven."

As Trina scurried off to fiddle with Tyler's stereo, Pat stood over Tyler with a stony expression.

"Look, man," Tyler started, "I don't want any—UGH!" Pat had kicked Tyler in the guts, hard. "You speak when you're spoken to, cream puff."

"Got it!" Trina said. "Against All Odds" blared out of the speaker system. "Louder!" Pat demanded. Trina cranked the volume. Pat crouched down and grabbed Tyler's face, twisting it around.

"You know something about this song?" Pat said. "Phil Collins recorded this for *Face Value*, his first solo album. It didn't make the cut. He didn't think it was good enough. He ended up giving it away for the soundtrack of some two-bit piece of shit movie. And you know something? He won the fucking Grammy for it. Knocked "Footloose" off the number-one spot. Probably one of old Phil's most successful, best-loved songs. And he almost ditched it altogether. What does that tell you?"

Tyler shook his head, confused. Pat grabbed him by the hair and slammed his skull against the floor.

"I SAID, WHAT DOES THAT TELL YOU, PRINCESS?"

"Uh . . . uh . . . Jesus Christ . . . ah—that . . . that you never . . . can tell?"

Pat laughed. He looked over to Trina and said, "You heard this dumb motherfucker? Can you believe this prick?"

Pat looked back at Tyler with a look that further chilled his blood.

"I'll spell it out for ya, cupcake. It tells you that your life can get fucked up by one bad decision. Phil Collins got lucky, because someone gave that song a second chance. Me, I don't give second chances. So you'd better make sure that whatever decision you make here today is the RIGHT fucking decision. I'm gonna ask you some fucking questions and I'd better get some straight fucking answers outta you, okay?"

He punctuated this by slamming Tyler's skull against the floor a few more times. Then Pat stood.

"Bring that chair over here," Pat said to Trina, pointing to the middle of the floor. She did as she was told. She didn't look at Tyler. He was just a shapeless mass on the floor. If she didn't look at him, then he couldn't look at her. She didn't want him to look at her.

Even when they both lifted Tyler by the armpits off the floor and onto the chair, she didn't look into his face. Tyler couldn't raise his head, anyway. He was oozing blood and snot from his mouth and his nose. He just slumped there.

"Tape," Pat said.

Trina retrieved the duct tape from her purse and handed it to Pat. He used the whole roll. The silver tape covered Tyler's arms and his legs in a cocoon, bonding him to the seat. His head was still slumped down, so Pat slapped his face a little.

"Wake up, pretty boy," Pat crooned.

Trina left and started rummaging through Tyler's bedroom, while Pat began to extract information from his victim. Immediately, she found a pile of meth on the nightstand. She cut herself a line and snorted it. It burned. Her eyes watered. Goddamnit. Then she started opening drawers, cupboards, looking under beds with a renewed vigor. In the next room she could hear the music blaring, not quite drowning out the other noises: thumps and staccato, high-pitched squeals like one of those toy dogs from Chinatown that barks and flips over. She didn't feel regret. She didn't feel anything. She felt excitement, she guessed. She mentally placed herself in Pat's car; both of them with the money and the drugs, heading off down the highway to a new life. No more Crazy Girls, no more Hollywood. Maybe they really would go to San Francisco just like Pat said. Maybe for once someone would keep a promise they'd made her.

When she got back in the room, there was a lot of blood on Tyler. He had a rag shoved in his mouth, and it had been duct-taped in place. The rag was deep crimson. Pat was on the other side of the room, arms folded, looking at Tyler impassively. Phil was now singing "You Can't Hurry Love."

"He don't wanna talk," Pat said.

"Oh. What do we do?"

"We make him talk."

Pat stood up suddenly and walked toward the kitchen.

"I wanna beer," he yelled over to Trina. "You want anything?"

"No. There's go fast in the bedroom."

"How much?"

"Just a little."

"Fuck it. I got my own."

Pat walked away.

When they were alone for a moment, Tyler started shaking his head, calling Trina over. She approached him cautiously, careful not to get too close. With a shaky hand, she reached out and unpeeled the duct tape from his mouth. Tyler spat the bloody rag out.

"Trina. Trina. Help me," Tyler whispered, as his glance darted between her and the door to the kitchen.

"It's too late for that," she replied, with something like regret in her voice. "Where's the money?"

Tyler glared at her. He was going to have this bitch hunted down and killed, he thought. That was the only comforting thought he could conjure right now. He would have her killed. They would find her in a garbage Dumpster. And he would make sure that the last thing she would do before they killed her was beg for mercy. And then she would be dead. Then Tyler looked miserably at his bound feet.

"Fucking Mexican beer!" Pat called from the kitchen. "What is it with these fucking hipsters and Mexican beer? What's wrong with Budweiser?"

"If you don't tell him," Trina said, "he'll kill you. I mean it. He'll kill you."

.   .   .

Pat strode back into the room, halfway down on a bottle of Modello. He looked at Tyler, at the bloody rag on the floor, and then at Trina.

"Is he talking yet?"

Trina shook her head, and walked away from Tyler.

Pat sighed. He came over, lifted Tyler's chin, and glared at him. He slapped Tyler across the nose.

"Where is it?" he said softly.

Tyler sniffled. Pat punched him suddenly, twisting Tyler around with a grunt. The chair, and Tyler still tied to it, went crashing to the floor. Pat roughly shoved the rag back into Tyler's mouth, sealed it back in place with duct tape, and then stepped back, admiring his handiwork. Tyler was looking at Trina's feet and crying. From somewhere in the room, Phil Collins was singing that "love don't come easy . . ."

Trina crouched down. One wide eye stared at her with uncomprehending fury.

"T, he'll kill you. I'm serious. *He's crazy.* He'll fucking kill you."

Something about the way she said "he's crazy" scared Tyler. She said it with awe in her voice. She said it the same way that someone might point out that her boyfriend owned a Fortune 500 company.

"Just tell us where the shit is, and you'll never see us again."

"You fucking bitch," Tyler mumbled through the bloody rag. He felt one of his teeth rattling around in his mouth, and he swallowed it with an involuntary gulp.

Pat grabbed Tyler and sat him up again.

"Give me your purse," Pat said. Trina hesitated for a moment, and then handed it over. She knew what was coming next. Tyler looked toward Pat for a clue. Pat went through the pantomime of looking into the bag and gasping in surprise at what he found there. Then he looked at Tyler and a long, cold grin spread across his face. He reached in and removed a pair of steel pliers.

"Well, look what I got here," Pat said.

Tyler started to scream, and even through the rag and the duct tape it was pretty loud. Pat ripped Tyler's T-shirt in two, exposing his chest. He sat down on Tyler's lap, facing him.

"Now, don't get too excited, faggot," Pat said. "I'm just sitting here to hold ya steady. If I feel anything start to grow down there, know this: I will cut it off and make you eat it. Do you understand?"

"Wait a second—" Trina said. "I gotta go pee. Wait till I'm gone."

She left the room, locked the bathroom door, and sat on the toilet, covering her ears with her hands. In the other room Pat said to Tyler, "Just you and me now, huh?"

He brought the pliers up to Tyler's chest. He pressed the cold metal against Tyler's left nipple. He squeezed it slightly, and a white-hot sensation burned through Tyler. ILLTALK-ILLTALK-ILLTALK. Tyler was screaming it through the rag. ILLTALK-ILLTALK-ILLTALK.

Pat heard. He didn't want the kid to think he was fuck-ing around, so he went ahead anyway and squeezed the nipple as hard as he could with the pliers. A scream came up from deep inside Tyler as the flesh split and the blood started to come. Then with one vicious twist, most of the nipple was ripped away from his chest altogether. As Tyler thrashed and vibrated, Pat held up the little piece of useless flesh still hanging from the jaws of the pliers.

"That's your titty," Pat said. "It could be your teeth. Or your dick. Or your nose. It could be anything that can fit between these fucking pinchers, an' that I can rip off of you. I'm gonna remove your gag now. I don't wanna hear shit from you, except for where the money is and where the drugs are."

Pat ripped the tape from Tyler's mouth and pulled the bloody rag from him. Tyler gasped. He hung his head and made a noise that sounded like it should come from a dying animal.
"The safe. The safe. It's behind the *Scarface* poster. The combination is 42068. Please stop. Please stop. Please."
"Good boy," Pat said, getting off of him. "You see? That's all you had to say."

There was a knocking on the bathroom door. "You can come out now," Pat cooed. "We're all done here."

A few moments later Pat emerged from the bedroom victorious, with Trina trailing after him like a puppy dog. He had the briefcase in his hand. The case contained almost ten thousand dollars in cash, the useless handgun, and a lot of drugs. A lot of fucking drugs. Tyler sniffled and stared at Trina balefully. She was looking anywhere but at him. The hole where his nipple used to be burned with an icy kind of fire. He could feel the blood congealing, still trickling down his chest in places. Trina's eyes were glued to Pat. The bitch was going to die. The fucking conniving, greedy, junkie bitch was going to die. There was a moment of silence before the next song, "Sussudio," kicked in. Pat silenced it by retrieving his CD from the stereo.

"Okay, let's go," Trina said, taking Pat's arm. Tyler felt himself slipping into unconsciousness. The pain was not receding but he was getting used to it now. He felt tired. Terribly, terribly tired. He watched them walk toward the door with heavy, out-of-focus eyes. They stopped, Pat's firm hand on Trina's shoulder. They whispered, frenziedly. Pat shot a glance toward Tyler, as hard as stone. Trina looked like a guilty child. She was sniffing a little, moving anxiously from foot to foot. Pat was whispering meaty, wet words into her ear. She nodded slowly, as if feigning understanding of a complex mathematical problem. She looked at Tyler with something approximating sadness, and then turned her back to him. Smelling death, Tyler began to thrash about madly.

Pat crouched down and removed the knife from the sheath concealed in his boot, straightened up, and walked over to Tyler. She did not look. She sensed the two of them behind her. She heard the bangs of the chair's legs against the floor, and Tyler's frantic grunts as he tried futilely to escape. She sensed the sudden movement of the knife. And then a sound, like piss splashing against porcelain. The thrashing intensified, and the grunting and groaning also. The rhythm slowed, slowed, and then a moment of silence. Pat's feet made a schlupping sound against the bloody floor. She felt his hand on her shoulder.

"Let's go," he said. She almost turned to see for herself, but Pat stopped her with his firm hand. "Don't look. Just walk away." She did as she was told.

TWENTY-FIVE

Trina was silent as she and Pat grimly walked back outside. They had barely gotten in the car when Trina said, "Why did you have to do that, Pat?" She was breathing funny, sounded like she was on the verge of some kind of panic attack. "Seriously—why did you do that? You didn't say you were going to do that!"

"You wanna do time?" Pat said, glaring at her. "'Cos I don't *think* you wanna do time."

"Pat—you fuckin' killed him! You shouldn't have done that, man! He already told you where the shit was and you killed him! I mean, Tyler was an asshole, but— FUCK, Pat—"

Without another word, Pat backhanded Trina across the face. The sudden blow silenced her. She cowered away from him, holding her hand to her burning cheek and shaking in terror. Pat was staring at her with eyes like black holes.

"I'm gonna write that one up to you bein' in shock or

some shit. You ever talk back to me like that again, bitch, and you ain't gonna like what you'll get."

"Pat, I'm sorry! I'm sorry, Daddy!"

"Don't be getting overfamiliar with me, girl. Nobody talks to me like that. Not you, not nobody!"

"Pat . . . I . . ."

Trina's mouth hung open for a moment. She was staring right past Pat now. Pat turned to follow her gaze. A car was pulling up in front of Tyler's apartment. "Shit!" Pat hissed. "Get down!" Trina hunched down, and Pat slid his ass to the very edge of the driver's seat so that only his eyes were peering over the steering wheel. He watched as Jeffrey got out of the car and slammed the door behind him. "Can you see that motherfucker?" Pat hissed. "Who is he?"

"Oh, shit," Trina said, "that's Jeffrey. He's one of Tyler's friends. Fuck!"

"He's a junkie?"

"Yeah. He just got out of rehab. I guess he came back for his bag. . . ."

"What bag?"

"He left his shit with Tyler when he checked in. Tyler said he left a bag of dope, valuables, all of his shit there."

Trina sensed Pat's body coiling tighter, a cobra about to strike.

"He was supposed to pick it up last night. That's why I didn't say anything, Daddy!"

They watched as Jeffrey rang the bell. Getting no answer, he pushed the door softly. Then he walked inside, leaving the door ajar.

·   ·   ·

Trina watched from the corner of her eye as Pat put his hand to his motorcycle boot, feeling for the handle of the blade. She kept her goddamned mouth shut this time.

"One Mississippi . . . ," Pat was breathing, "two Mississippi . . ."

As soon as the door had opened, Jeffrey knew that something was wrong. He stepped into the living room and almost slipped in the not-yet-congealed pool of blood that had spread out over the hardwood floor. He saw the body, lying there, duct-taped to the chair. He didn't even check if Tyler was still alive. There was so much blood. He was covered, fucking *drenched* in blood. His eyes were open, turned up toward the ceiling. Jeffrey choked back a yelp. He turned away quickly, before the image could be etched onto his psyche too deeply. He looked at his feet, but when he did he became aware of how much blood was on the floor. He fixed his eyes on the bedroom door and tiptoed toward it.

Inside, he saw the safe, yawning open, obscene and empty. The entire room had been turned over. Drawers hung open, clothes lay in piles on the floor. He looked up to the ceiling, toward the entrance to the crawlspace. It was still closed. He stood on the bed, leaving bloody footprints on the duvet. He reached up to the crawlspace entrance and pushed it aside. He put his hand there and felt around, thinking for one heart-stopping moment that the bag was also gone, before he touched the strap and pulled it down on top of himself. He found himself momentarily confused as he stared at a picture of Eddie Murphy in a space suit. Then he remembered Tyler's spiel about how this tote bag would be valuable one day. The memory sent Jeffrey's stomach lurching again. Tyler was dead. He was dead, right here, lying in the next room.

He felt the weight of the bag's contents and stepped down to the floor again. He didn't hear the front door creaking slightly as he peeked inside of it. Everything was there. The film canisters. The Ziploc baggies, stuffed with drugs. The handgun. He reached in and rested his hand upon the weapon.

"Don't fucking move," said a voice from behind him. "Don't fucking breathe. Listen to everything I say, or there's gonna be two dead motherfuckers in this house."

Jeffrey felt his guts turn to ice. He had the cool, heavy gun in his grip.
"When I say so," the voice said, "you're gonna turn around slowly, with the bag in your hand. Okay? Then you're going to throw the bag over to me. Do you understand? Say YES if you understand."
Jeffrey tried to say yes, but it came out as a dry croak.

"Pick up the bag."
Jeffrey slid his right hand with the gun still in it through the strap. He lifted the bag up, with the gun pointing forward.

"Now turn around, slowly."
Jeffrey did as he was told. He had never pointed a gun at another human being before. He knew that the thing was loaded, because Bill never kept an unloaded gun in

the house. But he did not know if the safety catch was on, or if it was, how to take it off. He knew that the gun's only real use was as a prop to intimidate the voice that was behind him. When Jeffrey rotated 180 degrees, he found himself staring at an unfamiliar figure.

The man was tall. Very fucking tall. He was dressed in grease-stained Levi's and scuffed motorcycle boots. His torso was muscular, with not an inch of fat on it. He wore a wifebeater that exposed a lot of that sinewy frame, and flapping open around his shoulders a gaudy Hawaiian-print shirt. There was a gold pendant around the neck, encrusted with jewels. The face was stony and emotionless, and there was no mistaking the lack of humanity in the eyes. They burned straight into Jeffrey. They were the eyes of death. In his right fist was a six-inch bowie knife, the blade curved upward slightly at the tip, and the backside of the blade had vicious-looking serrated teeth. Jeffrey's mind flashed to the bloody remains of his friend, out in the living room. Barely breathing, he stood there, dangling the bag from his right hand, keeping the handgun pointed at Pat.

There was no movement for a moment, as each man took in the other. Jeffrey waited for Pat to say something, but he did not. Pat seemed unperturbed by the grinning visage of Eddie Murphy looking at him. The eyes registered the gun—pointing straight at his chest—with barely a flicker.

"I want the knife," Jeffrey said.

Pat did not move. Jeffrey raised his voice a little and said, "Drop the fucking knife."

Pat extended his hand and held the knife between his thumb and forefinger, the blade pointing straight down.

Every movement was painfully slow, as if he were still toying with Jeffrey despite the fact that there was a gun pointing at him. Jeffrey tried to control the twitches and shivers that threatened to tear through him. Pat tossed the knife, and it clattered against the wood floor. It spun around, finally coming to rest between the two of them.

"Now back away. Slowly," Jeffrey said.

He watched as Pat started to walk backward, glaring at Jeffrey the whole time.

"If I was you, I wouldn't do anything . . . *stupid*," Pat said.

"If I was YOU," Jeffrey hissed, "I'd shut the fuck up in case I got myself shot."

Jeffrey walked toward Pat, keeping the gun on him. When he was standing next to the knife, he bent his knees slightly and picked up the knife slowly. He straightened up again.

"I'm going to back out of the apartment now. If I see you trying to follow me, then I'm gonna kill you. Now keep your ass put."

With that, he walked slowly out of the bedroom. He kept his eyes on Pat, who was as silent and still as a statue. Pat tilted his head slightly and followed Jeffrey's gaze out of the room like a hawk watching a mouse. Walking backward out into the living room, Jeffrey felt himself almost slip again on the blood. It was congealing, he could feel the soles of his feet sticking to the floor. He briefly considered shooting Pat just to be sure, but he knew that if the gun didn't go off on the first attempt he would be dead before he could figure out how to get the weapon to work.

When he was across the room and Pat was in danger of disappearing from his line of vision, Jeffrey made a break for it. He slammed the front door shut and sprinted across the sidewalk. He wrenched open the car door, tossed the bag inside, and took off with a squeal of tires.

Trina watched, dumbfounded, as a gun-toting Jeffrey made his escape. When Pat didn't come racing out of the house, she thought for a brief, mad moment that Jeffrey had hurt him. As she thought this, Pat burst out of the building and jumped into the driver's seat.

"What HAPPENED?"

"Shut the fuck up!" Pat hissed. "Where did he go?"

Trina pointed dumbly to the corner where Jeffrey had made a left moments ago and disappeared from view. With a squeal of tires, they took off. Gripping the wheel with white knuckles, Pat made a vain attempt at catching up with Jeffrey. Trina, hysterical, kept demanding to know what was going on. At the corner, Pat made a left and sped down the block before reaching another intersection. There was no sign of Jeffrey. Trina was still whining, and talking, and demanding to know what was happening. When he could take it no more, Pat locked his arms straight ahead to absorb the impact and slammed on the brakes as hard as he could. The car screeched to a halt, and Trina smashed face-first into the dashboard. She hit it with a sickening crunch and bounced back again into her seat.

"Jesus fuck! Jesus fucking shit fuck!" Pat was screaming.

Trina was holding her nose. The backs of her hands were slick with her blood. The shock of the impact made her mute for a moment.

"He's GONE. He's fucking GONE!" Pat hissed.

"I dink I boke my dose," Trina said.

"Shut up! I lost the bastard! Shit!"

Pat stuck the car into Drive again, and they took off. Trina started to sob as she felt the blood seeping between her fingers. The pain in her nose was almost unbearable. It felt as though she had hot needles inserted between her skull and her flesh. Her vision blurred, went gray. Pat looked at her, cursed, and then back at the road again.

"Now we got a problem," Pat muttered. "Now we got a real fuckin' problem. Fuck!"

———

In some faceless Hollywood bar full of yuppie scum, tourists, and dental assistants from the Valley, Jeffrey raised the glass to his mouth. He drained it. His hand was still shaking. *Jesus Christ.* He clutched the *Pluto Nash* bag tight to his chest. Feeling its weight against him comforted him a little. The bourbon burned at his guts, and nausea tore through him. He held it in. A woman laughed unexpectedly behind him, and he jumped as if he had heard a shotgun's blast. He took the bag into the bathroom and locked himself in the stall. He opened up the envelope full of heroin. He stuck his key in it and allowed himself a generous blast in each nostril. He sat with his head against the cool tiles, waiting until he felt the heroin come on, taking the edge off of the terror that burned inside of him. He started to feel anxious indoors, so he walked out into the streets again, holding the bag with trembling hands. Warmed over inside from the dope, he wandered Hollywood Boulevard, like a shell-shocked ghost. He needed to be surrounded by people. Anonymous, dull, unthreatening people. He found himself smiling at them. Smiling at the fat tourists who thronged around Mann's Chinese Theatre. Smiling at the street people, and the buskers, and kids out on dates. He did this for an hour, just walking, and smiling that lobotomized smile, and holding the bag to his chest like it was his own child. And then the shaking started, an uncontrollable shaking that wracked his entire body, and he walked as quickly as he could down a darkened side street. The whiskey vomit came, a violent purging. He vomited, and vomited, and when there was nothing left, he retched hopelessly while supporting himself against a skinny palm tree. When he was done the tears were streaming down his face, and he felt lightheaded and euphoric.

Oh God, oh God, he thought. *That is what Sharon Tate must have looked like when Bill saw her. Smeared bloody crimson. The smell of copper and death and fear. Ripped apart, gutted like a fucking animal. This fucking film is cursed,* he thought, *jinxed. I killed Tyler. He fucking died because of me. I should have left this fucking thing in Bill's safe. Walked away and never come back. Oh Jesus fucking Christ.*

He knew that there was only one thing to do. He had to go get as high as possible.

When they finally pulled into the motel Trina asked in a little-girl voice, "Are we dill goi-g do Dan Fra-disco?" Pat glared at her.
"No. Now we got something I have to take care of. . . ."
"We deed to get out of down, man! We can't day around here. . . ."

The blood was everywhere. It was all over her shirt, her hands, and her face. Goddamnit to hell. Pat shook his head.

"Where does this faggot live?"

"I dunno. Uh, shit, I don't know. He's dust a dunkie. He scores from Dyler. I don't know much aboud him." Trina was crying.

"He saw my face. He pointed a gun right at me. He took my knife. He's dead fucking meat."

Pat rolled the car into the parking lot. He killed the engine. He said, with something approximating tenderness in his voice, "Let me look at you."

In the gloom of the car, he removed her hands from her face. The nose was swollen grotesquely and was now pointing to the left.

"Iz id bad?" Trina asked in a whisper.

"No, baby. It's gonna be fine."

"Do I need do see a doc-dor?"

Pat shook his head. "No doctors. I can take care of this."

Trina's guts turned to ice, but she retained a cool composure.

"Am I dill pri-ddy?" she asked.

"Sure, baby doll. You're a knockout. Now let's get the fuck inside and figure out what the hell we're gonna do."

The Indian behind the reception desk watched them as they walked in. He picked his nose and turned his attention back to the TV before any trouble started.

In their room at the Motor Home Lodge with the TV on, the money and drugs spread across the floor, and the blinds drawn, Pat removed the ice pack from Trina's ruined nose. Trina was crying a little now because Pat was still insisting that he could fix the nose himself. "I just gotta crack it back into place," he was saying. "You won't even feel it until it's done. You wannit to set like that?"

"I wand some more heroin," she said, "I need more. I can dill feel id."

"I don't want you going over on me. You've taken a lot already. Let's just get this shit over with, baby girl. Watch the TV. Concentrate on the TV."

"Pad?"

"What?"

"I'm sorry, baby. I'm sorry for be-ig a bidch. I dow you dow bess. I was dust scared."

Pat nodded. On the TV was a black-and-white image of a 1980s porn star being sodomized. The top of the screen was distorted, like they were watching an old VHS copy of the movie. Pat straddled her, and with his weight on her chest she started to sink back into the mattress, the effects of the heroin cutting through even her terror, and she looked at the screen and tried not to think of what was coming next. She tried to find the part of her brain where the heroin was and focus on it. Focus on that warmth radiating out from there, focus on that and block out the feeling of Pat's thick, scarred fingers getting into position on either side of her nose. On-screen the woman's breasts were bouncing toward the camera, like pendulums counting down the seconds until the agony. Oh, Christ, just do it already. . . .

When the nose snapped, Trina's howl shattered the silence of the motel. In the room next door, a fat man in a greasy undershirt froze for a moment when he heard Trina's scream. Then he shrugged, turned his TV up, and pulled a beer from the fridge. On TV they were showing a *Cops* marathon. Perching on the edge of his bed, he looked at the screen and his face went slack.

PART TWO

TWENTY-SIX

Randal sleepwalked through his final two weeks at Clean and Serene before he checked out into the waiting arms of his brother. During the graduation ceremony, as he and twelve others received a fake gold coin with a Dr. Mike mantra stamped onto it—"It's as easy as simply saying NO"—Randal watched the doctor sitting at the back of the room, checking his watch and looking anxious to be elsewhere. Over the past week the doctor's involvement in the running of the place had become almost nil. Randal wondered if he weren't hard at work on another piece of shit TV series. He gave Johnny D a hug, and slapped the palms of several red-cheeked, track-marked guys whom he had become friendly with. "Good luck, baby." Johnny D grinned. "Be good. And if you can't be good, be safe. . . ."

"Hey, Harvey," Randal said as he slumped into the passenger seat of Harvey's Lexus, idling outside of the facility, "what's up?"

"What's up?" Harvey crackled. "My little brother was on fucking VH1, that's what's up!"

"What the fuck are you talking about?"

"*Detoxing America*, bro! I saw you, wolfing down those goddamned tacos, hanging out with the dude from the Nosebleeds. . . ."

"Aw, come on, man. They didn't show me, did they? That's the last fucking thing I need."

"Well, they blurred your face, but I'd recognize that skinny fucking ass anywhere. I TiVo'd it for you, man. You can check it out yourself. You look good, bro! You've put on weight."

"Great," Randal said, staring out the window, "that's just great. I smoke a little ice and you're disgusted with me. I end up on fucking reality TV and you're acting like I just won the lottery or something. Your value system is really fucked up, man."

Randal stared at his brother like a sullen child for a moment, and then cracked a smile. Harvey started laughing and gave his kid brother a playful slap as the car took off. "Keep it up, shitpants," Harvey grinned, "and I'll send your wise ass to Dr. Phil. . . ."

As soon as he was settled into his room at Harvey's Spanish-style villa in Brentwood, Randal started trying to get hold of Jeffrey. Only tracking down Jeffrey was harder than Randal expected. He initially answered his phone the first day that Randal called.

"Hey, man. Yeah, look; this is kind of a bad time. Huh? I'm in the Mark Twain. It's a hotel on Wilcox and Hollywood. I'm staying here. Really, though, it's not a good time. Huh? Room? 317. There's no phone here anyway. You can't call me here. Just call the cell. I'll call

you, bro. I'll call you. . . ." Then the line went dead. After that, Randal couldn't manage to get Jeffrey to pick up again. Something in Jeffrey's voice alarmed Randal. He sounded hoarse and frail, altogether different from how he had seemed inside of the facility. Randal immediately assumed that Jeffrey was using drugs again. Maybe he was ashamed and trying to hide it from him. But that didn't make sense either. Randal couldn't give two shits whether Jeffrey was getting high or not, but he sure as hell did care about the business proposition they had discussed inside.

Distracted with thoughts of Jeffrey and the tape, Randal walked down the marble staircase and found himself confronted with a most unwelcome sight. Harvey, his wife, Cheryl, and a jackass friend of Harvey's from the program were sitting around the dining table, grinning at him like lobotomized fools. "Randal," Harvey grinned, gesturing to his friend, "you remember Markie? My old sponsor?"

"Sure," Randal said.

"Well, Markie has nearly thirty years under his belt. I thought it would be a good idea for you two to get acquainted. . . ."

Markie was a rotund ex-boozer who enjoyed getting in the faces of the newer members, puffing his chest out, and generally acting like the big man in the meeting rooms. His sponsorship of Harvey had lasted a few months before Harvey tired of Markie's "in your face" persona and dumped him in favor of a more passive old-timer. And now here he was, like the lecherous husband-to-be at an arranged marriage, ready to take on the younger Earnest instead.

.   .   .

"Sit down, kid," Markie said.

Randal sat down.

"How ya feeling, kid?"

"Okay. You?"

Markie grinned. "One hundred fuckin' percent better than you, I'd bet! I'm enjoying the fruits of my sobriety! Here—lemme show you something. . . ."

Markie pulled out his BlackBerry and started playing with it. Randal looked at his brother and rolled his eyes. Harvey gave him a look that said, *"Sit still, and be nice, or there's gonna be trouble."*

"Look at this," Markie said. He shoved the BlackBerry into Randal's hand. Randal was looking at a picture of a beach, with palm trees, white sand, and an endless horizon of crystal blue water.

"Nice," Randal said, "you been on vacation?"

"No, kid. I own the fucking island."

"Nice." Randal handed the BlackBerry back to Markie.

"You look doubtful. You don't think that you can share in the dream. You don't think that you can pull yourself up by your bootstraps and make something of yourself. Well, I'm here to tell you, kid, you can. Thirty years ago I was a bum. A drunk. The only island I knew anything about was Rikers Island. It took the twelve steps to turn all of that around for me. You been working the steps inside?"

"Yeah. I have to do a fearless and searching moral inventory," Randal deadpanned, "then I got eight more steps before I'm cured and I get that island. Cool, huh?"

Sensing tension, Cheryl cut in by saying, "I saw you on TV, Randal. On *Detoxing America!*"

"Oh, yeah. Fun episode. Did the brawl make the final cut?"

"Brawl? I don't recall any brawl."

"You mind if I see it? You got it on TiVo, right?"

"Well, sure . . . I mean, if you're done here . . . ?"

"Oh, I'm done all right." He turned to Markie. "Nice to see you again, man. Take care. Have fun on that beach."

Markie smiled and said, "Yeah. I'll be seeing you, kid."

Randal moved to the TV room. His nephew, Alex, was in there watching some godawful reality show on MTV. It was rare to catch Alex anywhere outside of his bedroom, where he was usually sequestered, eating Cheetos and blasting shitty music. Alex was sixteen and his long bangs, dyed blue, covered one eye completely. He was wearing a My Chemical Romance hoodie and baggy jeans.

"Hi, baby!" Cheryl cooed. "What are you watching?"

"Goddamnit, Mom! I'm watching *A Double Shot at Love*! Get out of here!"

Randal looked over to the seventy-two-inch flat-screen television that dominated one wall. On-screen a girl in a bikini was licking tequila from the navel of another girl while a throng of fools hollered and cheered around them.

"I told you I don't want you watching that trash, baby." Alex scowled but did not move.

"Baby, Uncle Randal wants to watch the TV."

The kid did not move. When his mother grabbed the remote and flicked the TV off, Alex jumped to his feet and screamed, "You're ruining my LIFE! You're such a frickin' bitch sometimes!" Then he flicked on his iPod, pulled the hoodie over his head, and glided out of the room on sneakers with wheels.

"Sorry about that, Randal. . . ."

Randal watched the little shithead skate away to another part of the house. Elsewhere in the mansion Randal had counted a total of five flat-screen televisions, two bookshelves stuffed with cookbooks, self-help manuals, and the collected works of Tony Robbins, and abandoned last-year's-model iPods lying on couches and tables like discarded gum wrappers. The Ben Shahn lithographs that had pride of place in the alcoves and on the dining room walls were a constant source of amusement for Harvey, who was always willing to wax lyrical about the fact that they were as ugly as shit but had an appraisal value that kept creeping ever upward. After being under Harvey's roof for just over twenty-four hours, Randal remembered all of the things that had pushed him back into meth use following his last bout of sobriety. He actually found this lifestyle to be more soul-destroying than one spent waiting for death in by-the-hour motel rooms.

"Here we go!"

Randal sat alone, watching the show. First there was the "in case you missed it" montage of the celebrities turning up to their rehab, mostly drunk and stoned. A shot of the Nosebleeds guy pulling up in his Hummer and vomiting out of the passenger window was replayed several times. "America is sick," the narrator announced, " . . . but the doctor is IN!"

What followed was a total fiction—a reconstruction of reality, carefully put together by Dr. Mike and the show's editors. The "Reunion Special" bore no resemblance to the events that Randal had witnessed firsthand only two weeks earlier. When the celebrities were finally shown in the dining room of Clean and Serene, the camera angle, and cutaways made it seem as if they were surrounded by the regular population. There was a second-long shot of Johnny D grinning and shoving French fries into his mouth. Then they showed an edited version of Dr. Mike's speech in the cafeteria. At the moment that Running Deer fucked everything up they cut away to another scene, an "in house" meeting at Clean and Serene, filled with patients whom Randal had never seen before. The only familiar faces in the bunch were staff members who were posing as clients. Randal assumed that the rest were SAG-card-holding wannabe actors bussed in from two-bit Hollywood talent agencies for the day. The meeting had all of the false optimism and empty smiles of a self-help seminar, and Randal realized that this entire scene had been rigged to create the impression that the celebrities were now beacons of calmness, sobriety, and health. The final straw came when Sasha Jones smiled tearfully at the camera and said, "Thank you, Dr. Mike. Thank you for this experience, thank you for all of your hard work, and to you guys"—she gestured to the ringers in the meeting— "I wanted to thank you all for allowing me to share in your own journey. I now realize that an addict is an addict, whether they are an actress or . . . or a plumber. This disease does not differentiate. . . ."

Randal clicked off the TV, disgusted by the charade that Dr. Mike was engaged in. Over in the dining room, Harvey and Markie were no doubt discussing how best to keep Randal on the straight and narrow. He made a decision to start withdrawing money, a bit at a time, and squirreling it away in a separate bank account. One fuckup, and Harvey would have his credit cards canceled. He needed to start planning his escape.

It made him uneasy to think that the best hope he had for escaping his situation rested on a get-rich-quick scheme hatched inside of drug rehab with a junkie male prostitute whom he barely knew. When these niggling doubts surfaced he pushed them away. *What is my alternative?* his mind would demand. *Stay clean? Jesus Christ, a long shot is better than no shot at all.*

One way or another, Randal decided, while sitting there surrounded by the empty luxury his brother had amassed over the years, *one way or another, I have to get the fuck out of this place.*

TWENTY-SEVEN

"So . . . how's the manuscript coming along?"

"Manuscript?"

Dr. Mike looked around his office, grasping for information. He was distracted, and for a moment his agent's words meant nothing to him. This was the third day in a row that his frantic calls to Champagne's cell phone had gone unanswered. He had gone through the last few days on a kind of autopilot, his stomach fluttering, his thoughts always distractedly returning to her.

Was she okay? Was it over? Maybe it would be better if it were over.

He thought of the last time they spent together, in the hotel in Century City. He thought of her in her bathrobe, long dark hair plastered to her forehead, water dripping down the smooth skin of her neck, onto her chest. Whenever he thought of her, he would get a lightheaded feeling, a turn in the gut that was pleasantly nauseating. He thought of her smooth, hairless body. Her tits, her erect nipples. The thought made his cheeks flush red.

If you never see her again, it's for the best. You can't get hung up on someone like that.

"YOUR manuscript," the agent, Bob Rosen, repeated patiently. "*Teenage Wasteland: How Prescription Drugs Are Devastating Our Nation's Youth.* Have you spoken to the ghostwriter at all?"

"No, no, I haven't. Not recently."

"Hm. Well, I'll shake the tree a little. See if I can put a rocket up his ass. He's good, but he's a lazy motherfucker. He did a good job on your last book."

"Yeah, I heard. I haven't read it yet. . . ."

Occasionally other, more troubling thoughts would surface. Thoughts that would threaten to disrupt his veneer of professional calm altogether.

He thought of her splayed on the king-size bed. He thought of her full lips tightening around the stem, moving from the crack pipe to his cock with practiced efficiency. The Viagra had made his penis painfully erect, and he brutalized her asshole with it, the room heavy with the stench of sex and amyl nitrate. Both of them lost in separate worlds: Champagne in the throes of a crack- and Xanax-induced haze, and the doctor pumping into her with a chemically induced hard-on, holding the little bottle of poppers to his nose, huffing and snorting, his eyes rolling back into his skull, the glasses bouncing up and down on the bridge of his nose in time with every thrust. She was cursing and squirming underneath him, "Motherfucker! Ugh! Oh fucking CHRIST it feels so GOOD!" as she frantically jerked her own dick in time with his movements. All they had, the only point of connection, was his cock and her ass, the rest of it was all taking place entirely in the chemical cocoon of their minds.

He started in easy with the dirty talk: "You BITCH! You like it rough, you fucking WHORE!" When she responded by gasping, "YES!" he thrust into her even harder, grabbing her by the hair and twisting her face around a little, screaming into it, "You fucking CUNT! You fucking PIECE of TRASH!" as he pistoned into her. "You fucking FREAK of NATURE! You DIRTY FAGGOT SISSYBOY FUCK HOLE! You VILE JUNKIE CUM RECEPTACLE!" He felt her stiffen up as he screamed this, but he was too close to stop now. He saw a troubled look flicker across her face, and rather than disrupt his rhythm he just pushed her face back down into the pillow so he wouldn't have to look at it.

"You make me SICK, you PATHETIC fucking MONSTER! You HALF a fucking PERSON! You piece of SCUM—fucking HUMAN GARBAGE!!!" Uh—uh—he was close—uh—he huffed and huffed the amyl fumes—his vision breaking up into a thousand fractured points of light—and she was struggling now—no longer touching her own penis anymore—instead aware of an ache—not only the building ache in her bowels—but another ache—one that she usually only felt when she was alone and with no drugs—a terrible, empty feeling inside—"You WEAK PATHETIC FAGGOT JUNKIE CUNT OH JESUS FUCKING GOD I'M CUUU-HHMMMMIIINNNGGG—UH!—UH!—UH!"

The doctor fell back on the bed, naked apart from his socks and his glasses, slick with sweat, the full condom still on his raging hard-on. . . . He twisted the cap back onto the poppers, and let the bottle fall to the floor. He gulped back the air, and his vision started to clear a little. Next to him Champagne was still, breathing softly, facedown. After a few moments he touched her buttock, still slick with lube, and said, "Was that good for you?"

. . .

There were a few moments of silence. Then Champagne said, quietly, "Do I really make you sick?"

"Huh?"

Dr. Mike caught his breath. Was she . . . crying?

"You said that I make you sick. Is that true?"

"No! Not SICK! Not at all. . . . That was just . . . talk. I was just in the moment. I was just into it. Into YOU. That's all."

Champagne sat up and looked at the doctor. Her nose and eyes were wet, and she was sniffling. When Dr. Mike saw her like that it sent a shiver through him. She reminded him of his own wife for one horrible moment. Crying, drunk, saying, "You don't love me the way you used to!" whatever the fuck that was supposed to mean. This image cut through the effects of the Viagra, and he felt himself getting soft. He was about to comfort her, but stopped himself, fearing that it would set a dangerous precedent.

"You think that I'm a freak!" Champagne sobbed.

"No," the doctor said in a neutral tone. He put his arm around her, awkwardly. "Not at all. I mean, just to be clear, I could never be seen with you in public for many, uh, obvious reasons . . . but I do really enjoy having sex with you, and, uh, I want to continue to do it. And, uh, well, I was going to do this later . . . but I have a present for you. . . ."

He got up and started rummaging around in his briefcase. He started tossing pill bottles toward her, yelling the names out as he did so.

"Xanax . . . Dilaudid . . . diazepam . . . temazepam . . . !"

"Thank you . . . ," Champagne sniffed.

"Just be careful with all of that. Go easy. There's more where that came from. . . ."

The doctor crept over to her and finally removed the condom. He stood in front of her, naked, taking in her red, puffy eyes as she appraised *the bottles on the bed. He looked at her nude body again, hoping that he wouldn't have to cut this one loose too soon. She stood and put her arms around him, almost touching his lips with hers. He stopped her and reminded her that he didn't like to be kissed on the mouth. Instead, he pushed her back onto the bed and positioned his half-hard cock in front of her face.*

"Why don't you kiss that, instead?" he suggested, helpfully.

The intercom buzzed. "Excuse me," the doctor said, jerking out of his thoughts. He picked up the phone and said, "Yes?"

"Dr. Mike, there's a Mr. Lang on the line for you."

The name was unfamiliar, and the doctor said, "No calls right now, I'm in a meeting. Take a message."

"You seem tense," Rosen said. "Is everything all right?"

"Yes. I'm just so . . . busy right now. Juggling plates."

"Shit," Rosen laughed, "tell me about it. This is good! You're hot right now. We have to take advantage of every opportunity that comes along. I think we're close to a deal on season three. Oh—I meant to run something past you. I had this great idea . . . instead of doing the same thing next season, I thought that we could do a follow-up show called 'Out Patient.' See how some of the cast from season one are doing, maybe have you meet with them once a week. You know, I got a call from Terri Starr's people, and she's back on heroin. About to lose her apartment. I figured if we could get some cameras down there, get the whole thing on tape . . . I mean—this is a big story. It would create a lot of interest."

The intercom buzzed again.

"Damnit!" the doctor spat. "Hold that thought, okay? Yes?"

"Dr. Mike? So sorry to interrupt again. But Lang is still on the line and—"

"I told you—NO CALLS. Take a message, for goodness sake!"

"But, sir, *Detective* Lang insists that he speak to you right away. He says that it's an urgent matter."

Dr. Mike held the phone very close to his ear for a moment. His agent looked at him, noticing the whiteness spreading around his knuckles as the doctor's grip became tighter and tighter. All of the emotion drained from his face, and for a second Rosen thought that his client was about to faint. Then the doctor cleared his throat and said, "Oh. Well . . . I see. I suppose you'd better put him through then."

The doctor covered the mouthpiece and said, "Hey . . . I have to take this. Do you mind if I, uh, call you later?"

Rosen furrowed his brow and said, "Is everything okay?"

Dr. Mike just looked straight ahead and said, "I don't know. I'll call you, okay?"

Rosen stood, and said, " 'Out Patient.' " He tapped his forehead with a finger. "Think about it. Terri's already relapsed. I heard that David Seaborne is about to lose it, too. If we could get them on camera . . . I'm thinking an Emmy, Mike. Let it percolate, okay?"

And with that, the agent was gone. The doctor stared at the door for a moment after it closed. Then, from somewhere inside of his head he became aware of a voice saying, "Dr. Mike, are you there? Dr. Mike, this is Detective Lang, LAPD. . . ."

TWENTY-EIGHT

In the weeks since he had last seen Jeffrey, the idea of selling the sex tape had been needling away at Randal. It was what got him through the drudgery of his day-to-day life inside of the treatment center; it had gotten him through every pointless, airless meeting with counselors and life coaches. The tape itself had become infused with a talismanic power in his mind: it represented a chance for Randal to finally walk away from the wreckage of his life in Hollywood and start over somewhere else.

Since Randal's release, Harvey had taken it upon himself to be his younger brother's shadow. He accompanied him to meetings, to restaurants, even forcing him to the clinic for an AIDS/Hep C screening. Each successive AA meeting on the outside made the idea of the tape seem more and more urgent. The same wan, drunken faces, the same parade of misery and religiosity, the same shitty coffee and uncomfortable metal chairs in cold church basements. The longer Harvey had been sober, the more bitter, cynical, and unbearable he seemed to have become. If this was the kind of asshole that you turned into after experiencing a spiritual awakening, then Randal figured that God could keep that shit for Himself.

No, Randal wanted to be on a beach somewhere far, far away from here, somewhere where the cocktail in his hand would not fill him with a kind of uneasy guilt and shame. He wanted to start over as the person that he vaguely remembered from the time before the meth had taken him. He had come to understand, in an unspoken way, that his problem wasn't drink or drugs. His problem was Hollywood itself.

But ever since Jeffrey had vanished, a fear that the whole episode was over began to grow. *There is no tape!* his mind insisted. *And you're an idiot for even believing that there was!* Every futile, unanswered call to Jeffrey's cell made the voice louder and more insistent. Finally, in desperation, Randal decided to track down Jeffrey himself at the hotel he was supposedly staying at.

Randal was cursing to himself and sweating under the unforgiving desert sun when he showed up at the hotel, a crumbling, toxic hole called the Mark Twain on Wilcox, just below Hollywood Boulevard. Seeing the building, he got an ominous feeling about Jeffrey. The hotel had been standing there for as long as anybody could remember, yet had gathered none of the iconic status that certain bars, coffee shops, or diners that had stood in this city for much less time had earned. Nobody stayed at the Mark Twain unless they had no other option. At the end of many Los Angelenos' slow slide into destitution, the Mark Twain was waiting at the bottom like an open pair of alligator jaws. The building itself was an unappetizing salmon pink, and inside, the cool lobby smelled of decades of mustiness and degradation. He looked over to the front desk and it was empty. Despite a sign over the entrance that warned that visitors were not permitted inside, nobody stopped him. There was an old Indian snoring softly on a couch in the office beyond, while a daytime talk show softly bleated out of a black-and-white television.

Jeffrey was supposedly up on the third floor. The stairwell was dark and foreboding, the lime green carpeting and puke-colored walls oppressive and dreary. As he passed by door after identical door, he heard noises— sobs, laughter, thumps, groans, gasps, and retching— that hinted at the unfathomable horrors within.

Room 317. He knocked on the door. No reply. He waited a beat, and then knocked again a little harder. The flimsy door shook under his knuckles. Beyond there was a frantic shuffling, the scattering of feet.

"Who is it?" said a voice.
"Randal."
"Who's that?"
"I'm a friend of Jeffrey's. Is he here?"
A moment passed. Then a coughing fit. The person spat something up and said: "He ain't here."
"But he lives here, right?"

The person went away. There was more frenzied movement in the room. Whispered voices bled through the paper-thin plywood door. Then steps cautiously approached the other side of the door.

"He ain't here. There's no one here."

The voice had an unnerving, nasal quality to it. It didn't so much come through the door as seep through the keyhole. Just who the fuck was this?

"Can you give him a message?"

"Look, man," the voice said, "I'm busy. Why don't you write him a fucking e-mail or something?"

Randal punched the door in frustration and waited to see if there would be any retaliation. There was nothing. Randal pictured the person, standing on the other side of the door, waiting silently for the sound of Randal's retreating footsteps. He waited for a moment before dejectedly trudging away. So that was it. The game was up. As he walked down the stairs, he passed a young woman with a busted lip and a newborn in her arms, two sad-eyed children following behind her. The smell of rot here was stronger. Randal did not know what exactly had brought Jeffrey to this place, or who it was he was with, but he did know one thing without a doubt: he could forget about the Sharon Tate movie once and for all. Even if Jeffrey had been sincere inside of rehab, now he was lost, and there wasn't a goddamned thing Randal could do about it.

Downstairs, he knocked on the desk, rousing the old Indian from his stupor. He staggered over, his wife-beater exposing beads of sweat glistening on a graying mop of chest hair.

"Whatchoo want?"

"I'm looking for a friend of mine. Jeffrey. Does he live here?"

"Room is fifty-one dollars."

"I don't want a room. I'm trying to find a friend. Jeffrey. He's a tall guy. Skinny, tattoos. Black hair. I heard he was living here."

"Lotta people live here. Call your friend. Don't ask me. People like privacy. I dunno what or who. You want room?"

"No, thanks."

"Then go."

"Thanks. And fuck you."

After that, Randal returned to his brother's house and brooded for a while. That motherfucker! Randal wasn't sure who he was angrier at—Jeffrey, for sucking him in with that ridiculous story about the sex tape, or himself for falling for it. Randal sadly came to the conclusion that he had wanted a way out so badly that he had actually willed himself into believing Jeffrey's fairy tale.

Days went by and turned into weeks, and Randal attended meetings, and had stilted dinner conversations full of long pauses with his family. The idea of escape started to seem abstract and hopeless. At first there was sadness, then a flare of anger, but like everything it turned into a dull, sad resignation over time. Sometimes, hating himself for doing it, Randal would dial the number from pay phones, hoping to catch Jeffrey unawares, but the phone either rang and rang or it went straight to voice mail. Jeffrey didn't want to be found. Maybe the bastard was dead. Maybe the whole thing was a fantasy, a joke, the ravings of a detoxing junkie desperate to pass the time. But the fucked-up thing was that something about Jeffrey's story had resonated deeply with Randal. It had seemed solid, three-dimensional. It had carried with it the promise of a new life, a new beginning, like the scent of long-ago perfume on a spring breeze. He wasn't ready to accept that it was a fantasy. He wasn't ready to accept that he had fallen for a confidence trick, especially not one that was so outlandish. If the tape didn't exist, then in some strange way, neither did Jeffrey. If the tape was a fraud, then so was the story about Bill, the escape to Los Angeles, all of it a carefully constructed confidence trick . . . and Randal had swallowed it. But what Randal couldn't figure out was why Jeffrey would have done it in the first place. Just to fuck with a complete stranger? To take hope away from someone who was all out of that commodity already?

None of it made any sense. All that was certain was that until the day that the call from Jeffrey finally came, Randal had begun to accept that the scheme was dead before it had even begun, and had even started to try to understand all of the talk at the meetings. He took the term "fake it till you make it" to heart. He faked it for all he was worth. He faked smiles, he faked epiphanies, and he faked happiness. He collected chips of various colors and hung them on his keychain—talismans and testaments to his misery. And instead of waking up one morning somehow sane by osmosis, he woke up one morning and realized that he had become a fiction himself. He had faked his way into a pantomime of existence. He had become the ultimate fake, and he hated himself for it.

TWENTY-NINE

In the bathroom of a fast-food noodle joint called Yoshi-noya, right across the street from MacArthur Park, Spider locked the door behind him. Inside the air was heavy with the smell of shit, and the floor was swimming in a vile mixture of urine and sopping paper towels. Flies buzzed around the flickering fluorescent light. Spider fumbled with the baggie of meth, opening it, shoving his knife in there, and scooping up a pile of powder on the tip of the blade. He placed the tip under his nose and inhaled the rocky white substance. It burned his nostril, but Spider immediately sensed that something was wrong. It was a different kind of burn, not the intense, eye-watering, chemical heat of meth. This stuff was different from that. He noted a strange taste as the residue dripped down the back of his throat. Swallowing his doubts, Spider repeated the procedure in the other nostril.

He looked at himself in the mirror, managing to see some of his face through the tapestry of gang tags on the tiny square of scarred glass. He splashed water on his face. Waited. Nothing. He looked at the baggie again as he held it up to the light. When he saw the odd consistency of the powder up close for the first time, Spider cursed to himself. The shit was bunk. As soon as the thought surfaced Spider flew into a rage. "Fucking motherFUCKER!" he bellowed. It had been a week since he'd shown up at Tyler's house to score, only to find police tape covering the front door. Some motherfucker had offed his main meth connection. The first few times he'd had to resort to buying from the dealers who hung out in MacArthur Park, the stuff had been shitty but serviceable. But today he had just laid out fifty dollars for some shit that was weaker than Sudafed. He stormed out of the bathroom, nearly knocking over a Mexican girl with a tray of food, who cursed at him in Spanish as he made his way outside again.

Spider looked around MacArthur Park. A gaggle of mangy-looking pigeons congregated around his feet like crackheads looking for change. Across the lake, where flies buzzed around the garbage that floated on an oily surface of scum, he saw a familiar group of men standing in the shade of a palm tree. He stormed over to them, nearly upending a shaved ice cart. As he got closer he spotted the kid who had sold him the drugs earlier. He was tall and skinny, wearing an oversize Lakers shirt and a fake Rolex. Spider took a quick glance over his shoulder for cops, and then approached.
"Hey, homie!"

The kid turned. He was standing with several other ominous types—young gangbangers with low-slung jeans and baseball caps pulled down over insolent faces.

They looked young. Sixteen, seventeen, maybe.

"'Sup?"

"We got a problem. Remember me?"

The kid shrugged.

"The stuff you sold me was bunk," Spider said. "I want my money back."

The others looked at Spider and laughed. The kid who had sold him the fake meth looked pensive for a moment.

"I no understand," he said.

Spider held out his hand. In his palm was the baggie of powder.

"Your shit," Spider said, "is muy malo. You hear me? Muy fucking malo. I want my dinero. Here!"

Spider started shoving the baggie toward the kid. When Spider's hand got too close to him, the kid slapped it out of the way, knocking the baggie to the ground. The others straightened up, ready for trouble.

"Fuckin' puto!" the kid spat. "Don' put jour fucking hand near me!"

"That is bunk fucking shit, man. I want my money!"

One of the others stepped forward. A fat bastard, wearing a Virgen de Guadalupe T-shirt. "Get the fuck out of here, homie. Nothin' doin'."

"Hey, FUCK YOU. I ain't talking to you." Spider turned back to the kid and said, "Seriously. I want my money back. No fucking around."

"Jou gotta receipt for that?" the kid asked.

"Huh?"

"I said, jou gotta receipt for that? No receipt, no fucking returns, homeboy!"

The others cracked up. Spider stood there under the relentless afternoon sun, sweating toxic withdrawal sweat. He considered the walk back to the Metro, without his fifty dollars and without his drugs.

"You motherfucking beaners are gonna regret this," Spider said.

The kid looked to his friends. They shook their heads in disbelief. The kid took a bill out of his pocket and dangled it in front of Spider.

"Why don' jou take the money if you wan' it so bad? Crazy fucking white boy. Why don' jou try an TAKE it?" As he said this the others were gathering around Spider, cutting out the sunlight. Two options. Run or fight. Spider held his ground.

Later that day, Spider ambled across the parking lot of Crazy Girls. His face felt numb, puffy, like he had just had a shot of novocaine. He breathed a sigh of relief when he saw that Juan was working the door.

"Shit, Spider," Juan laughed, "what the fuck happened to you?"

"I had a little trouble. Got mugged."

"No shit! They done fucked you up good. You seen a doctor?"

"Nah."

"Your nose looks broken, dude. You should see a doctor!"

"Is Trina here?"

"Who?"

"Trina."

"Nah, bitch don't work here no more. She ain't been around in weeks."

Spider put his hand to his battered face and said, "Shit. Fucking shit!"

"Why you want her?"

"She used to score off a friend of mine. I'm trying to make a connect for ice but my regular guy got fucking wiped out, man. Someone came along, cleaned out his shit, and killed him."

Juan whistled. "Tough profession, man. You know, if you're looking for a connect I can put you in touch with my guy. . . ."

"He got good stuff?"

"It's great, man. He's reliable, too. Here—write your number down. I gotta call him and vouch for you, but you're good people. It'll be cool."

"I'm hurting, man. How quick can you speak to him?"

"I'll do it today. Give me your number and I'll call you."

Spider wrote his number on the back of an old receipt and handed it to Juan. He smiled painfully at the doorman and said, "Call me, bro. Seriously, call me."

"Will do. Stay lucky, Spider."

Juan leaned back against the door and watched as Spider trudged back toward Sunset Boulevard. Juan laughed to himself a little. He was always weirdly happy to see Spider walking away from him. Juan firmly believed that bad luck was contagious, like the flu or the clap or something. If you stayed around people like Spider too long, then their shitty fucking luck started to rub off on you. Juan clicked open his cell and found Pat's number. *Well*, he thought, *I guess Spider's luck is about to change.*

T H!R T Y

When the call came, he was drinking coffee with his brother at a pseudo-beatnik coffee shop called Bourgeois Pig, which looked out over the ludicrous splendor of the Scientology Celebrity Center. Harvey was slurping his second double espresso and talking a mile a minute about the intricacies of getting a project with Adam Sandler off the ground. There were mentions of bloodsuckers, cocksuckers, shit suckers, and plain old suckers. Harvey radiated toxic hatred. When the phone buzzed into life, Randal looked at it, and seeing Jeffrey's name, froze for a moment. He was paralyzed with something like fear. He had filed Jeffrey away and had been making a conscious decision not to think of the Sharon Tate tape any longer. This call threatened to disrupt this hard-earned yet wholly unsatisfactory cease-fire.

Harvey barely acknowledged the phone call, but Randal stopped him talking with the wave of a hand, and then picked up the phone and answered it, standing and walking out toward the sidewalk.

"Jeffrey?"

The voice on the other end was hoarse and weak, like someone who had spent a month wandering lost through a desert.

"Heeey, man . . . hey, Randal . . . shit, man, I'm so fucking sorry . . . I've been meaning to call, and . . . ah, shit, you know, I'm just sorry, man. I'm sorry."

"Where the fuck have you been? I thought, fuck, I don't know what I thought. . . . Man . . . how are you?"

Jeffrey laughed, a sad, weak noise.

"I'm fucked, man. I'm totally fucked. I just called . . . I just called to say sorry. I fucked everything up."

"What? Just tell me what's going on."

Randal looked back into the dim coffee shop. He could feel Harvey's dead, insect eyes on him, watching him like the fucking sobriety mafia. Goddamn. He dropped his voice to a whisper.

"Where are you?"

"Downtown. I'm with Damian, this guy I know, in his loft . . . what day is it?"

"Uh, it's Tuesday."

"Fuck. It's been a long week, man."

"So where *are* you exactly? I can come get you. . . . Do you need me to come get you?"

Randal listened to Jeffrey breathing sadly for a moment.

"Yeah," he said, "I need you to come get me. The place is downtown, near Pershing Square on Broadway. It's a loft, above some Chinese-Mexican place called Nuevo Taco de China. You know it?"

"No, but I'll find it. I'm on my way. Hang in there."

Randal clicked off the phone. He took a deep breath and walked back inside.

"I gotta go," he said to Harvey, picking up his coffee and slugging the last of it back.

Harvey looked at his brother and wrinkled his nose.

"Got a date with destiny, huh?" he growled.

"Something like that."

"Listen, shitpants. You're gonna use. It's all over your fucking face. I know that face. You're gonna get high."

Randal shook his head.

"Don't fuckin' bullshit me, man. You're gonna get high. Look at yourself, man! You're shaking."

Harvey tapped his head.

"Up here—you're already high. I can see it!"

Randal sighed. "Bro. Knock it off with the fucking recovery clichés, okay? If I was gonna get high, I'd fucking tell you. A friend of mine is in trouble, okay? I need to go help him."

Harvey snorted.

"Some fucking junkie, right? He'll take you out with him, bro. Junkies don't give a shit about anything except themselves. Your old friends, they ain't your friends. The only friends you have are your sober friends. The rest of 'em are dead, they just haven't realized it yet. They walk around this fucking city like something out of a George Romero flick, and you're too fucking stupid to see it. Sit down, dickweed."

Randal looked his brother in the eyes. His fists were shaking a little.

"Harvey," he said, "sincerely. Go. Fuck. Yourself. Okay?"

"If you go, you don't come back. You have been made aware of the consequences if you fuck up this time. I'm telling you now, bro, if you aren't willing to do this my way then you're on your own."

Randal stood there, very still for a moment. Then, taking a deep breath, he said, "Okay. If that's the way it's gotta be, then fine. Tell Cheryl thanks for the room. I'll call you about picking up the rest of my stuff. . . ."

And then, Randal was gone.

He found the restaurant, a shady-looking hole in the wall surrounded by shops selling votive candles and bootleg Dora the Explorer dolls. It had a grimy-looking C rating in the window, and the inside looked dark and empty. Outside a winehead loitered, looking for change. There was a door covered with gang tags, with three unmarked buzzers. He rang each of them in turn. Nothing. He tried again, holding each one down for longer. Suddenly there was a buzzing, and the door unlocked momentarily. Randal pushed it open and stepped into the narrow stairwell, letting the door close behind him with a heavy clunk.

The stairwell was bare concrete and dimly lit. Making his way up, he felt a familiar smell assault him, drowning out the background stench of stale urine. The smell of freshly cooked cocaine. His stomach knotted and unknotted in anticipation. As he made it up the first flight, the door immediately to his right opened a little, and a strange figure peeked out from the gloom. He was tall, at least six and a half feet, and dressed head to toe in black. Tight black denim jeans, cowboy boots that had been spray-painted black, a filthy black silk shirt open to the belly and exposing a corrugated, emaciated frame underneath. His face looked as though it were eating itself from the inside out, the sunken cheeks covered with coarse black hair that formed into a pointed goatee. The eyebrows were thick and prominent, the hair pulled back into a ponytail. The eyes seemed shocking amidst the monochromatic face—they were pale blue, like the iridescent glow of the ocean. They burned through Randal and made him feel breathless. In another life, this guy could have been the leader of a cult, or some kind of messianic figure. Randal approached him and said, "I'm here to see Jeffrey."

"Jeffrey is . . . indisposed right now," the figure said. There was no doubting the voice. The same creepy, nasal whine that he had heard in room 317 of the Mark Twain. Randal would not be so easily dissuaded this time.

"He called me and told me to come. I'd like to see him. Now."
The figure—Damian, for this must be his place—shook his head, but made no move to close the door. He was just testing Randal. Randal stood toe to toe with Damian. Damian had a few inches on him but was all skin and bone. Randal had no doubt that he could snap this motherfucker in two given the opportunity.
"Now," he insisted, leaving no room for interpretation.

He shoved Damian aside and stepped inside the cavernous loft space. It was dark. The windows had black cloths draped over them, and the only light came from the flatscreen television that was blaring some particularly intense kind of S and M porn. It smelled in there. It smelled something awful. Body odor, crack, and drying semen. On-screen a young boy was tied up and being throat-fucked by a fat, hairy man in a leather mask. Randal gagged a little. In front of the flat screen was a futon. On the futon lay a figure that looked for all the world like the survivor of a Nazi death camp. Randal edged closer.

All around the room were canvases, outrageously oversized canvases. The art was cartoonish, painted in vivid colors, and all with the same recurring visual joke. The largest one, the one that caught Randal's eye straightaway, depicted a nude man, shackled by handcuffs. He was kneeling in front of a devil, replete with red skin and horns. Where the devil's penis should have been, instead there was a huge, phallic crack pipe that was jutting out of the skin. The man was sucking on it with an agonized look on his face. The devil was looking toward the viewer, with a nasty grin. Scrawled across this image were the words SUCK IT, YOU SCUM in neon yellow cursive script. All of the canvases featured similar portraits of emaciated young men and women, either sucking on phallic crack pipes or with their own genitals transformed into limp syringes. They were the ugliest pictures Randal had ever seen.

Randal shuddered; he wanted to get the fuck out of this place right now.

He approached the figure and stopped. Around the futon were a few tripods—one with a rolling video camera focused on the figure, another with a still camera pointed toward the action. A pair of eyes, heavy and bloodshot, tried to focus on him. A cracked, bloody smile flickered across the lips. He was laying there in a cruciform position, the arms stick-thin, withered down to the bone, and the sallow chest exposed. The flesh of the arms was alive with red and purple weeping sores forming around the filthy, fresh injection sites. On the forehead was a large bloody welt that looked like some kind of grotesque, bleeding third eye. The hair was filthier and more matted than ever.

"Hey, man," the figure said, "long time no see. What's been going on?"

Randal shook his head and said, "Jeffrey. What the fuck did you do to yourself?" And when he said that, Jeffrey's smile vanished, and he started to sob a little. The tears wouldn't come, and his eyes stung; it had been days since he had drunk water or pissed, or did anything except suck on the pipe, probe with the needle, and wait for the morbid beating of his heart to stop. He tried to say, "I'm sorry, I'm sorry," but it came out all fucked up. Randal reached out to Jeffrey, and the odor that came up from him stuck in his throat, the smell of weeks without bathing, of weeks of sweat and filth and grime, of beating his penis bloody to pornography and filling his lungs with fetid, numbing crack smoke.

"We're getting the fuck out of here," Randal said. He sensed that Damian was behind him, so he turned.

"He's coming with me," Randal snarled.

"But I'm not finished with him yet," Damian said.

"Oh yes you are, fuckhead. Get out of my way."

"No, wait—look. . . ." Damian gestured to a canvas that was half finished. There was a picture of Jeffrey, nude and splayed, the track marks somehow more terrible when rendered in neon pinks and yellows, both hands reaching down to his crotch, where he played with an enormous glass phallus that was vomiting white smoke rings into the air.

"I call it *The Eternal Orgasm*. I already have a buyer for it.
He took it on the basis of the initial sketches. . . ."
"You mean people pay MONEY for this shit?"
Damian sighed. "Don't think that your philistinism
impresses me, because it doesn't. I am an artist. Jeffrey is
my subject. I've been working on him for weeks. Trying
to strip him down to his essential core. If I can't capture
his soul on the canvas, then the picture is a failure."

Randal looked around the loft.
"Your shit looks like the work of a sexually frustrated
twelve-year-old on magic mushrooms," Randal said,
"and your subject is coming with me. Come on, Jeffrey,
let's get the fuck out of here."
Damian shrugged. "Sure, whatever. He'll be back."
"Fuck you."
"What are you? His boyfriend or something?"
"Keep talking, shithead. I'll stick those fucking paint-
brushes up your ass!"
Randal turned away and helped Jeffrey to his feet.
"My shit," Jeffrey croaked.
"You don't need it."
"No! I mean, my bag. The stuff. Everything's in there.
Everything."

Randal scanned the room and saw a small canvas tote
bag stuck away in the corner. It was one of those goofy,
cheap canvas bags that they give away to promote movies, this one a comedy starring Eddie Murphy that had
become notorious in Hollywood for losing almost
ninety million dollars. Randal knew a few people who
had lost their jobs over that stink. Hoping that this
wasn't an omen, Randal grabbed the bag.

"Dude!" Damian said. "Leave your shit here. It's cool. You can pick it up the next time you swing by. . . ." Randal walked over to Damian and, without warning, punched him firmly in the face. Damian's nose exploded in a shower of crimson, and he collapsed to the floor. When he didn't move, Randal gave him a curious prod with his foot. Nothing. The bastard was unconscious.

"I knocked the fucker out!" Randal said, almost to himself. Then he looked at Jeffrey, as he shook his aching hand. "I thought you could only do that in the movies! Let's get the fuck out of here!"

As Randal carried the bag down the stairs and supported Jeffrey's stinking frame, he said, "What the fuck were you doing with fucking Lurch back there?" Jeffrey muttered, "Art, man. It's fucking art . . . ," his eyes turning back a little in his head. The coke was working its way out of his system, and unconsciousness threatened to take him before he had even made it to the car.

"Fuck me," Randal said as they took off, "I think I broke my fucking knuckle. That's the first time I ever punched anyone, you know that? You want to go back to the hotel? Jeffrey?"

Randal looked into the rearview mirror. Jeffrey was passed out, drooling slightly. As they crawled through the traffic heading toward Hollywood, Randal kept glancing in the rearview mirror. His hands were trembling. Jeffrey was snoring softly, and the bag was still there, a magical hangover from their days in the treatment center when the world had seemed full of possibilities, and the future theirs for the taking.

THIRTY-ONE

Dr. Mike was watching his wife's mouth move. He knew there were words coming out of it, but all he could really hear was the furious, paranoid beating of his own heart. The only words he could focus on were the ones spoken by Detective Lang yesterday.

. . . found dead . . . overdosed . . . hot pants fuchsia . . . cell phone records . . . prescription narcotics . . . repainting the guest bedrooms . . .

"Huh?"

Dr. Mike suddenly jerked out of his thoughts and looked at Anne, questioningly.

"Hot pants fuchsia. It's the color I want to use on the guest bedrooms. Marco says that hot pants fuchsia is really in right now and . . ."

"Yeah, I'm all for it." The doctor managed a weak grin. Anne looked at him sternly and took a sip from her glass.

"Jesus, Mike. Could you at least *pretend* to give a shit?

Marco said that with the housing market the way it is, a remodel like this would practically pay for itself. . . ."

The doctor nodded, watching her wet red lips flap up and down. Inside his skull the Voice started up again. The Voice had started up as soon as he'd hung up the phone yesterday with the promise that he would stop by Lang's office to answer questions . . . "informally." It was increasing in ferocity as the hours dragged on, scream-ing at him, *"You're SCREWED! Ruined! Nice move blowing up that bitch's cell phone! And leaving those fucking messages!"* The Voice assumed a whiny, mocking tone and blubbered, *"Oh, PLEASE, Champagne . . . ! Just call me back . . . let me know that you're okay . . . I want to HELLLPP you . . . !"*

" . . . And what's more, Marco says that he could get us a deal on the draperies. You know, he knows a lot of queens in the business. . . ."

As the doctor nodded dumbly, his mouth dry and his guts churning with that horrible childhood before-the-dentist feeling, the Voice demanded, *"Jesus CHRIST! How could you be so fucking STUPID? Such an AMATEUR?"*

And that was the worst part of it. There was noth-ing the doctor could do but agree with the Voice. He had gone over the moment so many times in the last twenty-four hours that the images were perma-nently engraved in his mind. He had turned it over all of last night as he listened to Anne's quiet, steady snores, praying for the relief of sleep. That moment, before the final liaison with Champagne, when he had looked over the bottles as he was shoving them into his bag, and he had actually thought, *I'd better remove the labels*. Why had he failed to act upon this notion? And when Champagne had asked for more prescriptions, that moment of hesitation before writing something that could be so easily traced back to him. . . . Why? Why had he shrugged away that hesitation and done something so bone-headed anyway?

This thought led him back to another memory worn smooth over the years with relentless, anguished replays. Ten years earlier, when Anne had been pregnant with Michael Jr. and coming back on an early-morning flight from Houston . . . and the girl, Tamara, had been ushered out of the house and into a waiting cab. As he had stood, watching the cab driving away, he'd suddenly thought, *I'd better check the bed*. Tamara was needy and young, and he wouldn't have put it past her to leave some token of her presence in their marital bed. And after thinking this, he had shrugged, went to the shower, and left for work as usual.

Back then, it had been a thong, scrunched up and shoved underneath Anne's pillow, that had blown his world apart . . . resulting in a separation that lasted until after Michael Jr. was born, five years of worthless relationship counseling that had left things in more of a mess than before, and the sexual stalemate that had defined the next ten years of their marriage. Replaying that incident over the years he had come to a conclusion that seemed terribly prescient now:

In some strange, unspoken way he had WANTED to get caught. And today, with this new tsunami of hurt about to engulf him, he knew that the only explanation for his behavior was that he had wanted to get caught again. He smiled a nauseated smile as he thought this, and the smile seemed to spur Anne on further in her monologue. She seemed utterly oblivious to how pale and weak her husband appeared.

Arriving at this conclusion, Dr. Mike felt as though he were standing on the edge of some great, gaping black maw. He felt a sense of desolation and sadness greater than anything he had ever known before. He knew that he had now gotten exactly what that rotten, fucked-up, self-flagellating part of his psyche had wanted all along. Instead of pitching himself into the void, the void would swallow everything around him. His wife. His kids. His career. Everything he had been building since his days as a radio host back in Santa Barbara. All of it was about to be sucked away from him. If he had been his own patient, he would have looked at himself with a knowing smile and said, "You have a narcissistic personality, with a deep, repressed masochistic streak. You also have some issues with sexual compulsion that I think we need to work on." But now that he was analyzing himself from the other side of the desk, the words seemed hollow, empty, and not at all encompassing of the complex, unique person he felt he was.

"Anne," he said suddenly, his own voice taking him by surprise, "we have to talk."
"We ARE talking, Mike. Jesus, can't you ever let me finish without interrupting? You do this all of the damn time and it's—"
"Shut UP! For Christ's sake, won't you just shut up and LISTEN to me!"

This silenced her, as effectively as a slap to the face. They looked at each other in silence for a moment. Now that he knew in his heart that he was about to lose her, she suddenly seemed beautiful to him once more. The coldness and the hardness that he'd long perceived in her face now seemed to melt away, revealing hidden traces of the woman he had fallen in love with all those years ago when they had met working in local radio. He removed his glasses and rubbed the bridge of his nose. He slipped them back on and his gaze met hers.

In a faltering voice, Dr. Mike said, "Anne. There's something I have to tell you."

THIRTY-TWO

Things had been bad all week. Trina had spent most of her time in the motel, waiting for Pat to return from prowling the streets, trying to get a lead on Jeffrey. His already terse style of communication had gotten even more tight-lipped than usual, so that he barely even grunted at her anymore. Trina began to fear that unless something changed, Pat could conceivably decide to take off without her. The one thing that Trina feared more than anything else was being abandoned. For once in her life someone had taken her in, looked after her. Now she felt as though she were incrementally losing Pat with each successive day.

Sometimes, alone in the motel room, she would pull out the briefcase that contained the money. She even tried to open it, but found that Pat had locked it and changed the combination. She pushed aside the dread feeling that this discovery gave her. More than once, the thought had crossed her mind to empty the case and split by herself. It sometimes seemed that it would be the only way to protect herself. If Pat beat her to the punch, she would be stranded. No job, no money, nothing. With this kind of money, she supposed, she could disappear. At the very least she could get her god-damned nose fixed.

•

But fear kept her rooted to the spot. Fear of having to start over somewhere new. But most of all, fear of Pat. He seemed to have a sixth sense about people, and she imagined that he could probably hear these thoughts as they went on in her head. Just thinking about leaving seemed like a dangerous thing to do. Sometimes she caught him looking at her. Not looking at her the way he looked at her when he wanted to fuck her, but in a different way. Looking at her like a butcher might look at a slaughtered pig, deciding the best way to chop the animal down into its component pieces. As soon as the thoughts of leaving would surface, she'd shout them down.

Pat is my man. We've gone through something together, something that means that you stick together for life. I saw him kill a man. I helped him to kill a man.

This is our life now. Like Bonnie and fucking Clyde.

This childish thought gave her some comfort. Sometimes, alone in the motel room, she would shoot some meth and stand naked in front of the bathroom mirror, playing with Tyler's gun. She'd point the gun at the mirror, admiring the way she looked holding it.

"Beg me if you wanna live, motherfucker!" she would whisper to herself. It made her feel good, it made her feel more *real* than she'd ever thought possible. For once,

her life was as colorful, vibrant, and REAL as the movies were. In those moments she felt what she guessed
was true love for Pat. Someone had finally liberated her
from the tyranny of dull, disappointing reality.

She'd feel good until the next time the drugs wore off,
and the nagging, black doubt surfaced again. The fear.
What the fuck WAS Pat capable of? She already knew
that he could kill without remorse. If she didn't have a
role to play, then why would he even keep her around?

Pat barely slept. When he did take enough downers that
he'd pass out for a few hours, Trina would watch him
dream. His fists would clench and unclench, his body
stiff as a board as he ground his teeth continuously.
Sometimes he would bark insults: "Cunt!" "Mother-
FUCKER!" "SHITsucker!" as he lay there, trembling.

She gave him a list of everyone she knew who frequented Tyler's place, and who might know Jeffrey away
from that scene. It was a pretty short list. Mostly part-
time meth users, crackheads, rootless musicians, and
barmen, people who operated on the periphery of the
city, scuffling in shady doorways and unlit streets. For
most of them, she had no more than a first name and a
description. The others, some sketchy details. One guy
who worked the door at a monthly S and M night in
a club downtown. A girl who worked the hostess bars
in Koreatown. A wannabe writer who lived in a motel
on Hollywood Boulevard. A guy who owned a bike repair shop over by Sunset and Benton. Each day Pat came
home, sometimes with a name crossed off the list, but
never any closer to finding Jeffrey.

"Nobody knows nothing about this guy," Pat grumbled, staring at the list one evening. "We're gonna have to rethink."

"Rethink what, Papi?"

"Just rethink. That's all."

And so it went, until the day that she heard the lock scraping back and Pat burst into the room. "The list," he demanded, "where is it?"

Trina had been examining her nose in the mirror, carefully peeling back the bandages, exposing the angry, swollen flesh underneath. She immediately stopped what she was doing and scurried over to the refrigerator. The list was held on there with a magnet in the shape of a California license plate.

"Here it is. Why?"

Pat glanced at it. Then a grin, long and slow, spread over his face.

"Spider," he said, "tell me more about this motherfucker Spider."

Trina shrugged.

"He's a cheap motherfucker. Creepy. He was always hanging around Tyler's place, trying to get freebies. He useta stop by the club once in a while. Christ knows why, he was into dudes mostly, I think."

"You said he knew the faggot pretty well."

Pat wouldn't say Jeffrey's name anymore. He referred to him exclusively as "the faggot." Tyler was referred to as "the dead faggot."

"Yeah. They were all queer boys together. I think they hung out. Why?"

Pat pulled out his cell phone and said, "Well, guess who's looking to make a connect for meth? Just got the call from Juan."

"No!"

"Uh-huh. Seems homeboy lost his last connection un-expectedly."

At this Pat laughed a little.

"What are you going to do?" Trina asked.

"I'm gonna be nice as fuckin' pie to him. Let's see how cooperative he can be. . . ."

Pat dialed a number and signaled for Trina to be quiet by raising a finger to his lips.

"Yeah. You Spider? Juan said you were looking for some, uh, materials that I can help you out with. Where you at? Oh. I'm pretty close to you. I can be there in twenty minutes. How much do you want? Uh-huh. Okay."

Pat clicked the phone off and said to Trina, "Get your-self cleaned up, baby girl. We got an appointment."

THIRTY-THREE

By the time they'd made it back to Jeffrey's room in the Mark Twain, Randal had clocked up seven missed calls from his brother. He turned the phone off. It was make or break time. The decision between living the life his brother wanted or risking everything on this long shot with Jeffrey was really no decision at all. He knew that one way or another he would never see his brother again.

The room was a far cry from his opulent digs in Brentwood. The brown carpet was threadbare, and the connecting door to the next room had a tiny peephole drilled into it. It was plugged with a piece of filthy cotton. There was writing on the walls, in spidery, obsessive script, crude cartoon reproductions of genitals, and places where the lime green paint had been scraped off altogether. Mystery stains covered the bedsheets, and the toilet was backed up. The windows didn't shut properly and looked out upon a parking lot and another flophouse hotel called the Cecil half a block down Wilcox.

Once Jeffrey was safely asleep in bed, Randal rummaged through the tote bag. Inside were the film canisters, old, rusty, and cool to the touch. In faint, barely there writing on the box was the date *Dec 1, 1968*. So it *did* exist. Randal felt a slight shudder work through his body. What he was holding was a genuine, honest-to-God slice of Hollywood history. He felt like an archaeologist, brushing dirt away from the remains of some unimagined, unfathomable creature.

Because of his industry connections, Randal had once been privy to a one-off screening of *The Day the Clown Cried*, a long-buried flick from the late '70s starring Jerry Lewis as a clown who leads Jewish children into the gas chambers of Auschwitz. . . . The film was a travesty, and Lewis had devoted much of his life to ensuring that it would never be seen publicly. It was a screening so shrouded in secrecy that Randal had been forced to sign a confidentiality agreement before being allowed to watch . . . but that was small fry compared to this, a piece of film that could change forever the way the world saw one of America's tragic icons. People KNEW about the Jerry Lewis movie. It was a staple of those stupid "50 Worst Movies of All Time" books. The script had surfaced on the Internet years ago. . . . But this, the Sharon Tate sex tape in Randal's trembling hands, was something totally different. This was a truly historic piece of celluloid.

Randal looked over to Jeffrey, still unconscious on the bed. He knew that it would be easy for him to walk out right now, taking the tape and the drugs with him. Even if the tape still turned out to be a fraud, there were enough drugs in the bag to make it worth his while. In a way Randal thought that it would serve the fucker right for disappearing like that.

He looked over to the door and imagined himself closing it gently, stealing out into the Hollywood streets below.

He looked at Jeffrey again, who was almost unrecognizable from the guy he had roomed with in rehab. Thin, pale, and totally ruined by drugs. And yet, in the midst of everything that had been going on with him, he had called Randal. Randal wasn't sure what that meant, but it gave him pause for thought when it came to ripping Jeffrey off.

Randal had made enough bad decisions in his life to know that every shitty trick you pull on someone will one day boomerang and hit you full in the face. No, for once Randal was determined to do something the right way. Even if what they were doing wasn't exactly legitimate, Randal decided that he could at the very least go about it in a dignified manner.

Randal silently replaced the canister. Also in the bag was a handgun. Randal picked it up and pointed it at the window. He whispered "blam!" to himself before replacing it carefully. Then he took out the drugs. He looked over at Jeffrey's still form, and then started to work out what he wanted to try first. There was no internal debate about whether he should use or not. Faced with the drugs, no debate was *possible*. He cut out a line of coke and inhaled it with a fifty-dollar bill. He sat back and felt the sensations starting in the back of his skull. *Oh, Jesus, yes.* He looked at the film canisters again and became filled with an urge to do something—to do anything. He started writing down names that would be helpful to them when it came to selling the tape.

———————

Even before he opened his eyes, Jeffrey knew where he was. It was the smell. The Mark Twain had a certain odor to it, a cocktail of mildew, cooked heroin, and metallic body odor that was all its own. He blinked, and his eyes adjusted to the mid-afternoon sunlight streaming in through the windows. The heat in the room was oppressive, unbearable. Outside honks, sirens, yelling, and the heavy rumble of drills on tarmac. He sat up and unpeeled his nude torso from the thin, wet sheets.

He saw Randal first, scribbling furiously onto a legal pad. Also on the table was Jeffrey's copy of the *Big Book*, with a pile of white powder and a rolled-up fifty-dollar bill on top of it. And there was Eddie fucking Murphy staring at him from the bag, which sat on top of the busted chest of drawers. Sensing movement, Randal looked up.

"Good afternoon," he said.
"Hey."
"How you feeling?"
"Like shit."
Randal nodded sagely. He pointed toward the book. "Wanna bump?"
"Sure."

Jeffrey flopped back onto the bed and ran his fingers through his filthy hair.

"How long have I been out?"

"A day and a half. I picked up some supplies. There's beers in the bathtub. And I got some tins of soup. I picked up some pizza, but it's cold now."

"Thank you."

Jeffrey got up and shuffled over to the table. He glanced at the pad that Randal was scribbling on. Then he focused on the pile of blow, scraping together a line with the credit card lying on there, and snorted it. He sat back on the bed, snuffling and shaking himself awake. When the coke started to make him feel better he looked up and said, "I'm kind of surprised to see you here."

"Oh, yeah? You called me, remember?"

"I know. It's just that somebody else might have decided to take the shit and split. You know? Just leave me here."

Randal shrugged. "Not me. I ain't a thief. But tell me, if you thought that I might have just ripped you off, why did you even call me?"

Jeffrey fell silent, and for a moment the image of Tyler's mutilated corpse flashed across his mind. He shuddered at the recollection. Jeffrey looked around the room and said, "You're the only person I could call. You're the only one I have left. . . ."

When Jeffrey started in with the garbled story of walking into Tyler's apartment to find his friend's mutilated corpse duct-taped to a chair, Randal initially thought he was suffering some kind of drug-induced psychosis. Still reeling from the two weeks of abuse he had heaped upon his body, Jeffrey didn't do much apart from sleep, eat, and get high over the next few days. Randal gave him the bed and set up camp in the rickety chair that comprised the rest of the furniture in the place. Sometimes in the night, he would wake up to the sound of Jeffrey moaning in his sleep. But after a few days' rest, the story remained the same. There was a twenty-four-hour newsstand on Cahuenga. Randal walked over and picked up a stack of porno magazines and newspapers.

Randal didn't expect to find anything in the paper about the weeks-old murder of some anonymous lowlife. The death of a drug dealer was about as newsworthy in LA as stepped-on cockroaches or rats run over by cars. But having nothing else to go on but Jeffrey's scrambled words, he looked anyway. Randal scoured the papers and finally found, at the back of the local news section, tucked away among rapes, dismemberments, and yesterday's winning lottery numbers . . .

No Leads in Suspected Drug Slay

AP—Police say they have no leads in the murder of suspected drug dealer Tyler James. Police found James's corpse after an anonymous phone call led them to the victim's apartment building. The killing appears to be a home invasion gone wrong, and police are not ruling out that James's death was drug-related. The victim had been convicted in 1992 for possession of methamphetamine and co-

```
caine, and police say that he was a
suspect in a drug ring that special-
ized in prescription medication.
```

"Home invasion, my ass," Jeffrey had snorted when he read that part. They had been in the room, getting high and drunk for two days now. Randal was fixing himself a stiff drink. He had bought several bottles from a liquor store on Hollywood Boulevard and kept the booze cool by stacking them in the bathtub, which he had filled with cold water. He winced, taking a gulp of vodka. It was four o'clock somewhere, he figured.

"Hm?"

"They say it's a home invasion. This wasn't a home invasion. They were looking for me. Either that, or they were looking for the tape. This shit ain't unrelated, man. This is bad. We need to unload this stuff and get the fuck out of town."

Randal looked somber. Ever since he'd dragged Jeffrey out of that loft space downtown, he had been muttering cryptically about needing to get out of town. When he tried to pin Jeffrey down on who exactly he suspected was looking for him, the story would change. At first he suspected rogue elements in the LAPD who had somehow found out about the tape and were trying to suppress it.

"Why would they give a fuck?" Randal had asked. "I mean, why would they care about the tape being made public?"

"Because it can be traced back to Bill. And if they find out more stuff about Bill, then it's a problem for the others. This shit goes way up to the top! I don't even know about half of the material those fuckers had access to. This isn't a fucking game! These are some cold-blooded killers we are talking about here. They are the kind of guys who shoot first and then plant a fucking gun in your dead hand later. Fuck, I mean . . . even in rehab . . . one of them was there. Leading a meeting. The Hammer. Old friend of Bill's, and he had a fucking grudge, too. I wouldn't be surprised if he recognized me, did a bit of research, and decided to come after me. . . ."

A rattling coughing fit wracked Jeffrey's body.

"They don't want this tape getting out. If this tape sells, they want to be the ones selling it, controlling the process, controlling who has access to it. You don't think that's worth killing me over?"

"But you can't be sure of that!"
"I know! That's what makes it worse. All I know is that we gotta stay away from the fucking cops. We gotta watch our backs, Randal!"

Randal was cutting out lines of blow on the nightstand. He looked up to Jeffrey.
"How do you know it wasn't a home invasion, just like the papers said?"
"Why would they wait around to chase me? I didn't see who they were. I didn't see nothing! I grabbed the bag, and suddenly some fucking hick psycho is threatening to gut me. If Bill's fucking gun hadn't been in my hand at that exact moment I'd be dead meat, just like Tyler. Why would anybody hang around after a fuck-

ing home invasion? They should have been long gone, man. No—they wanted the film. Or they wanted me. Or both."

When Randal heard Jeffrey talk like this, he'd get a sick feeling in his gut. He sounded like every crazed, paranoid crackhead he'd ever dealt with. It scared him, because he knew full well that sometimes crackheads just never get it back. One day something in the brain just overheats and blows out. When that happens, the change is irreversible. They go from being common crackheads to card-carrying paranoiacs and nobody can do anything about it. But . . . in some nook in the back of his brain Randal considered something even more disturbing. What if Jeffrey was right? Randal remembered the LAPD's Rampart scandal, where undercover cops basically became one of the most organized and out-of-control gangs in the city. They sold drugs, killed with impunity, and framed the innocent for murder. One of them had even robbed a fucking bank. In light of shit like that, Jeffrey's paranoia seemed almost justified.

"Either that, or . . ." Jeffrey trailed off.
"Or what?"
"Ah, it's nothing."
"Come on. Don't give me that shit. What's up? If we're going to do this thing, you gotta tell me everything. Okay? If there's someone else who knows about this, then let's get it all out in the open. . . ."
"Remember I told you that I had to leave London suddenly?"
"Yeah."

"Well, there was more to it than that. I left because if I didn't I was going to get murdered. I was working in Piccadilly. I was a prostitute. Sometimes they'd be so drunk I could empty their wallets without even having to touch their nasty old cocks. I had a few regulars, and one of them was Simon Price. You probably don't remember him. He had a big song in the mid-eighties called 'Flick the Switch,' with a band called Drone Cathedral."

"Weren't they one of those one-hit wonder bands, like Dexys Midnight Runners and shit?"

"Dexys weren't one-hit wonders back home. They were a good band. That fucking 'Come On Eileen' shit was not what they were all about. They had a bunch of great albums before they did that piece of shit. Drone Cathedral, on the other hand, yeah, they were a one-hit wonder band. Not a very good one. And, yes, that was Simon."

"Simon was at the height of his fame then. He was also one of the first people I met in England who knew how to freebase. Said some junkie hangers-on had introduced him to it during the band's first U.S. tour. He'd read all of these horror stories in the papers about this new killer drug that was sweeping the U.S. called crack, so of course he went out to find some the first night he landed in the U.S. It got to be so that Simon was seeing me most every night. Then I stopped asking him to pay. He told everyone I was his assistant. He wasn't out, not in the slightest. His band had this fucking fan base of fourteen-year-old girls who would have died if they knew he was queer. A queer crackhead, to boot."

.   .   .

Randal was rummaging around in the bag. Over the past few days they had managed to work their way through most of the drugs. The idea that the drugs would soon run out was finally forcing them into action. The tape would have to be sold as soon as possible.

"So you're living with a crackhead. And what?"

"Well, after six months or so, we were out of control. I mean, he had this great place in Earls Court, and it was just trashed, you know? It was a beautiful place. But we managed to make it look like the filthiest fucking squat you have ever seen in less than a fucking year. I mean, the place was *destroyed*. All we did was smoke and fuck. It was happy times.

"But it all fell apart . . . one night we had a big argument, and I ended up threatening to kill him. He said I was a junkie and I was stealing his money and that I was only with him because he was famous. He accused me of pawning one of his gold discs. I flipped the fuck out. We'd been up for days, you know? I was out of my mind on coke. I had him by the throat, naked, and was dangling him over the edge of his balcony. We were like six floors up. He was screaming, begging for his life. This was in a pretty nice neighborhood. The fucking neighbors called the cops and, well, as you can imagine, it ended pretty badly. The fucking *News of the World* were camped out there, the fucking BBC—I mean that story had everything. It was on the front covers for the next week and a half. He was big news already, always in the *Sun*, the *Daily Mail*, all of that bullshit. Now it was out that he was gay, that he was smoking crack, and of course it came out that I was a prostitute."

"Ouch."

"Yeah. After everything came out, he wanted it all back. The car, the apartment he'd rented for me. The jewelry. All of it. I told him to get fucked. I mean, my fucking life was ruined. I could never go home again. I was never out to my parents; we just didn't talk about it. When I turned fifteen I got the fuck out of Belfast and never came back. Now I was the most famous male prostitute in England. I wasn't about to be made homeless as well."

"He'd already stopped paying the rent on my flat, and they started eviction proceedings. He threatened me, said he had some heavy friends, but I thought he was full of shit. Simon was a poseur. He liked to surround himself with all of these pretend wannabe East End gangster types, but it was all just for effect. He was just a middle-class pop singer who got off on slumming it."

"One day, I'm getting out of bed and I heard a *boom*. Like my whole fucking bedroom shakes, shit comes flying off the walls, the whole bit. I thought there'd been an earthquake or something. I look out the window and people are running down the street covered in blood, screaming, car alarms are fucking going off all over the place. . . . You see, the night before I couldn't get parking on my street, so the car was two streets over. There was this old lady who lived in my building, Mrs. Sharkey, and she always parked right in front. Irritating old bitch, always banging on the fucking ceiling when I was listening to music. Where her car should have been, there's just a big hole in the ground with black fucking smoke spewing out of it. Glass and fucking metal everywhere. I realized that the cunt had tried to have my car bombed. Only the fucking arseholes he hired to do it blew up the wrong car. Mrs. Sharkey happened to have the same make and model as me, and when she turned the key in her ignition—*boom*. Blew her to fuck. I packed up and left the city that same day."

"Shit, did they ever get him for that?"
Jeffrey laughed.
"No, that's the kicker. They blamed the IRA, and the fucking peace process that everybody had been talking about in the news all year suddenly fell apart. The English thought that the IRA were launching a new campaign, and the IRA thought that the Brits had done it to discredit them. And all of it was because I had a fight with my boyfriend."

"So, what— You think that he might have something to do with this? He's come to fucking Los Angeles to kill you because of a ten-year-old lovers' spat?"
"Not him. Simon OD'd two years after all of that. But before I left London I tipped off the cops, mentioned a name that was close to him. A fucking psychotic bastard called Greebo, who was one of Simon's gangster friends. I heard he was sent down after I split London. I mean, he could be out of prison by now. Who knows what he's capable of? People like that . . . they don't let shit go."

"So what do we do now, man?"
"We need to sell the tape and get the fuck out of here. It's the only way."
The last of the cocaine was cut out into two fat lines. He handed the straw to Jeffrey. Jeffrey snorted it, rubbed his nose a little, and passed the straw over. Randal finished the rest.

"Pretty good shit," he said.

"I know."

"We can't fuck around anymore. We have to take care of business. I need to make a call. I know one guy who I'm pretty sure is gonna be able to help us. But I'm warning you—he's a whack job. He's for real—his family has been in the movie business for as long as anyone can remember . . . but he's kind of a black sheep."

"Can we trust him?"

"Yeah. I've known him for years. He's a fuckup, but he isn't a liar. But before I can deal with him, we're gonna need more drugs. A lot more drugs. You need heroin, right?"

"Yeah. More heroin."

"Okay. Heroin. Speed. You want coke?"

"Why the fuck not?"

"Okay, let's do this shit."

Randal felt that familiar old excitement rising in his chest. He picked up his cell and started making the calls.

THIRTY-FOUR

When Spider had originally answered the door and ushered them in, Trina wrinkled her swollen nose and whispered to Pat, "Jesus, it stinks in here."

She was right. Spider's apartment was a filthy, shambolic mess. He lived in a two-bedroom apartment in a run-down housing complex near Sunset and Bonnie Brae. Over the years the clutter inside had spread over every available surface: stinking clothes lay in unwashed heaps on the floor, and dishes with weeks-old food caked onto them piled up in the sink. The bedroom had gotten so filthy that Spider had abandoned it and moved into the spare room, where he slept on the floor.

Sometimes he'd consider moving the clutter from his abandoned bed so he could sleep on it again, but where would he put it all? Anyway there were more important things to consider. Like drugs.

.   .   .

In the weeks since Tyler's murder drugs were all that Spider could think about. Having a steady connection for meth had given Spider's universe gravity. With Tyler gone, Spider had devolved into a kind of feral state. He pined for Tyler's steady supply like a mourning widower. He didn't shave, his teeth went unbrushed, and the smell of his own body odor had become metallic, more pungent than usual.

With the arrival of Pat, all that had changed. Spider was so concerned with the meth that he barely acknowledged Trina's presence, beyond nodding, "Hey girl," totally unfazed by her out-of-the-blue appearance in his apartment.

"What the fuck happened to you?" Trina asked. Spider's face was still fucked up and bruised, one ear swollen and fat like a cauliflower, the cheeks raging purples and yellows, one eye cut and swollen almost shut.
"Got mugged by a fucking spic. What happened to you? You get a nose job or something?"
Trina put a protective hand to her nose, still painful and taped up.
"Yeah. Nose job . . . ," she said.

After the small talk and introductions, Spider stood in his ramshackle bedroom, his chin pointing upward, looking at his exposed throat in the mirror, as his trembling hand guided a needle loaded with Pat's meth into the fat jugular that ran down to his collarbone. He was talking the whole time.
"Ya gotta be careful going here. Hit my goddamned artery once. I knew straightaway, pulled out, and the

fucking blood was GUSHING outta me. I ain't kidding. Happened in the bathroom. If you peek around there ya can still see the stains. I mean that shit went everywhere. I scrubbed it off the best I could, but that was, shit, like a month ago, and I'm still finding bloodspots. On the fucking ceiling, behind the toilet, I mean, shit, man, it looked like fuckin' *Psycho* in there or some shit. . . ."

Pat watched Spider's shaky attempts at getting the needle into his vein, and an amused grin half formed on his mouth. Trina had to avert her eyes. She looked over to her left and saw a stack of porno: *Rectal Research, Twink Destroyer, Skater Boi Gangbang, Ali Baba and the 40 Cocks.* Catching her looking at one of the boxes in the mirror, Spider stopped what he was doing and said, "Some fucking friend of mine was crashing here, and he left a bunch of faggot porn. If you want it you can take it. I don't need it."

"No, thanks. I'm all good for gay porn, Spider."

Spider rolled his eyes and got back to work. With a grunt, he finally got a hit, and the black blood flowed lazily into the syringe. He pushed the shit in slow and easy. He withdrew the spike and leaned back against the wall, tilting his head a little, applying pressure to the injection site with his thumb. A thin train of black blood trickled down his Adam's apple.

He felt the rush, a tidal wave of pleasure building inside of him. He knew immediately that the stuff was top quality. His body reacted as if he had just skydived out of an airplane: a rush of adrenaline, terror, and pleasure that was almost overwhelming. He felt his skull crack wide open, and his brain expanding like a wet sponge.

He trembled, his eyes fluttered inside his head, and he murmured, "Oh, that's GOOOD shit, man. That's fucking GOOD shit. . . ."

Pat grinned and said, "I only deal with the best shit available. That's the finest-quality crystal meth on the West Coast. My chemist is a fucking genius. Ex-government scientist, top-notch equipment. This ain't no fucking Hells Angels shit cooked up in a trailer park in Riverside. This is fucking grade-A primo methamphetamine."

"Jesus Christ. Am I glad I met you."

"So," Pat said, getting right back to business now that Spider had a taste of the shit, "what do you think about this Jeffrey faggot?"

Spider opened his eyes to slits.

"Why do you want him so badly?"

"He has something that belongs to me."

"What?"

Pat walked over to Spider. Put his face real close.

"Listen, motherfucker. This ain't twenty questions. None of this is any of your goddamned business. I got an ounce of this shit I'm willing to give you, if you can give me the faggot. You don't have to worry about the wheres and the whys, okay?"

Spider raised his hands and tried to smile ingratiatingly.

"Okay. Look, I don't really give a fuck what you want him for. He's all yours, man. I can set it up, no fucking problem."

"Good boy." Pat slapped Spider lightly on his swollen cheek.

Pat backed off a little and cast a disapproving eye over the apartment.

"You are without a doubt the messiest fucking speed freak I have ever met. C'mon, sweet cheeks. . . ."

Trina stood and followed Pat to the door. A baggie of Pat's speed lay on the floor, next to Spider's spoon.

"What should I tell him?"

"Just meet up with him. Find out what he's up to; find out where he's staying. That's all."

Pat opened the door and ushered Trina out into the sunlight.

"I'll be in touch real soon," Spider said.

"Oh, you'd better."

And with that Pat was gone, pulling the door closed behind him.

T H I R T Y - F I V E

In the bloodred gloom of Musso and Frank's, where the ghosts of old Hollywood jostled shoulders with the tourists and the ghouls, Randal and Jeffrey sat nervously with Stevie Rox, who was currently lifting his shirt to expose a pasty, flabby torso that had a grotesque fresh scar running a good twelve inches up one side.

"Just got the staples out. Brand-new fuckin' liver in there. Got it down in South America. It belonged to some fuckin' eighteen-year-old Mexican kid. . . . The old one was all fucked up. The doctors told me I had to quit drinking and quit doing blow! Can you believe that shit? I pay those motherfuckers Christ knows how much per month so they can dispense their fuckin' wisdom upon me, and the best they can come up with is 'cut out the booze and the blow'? Fuck that!"

"So, I told 'em I wanted a new liver. I mean, I see all of these fucking moony-looking kids on charity appeals and shit, and they're doling out fucking livers, kidneys, hearts, all kinds of shit to them. So if it's good enough for them, then I'm fuckin' sure it's good enough for Stevie. . . ."

"I mean, these fucking American doctors are such pansies, with their fuckin' rules and regulations. . . . I had to go to South America to get the job done. Money still talks down there, I tell ya. Everything is for sale. They got a better working model for capitalism than we've managed up here, you know what I'm sayin'?"

Despite being born and raised in Los Angeles, Stevie Rox talked in an entirely affected British accent, for reasons that nobody could fathom.

"Sure thing, Stevie," Randal said. "I hear ya. The health care system in this country is FUCKED." He peered curiously at the scar. It looked moist.

Jeffrey was sitting there in shell-shocked silence. They had been with Stevie Rox for almost thirty minutes, ever since his pearl-colored limo had pulled up outside of the restaurant. He'd made a big show of getting out with a champagne flute in his hand and a bright orange, seemingly anorexic platinum blond woman with grotesquely enlarged lips and tits on his arm. They staggered in, causing a commotion, Stevie sticking one-hundred-dollar bills into the pockets of the lingering old men in polyester tuxedos who waited tables in the main room, before plunking themselves down at a booth and ordering a bottle of Cristal.

"Cristal, and hurry it up! I'm drier than a witch's twat in the desert!" Stevie had roared, before launching into a coke-fueled monologue about the music industry, the facile nature of musicians, how the quality of coke in the city was falling, and now the brand-new liver that he was waving in Randal and Jeffrey's faces. It looked like some kind of huge bloody mouth intent on swallowing them both.

"Jesus," Jeffrey said.
"Touch it!" Stevie ordered, edging his gut toward him, throwing out his chest.
"No, thanks!"
"Don't be such a faggot!" Stevie howled, loud enough for the whole room to hear. "It's healed up. Touch it!"

Jeffrey allowed his fingertips to brush the wound. This satisfied Stevie, who finally allowed his garish silk Gaultier shirt to cover his monstrous bulk again.
"Eighteen years old. He was still fresh."
"Wow, do you know what happened to him?"
"What happened to him? Fuck knows. For what I paid, they probably chloroformed him and snatched him off the fuckin' street. He probably woke up in a bathtub full of ice in a fucking motel in Tijuana. Anyway, it's all rather beside the point now, isn't it, because it's mine, and I can do whatever the fuck I want with it. Funny thing is, ever since getting the liver, I can fuck like an eighteen-year-old, too. Isn't that right, Baby?"
"Oh, yeah," the girl said in an utterly emotionless West Coast monotone. "He can fuck like an eighteen-year-old. He's wearing me out."

Randal smiled at her.

"We weren't introduced. What's your name?"

"You fucking deaf or something?" Stevie said. "Her name is Baby. Baby, say hello."

"Hello," Baby said.

As they guzzled the champagne, the waiter arrived to take their orders. Stevie ordered the minute steak with creamed spinach. Randal and Jeffrey, who were in the bathroom snorting rails of meth just before Stevie showed up, skipped dinner and stuck to booze. Baby asked the waiter if they had any lactose-free cottage cheese.

"Cottage cheese?" the waiter said, incredulous.

"Yeah, yeah, yeah . . . ," Stevie interrupted, "she's on a diet. Fat-free, fucking lactose-free, something like that. Something that don't taste of anything."

"No, sir," the waiter said, "I don't think we have anything like that."

Stevie pulled out another one-hundred-dollar bill. "Will you send someone out to pick some up from Ralph's?"

The waiter looked at the money, seemingly not comprehending. Stevie sighed and pulled out another bill. He pressed the two hundred into the waiter's hand.

"Very good, sir," the waiter said.

Baby said, "I want fat-free and lactose-free, okay?"

"Very good." The waiter nodded and shuffled off, presumably to order some unfortunate dishwasher out into the night to pick up the shit that Baby wanted to eat.

"So, boys," Stevie said, pouring himself another drink, "what was it that you wanted to talk about? Actually, wait—excuse me."

He turned to Baby and said, "Hey, honey. Why dont-cha go powder your nose or something and let us boys talk?"

"Sure thing, honey."

When Baby got up and *clip-clopped* toward the bathroom on her red heels, Randal said, "Goddamn, Stevie, you got her well trained."

"You gotta keep 'em in check, man. So what's the big deal you wanna talk about?"

"It's a movie. Celebrity porn."

Stevie rolled his eyes. "Seen it, owned it, bought the T-shirt."

"Yeah, but this one is different."

"Oh, yeah? Who is it? Britney?"

"Nope. None of that nouveau Hollywood trash. This is a historical document."

Stevie narrowed his puffy eyes to slits.

"You aren't going to try to sell me that tired old movie of Marilyn Monroe sucking someone off, are you? Because I've seen it, and it's crap. Women didn't know how to take care of a man back then. It was like watching your fucking granny suck someone off! I was watching it thinking, *'Get it down your throat, love. You're an actress! Act like you're enjoying it!'* Anyway, that fucker is off the market. In the hands of a collector. Some rich superfan who doesn't want old Marilyn's image ruined by a film of her sucking someone's meat torpedo going public."

Jeffrey leaned forward. "No, Stevie, it isn't Marilyn. This is an original sixteen-millimeter film that has never been duplicated and has been in the hands of the same private collector for decades. And now it has come into my possession. Do you remember Sharon Tate?"

Stevie laughed. "Do I remember Sharon Tate? Let me tell you something, kid. I AM Hollywood. You think old Randy here is Hollywood? My family has owned this fucking town since this place was all orange groves and Indian fucking burial grounds. My lineage goes right back to that fat fuck Arbuckle running around in his ill-fitting police uniforms, whacking some poor bastard on the head with a rubber truncheon. You got me? So, yeah, I know who fucking Sharon Tate was."

Jeffrey sat back and decided to keep his mouth shut. He found being around Stevie Rox a dizzying business. Randal stepped in, looking mildly amused by Stevie's outburst.

"What we have," Randal said, "is a twenty-minute film loop starring Sharon Tate, Mama Cass, Yul Brynner, and Steve McQueen. A gangbang. All of them getting high and fucking."

"How did this come into your possession, exactly?"

"He told you. A private collector."

"And how did this private collector get it?"

"He stole it. From the Tate house."

"And how exactly did he manage that, then?"

"He was one of the first people on the scene when they all got wiped out by Manson's goons. This guy was there to take fingerprints and mop the fucking blood off the walls, and he sees a tape. . . ."

Stevie Rox looked over to Jeffrey again. He leaned in close.

"How much did you pay for it?"

"He left it to me. When he died."

"Generous fucker, wasn't he? What, was he your boy-friend or something?"

"Yeah. He was my boyfriend."

Stevie nodded slowly. He looked back at Randal. "Have you seen it?"

Randal looked at Jeffrey. Jeffrey shrugged at him. Randal looked back to Stevie.

"Not yet. It hasn't been out of its canister since the early seventies. That shit is fragile. Old. We'd need specialist equipment."

Stevie finished his champagne. He emptied the bottle into his glass. "So what are you thinking? A collector?"

"Yeah. What about the Marilyn Monroe guy?"

"He's no use to you. He only gives a shit about Monroe. Your best bet is someone who is into the whole Tate legend. That won't be hard. I know some people. I know one guy in particular who might be useful to you. He's a freak. A memorabilia guy. A real fetishist. He's got money, too. But . . ."

"But what?"

"But . . . what's my cut?"

"I dunno, Stevie. If we make the sale . . . five?"

"Fuck off! It's not worth me writing his number down on a napkin for five. You know what this film could be worth? Millions. That sad cunt I knew paid two million for the Marilyn tape. I want twenty-five grand, cash."

"If he buys it."

"If it is what you say it is, then he'll buy it. And I want ten percent of whatever the tape sells for."

"Ten percent? Come *on*, Stevie. . . . How about five?"

"Ten, or I'm getting up and walking out right now. I hope you haven't dragged my arse all the way over here so you can waste my fucking time, Randy. . . ."

Randal looked over to Jeffrey. Jeffrey looked over to Stevie's blubbery frame one last time, shuddered, and gave the nod to Randal.

"Okay. Ten percent."

Stevie nodded, grimly.

"Randal. I've heard stories about you. Understand this: if you try to fuck me on the money, I will have your fucking balls cut off and fed to my shih tzu, do you understand?"

"Stevie, I'm clean. Look at me. I'm just trying to make an honest living, just like you."

At this there was a commotion as Baby staggered out of the bathroom and knocked into a table full of diners. She straightened herself, slurred an apology, and then continued on to the table.

"Oh, fuck me," Stevie said.

Her sense of direction was all off. She finally made it back to the booth, her head fell back, her eyes rolled up into her skull, and she was still.

"Jesus," Jeffrey said, "is she all right?"

"Oh, yeah. She's fine. She does this all of the time. It's the medication she's taking. She'll snap out of it in half an hour or so. Won't remember a thing. Fucking dumb bitch has got bats in her belfry. What a piece of ass, though."

With this, Stevie Rox wrote a name and a phone number on a napkin. He put his pen away with a flourish and placed a hand over the napkin. He looked at Randal one more time.

"I want my cut," he said, "I don't want excuses."

"If this guy buys, you get your money. Come on, Stevie, how long have we known each other?"

"Too fucking long. That's why I'm making sure you understand that I'm not pissing around."

Randal nodded. Stevie removed his hand, and Randal took the napkin, glancing at it before slipping it into his pocket. The waiter had arrived bringing cocktails, the minute steak with creamed spinach, and a small bowl with a pile of unappetizing-looking white goop in it for Baby.

Stevie nudged Baby. She seemed to stir for a moment.

"Wake up, Baby," Stevie said, "your food's here."

With that, Baby pitched forward and hit the table with her face, sending glasses tumbling and a steak knife clattering to the floor.

"Thank you," Jeffrey said, taking his drink from the waiter. He held the glass aloft, over the head of Baby, still facedown on the table.

"Here's to Sharon Tate," he said.

"Here's to my twenty-five grand," Stevie Rox gurgled, and they clinked glasses. Baby slept on.

THIRTY-SIX

As Trina and Pat lay in bed smoking cigarettes, they listened to their neighbors' disembodied voices through the paper-thin motel walls. Their bodies were bathed in a luminous sheen of postcoital sweat. Trina took a long drag and then exhaled a plume of gray smoke. It curled upward, hanging momentarily in the slats of neon light creeping in through the open blinds, before it was dissipated by the twirling ceiling fan.

"That was good, Daddy," she said. "You fucked me *good*."
"I aim to please . . ." Pat murmured.

"You know, baby, uh, I noticed how you never try to eat my pussy"—she felt his torso stiffen when she said this, so she quickly added—"and that's cool, baby. I ain't criticizin'. You fuck me better than any man's ever fucked me. It's just that . . . well, I've been wantin' to tell you somethin', an' it's never seemed like the right time before. . . ."

"Uh-oh," Pat growled, "sounds serious. You ain't missed your period, have you?"

Trina laughed, "Nah, baby. Nothin' like that. It's just that, uh, when I was a kid . . . well, my uncle Clay—my mom's brother—he useta live with us. After Gramma died, Clay couldn't live by himself anymore. . . . Uncle Clay was born kinda screwy, something in his genes Mom said, some kinda disorder that twisted his brain a little. Well, uh, when I was ten, Uncle Clay used to come into my room at night. At least once a week, sometimes more. An' he'd just stand there, lookin' at me. Starin'. I'd always wake up. Somethin' . . . some sixth sense would bring me 'round . . . an' there'd be Clay with his fingers to his lips saying '*shush* . . .' "

Pat sucked on his Parliament, thoughtfully.

"So, Uncle Clay useta screw ya?" he asked.

"No, baby!" Trina laughed, "Jesus, you're sick! He was my *uncle*! Nah, he used to get under the sheets and shimmy up the bed toward me an' put his mouth between my legs, you know? An' just lick me . . . like a dog. I guess he'd be, uh, y'know, takin' care of himself down there . . . 'cos after ten minutes or so he'd sorta . . . stiffen up. His whole body, just tremblin' all over. Then he'd just lie there pantin' for a while. I'd lie there real still, pretendin' to be asleep. After a few minutes he'd get up, wipe himself off on the sheet, an' kinda . . . slink outta there."

"Man. Did you ever tell your folks?"

"Oh, God, no! The first time it happened, I kinda thought that I'd dreamed it or something. I was watchin' Uncle Clay for clues at breakfast, but he was sittin' there eatin' his Capt'n Crunch like nuthin' had happened. The next time, I was too embarrassed to say nuthin'. After that . . . I guess I just kinda got useta it, you know?"

"Yeah, I hear ya . . . so what happened to Uncle Clay?"
"Nothin'. He's probably still at Mom and Dad's place, sittin' around in his underwear eatin' up all the cereal and watchin' Fox News. He useta watch that shit all day long. Motherfucker was obsessed with Bill O'Reilly, hero-worshiped him. He wrote a letter to him once, an' Bill read it out on the show, an' Uncle Clay just about creamed in his shorts."

"So he kept it up? Sneakin' into your room at night and eatin' your pussy?"
"For a while. When I was twelve I got my period. One time he snuck into my room an' got himself a mouthful of blood, that put a stop to it. He fuckin' ran out of there, an' I heard him retchin' and brushing his teeth like crazy in the bathroom."
"Ha. I guess ol' Uncle Clay more'n learned his lesson, huh?"
"I guess. So anyway, baby, the reason I wanted to tell you that . . . is ever since, I just can't stand to have any man put his mouth down there. It just turns me off. Leaves me cold. Bad associations, I guess."

Pat laughed his wheezy laugh and stubbed out his cigarette. He looked over to Trina. She was staring at the ceiling, a faraway look in her eyes. He kissed her on the throat.
"Well, no offense, baby"——Pat whispered against her hot skin—— "but I don't eat pussy anyway. Any man who says he enjoys eatin' pussy is either a fool or a fuckin' liar."
He bit her neck lightly, and Trina giggled, her body

breaking out in goose bumps. She took a final drag on her cigarette and stubbed it out in a coffee cup. She exhaled long and hard.

"Is that so? Well, aren't we the match made in heaven. . . . So anything else I should know about you, baby? Any stuff you want to tell me?"

"What? Sex stuff?"

"Yeah, sex stuff. Turn-ons? Turn-offs?"

"Only two things turn me off. One is when a woman talks too much about stupid shit. Another is when a chick tries to touch my ass. An ex of mine tried to stick her finger up my ass when we was fucking. Only once. I grabbed her by her fucking wrist and told her that the next time she tried that shit she'd pull back a motherfucking stump. I may be a lot of things, baby girl, but I sure as fuck ain't nobody's bitch."

Trina ran her hand across Pat's chest and said, "You can say that again, Daddy."

They lapsed into a contented silence for a while. Outside a siren wailed and then faded away into night. It sounded like the city was crying. Then Trina asked, "What are you gonna do when you find him?"

"The faggot?"

"Yeah."

"I'm gonna kill him."

Trina buried her face in Pat's neck, sniffing at his skin. "What about Spider?" she breathed.

"You leave Spider to me, baby girl. I don't like loose ends."

Trina didn't say anything. She continued to nuzzle Pat, before resting her cheek against his shoulder.

"Don't worry, sweet cheeks," Pat said. "It gets easier the second time. Just like with your uncle Clay. After a while, it becomes as natural as breathing."

Outside, the traffic on the boulevard sounded like the roaring of some vast, distant sea. Trina clung to Pat, imagining herself adrift on its endless inky darkness, clinging to Pat to avoid being dragged under the surface. Pat stared at the ceiling fan as it went around, *thunk, thunk, thunk,* his mind squirming with thoughts of blood and retribution. A silence fell on the city for a moment—no sirens, no alarms, no Spanish curses, no breaking glass. Just the soft, steady sound of the ceiling fan. The night had declared a cease-fire. Trina huddled closer to Pat and soon she was asleep.

TH!RTY-SEVEN

They were in the car outside of Rupert Du Wald's place. The radio was on, fading from some moronic top-forty rock into a news report. It was mid-afternoon, and the air-conditioning was on full-blast. Randal was smoking a cigarette and looking out the window distractedly while Jeffrey tried to fix with shaking hands. His knees were up on the dash, and he had his elbow tucked into his gut, repositioning the needle under his skin, trying to find a vein somewhere on his bruised forearm.

"Shit!" Jeffrey hissed as he withdrew the needle and a glob of blood trailed from his arm and spotted his T-shirt.

"It's four fifteen," Randal said.

"I know it's fucking four fifteen," Jeffrey snapped. "Stop rushing me. I'm almost done. It's a bitch to fix when you keep interrupting me."

Randal threw the cigarette out the window and exhaled

a plume of gray smoke into the balmy air. The bag with the film canister was sitting on his lap.

"Are you nervous?" Randal asked.
"Nervous? Why the fuck would I be nervous?"
"Well, the tape, man. It's make or break time."
"I'm not afraid. I know the tape is bona fide. There's nothing to worry about as far as that goes. Oh—wait. Here we go. Got you, you fucker. . . ."

Jeffrey got the hit, slid the needle out, and put it away with the rest of his shit in the glove compartment. He closed his eyes for a moment. His voice took on that dreamy tone it got when he was high on heroin, like he was talking half asleep through a mouth wadded with cotton.

"Fuck me. That's good shit. That's almost all of Bill's China white gone now. I'm telling you, it's gonna be tough to go back to using fucking Mexican tar after getting used to this shit."
"I thought you were gonna quit when we sell the tape? Why would you start using that shit?"
"Yeah," Jeffrey slurred, "yeah, exactly. I'm *definitely* going to quit once we sell the tape. I mean, I've only been using this time for like, what, two weeks?"
"Jeffrey, you got out of rehab like two months ago."
"Okay, a couple of months. I don't think I'll have copped a habit already. Maybe just a chippy little habit. No worries. . . ."
Jeffrey's head slumped toward his chest. Randal watched him for a moment, nodding silently. Then something caught his ear on the radio. He cranked the volume, rousing Jeffrey.

"What the FUCK, man?"
"Shhh!"

> Dr. Michael Schwartzki, better known to
> his audience as the so-called recovery guru
> Dr. Mike, has denied any involvement in the
> death of Joseph Khu. Khu, who lived his life
> as a female named Champagne, was found
> dead earlier in the week in East Hollywood.
> The twenty-year-old was allegedly a drug
> addict and a prostitute. Yesterday, the *National
> Enquirer* went public with allegations that the
> drugs that killed Khu had been traced back to
> the doctor, and that a message left by Khu on
> his sister's cell phone shortly before his death
> suggested that Dr. Mike and the deceased
> had been involved in a sexual relationship. In
> a statement issued today via his lawyers, Dr.
> Mike denied all the allegations made against
> him by the Khu family and the tabloid
> press. . . .

"Jesus Christ!" Jeffrey said. "You have to be kidding me!"
"I told you something about that motherfucker was off,
man. I could smell it a mile away. You can't go through
life with your shirt buttoned so tight without blowing
your top eventually."
He clicked off the radio.
"Anyway, enough about that motherfucker. Let's go see
this guy Rupert. What kind of a fucking name is Rupert?"
"What kind of a fucking name is Champagne?" Jeffrey
laughed.

They rang the bell and looked at each other for a moment, waiting for a response. A tiny, ancient Asian woman opened the door and peered at them.

"Yes?"

"Hello. I'm Randal, and this is Jeffrey. We're here to see Mr. Du Wald...."

"Yes, Mr. Du Wald is expecting you. This way, please...."

The entrance hall was huge, with two winding staircases leading off to other parts of the house. The floor and walls were constructed of what appeared to be onyx marble, giving them a translucent, fragile quality. The air was thick with the scent of orchids. Du Wald obviously had a thing for orchids, because they were everywhere: hanging from suspended pots, in vases; there were even vaguely sexual paintings of them mounted on the walls. The housekeeper led them into a main room, which had a grand piano set into a sunken floor. A huge window looked out over the city's smoggy horizon. Sitting at the piano was a strange little man holding a cocktail glass in his hand. He was short and fat, wearing a monogrammed dressing gown. He was at least seventy, and his skin was pulled back tight over his skull, giving his face a waxy, unreal look. He was wearing aviator glasses with brown-tinted lenses, and the strange head was topped off with a hairpiece that seemed—in the half-light—to be a shade of powder blue.

"Mr. Du Wald, Misters Randal and Jeffrey are here to see you...."

Du Wald held his hand up, and the housekeeper was silent. As he continued to pick out notes on the piano with his free hand she turned to them and whispered,

"He'll be with you in just a moment. Would you like a drink?"

Randal shook his head, and the housekeeper scurried off to some other part of the house. They watched as Du Wald put the glass of wine down on the piano and scrawled something on a piece of manuscript paper. Then he picked out a melody on the piano, singing along with gusto.

"We are the Teacup Family! Welcome to our HOOOOMMME!" Du Wald sang in an operatic voice.

He nodded and replaced the pencil. He turned to look at Randal and Jeffrey.

"Hello," the little man said.

"Mr. Du Wald? I'm Randal P. Earnest, and this is Jeffrey. . . ."

"Hello . . . ," Jeffrey slurred, his eyes rolling back into his skull slightly.

"Welcome, boys! Come in! Make yourself at home. . . . Is Lilly fetching you a drink?"

"Oh, nothing for us," Randal said.

"Yeah, we're cool . . . ," Jeffrey said, sleepily.

"My work," Du Wald explained, pointing to the music sheet. "Theme song for a new children's television show, *The Teacup Family.* For the English, of course. Only the English would write an entire show about the adventures of a family of teacups. . . ."

"I didn't know you were in the music game."

"Oh, yes! My whole life. Commercial work. Movies. Television. . . . Please, sit down."

Aside from the grand piano, and the leather corner sofa, there were several bookshelves stuffed with antique-looking hardcover books, and mounted props from the various movies and TV shows that Du Wald had worked on.

"*Murder She Wrote . . . Airwolf . . . Manimal . . .*" Du Wald recited, waving his cocktail glass around the room, "I worked on all of them at some point. . . ."

Randal's gaze was drawn to some paintings hanging behind glass. "Is that a Picasso?" He asked, peering at one of them.

"It sure is. You don't even want to know what that beauty is appraised for. Almost makes you feel sad when you think that there are people starving in this city. *Almost*, mind you. . . . But onto business, gentlemen. Mr. Rox informed me that you had something that I would be quite interested in. A piece of Sharon Tate memorabilia. Are you sure I can't get you a drink? I'm fixing one for myself. Then you can tell me all about it. . . ."

Randal looked over to Jeffrey. His chin was slumping down onto his chest again, the stoned lurch of the satiated dope fiend. Randal elbowed him in the ribs quickly, and Jeffrey jerked awake again, slurring, "What the FUCK, man?" Randal cleared his throat. Thankfully, Du Wald seemed entirely oblivious to how loaded Jeffrey was. He was standing by the bar, mixing himself a Tom Collins.

"Well," Randal said, "it's a home movie, shot in the late sixties. An orgy at the Tate house. A kind of sixties free love, pot brownies, and acid hors d'oeuvres kind of thing. Sharon Tate, Steve McQueen, Yul Brynner, Mama Cass."

"Uh-huh," Du Wald said, as if this was nothing out of the ordinary. "And this is the original copy?"

"Yeah. No duplicates exist. It's been sitting in a safe for the best part of thirty years."

"My goodness. And who owns it, exactly? You?"

Randal looked over to Jeffrey again. His head was bob-
bing, as if it weighed thirty pounds and his neck could
no longer support it. "Yeah," Randal carried on, "we
both own it. It's a partnership."

"And the source of the tape?"

"A contact in the LAPD, now deceased."

"Interesting."

Du Wald walked over to the door of the room and
shouted, "Lilly! LILLY! I HAVE SOME BUSINESS TO AT-
TEND TO, AND I MUST NOT BE INTERRUPTED!"

A faraway voice replied, "YES, MR. DU WALD!"

Du Wald closed the door and locked it. Then he walked
over to the bookshelf. Randal gave Jeffrey another dig
in the ribs and hissed, "Snap out of it, fuckwad!"

"Oh, uh, shit, sorry," Jeffrey slurred, standing up suddenly to clear his head. He saw the little old man in the
robe pulling a book from the middle shelf, and as he
did so, the entire bookcase popped away from the wall,
revealing a hidden steel door. There was a keypad to the
right of the door. Du Wald typed a sequence of numbers into the pad, and the door opened with a heavy-
sounding click.

"Jesus," Jeffrey said, "that's pretty cool."

"This way, gentlemen. . . ."

They followed Du Wald through the door. They found
themselves in what looked like a modern art gallery: a
large white room, cold and sterile, with marble floors
and a series of glass cases housing what looked to be
a ragtag collection of junk. Du Wald walked in between the "exhibits," throwing his arms in the air the-
atrically.

"Gentlemen—here are the star items in my collection!
Consider yourselves lucky—you may never see the
likes of these artifacts again. . . ."

They followed him for a moment, staring at the contents of the glass boxes.

"A toilet seat?" Randal said, staring at one of the items.

"A gold toilet seat?"

Du Wald smiled mischievously and raised his eyebrows.

"Not just ANY toilet seat. This is the toilet seat that the
King himself, Elvis Presley, died on. Did you know that
nobody has been allowed into the second-floor rooms of
Graceland since Elvis died in 1977? That the bedrooms,
the bathrooms have all been kept exactly as they were?
That the sheets are still full of Elvis's dead skin cells and
hair, the pillows stiff with the King's drool? Not even
President Clinton was able to get access to the private
rooms of Graceland when he requested it. In fact, the
only thing that has been changed since the day Elvis
died is this toilet seat."

Jeffrey placed a hand lightly on the glass.

"So Elvis died sitting on this?"

Du Wald nodded. "Quite right."

"How did you . . . ?"

Du Wald shrugged. "A lot of negotiation. And a lot of
money. But believe me, this artifact is totally authentic.
I was present for the removal and replacement myself.
This is the second most valuable thing in my collection."

"Oh, yeah?" Randal said. "What's number one?"

"This."

Du Wald was at the far end of the room now, looking
into the last glass case. Randal and Jeffrey followed him

and crowded around to take a look. It contained an old Cartier box, frayed at the edges. Inside, on a bed of white silk, was what looked to be a small piece of beef jerky, or maybe a dried eel. It was brown, and shriveled, and utterly unrecognizable. But Du Wald was staring at it in wonder, his breathing fat and labored.

"What IS it?" Jeffrey asked.

"This, gentlemen, is the penis of Napoleon Bonaparte." Rupert fell into silence again, allowing the words to resonate. He looked to his guests, who stared at the small, dried-up thing with mouths hanging open. He cleared his throat, and continued:

"There have been several fakes floating around the collectors' market over the past fifty years, but this one is the real deal. It was removed from the corpse by the emperor's physician Francesco Antommarchi and a priest named Abbe Vignali, on the island of Saint Helena. Now here's the rub: supposedly the penis was sold to a rare book dealer in 1916 by Vignali's descendants. That curio has passed through several auction houses over the years, finally ending up in the hands of a private collector who bought it in the late 1980s. However, back in 1821 a manservant called Ali was also present at the removal, and this artifact came as a package with Ali's diaries, which reveal that Ali substituted the penis with the mutilated corpse of a seahorse. The diaries also reveal that the priest was a shortsighted drunk, who was easily duped by his plucky manservant. This—the genuine penis—has never appeared on the open market and has only been in the hands of three collectors before me."

"It's so . . . *small*," whispered Jeffrey.

"Well"—Du Wald smiled—"if we were to remove your

penis, drain the blood from it, and mummify it for a century and a half, it may also seem suddenly less than impressive, yes?"

"Jesus Christ," Randal said, his nose pressed against the glass, "that is some crazy shit."

"Indeed. Now, gentlemen, enough small talk. I think that it's time for our featured presentation, don't you?"

They straightened up. Randal had the bag in his hand.

"You have the equipment ready?"

"Of course. Film makes up a large portion of my collection. This way, please. . . ."

"Um, do you have popcorn?" Randal asked as they walked through another door, leading to a small theater room. There were two banks of fold-up red velvet cinema seats, facing toward a small screen. In the center of the room was an ancient-looking sixteen-millimeter projector. Du Wald ignored Randal and placed a hand lovingly on the projector.

"Gentlemen," he breathed, "the film, if you will."

Randal passed the bag to Jeffrey. Jeffrey placed it on the floor and removed the canister. He looked at it for a moment and took a deep breath.

"Are you sure you know what you're doing?" Jeffrey said. "This thing is old. Delicate."

Du Wald smiled softly. "I will treat it as if it were my own child," Du Wald said, in a way that made Jeffrey feel extremely bad for Du Wald's descendants. Reluctantly, he handed the canister over. He watched as the old man opened the lid in the dim light and looked upon the reel of film within, awestruck. He took a deep breath, as if he were trying to inhale the essence of what this reel contained. His eyes were gleaming with anticipation.

He lifted the film from the canister and loaded it onto the front of the projector. With practiced movements, he clicked open the lens and turned it to one side. Then he took the film and gently unraveled around three feet of it, holding it up to his eye in the dim light, and nodding appreciatively. Randal and Jeffrey anxiously watched him feed the film through a series of cogs, locking the film in place with a small lever.

"Film is a tactile medium," Du Wald was muttering to himself. "I find this to be part of the appeal. I mean . . . *video* . . . there's no romance to video. I feel sad for the people who will come after us, don't you? Those people for whom video or CD will be the medium that documents their history? I mean, can you imagine someone getting genuinely excited by finding an old dusty DVD that had been misplaced over the years? Everything is available to everybody at the click of a mouse button, these days. The art of collecting is dying."

Creating a loop with the film, he lined it up behind the lens, fiddling with it, positioning it perfectly. Then he closed the lens over the film with a dull clunk. He repeated the process on the back end of the projector, looping the film through a series of cogs of various sizes with quick, nimble fingers. He threaded the film upward, until he was able to wind the film onto the empty reel, holding it gently in place while he started turning the reel slowly, wrapping the film around it. He tinkered with the machine for a few more moments, muttering about the framing of the movie, before he turned to his guests and said, "Gentlemen, we're ready. Why don't you have a seat?"

·   ·   ·

Randal and Jeffrey sat in the front row. Both stared at
the screen as Du Wald dimmed the lights further and
took up his position behind the projector.

"How long did you say it has been since anyone saw this
tape?"

"At least thirty years," Jeffrey answered.

"Goodness. In that case, gentlemen, we are truly privi-
leged. Ms. Tate . . . we are ready to be entertained."

With a whirring sound, the projector started up, and
a flickering image appeared. Indistinct figures danced
on the screen, out of focus in a psychedelic splash of
colors. The image sharpened, and a mouth appeared,
filling the screen. A perfect smile, full red lips, laughing
silently. As Du Wald continued to tinker with the projector, sound began to fade in, filling the small screening room with laughter, muted voices, and the musical
chime of glass on glass. The soundtrack of a long-ago
party filled the air, and Randal felt the small hairs on
the back of his neck rise. He looked over to Jeffrey, and
even Jeffrey was enthralled now, eyes fixed on the screen,
mouth half open in a mixture of awe and disbelief. A
male voice, mute for decades, now saying, "Okay, okay,
we're rolling. We're rolling . . . ," as a woman laughed
drunkenly in the background, and the camera pulled
back suddenly, and everyone's eyes focused on a familiar face on-screen.

"My God," Du Wald muttered to himself as the action
unfolded. "She really was beautiful. I suppose it's easy
to forget, amidst the ugliness of what happened to her.
But she *was* beautiful. Utterly *devastating*."

THIRTY-EIGHT

"Three million dollars," Jeffrey was saying again in a voice dripping with wonder. "That's a lot of fucking money."

Randal shrugged. "It is. One and a half million each. It's not bad. But then you gotta figure in Stevie's cut. Twenty-five grand finder's fee, and his ten percent. That's a pretty hefty chunk."

They were back in the Mark Twain now, Jeffrey on the bed, shirtless, fixing dope and Randal smoking meth, blowing the rank cat-piss-stinking fumes out the window. Randal watched Jeffrey as he slid the 28-gauge ½ cc insulin needle into his flesh, digging around under there, the thin rivulets of blood running down his stick-thin arms. So long as he stuck to just smoking meth, Randal could feel a little bit of moral superiority over his companion. He started to get the impression that whatever cut Jeffrey was going to make from this deal might well prove fatal.

. . .

There was something that struck Randal as almost comical about this moment. They could hear a pimp loudly beating one of his girls in the adjoining room. She was sobbing, begging for forgiveness, and occasionally she would let out a blood-curdling scream when one of his blows really connected with her. It sounded like he was using a belt buckle, because each blow had a heavy, metallic sound to it.

"Where's my MONEY?" the pimp kept screaming. "BITCH, where's my MONEY?"

Here they were, shirtless, bathed in sweat (the Mark Twain did not boast air conditioners), listening to all of this in one of the scummiest hotels in one of the scummiest corners of Hollywood, discussing their cut of a multimillion-dollar business deal. Below them some homeless drunks were fighting and cursing at each other in the parking lot.

Jeffrey got his hit, slid the needle out, and lay back on the bed. He raised his arm to his mouth and sucked away the excess blood with a contented grin.

"Still . . . ," he said, "it's a lot of money."

When Jeffrey said it this time, there was a hint of doubt in his voice. Something about Stevie Rox walking away with such a huge chunk of their money rubbed Jeffrey the wrong way. He hated people like Stevie. It seemed in America, whenever you made some money, there would be a queue of bastards like Stevie lining up to take their goddamned cut. Usually they only had two things in common: they were already as wealthy as shit and they had done nothing to earn their percentage.

You put your money in a bank, and they start cream-
ing shit off the top. You buy a house, and some asshole
wants a percentage of the sale just because they unlocked the door for you and gave you some rehearsed
spiel about what a great place it was. And here was Stevie Rox, no doubt right now snorting blow and banging
Baby in his four-poster bed, in some obscene mansion
up in the Hollywood Hills, about to take his cut because
he happened to write Du Wald's number on a napkin
for them.

With a sudden crash, the prostitute next door bounced
off of the connecting wall. "Well, you gone and done it
now!" the pimp screamed. "You made me go mess up
yo face! Stupid ho!"

"Aw, fuck this!" Randal spat. He got up and started
banging on the wall. He screamed, "Can't you beat her
quietly? Keep it down, man!"
There was a moment of silence, and then the girl started
screaming: "Mind your business, fuck face! My man has
a gun! He'll shoot your ass!"
"I gotta gun too!" Randal screamed back. "And I'm
halfway outta my mind on meth right now, so DON'T
FUCK WITH ME!"

As this was happening, Jeffrey's cell phone rang. It was
the third time tonight. Jeffrey was about to ignore it
again, but Randal said, "Can you like turn that thing
off? Or answer it? It's driving me crazy. What the fuck
is that ringtone? It's from the Tom and Jerry cartoons,
right?"
"It's called 'Arrival of the Queen of Sheba.' It's by
Handel."

"Handel? So he's the guy who did the music for those old cartoons?"

"Yeah, that's him."

Jeffrey looked at the phone, wrinkled his face, and said, "Oh, shit. It's Spider."

"Who's Spider?"

"Guy I know. Speed freak. Used to be in the porno industry. . . ."

"Oh, yeah? He knows porn people?"

"Sure, I guess. He used to work for the Russians, some guy called Dimitri Barakov. Big porn guy, financed a lot of shit."

"I know that name. Barakov. Yeah . . . he's pretty big. You think Spider could help us? I mean, get rid of the movie?"

"What, sell it to the porn industry?"

"Why not? What I saw tonight was pretty pornographic. I mean, if fucking Paris Hilton giving a half-assed blow job is worth millions to the porno industry, what about this tape? You saw the way that McQueen was drilling Sharon Tate and Mama Cass at the same time? He coulda had a career in hard-core, easily."

The song kept playing. "*Dada-dah—dada-dah—dada da-daaah . . .*"

"But you said that porno wasn't the way to go."

"But we have an offer on the table now. If we could get someone to match it, we could cut Stevie out altogether. It doesn't hurt to see what our options are. . . ."

"I guess . . ."

Jeffrey looked at the phone.

"Spider is kind of an asshole, though. . . ."

"Who isn't? You think I wanna go hang out with fucking Rupert Du Wald and play with his collection of mummified dicks?"

Somewhat reluctantly, Jeffrey picked up the phone. "Hello?"

"Jeff! Baby! You okay?" Spider's crackly, faraway voice said.

"Yeah. I'm good. What's up, Spider?"

"Nuthin'. I just, uh, wanted to give you a call . . . see how you were doing. . . . You know, I hadn't heard from you since the whole Tyler thing went down, and, uh, you know I got a new connection now. Good guy, good stuff. I mean he can get it all, and I mean I don't wanna talk bad of the dead or anything, but he's a much more reasonable guy than Tyler ever was. Guess I wanted to call and see if you needed to find a steady source, you know?"

"Spider . . . ," Jeffrey said, cradling the phone with his shoulder while he caressed the fresh tracks on his arms, "I just got out of rehab. You crazy or something?"

"Oh, shit! My bad. You still off the shit? It's been like two months already! I just assumed . . ."

"Well, don't. Actually, though . . . there is something I wanted to talk to you about. You around tonight?"

"Sure."

"You wanna meet me in the Spotlight, on Ivar? I got a friend I'd like you to meet. We got some business you might be interested in. . . ."

"Sure, sure, baby. Now?"

"Yeah!"

"Okay, I'll be there, man . . . Gimme like forty minutes, okay?"

"Sure."

With that Jeffrey hung up. Randal gave him the thumbs-up. Jeffrey still looked unsure.

"It'll be fine," Randal said. "We're just gonna shake the tree a little. If he can't help us, we call Du Wald tomorrow morning and tell him we accept. Either way, we're outta here by tomorrow night. What do you say?"

Jeffrey nodded. The staccato thump of belt buckle on flesh resumed next door, as the pimp got back to work straightening out his girl.

THIRTY-NINE

It was early evening in the Spotlight. At this time of the night there was an uneasy truce between the transvestites, the male prostitutes, and the speed freaks. Depending on what time of day you set foot in the Spotlight, one of these three social groups would dominate the bar. But at eight p.m., with the final rays of sunlight still creeping around the sticky black PVC curtain that hung in front of the door, and before the evening crowd had yet gotten good and drunk, no one particular group had dominance. A couple of lonely-looking men with five o'clock shadows and makeup melting off their faces sat close to the jukebox, sadly miming along to Sammy Davis Jr. singing "I Gotta Be Me." Their faces told silent tales of lives gone horribly wrong, of worlds that had long since imploded. By the bar, an alcoholic with a long-ago broken nose that had healed up in such a way it looked like a smushed piece of Play-Doh was trying to convince a female barfly that he had connections in the movie industry. It was the oldest hustle in the book, and they both knew it, but they carried on the dance anyway, the gestures and lines worn smooth over the years with repetition.

"You could totally be in the movies," he was saying to her, edging ever closer. He had been up all night already and his earlier bar friends were long gone. All he had going for him was a dog called Fuckface that was sleeping in the trunk of his car and three months of unpaid rent on the roach-infested hole he called his apartment. The object of his attentions looked to be in her late forties, and brightly colored patches of makeup gave her the look of a battered wife.

"Well, I do got legs," she was saying, stretching one of them out and looking at the calf admiringly. "My second husband was from the Dominican Republic. He used to go *crazy* for my legs. He was shot and killed three years ago."

"They are great legs," the man said. "Who shot your husband?"

"The guy who worked at the 7-Eleven he was robbing. I heard the guy was a Buddhist or a Hindu, or one of those fuckin' crazy things. The ones who worship cows and shit. Anyway, I thought those bastards were all pacifists. He sure as hell wasn't a pacifist when he blew poor Enrique away. Goddamn his soul."

"That's a tough break. . . . You got your SAG card? I know a guy who can get you one if you need it. . . ."

In the back room, under the glow of the Coors sign, Randal looked at Spider. Spider had a vaguely familiar look about him. Maybe it was that he reminded Randal of vermin. He had a long, pointed nose that seemed to be missing whiskers, but no—it was something else. He looked like a dwarf in reverse. Like somebody had transplanted a child's face onto an adult's body. Sure, it was wrinkled and fucked up, but somehow the features still looked childlike. He may have been cute as a kid, but now there was something grotesque about him, unnatural.

Spider drained a shot of Wild Turkey and washed it back with a slug of beer. He looked over at Jeffrey. "So what's the deal?" he said. "You said that you had some business for me."

"You still got those connections in the porn industry?" At the mention of his porn connections, Spider suddenly got antsy. He looked at Randal and said, "What's Jeffrey been telling you?"

Randal shrugged. "Just that you know some people. That's all."

"Be cool, Spider. Randal's good people. He's okay."

"I just don't like to talk about that shit," Spider said, glaring at his empty bourbon glass.

"Another?" Randal said, getting up before Spider had a chance to say yes. Before the meeting, Jeffrey had told Randal the whole story of Spider's career in porn. He heard that there had been some kind of a stink on an S and M video he'd done a few years ago that made him pretty much unemployable within the mainstream porn industry. Something to do with a strangulation scene that went wrong. The way that Jeffrey told it, nobody had even realized that the kid was dead until after Spider had ejaculated. The Russian mafia financed the films, and they had forced Spider to help dispose of the corpse. The dead kid was illegal, underage, and vanished as if he had never even existed.

.   .   .

"I mean, you gotta imagine the effect this had on him," Jeffrey had explained back in the hotel room. "Spider *supposedly* doesn't dig guys anyway. Now he has to fuck this Russian kid while tightening a leather belt around his throat. Afterward, Spider realizes the kid died and now not only is he a faggot for money, he's a necrophiliac, too. And it's all on tape. The guy shooting the video hands Spider a handsaw and tells him to get to work while he goes to buy a shovel and some lime. Let's just say that Spider didn't do movies for a while after that."

When Randal returned with the drink, Spider's mood had changed again. Jeffrey and Spider were having a conversation that, judging from the smiles on their faces, could only be about drugs.

"You got some go fast?" Spider said, shooting a gap-toothed grin at Randal. "You mind if I, uh . . . ?"

"Sure." Under the table, Randal passed the baggie to Spider.

"Be right back, boys!" he said, walking toward the bathroom.

Once he was out of sight, Jeffrey said, "I don't know why the fuck we're dealing with this guy. He's a total fuckup."

"I can see he's a total fuckup. But that's beside the point. He knows Dimitri Barakov, who is big fucking time in the porn industry. I've heard of that motherfucker— he's a billionaire. You won't hear his name mentioned at those fucking Adult Movie conventions, but he bank-rolls everything."

.   .   .

"Man, I just don't think that the fucking Russian mafia is the direction we should be taking this. This is movie history, man. We need to get it into the hands of a proper collector. . . ."

"I agree," Randal hissed, "but we don't got time for that. If we sell to Du Wald we have to pay out Stevie. There's no time to find another freak like Rupert. If Spider's porn connections matched the offer, we'd take one hundred percent. I mean, Spider might want a cut, but believe me, I can read people. This guy? He's a first-class moron. We could probably pay him off with some fuck-ing meth and he'd be happy. People are looking for us right now, you said it yourself. We need to cash this shit in and get the fuck out of LA. Right?"
"Right," Jeffrey conceded.

As soon as Spider returned, Randal took the baggie from him and snorted more himself. He shivered under the bathroom's short-circuiting fluorescent light. The chemical stench of the speed made his lungs feel as though they had been scrubbed out with Ajax. He was snorting more and more of it, just to keep the fear away. He knew that he was right around the corner from an-other insane, self-destructive bout. As many times as he had put himself through this and sworn that he would never do it again, Randal seemed incapable of avoiding doing the same fucking thing over and over. Once he started up on meth, he knew that he needed it daily. He needed it to get out of bed in the morning. He needed it to think straight. He needed it to fuel this whole caper, so that he could escape and never look back. He could sense that he was days away from starting up with needles again, and when that happened. . . . Snorting a huge nostril full of the burning powder from the tip of his car key, Randal again made himself a promise.

Once we sell the tape and get out of LA, I will never do this shit again.

He didn't laugh as he thought this.

He flushed the toilet and walked back out to the bar. His brain was frantically spinning off in many different directions.

He slid back into his seat, his eyes burning holes through the ozone. As he sat down, it came to him in a moment of idiot genius. Why Spider's face was so familiar.

" . . . toldja what that motherfucker did to me. You know they sold that fucking clip, anyway? Out there somewhere, some corpse fucker is using it for jerk-off material."
"That's rough."
"But you know . . . I could make the call. It would have to come through me. But you know, I have a relation-ship with those guys, so if I'm gonna put my good name out there . . . there'd better be something in it for me. So what is it? What's this big deal that you're trying to unload? It is porn, right?"
Jeffrey nodded his head. Spider dropped his voice down.
"Specialist stuff, huh? What is it? Kids? Animals? It's okay. I'm broad-minded. You won't offend me. . . ."

"Little Wonder!" Randal finally blurted, when he could hold his tongue no longer. "You were in *Little Wonder*. You were Jimmy! The neighbor's kid!"

At the mention of these words, Spider's face collapsed in upon itself. He scowled and then emptied his glass with a flourish.

"What the fuck's a little wonder?" Jeffrey asked no one in particular.

"Yeah, that was me. So fucking what?" Spider spat.

"*Little Wonder* was this great TV show. Back when I was a kid. Ahead of its time. Too fuckin' dark for network TV. Didn't the scientist . . . Mr. Fester . . . didn't he murder his son during the opening credits?"

"It wasn't murder. It was an accident. In the lab."

"Right. He kills his son in some kind of terrible accident. Remember, this is a sitcom aimed at the same audience as *Punky Brewster*. He kills his kid and then attempts to hide the crime by building a replacement. A robot kid. Little Wonder!"

Jeffrey looked at Spider through slit eyes.

"You played a robot on a TV show?"

"No!" Spider sneered, as if the very idea were preposterous. Then he quietly added, "I played the kid who lived *next door* to a robot. The one that knew that the kid was a phony. I was always trying to catch out Mr. Fester."

"Shit," Randal said, shaking his head in wonder, "how long did you guys last? A season or two at most, right?"

"Seven episodes."

"Jesus. Seven episodes. It was like a fucking Shakespearean drama, I'm telling you." Randal slipped the baggie of meth to Jeffrey. "It was ahead of its time. People weren't ready for that shit. Today, on HBO, maybe. You can get away with weird, dark shit like that. But back then on the networks . . . "

"They killed us," Spider said, matter-of-factly. "*Killed us.* I never worked again. Landon Bruce, the guy who played Mr. Fester . . . he did a few episodes of *The Love Boat* and then burnt his face up in an accident on the set of some Italian movie about cannibals. After that . . ." Spider shrugged.

"What about the kid? What about Little Wonder?"

"AIDS. Heard the chick he married was a junkie. You know how that goes."

They sat and considered this for a moment. Over by the bar, the guy with the broken nose was rubbing the thigh of the barfly and whispering filth into her ear. She was giggling and for a moment she looked like a fourteen-year-old girl. Jeffrey said, "I'm gonna powder my nose," and split for the bathroom.

When they were alone Randal said, "You should write a book, man. One of those fucking tell-alls."

"Fuck off," laughed Spider. "Get me a drink."

"I'm serious! Think of all of the kids our age who were scarred for life by that show."

"They don't wanna hear stories like mine!" Spider growled. "They want shit that'll make them feel warm and gooey inside. Shit that won't make 'em think too hard. They'd want me to say how I found God, or love, or golf, or fuckin' L. Ron Hubbard, or some shit. You know something, man? I'm already where I want to be. I got sixty dollars in my pocket, and I'm gonna pick up an eight ball of meth when we're done here. I wouldn't switch places with Leonardo DiCaprio right now. I got everything I need. Nah . . ."

He looked around the bar once more and grabbed Randal's shoulder with a pleading, shaking hand. His voice dropped to a hoarse whisper.

"They don't want that! They want the candy-coated, low-fat, mocha latte garbage that they're used to! They like their junkies nice and presentable. They like 'em sorry. They like 'em boo-hooing and asking for forgiveness. Well, fuck that. Fuck writing books. Now . . . are you gonna buy me a fucking drink?"

Jeffrey sailed across the dirty floor like he was ice skating. He knocked on the table and said, "Well, ladies, what did I miss?"

FORTY

It was later that evening. Spider clutched the phone. He listened to it ring. *Nobody is going to pick up,* he thought, *maybe nobody will pick up.* He was not sure if that would be a good thing or a bad thing. Suddenly there was a click, and a voice said, *"Yeah?"*

"Hey, Jeff. It's Spider. Uh-huh. Yeah, I'm calling about that thing. The *THING*. The thing we talked about, your *MOVIE PROJECT*?"

"Yeah, well, I spoke to Dimitri. Dimitri Barakov, yeah. Uh-huh. Anyway, this dude's interested. Really interested. He's a high roller, man. You know those porn guys. He finances the shit. Uh-huh. Out in the Valley someplace . . . someplace where, uh, rich white people live, I dunno. He doesn't have me over for dinner or anything. Anyway, look—are you interested? He wants to meet."

"Dimitri. D-I-M-I-T-R-I. That's all you need to know. Projector? Yeah, sure, he's got all of that. He wants to meet you first. He wants to talk to you. He wants to see the item."

"What? I dunno about that. Can't he just come to where you guys are? Mac—Mac—really? MacArthur Park? Come on. This guy don't wanna. He don't. He . . . hold on."

Spider covered the mouthpiece and said, "They want to meet in MacArthur Park. They're as high as fucking kites right now, all tweaked out and shit. They're paranoid. They wanna do it in public. *'See the whites of your eyes,'* he said. . . ."

Spider was careful as he recited this, very aware of the gun that was resting on Pat's lap. He got the nod. Took his hand off the receiver.

"Okay, I'll tell him. Lemme get a pen."
Spider said this even though there was a pen and a notepad laid out for him already. He picked it up and started to write. When he was done he said, "Okay, I got it. When are we gonna talk about my fee? Oh, yeah, this guy's serious. He'll take it right off of you if it isn't bullshit. Okay. Okay. I'll speak to you tomorrow, right after you guys are done, okay? Peace."

Spider replaced the handset. Everything was silent in Pat's motel room for a moment. Then Trina walked out from the bathroom, clapping her hands slowly.
"Fucking bravo," she said.
Pat cocked the gun, pointing it away from Spider.

"Good," he said, "you did good."

Spider passed the notepad over to Pat. "Tomorrow, at noon. This is the address. It's a fast-food joint."

Pat looked it over. "Fuckin' MacArthur Park, man. There'll be cops all over the place. This is gonna require some fucking diplomacy."

Spider shrugged. After a moment he said, "So I guess we're done here?"

"I guess."

"So is it cool for me to, uh . . . ?" Spider looked toward the door.

"Sure," Pat said, cracking a grin. "Go right ahead."

Spider looked at Trina, doubtfully. She smiled at him. Spider stood, slowly, wary of making sudden movements, considering the loaded gun in Pat's hand. Spider shrugged and looked around the room one more time. His eyes fell on the pile of meth that was heaped on the nightstand.

"Hey, Pat, you, uh, mind if I . . . ? You said I could get an ounce."

Pat grinned even wider.

"Sure, baby. You wanna take it with you now?"

Spider nodded slowly.

Pat gestured to the bureau. "There's some packages weighed out in there. Take one."

Spider looked at Pat again. Pat was grinning still. "Okay, cool," Spider said, "thanks, Pat."

"Anytime. I appreciate the help, Spider."

Spider walked over to the bureau and opened it. Inside were several fat packages stuffed full of meth. Spider took one, held it up for Pat to see, and then pocketed it. He looked at Trina, who was leaning against the wall, arms folded, regarding Spider with curious indifference on her face.

"Well," Spider said, straightening up and walking toward the door, "I guess I'll see you two around."

"Lemme see you out," Pat said. He stood and walked toward Spider. Spider tried the door, but it was locked.

"Ya need to open that dead bolt, up there," Pat said, pointing upward.

Spider reached up, and as he did so, Pat clubbed him on the back of the skull with the handle of the gun. With a grunt Spider fell to the floor. Pat sat on top of him and smashed the gun into Spider's skull several times, with brutal grunts. The flesh split, exposing bone underneath, and blood sprayed lightly on Pat's face. When he was done, Spider was bleeding and unconscious.

"Can you believe that motherfucker?" Pat said to Trina as he washed the blood off his face in the bathroom sink. "Thinking he was gonna walk out of here with an ounce of my shit!" Pat laughed his wheezy laugh.

Trina peered down at Spider. Pat was right, she thought, it's easier the second time. Her squeamishness was all gone.

"Stupid bastard," she said.

"He had balls, though, I'll give him that. I hope to fuck he doesn't have AIDS or some shit. Motherfucker bled all over me."

"Balls are overrated," Trina said.

"Gimme the thing. The needle."

As much as Pat hated to waste drugs, he used a massive overdose of an opiate called fentanyl to finish Spider off. He put the needle into the scarred, bulging vein running down Spider's neck and fed the shit in slow. When Spider stopped breathing, Pat went down to his car and removed a tarp from the trunk. They wrapped the body in the tarp and carried him downstairs. They passed a woman on the stairs, and Pat said, "Howdy, ma'am," to her as they passed. The woman ignored them and carried on upstairs. They stuffed Spider's body in the trunk.

"Now where?" Trina asked, slightly out of breath.

"First we drop our friend off," Pat said, nodding toward the trunk. "I know a Dumpster by Fifth and Alameda where homeboy will fit right in. Then . . . you in the mood for Korean food?"

"Sure, baby!"

"Good. I know a kick-ass place down there. We're celebrating. Shit, I don't know much about celebrity skin flicks, but if this thing is as valuable as homeboy said it was . . . we're gonna do all right outta this. Tomorrow, we leave for San Francisco, rain or shine."

Trina squealed and threw her arms around Pat. She crushed her lips against his.

"I love you, Daddy!" she said.

"I love you, too, sweet cheeks. Now, let's drop this trash off and get some eats."

———————

Back at the Mark Twain, Randal looked up from the newspaper and said, "All good?"

"Yup. Noon tomorrow. Hey, let me read that shit now!"

They both huddled around the paper, laughing at the picture of Dr. Mike and the glorious header:

The Doctor is Out:
Recovery Guru Dropped
by Network Over Death of Lover

"I want to apologize to the public,
to my colleagues, and most of all to
my family."

"That motherfucker is FINISHED," Jeffrey said. "Gone!"

"It says there's charges pending for distributing prescription drugs illicitly. Good fucking riddance. You know, you can never trust anybody that straitlaced. At least people like us . . . we're honest about what's inside of us. Assholes like that, they try to keep a lid on it . . . but it's not possible. The pressure builds and builds, and then, one day . . ."

"Boom!" Jeffrey laughed.

"Yeah, exactly . . ." Randal placed a finger on the black-and-white picture of a harassed-looking Dr. Mike fighting his way through a throng of photographers. "BOOM!"

FORTY-ONE

Randal and Jeffrey pulled into the parking lot of USA Donuts and left the engine running. It was twenty minutes before they were due to meet Spider's connection.

"So what are we going to do when we see this guy?" Jeffrey asked.

"Well . . . we check him out. If he seems on the level then we go with him and get this shit over with. Easy-peasy."

"I don't know, Randal . . . ," Jeffrey said quietly. "I'm beginning to think we should have just taken that shithead's money, split, and fuck Stevie Rox. I mean, what's he going to do? We'd be long gone. You really think he'd be together enough to chase us down?"

Randal looked over to Jeffrey and said, "We'd be dead meat. Stevie might be a fuckup, but money talks. He could have us taken out like THAT."

"This feels sketchy. I don't like it. Spider's a total asshole, man. I don't trust him."

"That's why we're doing this shit out here. Everything right out in the open. No funny business."

A kid started hammering on the window, making Jeffrey jump. "Jesus!"

"Chill the fuck out!" Randal said. "Stop being so fucking jumpy!"

He rolled down the window and the kid, maybe sixteen or seventeen years old, stuck his head through and said, "Watchoo need?"

Randal handed the kid forty dollars and said, "Rocka." The kid spat a bundle of aluminum foil into his hand and passed the slimy package to Randal. Randal rolled up the window as the kid walked off.

Jeffrey stared at Randal. Randal had a big, dumb grin on his face as he checked the merchandise. "What are you doing, man?"

"You wanna take a blast before we do this?"

"You want to smoke? Now?"

"Sure. Why not? You got other plans?"

Jeffrey sighed, resigned. Now that the crack was in the car, his modicum of self-restraint was gone. "I don't even have a pipe on me. You have a pipe?"

"Hold on."

Randal got out of the car and walked past the doughnut stand, over to a convenience store on the far side of the parking lot. The gaggle of dealers by the pay phones regarded him blankly. The bell over the door tinkled as Randal walked into the gloomy, cool interior. He walked around the narrow aisles as tinny speakers blasted Arabic house music, and a security camera recorded his every move. There was no Chore Boy on the shelves. He walked over to the counter. A fat Turk sat back with the bottles of liquor and the lighters watching *The Price Is Right*, his shirt soaked through with sweat. A fly landed lazily on the back of his hand, and he waved it away. Randal cleared his throat.

"Hey. You got any Chore Boy?"

The guy looked at Randal for a moment and then reached underneath the till. He retrieved the Chore Boy and tossed it on the counter. "Two dollar."

"You got any Love Roses?"

The clerk looked at Randal for a long time. Randal had not slept in many hours. He emanated the lonely scent of by-the-hour motel rooms. His clothes, wrinkled and unkempt, reeked of ammonia and desperation, and his lips were chapped and bloody. The clerk smiled coldly and reached under the counter again. He produced a four-inch glass tube, a cork in each end, and a tiny, dried rose inside.

"You need lighter?"

"No. I'm good."

"Five dollar."

Getting back in the car, Randal threw the paper bag over to Jeffrey and said, "Hook this up, will you? I'm gonna drive around the block."

Once they'd pulled out of the parking lot Randal sighed. "Fucking clerk was giving me the eye. They're all nervous 'cos some asshole reporter did a story about the whole Love Roses thing. Saying how they're selling crack pipes under the counter. Everybody's howling and now the cops are trying to bust them on paraphernalia charges."

"Jesus Christ. That fucking sucks."

"Right? Like if they get rid of all those fucking pipes people are gonna stop smoking crack or something."

"Uh-huh. They'd have to stop people from selling ball-point pens and fucking lightbulbs next. You can make a pipe out of anything. If I got dropped on a desert island with some crack I could find a way to smoke it."

"What would happen if you shoved it up your ass? Would you get high? I mean, if you shove heroin up your ass, it's fucking wild, man. Hits you like a fucking Mack truck."

Jeffrey laughed. "I don't know. Crack is one of the few things I haven't got around to shoving up my ass yet."

As they talked, Jeffrey had removed the corks from each end, shaken out the rose, and started ripping a section of the Chore Boy away so he could stuff it into one end of the tube. The crack pipe was assembled in a matter of moments. He said, "Ready to rock."

"Cool. I'll pull over here. Keep an eye out for the five-oh, man."

———————

Jesus and Angel were standing at the counter, waiting for their food, when Pat walked in. Jesus glanced over at the tall, muscular guy with the Hawaiian shirt, and then looked back to the counter with a sniff. He pinned him as another *viciouso*, come into the neighborhood to meet a drug connection. Angel's gaze followed Pat as he took a table by the window, looking out over the chaos of Alvarado Street. Outside vendors were selling cheap, imported trinkets. Baby turtles splashed about in a plastic tub of green, filthy water. A Bolivian chol-ita, wearing a tiny bowler hat and a pleated skirt, sold Mexican antibiotics from a child's stroller. An LAPD prowl car sailed past, making sure that nobody was killing each other. The sun beat down, furious and indiscriminate.

Angel looked away and barked at the guy making the tacos *"¡Para ir!"* The old guy nodded and wrapped them to go. He placed them on the counter, and Jesus said, "Put them on the tab."

They walked out to the street. Angel said, "You see ese chango? The blanquito in the ugly shirt?"
Jesus went to look over his shoulder, and Angel elbowed him in the ribs. "Don' look, dumbshit! You saw him—yeah or no?"
"Yeah. I seen him."
"You see what he was wearin'?"
"Yeah. An ugly ass shirt. So what?"
"Nah, pendejo! The fuckin' chain homeboy was wearin'. You see it?"
"No. What's the big deal?"
"He was wearing a Malverde pendant."

They walked in silence toward Sixth Street against the tide of people. Jesus looked toward Angel, who was tearing at his taco de lengua hungrily and said, "Iz that silence because you iz thinking, or because you a dumbshit?"
Angel scowled, his mouth smeared with salsa verde. "So he was wearing a Malverde. So what? Those fuckin' gabo hipster stores on Melrose sell pictures of Malverde now."
"¡Pinche hijo de puta de mierda—shingado pendejo! What I'm saying is it looked familiar. All the fucking jewels on it and shit. It was a custom job. It looked a lot like the chain that got taken from Xavier, ese."

"Oh, shit! You think that's the fuckin' guy that fucked Xavier up?"

"Yeah, genius, I do. They said it was some crazy fuckin' white dude smashed his face in an' stole his shit. This has to be the same dude. Vamanos! We'd better tell Gordo before this puto splits."

Pat sat there, checked his watch again. Ten minutes before they were due to show. A girl brought Pat a beer, and he clicked open his cell and dialed the room. Trina picked up after the first ring. She was sitting on top of a suitcase, smoking a cigarette and absently watching *The Young and the Restless*.

"Hey, Papi," she said, "is everything okay?"

"Dandy, baby. I'm just waiting."

"Call me as soon as you're done, okay? I got everything packed up, ready to go."

"Good. We'll be in Frisco before the day's out. Just sit tight and wait for me, okay?"

"Okay."

Pat clicked the phone off. The gun, tucked into the waistband of his jeans, put a subtle pressure on his gut. It felt good. His mind was cool, emptied of all thoughts but the upcoming confrontation. He drained the beer, burped, and checked his watch one more time.

———————————

"What's this puto look like?" Gordo said, squinting his eyes against the sun.

"White. I dunno. He looks white. He has the Malverde on. Wearing some fucking ugly ass shirt, like the shirts that retired gringos down in Florida wear."

"Has he got hair?"

"Nah, he shaved it. Gotta mustache, though."

Gordo looked around. The street was quieter than usual today. Something in the air had scared the junkies. He said, "That sounds like the guy. Fucked Xavier up good. Grabbed him by the fucking throat, pulled his head into the car, and took off. Dragged him four blocks before the chain busted, and he let him go. Smashed homeboy's fucking teeth out with the handle of a fuckin' hunting knife."

Angel puffed his chest out. He knew that locating this fucker for Gordo, even by accident, would have to be good for an ambitious kid like himself. "Well, he's there. Right now. He just walked in an' ordered a beer."

Jesus shuffled from one foot to the other. He was ready to get the fuck out of here. Gordo was an unpredictable motherfucker, and being around him made Jesus nervous. There was only one reason why a young kid like Gordo could rise up the ranks so quickly—utter ruthlessness. Gordo scared the shit out of a lot of people, and Jesus was no exception.

"Good. You did good, Angel."

When Gordo said this, Angel nudged Jesus in the ribs. He gave him a look that said: *Told you so. Stick with me and you'll go far.* Jesus just smiled ingratiatingly, looking dumb, as usual.

"Come here," Gordo said, putting his arm around Angel's shoulder. They walked a little farther up the street, to a raggedy palm tree that had a gang marking spray-painted on the trunk.

"You did good, man. I need you to take care of something for me. Here."

They were standing in the shade of the tree. Gordo looked around one more time, and then bent over, retrieving something out of a hole in the dirt that was covered with a brown, dry palm leaf. It was wrapped in a rag, but the moment Gordo placed it in Angel's hand his guts fluttered at the recognition of what it was.

"Take the dummy with you if you like. Either way, I don' wanna hear that this motherfucker walked away from here again. Bring the pendant back to me. And don't get caught, okay?"

Angel held the gun in his hand for a moment. He felt nauseous, and his chest became light and fluttery. He said, "Sure," and stuffed the piece into the waistband of his jeans. His baggy T-shirt concealed the weapon easily. He walked back to Jesus and said, "Come on. We gotta go."

As they walked back toward Alvarado, Jesus said, "What's up? What did Gordo say? Is he happy?"

"Yeah. He's real happy. We gotta do something for him, though."

"What?"

"We gotta take care of this dude."

Jesus stopped. "What? Out in the open? What are you, fuckin' crazy?"

"Nah. Are you? This is boss's orders."

"Nah, man. Guadalupe is gonna kill me if I get fuckin' arrested again."

"Then don't get arrested, shithead. You don't got a choice. Gordo said that you and me gotta do it. That's it. You wanna go back there an' tell Gordo you pussying out?"

Jesus was silent for a moment. Then they slowly started walking again.

"Yeah. That's what I thought. We just go in and out. Hopefully homeboy's still eating his fuckin' taco. Nobody will see nothin', chill."

———————

Hidden away off of Burlington Avenue, Randal and Jeffrey sat in the car, desperately trying to fan the cloud of white smoke out the windows. Sweat stood out in beads against their foreheads. Randal was hunched down in his seat, sucking on the end of the pipe, trying to find some cocaine residue that was left over. Jeffrey watched him, his right foot tapping a steadily more insistent tattoo. "Did you get anything?"

"Nah. That's it. We fuckin' killed it."

"Shit. You wanna get more?"

Randal looked at his watch. "We got five minutes. We'll be late . . . *fuck!*"

"What if we just pick some up? For later. We pick it up, take care of business, and then we can have it once we're done. To celebrate."

Randal nodded. "Yeah, yeah, we can totally do that."

"But we gotta go meet this fucking guy. Seriously. Let's not, uh, you know, get all fucking distracted or something."

"Yeah, yeah," Randal said, desperately licking his dried-out lips. His mouth felt like it was stuffed with wads of cotton. He found an old can of Coke that was in the drink holder and took a gulp. It had been sitting there since yesterday, flat and warm. The taste made him gag.

"Drive, man," Jeffrey said, "we need to air this place out. Looks like a fucking sauna in here. What if the pigs see us?"

"Jesus," Randal said. His heart was pounding. He could feel it in his throat. He looked all around for cops. There was nothing. He took off and circled around the block. Made a left at Third Street, and then left again on Bonnie Brae.

"It was good shit, right? We should find the same guy. That was good shit." They rode down the block slowly. A fat, ominous-looking dealer watched their car with the flat, expressionless eyes of a lizard.

"This fucking place creeps me out, man," Jeffrey said.

"Huh?"

"Creeps me out. So fucking sketchy. I hate being down here. The pigs are crawling all over the place."

Randal snorted. "So long as the fucking Eighteenth Street remembered to pay off the cops this month, we're cool."

"I hate it, though. It's fucking depressing. The poverty. I mean, Jesus, imagine raising your kids here?"

Randal laughed. "Listen—nobody gives two shits about these people. They don't care how these people's kids grow up. This place is totally abandoned by the rest of the city. I mean, there are people I know who have never so much as driven through this neighborhood. It doesn't really exist to them. Imagine, a whole section of the city they call home, and it may as well be fucking deepest Africa or something. That's why the fucking subway stops at Beverly. It's not just because the rich fuckers don't want to come here. It's because they want to keep these people contained. This city is fucked up, Jeffrey. It's a fucking cesspool. Calling this place the City of Angels is a horrible fucking joke. It isn't a city of angels. It's a city of fucking whores. The thing is, you can't act like this neighborhood is the problem and over in Beverly Hills everything's hunky dory."

"Beverly Hills might be a fucking cultural black hole, but at least I don't have to worry about getting my throat cut for my wallet over there. I don't like it. If I didn't need drugs, I'd happily never set foot around here again. I grew up around poverty. It depresses me."

They pulled into USA Donuts again. Randal rolled down the window and signaled to the same kid to come over. *"Cuarenta blanca."* He handed the money over and took the rocks. The kid tucked the money into his shoe and split. Randal looked at his watch. "We still got a couple of minutes."

"Where we gonna leave the car?"

"You wanna drop it over on Fifth Street?"

"Okay. You know, I think we have time for a quick blast. Just to take the edge off. . . . He'll wait, right?"

———————

Pat tossed a five on the counter and stepped out onto Alvarado Street. He looked all around him. He knew that if the faggot happened to see him first it could cause all kinds of problems. He didn't want to be chasing him down at gunpoint on a crowded street. Too many random factors. They had arranged to meet at Yoshinoya, a noodle place that looked directly over the park, so Pat took up a spot across the street, leaning against a wall, trying to take advantage of the sliver of shadow created by a pawnshop's awning. The plan was simple. When they were in position, he'd walk in through one of the two entrances to the place, stick the gun against the faggot's back, and tell him to be cool. "Nobody moves, nobody gets hurt." The only problem would be convincing himself not to blow that shit stabber away after he had taken the bag from him. The memory of the bastard pointing a gun at him, taking his knife from him, still niggled away at Pat. Maybe it would be easier just to splatter his brains all over the Formica tabletops in there, just do it in front of every motherfucker that happened to be sitting there. The cops were so fuckin' slow they couldn't catch a cold, and Pat knew that he would be heading north long before they had even begun to collect witness statements. People ended up in body bags around this neighborhood all the time. Wasn't nobody going to go out of their way to solve the murder of a dead faggot junkie.

Pat stuck a cigarette in his mouth, lit it, and leaned back against the cool bricks. He watched the streets, watched the people choking the sidewalks. Halfway up the block some fucking spic had rigged up a shopping cart with a butane heater and one of those aluminum trays so she could sell some unappetizing-looking fried meat. Same kinda shit his ex-wife useta eat. All the bits of the pig they shoulda tossed, fried up and served with some fucking bananas.

Pat checked his watch. The motherfuckers were late.

———————

Coming down Alvarado toward Yoshinoya, Jeffrey could feel the sweat beginning to trickle down his back. His T-shirt was soaked and clung to his skin. The crack had totally fucked him up. His heart pounded against his ribs, like a starved rat trying to escape a garbage can. It seemed that only moments ago they had been in the car, finishing off the rest of the rock, yet a chasm of drug need was already yawning open inside of him. The faces he saw on the street seemed to glow with malevolence. Everybody looked like an undercover cop.

"Jesus Christ," Randal said, glancing over to his partner, "you're sweating like a pig. Calm down."

"I don't fucking like this," Jeffrey said, almost staggering up the street with the bag in his arms. "Something's wrong. I can feel it in my gut. Something is really wrong here."

"Come on, man. It's the coke. Take a deep breath. We're cool."

"No! I'm telling you, something doesn't feel right. Why wasn't Spider answering his phone this morning? Huh?"

"Because he's a fucking speed freak. You're being paranoid. It's too late to start all of this shit. We're here. Let's just get this over with."

They were half a block away from Yoshinoya now. Jeffrey's eyes darted around the place. He could hear sirens occasionally drowning out the sound of his pounding heart. He felt his guts loosen, the urge to shit his pants growing. Oh, Christ. He stopped walking.

"I can't do it," he said. "Here."

He shoved the bag into Randal's arms.

"What the fuck, man?"

"I'm serious. I'm too tweaked to deal with this now. I'm too fucked up."

Randal shoved the bag back into Jeffrey's arms.

"You need to fucking quit it, man. You're gonna fuck everything up. I need you here! This is your fucking tape. Your fucking contact! What do you mean you can't do it?"

"Let's just go back to the collector. Give Stevie his cut. Forget about this. I got a real bad feeling."

Jeffrey sniffed. He felt pathetic, overwhelmed. He had lost his nerve, and there was no going back now. His coke paranoia could no longer be reined in. "Do you even know what ten percent of three million is? Do you? Is your bad feeling a three-hundred-fucking-thousand-dollar bad feeling? Not to mention the twenty-five fucking grand he's going to take just for writing down that motherfucker's phone number? You're really gonna walk away now and just give away three hundred twenty-five thousand dollars because you have a bad feeling?" Jeffrey shoved the bag back to Randal. Now, as their voices got louder, people were beginning to give them a wide berth. As the shouting and the screaming continued, eyes started to turn to the two crazy crackheads screaming about three hundred twenty-five thousand dollars and playing pass the parcel with a canvas bag.

And it continued, back and forth, right up until the explosion happened only feet away from where they were arguing. The boom, as the propane heater rigged up in the shopping cart full of chicharrones overheated and exploded, caused the entire block to freeze for a moment. A twelve-foot-high column of sooty black and orange flame shot up into the desert sky, and burning pork rinds vomited over the sidewalk. Jeffrey howled in terror and barreled into Randal, sending the two of them tumbling to the ground, the bag containing the film forgotten for a moment as it too hit the sidewalk.

———————

Pat saw several things at once. He saw the column of flame shoot into the air. He saw motherfuckers hit the ground, thinking that a drive-by was taking place. He saw the woman who had been tending the cart running out into the traffic of Alvarado Street with her hair on fire, causing an Oldsmobile to swerve to avoid her, mount the sidewalk, and come crashing through the window of a botanica. But first and foremost he saw the faggot, lying on the sidewalk, next to the bag.

Throwing his cigarette to the ground, Pat pulled the gun from his waistband and took off, heading straight for the chaos. As he picked up speed, he saw the entire world cropped down to its bare essentials. The chaos around him, the people fleeing the flames, and the shattering glass became invisible. A woman who didn't clear out of his way fast enough was shoulder charged and sent sprawling to the ground, where she was trampled by the people running behind her. There was nothing else in the entire universe but the weight of the gun in his hand, the faggot sprawled out on the sidewalk, and the three-million-dollar bag that lay there, totally unattended for a moment.

"What the FUCK?"

"Hurry up, man!"

As they rounded the corner in the aftermath of the explosion, Jesus and Angel saw a scene of utter chaos. A woman was lying in the middle of the street, surrounded by cars, her hair and clothes dancing with Halloween oranges and Christmas reds. Somebody was standing over her, trying to put out the flames with his jacket. A few steps away some kid was filming the scene on his cell phone. Halfway down the block, the sidewalk was covered in shattered glass, and the back end of an Oldsmobile was sticking out of a storefront. Jesus had frozen in his tracks.

"Fuck this, man!" he screamed.

Angel grabbed him by the arm. "Come ON, motherfucker! Now!"

But Jesus pulled his arm away and started backpedaling. "I ain't goin' back to jail, homie! Fuck this!"

Angel was about to tell that stupid motherfucker that he would shoot him himself if he didn't stop acting like a pussy, but it was too late. Losing whatever nerve he had left, Jesus took off running away from the scene. Angel watched him go and then looked back toward the chaos on Alvarado Street.

"Fuck," Angel said to no one in particular. He took off running straight for the action.

———————

"Jeffrey? Jeffrey? Are you okay?"

Randal felt his partner on top of him. He looked to his left. The sidewalk was covered in broken glass and burnt chunks of pork rind. He shook Jeffrey again. Jeffrey coughed and said, "Yeah. I'm cool. I think I'm okay. . . ."

Jeffrey rolled off of Randal and lay on the sidewalk for a moment. Screams. Alarms ringing. What the fuck was going on? Suddenly the sunlight against his eyelids vanished, as something blocked it out completely. He opened his eyes. Someone was standing over him. Someone familiar.

"Oh, shit," Jeffrey breathed.

Randal sat up. He looked up at Pat, standing there with the bag dangling from his left hand, and in the right, a gun pointed at Jeffrey.

"Tough break, faggot," Pat said.

There was a moment of shocked silence. Jeffrey started trembling.

"Don't kill me," Jeffrey said. "Whoever the fuck you are . . . just please don't kill me."

"Too late."

Randal looked at Pat's face. What he saw terrified him. All around him were screams and flames, pandemonium. But Pat was darkly calm, his face untroubled by what was going on. The eyes were voids, killers' eyes; the only life in there seemed to be the flames and the chaos that reflected on their dark lenses.

Randal tried to move, but his muscles were frozen in the face of death. He recognized something in those eyes. Randal realized that he was staring into the eyes; of something primal, prehistoric. Something that could eat him alive if it decided it was worth the trouble. Randal knew that killing him and Jeffrey both would be of as little consequence as scraping gum from the sole of his shoe. Pat cocked the trigger.

Jeffrey closed his eyes.

It was all fucking over.

He expected that his life might flash before his eyes, but it didn't. The last coherent thought was a fleeting regret for stealing twenty pounds from his mother's purse when he was nine. Then, with a boom, Pat's face seemingly exploded from the inside out. The whole skull looked to expand and distort for a fraction of a second before it erupted like an overripe watermelon, spraying Randal and Jeffrey in stinking black blood and the jellied contents of Pat's head. All that was left intact was the lower jaw, and the half-mouth flapped open for a second as if to express surprise, tongue waggling wildly, probing the air, before Pat fell to his knees and flopped lifeless on the sidewalk.

.　　　.　　　.

As they sat there, dumbfounded, the young kid who had walked up behind Pat and blown his face off cursed in Spanish, then reached down to the bloody mess on the sidewalk. He grabbed the chain from around his neck. It came away with a tug, and as quickly as he had appeared, the kid took off, running for the warren of backstreets that surrounded the park.

Randal looked over to Jeffrey. They were both covered in the contents of Pat's skull. They looked to the bag, which lay there with Pat's fingers still curled around the strap, splattered red but undamaged. Randal tried to say something, but nothing would come.

"What the fuck just happened?" Jeffrey whispered.

"I don't know."

They got to their feet and looked around. People were running in all directions. Sirens were approaching, but the entire street was blocked with traffic. Somewhere off in the distance, a woman was crying and screaming in Spanish, and just ahead of them, a man staggered out of the car that had gone through the window, his face crimson and soaked through with blood, and collapsed on the sidewalk after a few steps.

As casually as possible, Randal picked up the bag and they began to walk away. Nobody paid them any mind. The farther they walked, the faster they walked. By the time they made it to Fifth Street, they were running. Jumping in the car, they slammed the doors after them, and Randal took off with a screech.

"What the fuck are we going to do?" Randal said.

"We're gonna call the collector. I'm done, man. I'm done. My fucking nerves are shot."

They drove in silence for a moment.

"Do we have any stuff back at the hotel?"

"Yeah, a little."

"Good. I think we fucking deserve it. Don't you?"

_____

When Trina called Pat's cell for the second time and it went straight to voice mail, a cold panic took hold of her. She looked at the clock again. Motherfucker! It should have been all over by now. Where the fuck was he? What was going on?

She went over to the briefcase they had taken from Tyler. Of course, it was still locked. After she had realized that fucking Pat had reset the combination on it, she had been too scared to ask him what it was. But he had left it here, hadn't he? That showed that he trusted her. She lifted it. It felt heavy. The locks themselves looked weak, though. She figured that she could easily jimmy it open. But then what? If—WHEN—Pat returned, he'd see what she had done.

She tried the phone again. Straight to voice mail.

What if he isn't coming back? a small, nagging voice inside of her asked. *What if he's been busted?*

Her mind turned this over and over while she paced the room, her stomach knotting, cold sweat forming in beads on her forehead. She thought of Pat leaving LA without her, abandoning her, striking out alone with the tape.

But he wouldn't! He wouldn't leave the money behind! He wouldn't. . . . She looked over at the case one more time.

Fuck it!

She hunted around and found one of Pat's screwdrivers. She took a deep breath and used it to lever one of the locks open. It popped easily. She tried the next. Crack. The case was unlocked.

She opened it slowly. She stared inside for a moment, barely comprehending. The case was stuffed full of old skin magazines. She lifted a few on the top layer, praying that she would uncover the money underneath. But no, the more magazines she pulled away the more she found. *Barely Legal. Penthouse. Euro Sluts. Juggs. Swank.* She started to scream as she tossed the magazines aside, scream and scream in fury, hopelessness, and frustration. Unbeknown to her, somewhere across town, the ten thousand dollars sat in the trunk of an abandoned Toyota Corolla, tucked away on a shady side street, noticed by no one during all of the chaos unfolding a block away.

EPILOGUE

ONE

Randal woke up, suddenly aware of a pressure on his chest. He surfaced from some half-forgotten dream. Only flashes of it remained. A large black mass, pressing down on him, like some horrible combination of the monster from that Steve McQueen movie *The Blob* and a vast, black, malevolent rubber air bed. He opened his eyes. He was looking at a wet patch in the ceiling in room 314 of the Lamplighter Motel, downtown Las Vegas.

Randal groaned. It felt as if something was trying to burrow out of his skull. Whatever demon was trying to escape, it seemingly was using a rusty dentist's drill to do it. The pain was very sharp and focused entirely behind his right eye. There was another pain, deeper and throbbing. It was in the soles of his feet. Randal wiggled his toes, and the movement made him wince as the pain sharpened and then faded back to a dull ache.

There was a noise, steady, like someone sawing wood. He looked down to the source of the weight that bore down on him. He saw a head on his chest, snoring loudly. He was looking at the crown of the head. White skin peeked through thin, matted hair like some kind of bird pushing through the embryonic cocoon of its shell. Membranous and greasy. Long, black hair, with gray steaks. Suddenly his stomach convulsed, as the first images of last night came back to him.

He'd started the evening at a dive called Western Hotel and Casino, playing the three-dollar blackjack tables, waiting for the connection to show. When Jake, a skinny ex-biker with a prosthetic leg, placed his hand on Randal's shoulder, he was already ninety dollars down. They did business in the bathroom—Jake popping off his leg at the knee and pulling out an eight ball of meth and a strip of Xanax, laughing about a mutual friend called Macho who was shot in the ass three days ago outside of a liquor store on Freemont. "He's walking around already," Jake laughed, "and he said it cleared up his fucking hemorrhoids, too."

It wasn't always this way. When Randal had fled Los Angeles for Vegas one year ago, he had checked into the Mansion at MGM Grand, using his family's connections and his new American Express Centurion Card as collateral. The trip was meant to be a stop-off—a chance to unwind and plot his escape from America altogether. He was picked up at the airport in a black Rolls-Royce Phantom and taken to a room that—even by the opulent standards his family was used to—seemed grandiose. The bathrooms were bigger than most luxury hotel rooms, the floors heated, the indoor pool always at a perfect temperature. Butlers waited on him hand and foot, and that night he hit the casinos looking for action. He found it, too, winning almost ten thousand dollars playing roulette and meeting a drug dealer who went by the name of Nixon. Nixon appeared at Randal's door within twenty minutes of being paged, wearing a black Armani suit and looking more like a male model than a drug dealer. He was carrying a black leather briefcase containing a mind-blowing array of chemicals and herbs. Ten different strains of marijuana. Pure Colombian cocaine. Tar heroin. China white. Every strain of methamphetamine imaginable—from pink champagne to peanut butter. Pharmaceutical methedrine. Painkillers. Sleepers. Stimulants. Ecstasy. Viagra. Antianxiety pills. Stocking up for the weekend, Randal dropped almost four thousand dollars on drugs alone that first night. And this insane consumption continued into the second, third, fourth, and fifth week. It continued after he decided to downgrade his room to save money. It continued after he was tossed out of the MGM Grand altogether for nonpayment. It continued after Nixon cut him off, and he had to head downtown to check into the Lamplighter, trawling the underbelly of Vegas to find another connection for meth. His plans for moving on from Vegas fell by the wayside, as he found himself sucked back into the petty aggravation of sustaining and maintaining a habit. There were . . . how many escort agencies that wouldn't take his calls now? Three? Four? Randal had vague memories of a blond called Sasha whom he choked into unconsciousness during a sex game. Of a pimp called Charles who broke out some of his teeth when he tried to argue with a hooker who couldn't coax his meth-numbed cock into a climax but still wanted payment. There was no way out anymore. The idea of getting on a plane was alien, terrifying. The drugs had frozen him into inaction.

It had gotten to the stage that Randal didn't check his bank account anymore. He already knew that the news wasn't good. What he had warned himself about since the first day—that one million and change could easily be pissed away by a drug addict in Vegas—was now coming to pass. Every day that the ATM still dispensed cash to him was a little miracle all its own. He'd type in his request, breathless, always expecting a white slip indicating a negative balance. There would be an urge to get down and kiss the ATM, when instead it delivered the forty or so bucks that he requested. But he knew that the money couldn't last more than another week. Randal supposed that he might eventually die in Vegas and was okay with that. He liked the garishness of it. He wondered what Harvey would think when he got the news that his brother had been found dead in a Vegas dive hotel. This thought, at least, still brought him some measure of comfort. It meant he still had some sway in this world. He had the power to disappoint people.

Last night was just another incident in a catalogue of atrocities that kept coming and coming. The more he gambled, the more shitty-ass beer they brought to his table. After a lot of meth, and maybe thirteen or fourteen cans of Schlitz, topped off with flat well whiskey and cokes, he had met a woman at the casino. He could not remember if he had negotiated a price for her or if she had just been so drunk that she actually wanted to sleep with him. One of his last memories of the Western Hotel and Casino was a security guy hammering on the bathroom door and demanding that they get the fuck out of the stall. After that, the images faded into a numb blackness.

Randal slowly pushed the head from off of his chest. He didn't want to wake this woman up. When he finally maneuvered her onto the pillow, he got a glimpse of her face. She looked older than he remembered. Her skin was pitted, scarred, and something else came back to him suddenly. He remembered going down on her, and the yeasty, vinegary taste that had almost made him gag. She was shaved bald down there, and her cunt hung almost inside out between her legs. Randal started to wonder what horrors this pussy had seen, and suddenly his guts lurched again. He burped and tasted tequila.

Tequila. The tequila fumes brought more memories trudging guiltily forward, like shame-faced suspects in a gang rape lineup. That's where they had gone afterward! They had staggered to some backstreet Mexican bar that had a few lonely-looking prostitutes in it. It was dark in there. Empty, too. Juan Gabriel was on the jukebox, singing "Querida." He had remembered that much. "I love this song," she had said. It was dark, and she had seemed passable. Petite. Randal looked at the shape of the body in the bed next to him. What had seemed like petite in the bar now seemed borderline dwarfish. Did she even hit the five-feet mark? Her face was half turned away from him, but from what he could see from the shape of her forehead, her bone structure, there was something abnormal about her. Some kind of genetic disorder. He thought back to the bar again. An old man had stood up, and was doing a strange slow-motion dance, his thin wet lips silently mouthing the lyrics, his eyes fluttering behind half-closed lids. She had said, "I have drugs, let's go do them," and there, under the bathroom's bloodred light, they had locked the door and snorted something that might have been ketamine. Whatever it was had had a strange effect on him, and the rest of his memories seemed to throb with a psychotic glow.

The next memory was a flash of being thrown out of a supermarket and shouting death threats at a manager wearing a polyester shirt. There were threats that the cops would be called. Had he bought condoms? He had no idea. The next memory took place in the hotel.

Randal sat up. The room he stayed in was totally bare, except for the bed. All over the threadbare carpet lay electrical cables, thick, strong, black electrical cables. Where had they come from? There was a backpack on the floor. So, she was wearing a backpack last night. Was she carrying electrical cables around with her? Why would she . . . ? Oh, yes. He remembered now.

"Tie me up," she had demanded, "tie me up and fuck me!"
Randal had a hazy memory of trying to tie this woman up. Randal had never been much good at knots, and the more he tried to secure her with the cables, the more they had slipped. And she was loud, hectoring. "Jesus Christ, tie me up! Fuck me! Treat me like a bitch!" When he finally had her trussed up, the cables kept coming loose. It had taken almost half an hour, and if it wasn't for the meth, his hard-on would have long since vanished. He remembered taking a long look at her stumpy body, then the short, thick legs, which seemed to nar-

row down into points like pig trotters, the arms, which were too short for the body, the unnaturally long torso. The large head, sloping forehead, pug nose. Everything about this woman seemed out of proportion to Randal. He thankfully remembered that he had turned off the light next, and everything else unfolded in the forgiving glow of the streetlights outside.

And then he recalled what she said when she was trussed up with those electrical wires.
"I'm getting married this weekend. I wanna have one more night of fun. Fuck me, Mike!"

Randal had almost corrected her and then decided against it. He looked down at his throbbing, chemically induced hard-on. He silently apologized to his dick and then advanced toward the thing on the bed. She was on her belly. Even in the dim yellow light, he could see that her back was a grotesquerie of bumps, blemishes, liver spots, and dead center a large black mole with a single hair sticking out of it.

He remembered sliding his prick into that terrible, meaty hole. She had turned to face him, that little squashed-up nose, those gerbil eyes too far apart, and that huge forehead contorted with rage as she spat, "What the fuck is this? A Nicholas fucking Sparks novel? Are you trying to romance me, cocksucker? I told you, I'm getting married. Fuck me, Mike! Hurt me! Do me nasty!"

Randal started pumping hard into her, his dick totally numb. He was receiving so little sensation from this, he knew it would be hours before he'd be able to come. He started wondering if he could fake an orgasm using the dim light as a cover. It had been done before.

The more he pumped into her, the more she hectored him. *"What the fuck is this? Rape me! Tear me apart!"*

As she said this, he became aware of the smell rising from her. Some hideous mix of Bengay and a rank, acidic body odor. He looked over to the windowsill. A half-empty bottle of Olde English sat there. He pulled out, walked over, and brushed a roach from the neck of it. He finished the bottle. It was lukewarm and totally flat. He shivered.

"You fucking faggot!" the girl had screamed. "If I wanted this kind of shit, I'd have fucked my fiancé! You fucking shit sniffer! Cocksucker! Fucking pretty boy shit eater!"

Randal recalled throwing the bottle on the floor and screaming at her. The bottle shattered. Someone started beating against the wall. He advanced on her.

Now he looked over the side of the bed, and there was the broken glass, and a bloody footprint, too. So that explained the pain in his feet. Jesus Christ.

There was more. He'd walked over to her, crunching the glass underfoot. If she wanted it, she was going to get it. His dick jutted toward her like an instrument of destruction. He was going to shut her up, once and for all. He spread her ass cheeks, spat a great phlegmy wad straight into the asshole, and then shoved his way in suddenly and violently. That had done it. She had tried to fling him off, but he grabbed hold of her meaty hips and thrust into her quickly and brutally, and she actually struggled against the constraints, but he held on to her hip with one hand and pressed her face into the pillow with the other, and the relentless meth-induced hammering into the thing on the mattress went on for so long that Randal felt himself coming in and out of it. Days passed. The sun rose and set on the walls. Governments rose and fell. The universe contracted, and all that was meaningful was the pistonlike movement of his cock as it thrust in and out and in and out. Everything was an abstraction. The room. The woman. The emptiness inside of him. All of it dissolved around him, until there was nothing but his prick, and the hole he was shoving it into.

Her screams turned into cries of passion, curses, insults, until, sometime before he himself made it to orgasm, she seemed to have simply passed out altogether. When he'd finally filled her rectum with come, he had flopped next to her on the bed, bathed in stinking chemical sweat, and the blackness that had been threatening him all night finally enveloped him.

That was it. When the full story came back to him, Randal hopped out of the bed, across the bloody pile of glass, and crept toward the bathroom. He shut the door and vomited as quietly as he could into the toilet. When the heaving was over he noticed the smell rising from his crotch. He looked down.

His penis was smeared brown. He touched it. It had mostly solidified, but there was no doubting it—he was covered in shit. He gagged again, and more stomach acid came.

Shaking, trying not to breathe through his nose, Randal washed the stuff off of himself the best he could. As he did so he caught sight of himself in the mirror. His skin looked gray, ashen. The knocked-out teeth had aged him terribly. He saw his father when he looked in the mirror, all shriveled up, sucked in, and eaten alive from the inside out. He looked at his prick again. He spotted something solid and half digested glued to his flesh. After that, he did not look down until it was all off and the sink was full of muddy-looking water. He crept out of the bathroom and found his clothes, piled up in a corner. He slid his underwear on and then his T-shirt. He picked up his pants. As he picked them up, the wallet, keys, cell phone, and a few dollars in change fell out of the pockets and clattered onto the hardwood floor.

He froze. He looked over to the sleeping mass on his bed. She turned, quieted down for a moment, and then started snoring again. Randal picked up his cell phone. He glanced at the screen and was surprised to see a missed call. He wasn't exactly Mr. Popularity these days. YOU HAVE I TEXT MESSAGE, the screen said. He pressed a button. The screen read, FROM: JEFFREY.

Randal stared at the phone for a moment. He hadn't spoken to Jeffrey in a long time. They had halfheartedly kept up communication in the first few months following Randal's departure, but then as the drugs had taken over they had drifted out of contact. The last he had heard was that Jeffrey was planning to return to England. Seeing the Los Angeles area code, Randal guessed that Jeffrey's plans had changed. Scrolling down to see the message, Randal felt a shiver of recognition. It simply read, STEVIE ROX DEAD. FUNERAL THURS-

DAY @ 3PM BLESSED SACRAMENT CHURCH, HOLLYWOOD. R U
OK? X JEFFREY.

Randal looked around the room. This run-down hole,
with its threadbare carpets, by-the-hour rates, and regular visits by the LVPD had been his home for a long
time. He thought of Stevie Rox, and Jeffrey, but most
of all about Hollywood herself. No sooner had he resigned himself to one fate than she came calling again
like some insane ex-girlfriend he couldn't drink or fuck
out of his mind. Just thinking about stepping foot in
Hollywood again, for any reason at all, filled him with
a curious kind of thrill. Maybe Jeffrey was doing better
than he was. Maybe he would have some money to loan
his friend. But as soon as the thought surfaced, a wave
of anxiety shuddered through him. The idea of returning to Hollywood penniless and hopelessly strung out
again terrified him. Then he could no longer deny the
fact that he had fucked up his last opportunity. That he
really was what his brother had called him for so long: a
world-class, grade-A, prime piece of fuckup.

Should he stay? Should he go? He looked up to the wet
patch on the ceiling and said, "I need a sign. What the
fuck should I do?"

"Wha?" said the woman on the bed.
Randal started putting the trousers on as quickly as
possible. Goddamnit, where were his socks? He grabbed
the wallet. Grabbed the car keys. She was sitting up in
bed, rubbing her eyes.
"Hi, lover," she said, "where you going?"
"Beer," Randal stuttered, "I'm going to get beer."
She smiled at him sadly.

"Well, you sure had fun last night," she said, "I guess you enjoyed it more than I did. Not that I'm complaining . . . but, you know . . . you were kinda *selfish*."

Randal shivered. "That's me. Selfish. Listen, uh, I'll be back, okay?"

"Sure."

She looked at him with a puzzled, sleepy expression on her face as he searched around for his socks. Then, deciding fuck it, he grabbed his shoes and shook them. A fat roach fell out of one and scuttled into a hole in the wall. He stuck his shoes on without socks. The chunks of glass still buried in his foot made him stifle a sob.

"I'm getting married this weekend," she said, "and that's it. I'm gonna be faithful. Magnanimous. You don't think I'm a bad person, do you?" There was something tragic about the way she said it that made him almost reconsider leaving. Part of him wanted to go over to her and give her a hug. But only a small part.

"No. I don't think that. I'm sure you'll make him very happy. Good for you," Randal said, and he opened the door.

Randal stopped in his tracks. He was frozen by what he saw. He had been half joking when he'd looked up and asked for a sign. He wasn't expecting one so blatant, so shocking. He stood there, mouth hanging open, rocking back and forth on his heels for a while.

"Hey, Mike!" the voice called from inside.

Randal continued to stare out of the doorway dumbfounded. Then he croaked, "Yeah?"

"Get me some Cisco, will ya?"

"Sure thing."

"The red one!"

"Okay."

"And make sure it's cold!"

At this Randal started to laugh. He closed the door behind him, now knowing that he would never step foot
back in room 314 again. *It'll be cold all right,* he thought.
He closed his eyes, opened them again, and looked at
the absurd panorama before him. The streets of downtown Las Vegas were covered in a thick white blanket
of snow. The cheesy neon genie lamp that advertised
the motel to the prostitutes, johns, and down-on-their-
luck addicts who frequented the place had a fat layer
of white on top of it. The walkway and the parking lot
were covered under a silent, heavy carpet of frost. The
snow was still falling, thick, intricate flakes heading
downward in arcane patterns. All of the filth, and the
shit, and the human wreckage of downtown were hidden for a moment. For a moment, the streets almost
looked beautiful.

Randal shivered, walking out into the white toward his
car. The air was clear and sharp, and it made his lungs
feel freshly scrubbed out. His feet crunching into the
frost was the only sound. The room had two more days
left on it. Anything of value had long since been stolen,
lost, or pawned. All he had was his wallet, the clothes
on his back, and a car that might not make it all the
way to Los Angeles. He sat down in the driver's seat and
fumbled with his wallet. Finding the last of the meth,
he took out his keys and inhaled a generous blast in
each nostril. Then he stuck the key in the ignition and

turned the engine over. What was that great rallying cry of the American spirit? "Go west, young man!" Randal looked at his shriveled face in the rearview mirror. He turned the radio on and caught the end of a Missing Persons song, "Walking in LA." Deciding that maybe old men can go west, too, Randal stuck the car in Drive and started on the road to home.

TWO

Somewhere in the church, over the lilting melody of the pipe organ, a noise, a barely human noise, was building in waves, growing louder, stifling out everything else. In the pews, supported by her tarot reader and her hairdresser, Baby was wailing, inconsolable, playing the grieving bride behind a black veil perfectly appointed to match her Armani suit. And front and center was Stevie Rox, as ugly in death as he was in life, bloated, stuffed, plugged, painted, and rigid as a board. The coffin was dark mahogany, with a white silk interior. Ray-Bans shielded his extinguished eyes. Chubby hands clutched a crucifix to his chest, all decked out in a three-piece Yves Saint Laurent suit and a garish, European-style silk shirt.

The mourners lined up around the coffin, passing by him in turn, and each remembered how Stevie had touched their lives. They were a particularly Hollywood mix of actors and celebrities, businessmen, drug dealers, adult movie stars, and other rootless, wasteful children of Los Angeles. An Oscar winner stood over Stevie: once famed for his intense, soul-searching performances in the first wave of great American independent cinema, and now relegated to playing lovable curmudgeons in romantic comedies pitched at aging baby boomers. His iconic features were now shriveled as a prune. He let his hands dance over the white silk as he whispered his good-byes, remembering the prostitutes that Stevie would send over to his house, unannounced. The next day Stevie would call him up, cackling. "How did ya like the flowers I sent over last night?" That's what he called them, "flowers." "Oh, sure, they were beautiful, Stevie. The nicest arrangement yet."

Next there was a young woman who looked down on Stevie's corpse with a cold smile. She thought of screen tests and hush-hush abortions. She whispered, "I hope you burn in hell, you rotten cocksucker . . . ," before walking on. Stevie's coke connection was next. He slipped an eight ball of cocaine into Stevie's top pocket, a promise he'd made to Stevie a long time ago, and one that he had decided to keep. Stevie was ambivalent about the thought of an afterlife, but he had wanted to make sure that, just in case, he'd have some blow for the long eternity ahead. Stevie had paid for his dealer's house, his cars, and his daughter's college tuition. It was the least he could do. "Godspeed, Stevie. . . ." And then came a skeletal figure who had only met Stevie twice. His lank hair was combed back, tight against his skull. His skin was gray. The light in his eyes was all but burned out. It looked as if he were the one who should have been in the casket. Jeffrey shook his head slightly, amazed that he had outlived Stevie Rox. Stevie Rox, who had, in his own little way, helped to bankroll this last, final spiral into utter hopelessness.

.   .   .

Looking down at Stevie, he remembered the last time
he saw him, sitting on the edge of his indoor pool, in
that monstrous villa in the Pacific Palisades, smoking a
cigar and casually flicking the ash into the water. The
way he had looked at the envelope of cash they had
handed to him. That wide, bloody smile.
"Boys," he had said, "I guess this is what they call a win-
win situation."

And now, just over a year later, Stevie was dead of liver
failure. The morticians had done their best to play down
just how yellow Stevie had looked in the last weeks. Jeffrey was standing there in a borrowed suit, wondering
where exactly he would get the money to score when he
finished with the last of his heroin. The thought brought
about a twinge of psychosomatic withdrawal: a shudder
in the gut, a loosening of the bowels, an internal chill
that shook him with a wave of nausea. He tried to catch
his breath. As he did, he felt a hand on his shoulder.

"Are you a friend of Bill W.'s?" a familiar voice asked.

Jeffrey turned. He blinked his eyes, as if to adjust his
focus. He found himself staring into a face transformed.
The features were almost the same, but the face seemed
to have aged terribly in the preceding year. Maybe it was
the missing teeth that did it. It made the cheeks seem
even more sucked in, the mouth more puckered, like a
little old man. Almost every last trace of that remaining youthful beauty was now gone. The bleached hair
was thinner now, the skin blotchy.
"I know, I know," Randal laughed, "I look like shit. If it's
any consolation . . . so do you."

．   ．   ．

With that, they hugged. To the others in attendance they were just two old friends brought together by grief. People saw them standing there, hanging on to each other, and thought, *They must have really cared for Stevie.* They weren't to know that all of their grief was reserved for themselves.

———————

After a long church service, enlivened only by a eulogy from Tatum O'Neal and a graveside meltdown from Baby, who threw herself onto the coffin before fainting outright, Jeffrey and Randal sat in the half-deserted gloom of the Spotlight bar on Ivar. The place still smelled the same—a musty, long-ago smell, with an undertow of bleach. The place had the usual crowd of male prostitutes, worn-down transvestites, and other lost souls. They had the table by the jukebox.

"So his liver gave out, huh?" Randal said. "Goddamn."

"Uh-huh. He refused to stop drinking, even when the doctors told him that the thing was failing. He couldn't get his head around the fact that he could fuck up an eighteen-year-old's liver in less than a year. Thought they were lying to him. Even when he turned yellow as a fucking block of Velveeta he refused to give up his vodka gimlets for breakfast."

"How come you got to know Stevie so well?" Randal said. "You used to think he was a fucking asshole."

"He was a fucking asshole. He was Damian's friend. They took quite a shine to each other toward the end. He did a portrait of him, not so long ago. . . ."

"Shit," Randal said, looking over to the bar, where Damian was waiting to get the drinks, "I can't get over that motherfucker. Look at him! A fucking *artist*. How the fuck is that prick making a living as an artist?" As he said that, Jeffrey let his eyes move toward the bar where Damian was standing. His six-foot-six frame was draped in a leather trench coat. His stick-thin legs were clad in black denim and tucked into a pair of ostrich-skin cowboy boots. He dropped the money on the bar and started walking back toward them, drinks in hand.

Randal looked Damian up and down, still shaking his head.

"No offense, man, but I'm still finding it hard to believe that you're paying your way with those fucking paintings."

Damian smiled, with no real humor. He slipped a glass of Johnny Walker over to Randal.

"You might dislike my art," he said, in that nasal whine, "but it just paid for your drinks."

"Damian has a patron," Jeffrey said, raising his own glass to his lips, "a very generous patron. He has been buying up every canvas that Damian can produce. You know him, actually."

"Oh, yeah?"

"Yeah. Rupert Du Wald. The collector. He says that Damian is possessed by genius."

Randal looked at Damian, and then at Jeffrey. He noticed that Damian's yellow teeth had been replaced with fancy platinum and white diamond numbers that made him look even more ludicrous than before. Randal croaked, "Excuse me," and stood, walking toward the bathroom.

When Jeffrey followed him in a moment later, he could hear Randal snorting meth in the cubicle. He knocked on the door softly and said, "You got room for a little one inside?"

"Sure, come in."

"Thanks."

Bunched together around the filthy toilet, Randal held the key with a mound of meth on the tip up to Jeffrey's nose. Jeffrey took a blast in each nostril, making his eyes tear up.

"You heard the latest about Dr. Mike?" Jeffrey asked.

"He's in prison, isn't he? Over those prescriptions?"

"Nah! He was out after three months. No, I mean the billboards are up all over the city. DR MIKE: RECOVERY AND REDEMPTION. The motherfucker has landed a new show on VH1. About how he found God in prison, and now he's gonna use the lessons he learned inside to help others, and blah, blah, blah. . . . He's on *Oprah* next week."

Randal laughed, sadly.

"I guess you can't keep a good man down. . . ."

"I guess. So listen . . . Randal . . . Damian and I . . . we have something to discuss with you."

"Damian and I? Why exactly ARE you hanging out with this dick again, man? Seriously, the guy's a fuckwad. A talentless, know-nothing asshole. Just because that wannabe freak Du Wald is buying into his shit doesn't make it any better, you know."

"Randal, I'm broke. Totally, utterly fucking broke. I never made it back to England. I never even made it out of Hollywood. Every bit of that money went into my arms. Look at this."

Jeffrey pulled up the sleeves of his jacket, exposing his long, pale arms. They were a tapestry of needle marks, running from an angry purple welt at the crook of the arm all the way down to the bruised, swollen wrists. Then, for the coup de grace he tilted his head back, exposing a trail of angry-looking needle marks dotting the length of his throat, barely hidden with thickly applied makeup.

"Jesus, Jeffrey," Randal breathed, "what the fuck did you do to yourself?"

Jeffrey let his chin drop again.

"Speedballs. I got hooked on fucking speedballs. The coke took me down so fast, man. So fast." Jeffrey clicked his fingers. "Like THAT. . . ."

"Are you still using?"

Jeffrey shrugged. "I'm on the methadone program. There's a clinic in Hollywood. I go there every morning to get my dose. I can barely afford that. That's why I've gone back to working for Damian. He pays well. He did a whole series of abstract pieces based around my tracks. But listen, there's something else."

"What?"

"You remember some of the shit that Du Wald had in his place? The collection?"

"Sure."

"Damian has been spending a lot of time with Du Wald. They're real friendly these days. He managed to get these. . . ."

Jeffrey reached around to his back pocket, pulled out a small notebook, and handed it to Randal. Randal flipped the pages. There was a sequence of numbers, scrawled in spidery handwriting. "So what? What the fuck is this?"

"There are pass codes to every door, safe alarm, and case in the fucking house. All of them."

Randal looked at the book again, feeling his throat go dry.

"And that's not all," Jeffrey was whispering. "He knows someone. Movie executive. Real interested in something that Du Wald had. The penis. You remember the penis that he said belonged to Napoleon Bonaparte? Well, this guy is offering six mil cash, no questions asked. All we'd have to do is get it."

"But . . . but . . . what about Lurch?" Randal stammered. "Why doesn't he do it himself?"

"This weekend, Du Wald is taking him to meet some of his art collector buddies in Italy. They're going to be gone for seven days. If we're going to do it, we have to do it then. Damian needs to have an alibi. Du Wald has no fucking idea that you and I are still around. As far as he's concerned, we took the money and split a year ago."

"But what's going to happen . . . I mean, shit! How the fuck could we get away with it?"

"We got the pass codes. Who knows how long it would be before he even realizes that it's gone? Damian has secured another vintage Cartier box, exactly like the one that Du Wald has the dick in. He's even come up with a fake dick that looks pretty close."

"How did he make a fake Napoleon Bonaparte dick?"

"With a blowtorch and some beef jerky. It looks exactly the same to me."

"Well," Randal said dryly, "he IS an artist after all. You said six million?"

"Six million. A chance to start over. We take the dick, and when Damian gets back we sell it to his contact. Then all three of us go our separate ways. Just like that."

When they made it back to the table, Damian was looking intently at something small, squirming on a beer
mat. As they took their seats Damian said, "Get a load
of this."

They looked down. It was a cockroach. It was on its
back, six legs squirming madly in the air.
"Fucking thing tried to crawl into my rum and coke,"
Damian said.
Jeffrey went to brush it away, but Damian grabbed his
wrist and said, "Wait."
Damian took a finger and flipped the roach right side
up again. It froze for a moment, as if barely believing
its luck, before making a break for the edge of the table.
With a lightning reflex, Damian flicked it again, flipping
it up into the air, landing it on its back once more. The
legs resumed their wiggling.
"I love cockroaches," Damian said, "I love their hard-
headedness. Look at that fucking thing, squirming
away, trying to right itself again. You know it would
squirm and squirm for days if you let it? And then, if I
flip it again, it will make a break for it. I used to do this
for hours, when I had a dope habit, and my only friends
were the roaches. Flip 'em. Watch 'em squirm. Flip 'em
back. Watch 'em run. Flip 'em . . ."
"Yeah," Randal said, "good times."
Damian looked up. "Do you know that a cockroach can
live for up to two weeks without its head? You cut its
head off, and it's so determined to live it doesn't even
realize that it's dead already."
Randal shrugged. "I fucking hate roaches."
"Everybody puts the cockroach down. But it is the most
tenacious, hardheaded motherfucker out there. Its sur-
vival instinct is amazing. No other creature on earth

comes close. The humble fucking cockroach. A lesson to us all. Off you go."

With that, Damian flipped it over one more time, and they watched it crawl to the edge of the table and fall off of it, scuttling away to some shadowy corner. Randal smirked at Jeffrey and said, "Deep, isn't he?" They followed the roach's progress for a while before turning back to Damian. Damian smiled.

"So, do we have something to talk about, boys?" he asked.

"Yeah," Randal said, "I guess we do. We got about six million things to talk about."

Damian laughed coldly.

"Before we get down to it, would you boys like another drink?"

Randal drained his glass, and Jeffrey did the same.

"Sure," Jeffrey said, "a drink would be good."

Damian nodded and stood. He stretched like a cat and sauntered over to the bar. Jeffrey looked at Randal.

"You getting cold feet?"

Randal shook his head.

"No."

"If this isn't for you, you can walk. No hard feelings. I could find someone else. I just thought . . ."

"No. I want this. I need this. We both do."

They pondered this as they watched Damian order the drinks, and a stray beam of sunlight illuminated the bar as someone left, casting a sudden focus on the gray, spectral faces inside. Randal had the fleeting impression that this moment had somehow been captured, preserved in amber: his hand hovering over an empty glass, the sad-faced transvestite with the five o'clock shadow pushing a coin into the jukebox, a Cuban Chinese scowling at the barkeep, the dust particles hanging suspended in the stale, musty air.

They looked at each other: Jeffrey lurking in a borrowed suit two sizes too big for his starved frame, open sores running the length of both arms; Randal's puckered mouth, toothless, and penniless, eaten away from the inside by the ravages of meth and booze. For a moment they smiled. Looking past their desperate circumstances, their physical deterioration, their battered faces, in that instant they looked like two children, eyes burning with barely contained excitement. Just as a toss of the dice had once taken everything away from their own mentor, Dr. Mike, another toss of the dice now promised them a way out of the hell they had created for themselves. With all of the wealthy perverts, sickos, collectors, and freaks that this city seemed to breed, opportunities were everywhere. You just had to have the right kind of eyes, and you could see them, lurking in shadowy doorways like opportunistic crackheads. With a bit of luck, something would come along eventually. Shit, sometimes one toss of the dice is all you need.

Then the moment passed, and the bar seemed to come alive again. With a clunk, the jukebox whirled into life and a familiar song began to play. They sat and waited for Damian, waiting for whatever madness would come along, tapping their glasses absently with their fingers, alive again, truly alive for the first time in as long as they could remember.

ACKNOWLEDGMENTS

Notes from a Mexican bar, somewhere in Los Angeles, Sept. 2009
Vanessa and I are sitting in El Chavito, a Mexican bar on Hollywood near Vermont that looks like a concrete bunker, drinking cheap happy-hour margaritas. On the jukebox, Chet Baker sings about falling in love too easily. The diet pills are starting to kick in, giving my stomach a strange, disembodied feeling. The last time we got drunk here we ended up in the Valley with Ron Jeremy, partying with porn directors and watching a deaf girl with enormous silicone breasts cane Ron's ass with a riding crop. Writing is a dangerous profession, as William Burroughs once observed, and when you throw cheap, potent margaritas into the mix the danger is magnified exponentially.

"So what are you going to write for the acknowledgments?" Vanessa asks. "You keep saying that you're going to write them, but it's been weeks now."

"I don't know. Nobody ever reads the acknowledgments, do they? I've been agonizing over it, and the worst part is that nobody is even going to notice. Maybe I'll get inspired if we drink more."

"What do you have so far?"

I pull out a notebook full of spidery, handwritten notes. I look up for a moment. Over Vanessa's shoulder I notice a crazed-looking man staring at me. From the sidewalk, he peers into the bar through the open door. He has dried vomit caked around his mouth and a T-shirt that says, MY OTHER GIRLFRIEND IS A MODEL. He beckons me over. I put the book down, walk over, and talk to him for a few moments. I come back.

"What did that freak want?"

"He said he needed a dollar to pay for his headshots. I guess even the fucking bums are actors around here."

"Did you give it to him?"

"No. I told him I'd give him the dollar if he'd sign an exclusive management agreement with me, but he refused and stormed off."

"I can't blame him. So what do you have?"

"Um, okay." I start reading. "*I would like to thank my wife, Vanessa, whose patience and support helped to make* Sick City *possible.*"

"Do you mention that I saved your life?"

"What? Uh, no, I just say that . . ."

"You should put that I saved your life. You were injecting heroin and smoking crack when you met me. Put that in there. The only thing you were writing back then was phony prescriptions."

"Okay. I'll put that in. *'Phony prescriptions.'* Anyway, the next bit goes, *'My agent, Michael Murphy, at the Max and Co*

Literary Agency and Social Club, who is so much more than just an amazing agent, he is a tireless campaigner on my behalf for all of my craziest suggestions, a formidable ideas man, a pit bull when he needs to be, a teddy bear when he thinks no one is watching, and most of all a 100-percent, for-real, wont-let-you-down-in-a-crisis, always-have-your-back-no-matter-what kind of a friend.' Man, that's a long sentence. I'd better break it up or something."

"Do you think he'll get mad because you called him a teddy bear?"

"You think he might? I meant teddy bear in a nice way."

"What man likes to be called a teddy bear, Tony?"

I sigh and cross that line out.

"Okay, how about this bit? *'My editor, Michael Signorelli, who edits with a surgeon's grace and an artist's sensitivity . . . Thank you. You always leave the place in a better condition than you found it.'* "

"That's good. Are you going to mention that night we got him so drunk he ended up dancing to Whitney Houston's "How Will I Know" in some sleazy Avenue A eighties club?"

"No. I don't think he'd like it if I mentioned that. The last thing I need is my editor pissed off at me. Wait, I need more drinks."

I go to the bar and get another round. The jukebox has segued from Chet Baker to David Bowie's "Cracked Actor." Walking back from the bar, I notice that the guy with the dried vomit around his mouth now stands forlornly across the road, outside of the medical marijuana dispensary. He sways dangerously and looks like he's about to fall flat on his face.

"Okay, the next line is, *'Carrie Kania, whose belief in my writing really changed everything for me. Carrie really is one in a million: she possesses that rare mix of vision and the street smarts to make her vision a reality.'* "

"That's good. Wow, Carrie, me, your daughter . . . you got a lot of strong women around you. That's good. No wonder you're still alive."

"*In fact, all of my friends at Harper Perennial: Alberto Rojas, Amy Baker, Michael Morrison, Milan Bozic, and everyone who was involved in putting this book out. After all, my job was easy. I drink cocktails and write stories. You guys do all of the legwork, and I really appreciate it.*"

"You got to lose that. That line is terrible. You make it sound like you sit around getting drunk all day, and the books just write themselves. You know your problem? You're kind of like those people who are totally against drugs and try to ram it down people's throats. Except you're the opposite. You're like a preacher or something: 'Getting loaded is great!' Tony, nobody likes a preacher."

"I was just trying to liven it up a little. You didn't think it was funny?"

Vanessa shakes her head at me, half-smiling.

"Goddamnit." I start striking out more lines. I wonder if maybe I *should* become a preacher. That's where the real money is.

"All right. Okay, the next bit is, *'I want to thank George Lewis, whose conversations about Hollywood folklore were the initial inspiration behind* Sick City.' "

"He was the one who told you about the sex tape? So, is it real or not?"

I shrug. "It doesn't matter. It's just the idea that it exists that's exciting. Who cares about reality? Reality is boring. Hold on, there's more. *'Jesse Flores, who coached me in Spanglish and taught me all kinds of filthy Mexican curse words.'* "

"Good, I was going to remind you to thank Jesse. Mexican Spanish is totally different from the Spanish I know. They have a strong accent, a different way of speaking. You can't have all of this proper Spanish in there, it wouldn't be right. I can't believe that in all the years you lived in LA you only learned one phrase in Spanish."

"*Vente blanco, vente negro,*" I sigh, nostalgically.

"*The following writers and artists supported me at the outset and really helped me out with advice and encouragement when I needed it: Dan Fante, Zsolt Alapi, Tommy Trantino, Jerry Stahl, Dennis Cooper, Sebastian Horsley . . .*"

I drift off for a second. Something has caught my eye outside. Vomit Mouth across the road is pissing in the street now, waving his pecker around and shooting his urine up in the air like a gardener watering the lawn. I look away and back to the notebook.

"Is that it?"

"No, I just have this part . . . *'I would also like to acknowledge the presence of many of my old friends and enemies, both living and dead, faces from the dope scene, shooting buddies, dealers, nutcases, thieves, prostitutes, and professional fuckups whose faces and memories haunt these pages.'*"

Out of the corner of my eye, I think I see an old ghost from my dope days staggering across the road wearing a Mexican wrestling mask. I look up, startled, but there is nothing out there except the California moon, Vomit Mouth watering the palm trees, and the steady rumble of traffic down Hollywood Boulevard.

"Well," Vanessa says, "you are right about something. No one ever reads the acknowledgments. So I guess you can pretty much write what you want."

"That's true. Unless there's some kind of weird acknowledgment-reading freak out there."

I take a slug of my drink and check my watch. The diet pill makes my brain whirr like an overheated motor, and my fingers are icy cold. Seized by sudden inspiration, I jot down the phrase "*JUST SAY NO TO THE WAR ON DRUGS.*" I close the notebook. A few more drinks and maybe it will all make sense. The night is still young and full of possibilities.

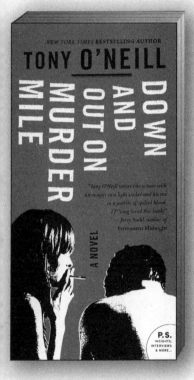